The Demon's Collar

The Bard's Demon Trilogy

Book 1

Lyra Sterling

Content & Trigger Warnings

The Demon's Collar is a dark fantasy romance with heavy themes. Reader discretion is advised. This book contains:

- **Sexually explicit content**
- **Dubious consent**
- Demons (including the MMC)
- Devils (mentioned)
- Magical compulsion
- Mention of (off-page) sexual assault
- Attempted (on-page) sexual assault (not by an MC)
- Child neglect and abandonment (remembered)
- Some blood and gore, including descriptions of violent death (in a fantasy war setting)
- War setting
- Violence
- Fire / burns / violence with fire
- Bondage/chains
- Kidnapping

Content & Trigger Warnings

- Punishment / spanking / strapping
- Butt stuff
- Fear play
- Primal play
- Bullying
- Hazing
- Branding
- Contemplation of mental health
- Hearing voices
- Imprisonment with torture (limited)
- Alcohol consumption

If you're sticking around, fantastic. Game on!

Chapter 1
Ero: The Wrong Book

Bardic Advice from Eroithiel von Dua to future generations: Learn to use your weapons...before you need them.

As I crouched in the tattered wardrobe listening to my entire adventuring party's gruesome slaughter, I realized I hadn't made the best choices that morning.

Screams rent the air. Metal clashed on metal—almost as though a proper fight was afoot. But there was no question about who was winning and who was dying.

Thunk!

We really hadn't come to fight.

Screech!

I held my breath.

Clang!

Hells, we'd barely come armed.

Of the party, I was the *most* armed, and I was hidden away, listening to the slaughter like a coward.

I blew out a slow, shaky exhale and sucked in a dusty breath.

A cough threatened. I swallowed it.

These caverns were supposed to have been picked over already, containing only scraps and books that hadn't been worth the effort for the myriad bands of raiders who'd come before to haul away.

It was the books that had drawn me. I didn't need shiny magic tomes. Nothing that might catch a sorcerer's eye or fetch a halfway decent price. I needed the dull stuff—the histories of a dying land that no one but me cared to read. *The key to your legacy lies in a centuries-old book*, the Temple Mother had whispered into my greedy ear nearly one year ago. And I took that challenge seriously.

I knew that the key to my legacy began with finding my father. I knew it bone deep. To do that, I needed a book of histories that could fill in the gaps my mother and my people refused to fill for me.

And so, I'd come. And so...I would probably die. Before I even got to solve the mystery.

Tragic.

The screech of battle felt like it'd been going on for hours by the time silence fell. If I had to guess, it'd only been minutes.

There was a fresh *thunk* on the outside of my wardrobe. Someone had leaned against it.

"Nasty cut, that," said a gruff voice.

"It's nothing," said another, nearer, in a growl so dark I vowed to simply asphyxiate rather than risk another breath. "Check for stragglers. I'll strip the corpses."

A grunt was the only answer, followed by footsteps retreating. A soft hiss of pain gave the lie to his *"it's nothing."* But the man couldn't have been hurt too badly, because the next sound was that of a nearby door being wrenched off its hinges.

I swallowed, listening to the wounded man rifle through one of the other wardrobes. If it was anything like my hiding place, there wasn't much to find. I'd jumped in at the first sign of trouble, only to discover absolutely nothing to use for cover.

A few footfalls later, I knew it was over. He stood outside my door. My heart stuttered.

I wanted to lift my crossbow. Unfortunately, I hadn't gotten around to learning how to use it. I felt extraordinarily stupid dying with the beautiful weapon on my lap. I'd brought it for luck, mostly—with little thought about what kind of luck it might bring. It *was* emblazoned with a black fist on silver—the seal of Haz, God of War and Peace.

At the last moment, I forsook the weapon in favor of my lute. I wrenched the instrument from my back and held it tight against my chest for comfort.

The door shattered.

Splinters rained down on me. I stared up at my angel of death. In the low cave light, the dancing shadows made him loom larger than life. Black leather hugged his cut frame, rippling with every motion. Firelight played tricks with his dark eyes, here giving them a black glint, there a fiery red.

Gods, devils, angels, and demons—at least I was going to die beautifully.

I was too transfixed even to beg for my life.

He glared down at me like I'd personally offended him by existing, because now he needed to go to the effort of lifting his knife again. He did lift it, though. And pointed it at my heart.

"I can heal you," I heard myself say.

No. I heard myself cry it, like a child. (I was decidedly *not* a child. I was twenty-one. An *entire* adult by human standards, thank you.) I whimpered at the way his hard eyes narrowed.

Was this real? It didn't feel real.

He reached for me. I shrank back. But I had nowhere to go. He grabbed my arm and used it to lift my wrist up into the light. His gaze fell on my leather cuff.

A fresh wave of fear sliced through me.

The gold tree emblazoned on green falsely implied that I was a sworn member of the Huntress faction. That alone would have sealed my fate, had it still been in question. The factions were merciless toward one another.

Only, I *hadn't* actually joined that faction. I'd stolen the cuff and volunteered for this party because I wanted some measure of companionship while I searched the creepy caverns. I had proof, too—because anyone who'd truly pledged any faction had ink to show for it. My only tattoo was the gloved fist on my forearm that matched the one on my bow. It was temple-given, permanent ink. A religious vow. In contrast, the tree below it was comically smeared, obviously drawn on. My party had known, of course, but they'd allowed me to come because I really could do some small measure of healing—and every party could use that. Not that it would do them any good now.

I don't recall saying any of this, but when I looked up, my captor held my leather cuff in his hand (I must have stripped it off in my panic), and stared at my smeared, false tattoo. I heard myself babbling words in an undignified rush.

"Stop talking," he growled.

I stopped.

He tossed the cuff aside, lifted my trembling wrist again, and used his torn shirt to wipe away the last of the ink I'd so cleverly (or stupidly) used to win my place in this ill-fated party.

And then he lifted his knife again.

"But—" I said.

A warning grunt stopped the protest in my throat. His glare broadcast something to the tune of *"Make me repeat myself and die screaming."*

He used the knife to cut a length of rope. Then he snatched my wrist again and gave me a pointed frown. Apparently, I was to read his mind now. I stared for a too-long beat as his eyes darkened like the sky before a storm. Before the storm broke, I realized what he wanted. I balanced my lute on my knees and thrust my other wrist to him. He bound them in a single expert motion and dropped them onto my lap.

Well.

I wasn't...dead.

Yet.

I chanced a quick glance around. The people I'd spent my morning making small talk with lie in pieces on the ground. My breakfast threatened to join them. I closed my eyes. The rough wood from the bureau's shattered door dug into my knees.

When I looked up again, my captor stood examining my crossbow. A twinge of anger burned in my gut. The crossbow was *mine*, even if I didn't know the first thing about using it yet. I would, just as soon as I found a worthy instructor. The weapon was a gift from the temple. A (perhaps outsized) reward for doing the bare minimum—turning up yearly on the anniversary of my birth to tithe a drop of my blood to their altar. I knew little about weapons, but it was a beautiful one. I knew plenty about beauty.

Speaking of which, my captor dropped the bow and lifted... my lute.

"Don't fucking touch that," I hissed before gods, sense, or anyone else could still my tongue.

His sharp gaze cut to me. He didn't look as angry as I'd have expected. He looked intrigued—perhaps a bit perplexed. The interest set ice pooling in my stomach. He gripped the lute by its neck, and I saw visions of its silky wooden curves splintering against the cave floor.

"I'll do anything," I said quickly, pivoting in my panic. "Please."

Half a dozen debauched ideas flashed through my mind. Offers I would never make aloud or admit to the gods.

He stared for a long moment and then gently set the instrument aside, laying it on the chest of a dead man. I supposed that was better than the grimy cavern floor, but I didn't love it.

His hand disappeared into his cloak and emerged again holding a collar of black leather woven with fae silver, ornamented with forest green gemstones.

The air fled my lungs.

I'd heard that collar described in stark detail once, by an acolyte at the temple who'd been chased off and scolded for saying more than he ought to in my presence. Had he known this moment would come? Were our fates *really* set in stone?

Dark power radiated from the collar. I didn't need to ask what it did. Before the gemstones were added, several collars like this one were made for hounds. They allowed the owner to compel the beasts. Perfectly obedient hunting dogs would have been a commodity in our war-torn land, had the magic worked as intended. It had not. Faced with losing their will, the hounds had gone mad and torn their masters apart.

The collars were supposed to have been destroyed. But as the acolyte's gossip suggested and the collar's presence here confirmed—one had been altered instead.

"Put it on," he said.

That quickly, my devotion to my beloved lute failed. Never

mind that I had attuned it to my own personal brand of magic over many grueling years, never mind that I'd perfectly molded it to my touch and could now produce the sweetest sound with a mere flick of my fingers. Technically, at great personal cost, I could replace the lute. In time. I couldn't replace my mind.

"No," I managed. "No, I can't."

He looked bored. I didn't yet know to fear that look more than his anger, but I would learn. I expected him to smash my lute then. But I also didn't yet know how impossible he was to predict. I would learn that too.

"Then shut your mouth," he said. "You'll be conveyed to the mines."

I blinked several times, digesting those words. The mines were full of slaves taken in the war, trapped underground, condemned to lifetimes of hard labor. Even when a mine changed hands, there was no relief for those inside. The factions all needed supplies. Being down there would be worse than a death sentence.

My captor had already turned away. He smashed the door of another wardrobe and pulled out a set of moth-eaten robes. A hiss of pain escaped as he withdrew. He dropped the robes and grabbed at his hip wound. His fingers came away wet with black blood.

Demon blood.

No wonder he'd been momentarily intrigued by me. I didn't know much about demons, but I knew they loved puzzles. And here I was, wearing a false faction tattoo, traveling with a party I clearly didn't belong to, holding an elite weapon I couldn't use, and clinging to a lute I cared about more than my own life —if not my sanity.

And then I'd told him no, and he'd grown bored.

Noted.

Voices echoed on the cavern wall, moving toward us. Grumbling and cursing. I gathered from the bits I could make out that the Fated had taken the area and these adventurers were charged with clearing the caves for their faction's use. They were irritated because they had found nothing shiny below to sweeten their task.

It didn't take an oracle to see how this would play out. They would round the corner. They would find me, use me in all the ways I had always been warned bad men could, and then take what was left of me to the mines.

A tiny spark of arousal sent shame racing down my spine. Dear gods, what was wrong with me? Sure, on long nights in the pubs, I loved to let my gaze linger on the brawny rangers and barbarians passing through—to imagine encountering them alone in the woods, putting up a bit of transparent resistance, and then giving myself to them. But this was not that. My private fantasies didn't involve a whole band of them at once. They *certainly* didn't involve being conscripted to the mines after.

I snapped myself out of it. This was no fantasy. It was also absolutely not how I intended to meet my end. From a purely story perspective, a bard could not endure it.

"I'll wear it," I said, loud enough to carry.

I didn't beg, because I didn't need to. If he'd wanted me moments ago, he still would.

"But don't compel me," I rushed on, steady now that I had the beginnings of a plan. "You wouldn't enjoy it anyway, and I'd be less fun if I went mad."

My words had the desired effect. His gaze conveyed quite clearly his irritation at my presumption. It also conveyed his renewed interest. One point to me. Perhaps I was playing with fire—but at least I had his attention.

The demon stalked toward me. The voices were just around the bend now. He held out the collar, his lips set in a cruel line. He wasn't making promises. My heart raced. Would I believe him if he did? Demons weren't exactly known for their honesty.

The moment I put the collar on, he would have the power to compel me to do whatever he wanted. And if he did, my mind would fight itself—possibly destroy itself—if I tried to refuse.

Was donning the collar my best plan?

No.

Did I see an acceptable alternative?

His silence held. The shadows of the adrenaline-riddled men grew on the cavern wall. The demon's brow arched in silent challenge, and I was certain this time what he wanted me to understand.

Now or never.

I lifted my bound hands and snapped the collar around my neck with a decisive *click*.

Chapter 2
Bǔk: A Stray Arrow

**Demon Binding Code 15: The bound shall
not do non-incidental harm to civilians
without consequence.**

The main difference between Hell and Earth, if you ask me, is the degree of irritation one must endure. In Hell—minimal. On Earth? *Endless.*

We rode into those caverns with a simple mission. The Fated's strength lay in its network of camps. Having exceeded recruitment goals steadily for months, the faction needed a quick and convenient place to house its most recently developed regiment. The caverns were a prime candidate. They'd served as barracks long ago. They were structurally sound, if littered with corpses and garbage. Not to mention, they were in stale gray territory that the Huntress faction held only by default and made little effort to defend due to the general uselessness of the surrounding land.

It should have been an uneventful day. But like I said, Earth's hallmark? *Endless* irritation.

We watched the meager Huntress party gather loudly and clumsily at the cave system's mouth. I'd personally hoped I was witnessing something of a land tour. *And here you see a bunch of empty caves. Nothing much of interest. Let's move along to that sad clump of trees in the distance.* But no such luck. They were there to "plunder" the many, many-times plundered caverns. The precise ones we were there to clear and claim.

The bloodlust ran hot in my party. Never mind that our targets were clearly Huntress in name only. Not a single one of them looked fit for a fight.

Well, perhaps one did. A young woman in an impractically colorful cloak possessed a weapon that, even from a distance, I could tell was blessed beyond any object I'd ever expect to find in the graylands. Its aura emanated a dark, thorny, unreadable power entirely at odds with its wielder's colorful knot of magic. But that was not unusual. Opposites attract—a truth to which fighter and weapon are far from immune.

And then I noticed her lute. *Haz's saggy sack.* A bard. Just my luck.

I'd been painfully bored by the idea of the encounter to begin with. It figured that my one hope for momentary intrigue would be a double-edged sword.

I sighed. I hated when civilians played at war. I hated when people got in my way. And most of all, I hated bards.

Naturally, I was in a foul mood.

The others babbled with excitement. As a scouting party, we saw more action than most of our regiment, but it had been a good while since we'd dirtied our blades. Our travels of late had been mild and dull. My party was excited to bring down this gazelle of a group, however grandmotherly she was. The should-be civilians had gone and received the Huntress's mark, and in doing so, had sealed their fates. There was nothing for it now but to get it over.

I will admit, my ill humor coupled with the certainty of their impotence made me...less careful than I ought to have been.

I entered the slaughter last, uninterested in participating lest I trigger some little-known subclause of my contract and end up in a psychotic state of torment. (Long story.) By then, death rattles sounded all around. I did not see the old man with his holy blade crouched in the shadow. It wasn't even a holy blade, in truth. It was a dull, rusted saber with a bit of holy water dumped on top. Ironically, that was one of the few things this meager party might have possessed that could have done my human form any real harm. Had I not been busy drowning in self-pity, I would have sensed and avoided it without hesitation. But I *was* drowning in self-pity, and I did *not* avoid the blow.

The holy water seared through my flesh, clearing the way for the rusted blade to burrow deep. I froze for only a fraction of a second. My furious gaze met the man's. He saw his death in the flames deep within my eyes. He was ash before he could scream. But unlike most of his companions, he didn't die without leaving a mark.

I yanked the saber from my human flesh and watched my blood spill from the gash. My party made quick work of the others as I attempted to glower my wound into submission.

"Nasty cut, that," Brü said with the irritating weight of an oft-recycled argument once his part in the conflict was done.

Brü had petitioned several times to add Aelith to our party. Aelith, being a true healer—and the woman in whom Brü liked to bury his cock anytime we weren't actively raiding. (If he could figure out the logistics, I'd bet he'd have it buried in her during raids too.) He acted like I was the one preventing her addition to our ranks, simply because I found her insufferable and she, in turn, loathed me. But I was not in charge of the colonel's decisions, whatever anyone liked to think.

"It's nothing," I said, and I knew my tone conveyed how not in the mood for this conversation I was. "Check for stragglers. I'll strip the corpses."

He didn't have to listen. I had zero authority here—by contract. But give an order with conviction, and you'd be surprised how quickly people jump to follow. In Brü's case, I think he just liked me. I couldn't begin to guess why. I was not *likable,* nor did I make any attempt to be.

When the others were gone, I knew even in my injured and distracted state that I had an interesting problem. The bard was alive. And hiding.

From my perspective, it was akin to watching a child cover their eyes and bask in the confidence that because they couldn't see you, you couldn't see them. Her aura radiated from the wardrobe like a beacon. Her panic made her colorful magic undulate in an inviting wave. And oddly, I thought I tasted a hint of citrus in the air that suggested mild arousal. Perhaps a misread. Even *my* senses could be flawed.

Demons tend to specialize in their brand of work. Punishers, for example, like to cause pain wherever and however they can. They smash the vulnerable. Guzzlers prefer to leach the will from their subjects until there is nothing left to take. They drink sentient beings dry. I have...more particular tastes. I am a Tormenter through and through. High emotions draw me like a moth to the flame. I like to taste them—to cause them—and, most of all, to see how high a pitch I can tease them to reach. I like people under my thumb. I like to squeeze.

My loathing for bards and my fury over the wound at my hip only made my hunger that much riper. I wouldn't get the pleasure of teasing the moment out the way I would have liked. Wouldn't get to enjoy the entire meal, so to speak. But I could take a bite.

I let her terror hang in the air. I needled it with a slow examination of the neighboring wardrobe, hearing her heart thud as I took my sweet time.

Then I pounced.

Before I shattered her door, I solidified my shadows to shield against the arrow I expected her to have readied. I'd seen the stunning bow after all. The shielding took effort with the wound draining my focus, but I wasn't about to take a second blow today.

Surprisingly, my shield turned out to be unnecessary.

The bard sat statue-still at my feet, eyes as wide and shiny as a kitten's—not at all the hardened adventurer she'd appeared from a distance. The weapon that might have given her a fighting chance lay utterly discounted on her lap. Instead, she clutched her lute as if it would save her.

I can heal you, she cried, but strip away the words and the utterance was an obvious plea. *Don't kill me. Don't hurt me.*

She would have to settle for one of the two.

If she'd played that thrice-damned lute then, I might have slain her. Luckily, her panic led her down a less strategic path. Her words spilled out in a barely coherent rush. I didn't need to do anything but stand there. She tormented herself. Just watching her come apart made my infuriating human cock pulse. Her tears made me rock hard.

I didn't care about most of what she had to say, but there were two things that stood out that I did care about.

First, she was not pledged to the Huntress.

I held the stolen cuff as she wiped demonstratively at her smudged ink. It wasn't hiding another faction tattoo. She wasn't faction *at all*—which meant that I couldn't kill her.

That was irritating.

It was also irrelevant, because the second truth made killing her out of the question.

The bard was from Finchton.

It was in the peaks and valleys of her vowels. The delicate inflections, the soft, unique flavor of the words as her tongue caressed them. Only a Finchton native spoke like that.

Although today's purpose was to perform menial tasks on behalf of the Fated, the reason I was *here*—existing on this mortal plane, trapped in human form—was to help the warlord who'd bound me win his war. In that task, I'd hit an infuriating wall. And it all came back to Finchton.

So, the bard would come with me. That much was settled, even if she didn't yet know it.

"Stop talking," I ordered.

I lifted my knife to cut a length of rope and scowled when she opened her mouth to protest. Bold little bard. In a flash, I envisioned half a dozen ways to teach her to listen the first time —and then realized that I would have to show *some* restraint if I hoped to elicit information from her.

I tied her wrists and examined the crossbow absently while I considered my options. The bow was just as impressive up close as it'd been from afar, dripping with enchantments. I didn't require a weapon, so it wasn't of much use to me. I reached for the lute, even less interested—but her immediate fury spiked in the air like volcanic gas. *That* intrigued me.

Don't fucking touch that.

I carefully masked my pleasure. There were people I spent years working to get that kind of reaction from. Show me where to hurt you, I begged them. And nothing. Not my little bard, though. She hissed like the naïve kitten she was, too angry to be wise.

I'll do anything. Please.

Her rising panic was the first salve to the wound that was my day. I breathed in her desire for a quick resolution. It tasted of bitter roses. She yearned for me to force the matter, to shove my cock down her throat or demand a healing song in exchange for my mercy. Neither tempted me. I couldn't break her...yet, but her words gave me an idea. She would do *anything?* I set the instrument carefully aside and reached for the artifact in my pocket.

I'd never intended to use it. It turned up in a raid and latched onto me. Darkness called to darkness and whatnot. I'd planned to hold it for trade. What did I want with a human pet, anyway? With all the rules imposed by my contract, it would just as soon be a nuisance as a toy.

Except. It *would* settle any concerns I had about the Finchton matter. One order when we reached the base camp, and she would sing.

To my surprise and further irritation, though, she refused.

How much did the bard know about the collar? Clearly, she recognized it. Did she know I couldn't simply clap it on her? That it would be nothing more than an expensive necklace unless she *chose* to submit and don the piece herself?

Not that I wanted to force her. Not really. My favorite flavor of submission is the kind my subject begs for. I strongly prefer manipulation to force.

I turned away, snapping an empty threat about the mines. She could chew on that while I spun my web.

I gave the rest of the gutted barracks a lackluster search— just to call it done—while I turned over what I knew about the bard. She was bold, to be sure. Brave too, considering the way she'd snapped at me. But not a martyr. She *had* chosen self-preservation in the face of imminent death.

I turned. I knew my path.

But before I could pluck her chords, she played them herself —again.

I'll wear it.

Her voice trembled as she attempted to elicit assurances I would not give. It didn't matter. She'd decided. My party had returned, and although I knew they wouldn't touch her—she'd convinced herself otherwise. I merely arched a brow and let her fears carry her across the finish line.

The collar snapped into place.

Her iridescent ribbons of magic flared against the stranglehold of the dark enchantments. I didn't push the collar. Her magic didn't fight it. It was a standoff—an impasse. Invisible to the human eye. A light show just for me.

She closed her eyes in anguished defeat. I'd never tasted anything quite so sweet. I was enthralled. I was addicted. The Finchton matter was a boon, sure—but I knew the real prize was the fact that now that the little bard wore my collar, I would get to break her a thousand times more.

I was so certain.

Of course, the adage would eventually ring true: A fool and his certainty are soon parted. Or whatever humans say.

Anyway, I can tell you now that I...underestimated the bard.

Chapter 3
Ero: Stubborn and Reckless

"They say to always bet on yourself. I say maybe consider all the options first if your "self" is someone who tends to overestimate her abilities." - an excerpt from the journal of Eroithiel von Dua, 1313 B.A., before the Great War

The rest of the party emerged as the clasp slid into place. The pitch of the complaints morphed into ribbing when they saw me. My crossbow quickly became the commodity of debate, and the man who won it in the mess of banter slung it over his shoulder as if he very much knew what to do with it. He did not even look at me.

I feared my lute would meet the same fate, but my captor casually picked it up and slid it into his cloak. If anyone noticed, no one bothered to challenge him about taking more than his share of the spoils.

A man with strawberry blond hair and an impish smile

dropped to the ground before me, eyeing the bloody corpse that had served as a table for my lute a moment ago.

"Ho, good sir!" He prodded the dead man's crushed skull with the tip of his dagger. "You look like you've got a *splitting* headache."

Disgust bloomed in my throat. I looked away.

I hadn't known the dead man for long. He sold spirits in town and had an endless well of tales about the travelers who visited his pub. He said he'd joined the Huntress faction for adventure, though he was clearly past his adventuring prime. On the walk to the caverns, he'd confided that his greatest desire for the day was to find a few interesting bottles to spruce up the decor for his patrons.

He didn't deserve to die.

When I failed to react to the grotesque show, the man gave up his game and cast an appraising look at me. Fresh alarm prickled my spine.

"Mammoth in the room, Book," he said. "You going to share?"

Book, it seemed, referred to my captor—who was busy speaking with another man. I spotted the sewn patch on his faction-issued cloak. *Bǔk*, not Book. Still, the irony was acidic. It seemed I'd gotten just what I'd come for. Wasn't that so often how life worked? Perhaps only for me.

The entertainer—*Flər*, according to his patch—stood when Bǔk failed to respond, adjusting himself suggestively as he padded closer to where I still knelt. I tried not to flinch away.

Flər lifted my chin and brushed his bloody, grit-smeared thumb across my bottom lip. "I'd settle for the mouth," he added, louder now. "Promise to give it back in top condition."

I fought for calm, but my unsteady breathing made it

obvious I was anything but. Hot tears welled in my eyes—and despite furious blinking, one slipped out. I'd put on the collar, and it hadn't even saved me. What garbage.

Abruptly, the hand disappeared from my face, and a grunt of pain hissed from my assailant's lips. We were eye to eye in a flash, he on his knees across from me, before I even registered that Bůk had moved.

"Do you see that collar?" Bůk asked Flər, his tone cold but so explicitly disinterested that he managed to sound bored. "Touch what's mine again and you'll lose a hand."

Flər glowered at me. Basic survival instinct told me to drop my gaze and wait for the situation to resolve. But give me even one single ounce of advantage, and I will abuse it. It's what I do best. Especially if you've recently made me cry. And yes—even if I, too, am still on my knees at someone else's mercy. So rather than look away, I stared directly at Flər and smirked.

Fury twisted his face. He looked like he wanted to spit at me —but he got to his feet and returned his attention to Bůk with a forced laugh instead.

"Hadn't noticed the collar," he said, chuckling louder for good measure. "All yours, Bůk. Wouldn't dream of touching your pet."

He sashayed away, casually sliding right back into conversation with the others as though he hadn't just been threatened with dismemberment.

I could feel Bůk's eyes on me. Pretending them away didn't work. Finally, I slid my gaze up to meet his.

He brought his knife to my cheek and scraped it gently against my skin. His focus narrowed on the glistening tear now at the tip of his blade. His tongue flicked out to lick it off. My stomach hollowed.

"Careful with those claws, kitten," he said in a low tone just for me. "Might come a day you'll wish you'd made a friend here."

Horses awaited us just outside the cavern. But before we could mount up, a massive, orcish-looking man begged for a short rest. Squabbling broke out. Some of the party were eager to get back to camp. Others agreed with the brute they called Hammond that food was in order.

Bůk's side lost.

He waved off his portion of the food and stalked into the woods alone without a backward glance.

I kept a wary eye on Flər, but he pretended I didn't exist. Most of the others followed suit. Brü—the apparent leader— handed me a hard bread roll. I spent the next fifteen minutes nibbling it and thinking about how nonsensical it was to put someone named Brü in a party with someone named Bůk. From a lyrical standpoint, I mean. What a mess. Faction leadership clearly didn't take input from bards.

When I finished eating, I got tentatively to my feet— waiting for someone to tell me to stay put. No one did, so I stretched my legs and took stock of my situation. The little town I'd inhabited for the last month or so would not miss me. They probably wouldn't even notice I'd gone. That was the unfortunate part about being a roaming bard. It was so common for my kind to come and go, people didn't notice or care much when we left.

I chanced a glance over my shoulder and wandered farther from the chattering men.

I'd always been good at adapting—finding the boundaries of a situation, settling into them, pushing where I found give. It took a specific combination of observational skills and existential uncertainty. If you never defined yourself, it was much easier to become something new over and over. Here, I thought, I would need to be clever. Outfoxing a demon would be no small task.

Speaking of the demon.

Bůk didn't make a sound. He simply appeared. His knife flashed out, cutting the ropes binding my wrists. He towered over me with his dark, glittering eyes and their all-seeing glare.

"We'll share a horse," he said, jerking his chin toward the beasts. Although the words were neutral, pain pulsed through each one. Bůk avoided wincing outright, but he couldn't conceal how badly his injury was affecting him.

Right. Sharing a horse with a grumpy, wounded demon was not on my list of hopes and dreams.

"I could still heal you," I said.

"You can't," he bit out, again seemingly irritated at me for forcing him to speak.

"How do you know?" I challenged.

The air grew several degrees cooler. I don't mean that figuratively. I wasn't imagining it. His mood *changed* the air. The wound must have been worse even than he let on, because when I sucked in that first frigid breath, it blistered my lungs like poison.

Bůk wiped a drop of blood off my arm, which I'd nicked on the wardrobe. He held it up, examining its bright red color pointedly, and I knew exactly what he was thinking. A healer like me, with human and fae blood, ought only to be capable of making his wound worse. Our kind weren't meant to *heal* demons.

"If you're wasting my time," he warned, "I'll compel you to serve the jester after all."

"Don't. Compel. Me."

Bůk used his blade to tip my chin until he had firmly ensnared me with his gaze. "Then I'll *tell you* to serve him. Is that better?"

The answer was obviously *yes,* in the sense that my greatest concern was the mind-eating spellwork and how it would unravel my sanity if he used it. But I couldn't *say* yes, because it also clearly *wasn't* better regarding the outcome of the situation. My silent swallow seemed to please him well enough.

"May I have my lute?" I asked.

"Can you heal without it?" he taunted.

I clenched my teeth. He was setting me up to fail. The truth was, I didn't know if I really *could* heal him, even with the instrument. It was foolish to have offered, and more foolish still to have pressed. But a wounded man is prone to bad temper— and a healed man ought to, at least on some level, be grateful. Right? It stood to reason that demons were similar. So, I'd let my mouth choose my path. Per usual.

Regarding the heal, I had a theory. I knew how to dispel holy water. I also knew how to close a wound by drawing on the elements rather than the heavens—a necessity if one hoped to help an unholy being. But I hadn't exactly *practiced.* And I wasn't sure dispelling the holy water would work inside a wound. And on top of all of *that,* I'd grown quite used to channeling through music rather than trying to force my magic to obey without it.

"I don't know," I confessed.

His lips set in a cruel smile. "Try."

I swallowed hard. Would he *really* give me to Flər if I failed? What even constituted failure? Certainly if he wanted to, he might call a scar *some* measure of failure.

The air chilled several degrees more. He didn't have to say a word. I knew I was out of time. I blinked away my doubt and raised my hands.

Rather than diving in with no melody at all, I hummed. It was nearly impossible to do even the first task with his dark glare trained on me. But the hum drew out the wriggling tendrils of power that lived deep in my chest. They were always temperamental about answering my calls. Perhaps my fear helped, though, because this time they came to life.

The holy water slowly fizzled and burned away. With my focus on the wound, I prodded at the tender parted flesh and sensed my way through the cleanup, methodically eradicating every drop of foreign moisture.

That turned out to be the simple part—relatively speaking.

The flesh was still burnt, and that reaction could not simply be undone. Worse, the exhaustion of the morning and the magic use so far was unraveling me from the inside. But I had no choice now. Not really.

And, fine. Maybe the challenge thrilled me a *bit*.

I closed my eyes and pushed. The dancing tendrils in my chest flowed through my fingertips into Bůk's gnarled skin. That part felt right. But inside, my body was aflame. I redoubled my efforts to focus. My attention narrowed to the sole task of cinching his flesh together, stanching the blood that got in the way.

I think I was making some progress. *Some*. But then I coughed. My tendrils scattered in a flash, and all that carefully held power fizzled far from my reach.

I gasped for air, mercifully free of Bůk's poison this time, and panted in a panic. He'd not given me a deadline. If I could catch a breath, I could try again—harder.

I looked up at him as my vision blurred in and out. The

wound was still there. There was still blood. Did it look better? I couldn't even tell.

I tried to speak, to explain that I only needed a moment, and that I hadn't given up.

Colors pulsed in my vision. That was new. Then they exploded, white-hot, through my body.

Everything went black.

Chapter 4
Ero: Marked and Fated

"The illusion of choice is addicting. But as addictions go, there are far worse." - a fragment of correspondence from a Temple Mother, preserved in the journal of Eroithiel von Dua

I woke up rocking to the beat of hooves beneath me. My entire body hurt. Probably because I was tied to a horse's ass like a saddlebag—and had been for gods and devils only knew how long.

I groaned. Although Bůk stiffened momentarily, he made no move to stop.

When I realized my situation wouldn't improve anytime soon, I closed my eyes and wrote a song in my mind to the horrid beat. The ride thudded on and on, and so did my song. By the time we slowed, I'd mastered the thing and almost wished I could try it in a drum circle. But I had greater concerns, obviously. Among them was how the bet—if you could call it that—would resolve. How was Bůk's wound? The question filled me with dread as the beast below me finally stilled.

Of one thing, I was absolutely certain. If any part of Flər entered my mouth, I would bite it off. Consequences be damned.

Bůk leapt from the horseback and hauled me unceremoniously to my feet.

"What do they call you?" he demanded without looking at me as he relieved the actual saddlebags of their contents and loaded them into his many pockets.

"E-Ero," I gritted out through muscle spasms.

"Arrow?" He lifted a brow, musing, probably the same as I had when I'd heard him called "book." I, an arrow that couldn't shoot. He, a book I couldn't read.

"With an E," I groused.

He snorted softly and adjusted the pack that covered his wound. My gaze fell to it nervously.

I'd never been a fan of mystery or anticipation, so I simply asked, "Is it better?"

He stepped toward me, and I stepped back—which placed me dangerously close to the tired horse's hind legs. Bůk didn't smile or even smirk, but I caught a glint of amusement in his gaze.

"A bit," he said.

I swallowed. What did that mean for his threat? Based on his expression, my anxiety was the point. The fucker was toying with me.

I dropped my gaze. Fine. If he wanted to draw it out, I would wait.

He made an approving noise. Clearly, he liked my deference. After a moment, he slid my lute out of his cloak and held it out to me.

"I'm not carrying this," he said. "Put it on. And do not play it unless I give you express permission. Do you understand?"

I took it, barely stopping myself from running my fingers over every inch of the polished wood. Gods. I'd missed it. I wanted to wax the wood and flick the strings and scream all at once.

Get it together, Ero.

The air chilled, and I looked up to find him still waiting for my answer to what had apparently not been a rhetorical question. His onyx eyes glittered with warning.

"I understand," I said, before he could reconsider and pluck the instrument from my hands.

It was only then that I realized he'd given me a direct order, and I'd felt no compulsion from the collar. Not that I knew exactly what that would feel like, but I supposed it would feel like *something*. I'd made a choice not to run my fingers over the lute. That wouldn't have been necessary if he'd compelled me.

So...did that mean he was honoring my request?

My heart beat faster. Stupid heart, in its quick search for hope. It'd always been my least reliable organ. My gut—*that* I could rely on. My gut told me the lack of compulsion didn't *mean* anything. At best, it meant I would have a little bit longer with my mind intact—assuming I did everything he asked willingly—and didn't bore him enough to make him seek a new form of entertainment at my expense.

"Come on, better to do the branding tonight than just before a ride," he said.

I turned to follow for a beat before his words sank in.

"Wait. The *branding*—?"

A scream rang out from the fire pit. Haloed in the evening gloom, a short line of prisoners in various states of ravishment lined up, eyes trained on the front of their line where the screamer stood held in place by two men as a third pressed a red-hot metal brand to his forearm. The blood drained from my face.

"In line," Bůk said.

He watched me curiously. I did not move.

The air thickened with his anticipation.

"Why?" I hissed. "I have the collar. I—you've already—"

"The collar is *mine*," he pointed out. "You cannot stay in a Fated camp without belonging to the Fated."

I scanned our surroundings, desperate for something I could use to get out of this. Of the many forms of torture, burning was second only to madness on the grand list of Things Ero Avoids.

The factionites in the camp largely ignored the screamers. Likely, they were commonplace after a day of raids. These must have been prisoners someone had opted to keep rather than sell to the mines. At a glance, I could guess what some were being saved for. There were those with obvious brute strength who would do good work keeping the animals and carts moving. A few pretty ones whose fates I didn't want to think about. Still others who looked wary but intelligent. Perhaps they'd begrudgingly leveraged their healing or magic talents to keep themselves above ground. One creature with horns looked rather like he might have secret plans to burn the whole place down. Best of luck to horn guy.

Around us, people settled and set up tents, made smaller fires, and arranged makeshift tables for their dinner. On the far side of the main fire pit, I spotted another line. A woman straddled a bench, inking initiate lines on a young man's arm while two others waited.

"If I have to—" Bůk started, and I tasted his lazy growl.

"Ink me," I blurted. "I'll speak the oaths. I'll join properly."

What did it matter to me? I'd pretended to join the Huntress faction before only because doing so in truth would have rooted me for too long in one place. But I had neither loyalty nor aversion to any particular faction. Unless the alleged "great war" doomsayers liked to wax on about actually materialized—which seemed unlikely—being faction might have its perks. Anyhow, if I would belong to the Fated by evening's end one way or the other, why shouldn't I join willingly rather than allowing them to brand me as a slave?

Bŭk stepped toward me. He seemed to quite enjoy using his size and proximity to intimidate. This time I didn't step back. I just looked up at him. I even tried to do the doe-eyed thing softer, prettier girls used on adventurers in the pubs. Just for a little pizzazz.

I softened my voice considerably. "Please?"

"I suppose you did heal me," he said. "However inexpertly."

It wasn't a yes. And I wasn't stupid enough to think anything was guaranteed. I held the demure pose.

He took my wrist and turned it over. His thumb traced the outline of Haz's mark. I shivered.

The air grew heavy and almost warm just for a moment. Was that a sign of his pleasure? Of acceptance?

"Alright then," he said. "Get in *that* line. Find me after you're marked."

It turned out I was supposed to know the vows stepping up to that line. Lucky for me, the man ahead of me was a Nervous Nester and mumbled them under his breath over and over for a good ten minutes before it was his turn to speak them.

When the woman stood ready to accept my vow, she stared

with obvious interest at my collar first. She looked back in Bůk's general direction and then to me again—but she did not ask whatever was on her mind, and I did not volunteer information. I simply spoke my vows.

Death to the old ways.

Death to the life before.

Live will I in the light of wartime.

Live will I under the Fated's gaze forevermore.

They were stupid vows.

But then, to my mind, most vows were stupid. Vows were promises uttered in the heat of a moment, meant to last for some alleged "ever after" when in reality people changed all the time, minute by minute. Desires changed. Nothing was ever more than temporary.

"Careful," the woman murmured, even as she pricked my skin with the first drop of ink. "Your mind is unguarded, and your face might as well have writing across it."

Warmth flooded my cheeks. It wasn't the first time I'd been accused of lacking even the most basic gambling face. I could *lie*, of course, when I wished to. Yes, with effort I could put on a good show. But most of the time, I knew my face spoke my thoughts. I just hadn't expected their meaning in this moment to be so obvious.

"You belong to Bůk," she stated—not a question. "Interesting."

I hissed when her needle struck a sensitive patch. I hoped that obscured whatever my face might have had to say about my "belonging" to Bůk.

The tattooist finished the outline and looked up at me. Scars marred one side of her face. That wasn't uncommon across our war-torn continent, but the dark curved pattern of these scars made me uneasy.

"Free advice," she said so quietly that I knew the man behind me could not hear. "Don't underestimate him. Lord Austvix's wrath is fearsome. Bůk's is deadly."

I stepped back. Whereas my face showed all, hers was a perfect mask. Had he done this to her? The bitterness in her tone suggested so.

I had so many questions, but the woman turned to the man behind me and motioned him forward into a space that he could only occupy if I stepped aside. She'd intended to end a conversation, not begin one.

I turned back toward the camp with a renewed sense of unease.

Run, both my heart and gut said. It was so rare to find them in agreement that I faltered.

Bůk was nowhere in sight. No one was watching me. He had not compelled me to stay. I wouldn't be able to remove the collar—but how far could it reach? Surely he couldn't bid me return from just anywhere.

My heart galloped as I moved through the crowd. I walked fast, but I didn't run. I flowed with the others, allowing their momentum to push me deeper into the encampment. I wasn't sure when I crossed the line from considering to doing, but at some point I knew I'd already made my choice. Once I realized that, I drew my lute into my hands and strummed.

Under my breath, I sang a song imbued with luck. Its familiar flutter lightened my heels and pushed me on, occasionally guiding my step away from something as small as a puddle of muck or as treacherous (presumably) as a wrong path.

The tents lined the sprawling field right up to the edge of a dark wood. I stepped into the trees without hesitation, trusting my song to guide me true. Toward freedom, away from wolves and demons and worse.

My mind skipped three steps ahead as I ran. I could deal with the new ink on my wrist later. It was fresh and would take time to fade—but it *would* fade. My skin did not hold ink well. I'd gotten Haz's gauntlet refreshed on my wrist every single year at the temple, and even so, by my next birthday I knew it would be as pale as a normal person's decades-old tattoo.

The deeper I got in the woods, the louder I played. It seems counterintuitive, I know, but luck told me the way—and I had to trust in her.

After all, luck had never yet betrayed me so deeply as she would that night.

Chapter 5
Bůk: Thrill of the Chase

An excerpt from The Adventurer's Compendium, entry on Demons: "The best strategy for evading a demon is to avoid eliciting interest or any other strong emotion to begin with. The second-best strategy is to pray."

"There was no resistance at all?" Colonel Astrada demanded of our scouting party. "Not even a minor conflict?"

After I sent the bard to get her ink, I'd *hoped* for a moment of silent respite in my tent. I had plans to make, now that I had a fresh lead on the Finchton matter. Unfortunately, Astrada decided the debrief couldn't wait. Her minions herded us unceremoniously into the command tent, and there we sat, reporting all the nothing we encountered in great detail.

Flər opened his scroll and gestured to the two measly paragraphs he'd recorded, then said in a tone bordering on impertinence, "It's right here, Colonel. That band of townies was the whole of it, and I'd bet my left nut the Huntress didn't even know about them. They weren't fit for target practice, 'cept Bůk's new little pet."

Flər looked triumphant about his report, because Flər was an idiot. I saw what he did not—the growing uncertainty and concern in Colonel Astrada's icy blue eyes. She smelled a trap.

Astrada ran a hand through her silver locks, which hung uncharacteristically loose. She and the rest of leadership had been close to turning in for the night when we'd arrived. I'd never seen Astrada's hair out of its typical skull-tight bun. The effect was disconcerting. My thoughts wandered briefly to the bard's erratic auburn braid. Lingering notes of her salty tear teased my tongue. I clenched my fist, imagining how it would feel to grip those silky tresses—to wrench her head back. What precisely would it take to make her scream my name?

"Bůk?"

Astrada stared pointedly at me.

"Apologies," I said drily. "I find it taxing to pay attention when the jester speaks."

Flər flushed. Colonel Astrada smirked faintly, but there was no humor in her sharp eyes. She held my gaze.

"I asked if you had a sense of the Huntress's intentions," she said—or, probably, repeated. "Is it possible she actually abandoned the area wholesale? Or do we have reason to expect conflict in the pass?"

Colonel Astrada was cleverer than most. She would make her choices independent of my recommendations. It *was* unusual for the Huntress to abandon large swaths of land. We *would* need to move cautiously as we crossed the contested territory to rejoin our base camp. But what Astrada really wanted to know was if I'd had any precognition about the enemy's plans. I was no oracle. My ethereal gifts were more temperamental than that. I could taste desire like a sixth sense —but intention, I had to work to unravel. Unfortunately for the colonel, I hadn't yet had a moment of peace to do so.

"I'll do my best to have an answer by morning," I hedged. "Barring that, as Flər noted, we saw little action on our run. We're more than capable of scouting in the morning."

Flər's expression darkened. Technically, we were owed a few days of light duty. There were other scouting parties Astrada could send. But aside from the fact that we were the best, any hope I had of reading the Fates would be exponentially more successful away from the larger group and their aural interference.

"As Bůk said," Brü cut in, "we can go."

"I'm afraid that would be best until we get a stronger sense that our path is clear," Astrada said. "We've lingered here long enough for our enemy to make plans. I mislike that. Not to mention, we'll be hauling a lot of supplies with relatively few soldiers to protect them."

I kept my face carefully neutral, though the delicate criticism of faction leadership amused me. Astrada had to follow orders—but she knew damned well that it would be her head if those orders were flawed. And they clearly were. We'd ventured this way with three hundred bodies. Two hundred would remain behind to populate the newly established outpost in the caves. That meant there were only a hundred in the returning party to protect the train of carts bursting with the logs, crops, game, and raid spoils we'd amassed from the contested lands. I couldn't have designed better bait if I'd tried.

"Bed down, crew," Brü said with finality. "We'll ride ahead in the morning and clear the way."

Flər shoved out of the tent first, leaving no doubt what he thought of the plan. Brü was less of a child about it, but he too looked frustrated. After weeks in the saddle, he was ravenous for some time with his woman. How frustrating it must be to have human attachments.

I stepped out into the clear starry night, hoping once again to find my solitude.

From the dim path, I surveyed the camp, listening to its unique pitch. No two camps ever sounded quite the same—even if they contained most of the same factionites doing most of the same things. The audible hum of energy in the air was an alchemical combination of the place, the moment's weather, the alignment of the stars, and yes—the people with their ever-shifting arrays of emotions and intentions.

I listened, knowing that if I could spare just a moment for stillness, I might catch a thread that would tell me everything Astrada hoped to know.

And that's when I noticed the silence.

Not in the camp—that was as loud as ever—but in the pitch of energy around me. An absence. Where the bard's colorful hum had been since I entered those caves, there was... nothing.

The tent flap rustled as Brü, who must have lingered to have a private word with the colonel, came out.

I ignored him and strained, listening with all my senses, earthly and otherwise. Through the wild, tangling thicket of vibrations, I finally sensed it. Faint—and growing fainter.

She was running.

"What is it?" Brü said darkly, noting my expression.

Fury bloomed in my chest and flowed to the tips of my fingers. I gritted my teeth, forcing a calm I didn't feel because I knew everyone around us would be privy to my emotions if I didn't rein them in quickly.

"Go to Aelith," I bit out dismissively.

Brü frowned. He wanted to listen—obviously. But he was too attuned to me to pretend he had noticed nothing.

Knowing he wouldn't leave it at that, I snapped. "The bard ran."

The flash of sympathy on his face was clearly *not* for me. Brü knew damned well the bard wouldn't get away. Leave it to him to feel sorry for her.

"Try to enjoy the chase," he said cheekily, a hell of a lot more relaxed now that my fury didn't require his attention. "Just don't go mad? And don't exhaust anyone we need."

I grunted. I might have told him to fuck off, but a flash of blond hair accompanied by a feminine squeal announced Aelith's arrival. She hated foul language. I *tried* to avoid provoking her, purely as a favor to Brü for not being half as irritating as every other human on the continent. It was a delicate balance.

Brü caught Aelith midair as she leapt into his arms and wrapped herself around him. But for their clothes, they probably would have copulated right there on the path. The tenor of their mutual desire sang so loudly it drowned out everything else.

I walked away.

My anger grew steadily as I stalked into the dark, giving the tents a wide berth so that I might let my rage flow freely without starting a fire.

I'd been *more* than fair with the bard, hadn't I? I wouldn't pat myself on the back for keeping scum like Flər from touching her—the emptiest threat I'd ever issued—but I would have been well within my rights to claim that precious lute of hers. Or to smash it. She'd been foolish to parade around as faction. I could have branded her for that, too. I could have caged her. I could have—perhaps should have—used that collar to compel her obedience.

My mood soured further at the thought. How dreadfully boring that would be. To put a will as strong as hers on ice. No, souls like hers were designed to be tamed—twisted and teased and bent until they broke. Then repaired and broken all over again. The collar was supposed to be a fail-safe, *not* a necessity. Yet she'd had the audacity to cry and beg and sing empty promises—and then spit in my face at the first opportunity.

I'd shown restraint with her in the cave. That was over now.

As I circled back to the barracks to gather a handful of initiates to man the hunt, a flicker of something...not exactly *happy*, but satisfied grew in my chest. Damn Brü. He knew I would enjoy this. Knew I'd been longing for entertainment outside of the slog. *Try to enjoy the chase,* he'd said. I wouldn't do that. But I sure would enjoy the catch.

I led my little party of initiates into the woods, content in knowing their nervous energy didn't come close to what I would tease from my kitten when I caught her. Her pain would be the sweetest salve for my weary bones—and by morning, I would drink that inflated will dry.

The bard was about to learn a lesson.

Chapter 6
Ero: Invoking His Wrath

Bardic Advice from Eroithiel von Dua to future generations: No one in the realms can humiliate you as thoroughly as you can humiliate yourself.

The woods glittered with possibility.

I breathed in the musky air, feeling more alive for the way it stung my lungs as I sang. What was triumph without a *little* pain, anyway? My feet fell silent and sure, wringing every ounce of advantage from the fae half of my blood. *Too bad for you, Mother,* I taunted, *I got this one small boon from you after all.* Oh, how she would hate to know she'd helped me.

The more distance I put between myself and the Fated camp, the more paths unfurled in my mind. Honestly, I'd been overdue for a change. Playing the same pubs in that town, seeing the same faces—friendly but never *friends*. And who was to say the book I needed wasn't leagues away, anyhow? Histories traveled.

Or, so I told myself as the other options went to ash behind me.

I sure *hoped* the book I needed was far away, because it would be a long while before I came back. Bůk knew my real name. Even if it was only "Ero" in place of the supremely more trackable "Eroithiel von Dua," it would require sprucing wherever I went next. Perhaps I could be Eve or Tyla or Daphne. Those had a nice ring.

My foot splashed in a shallow stream. I leapt featherlight over a fallen tree and followed a moonbeam into a clearing. For the first time all night, I paused. The crisp air kissed my skin like an old friend. My heart swelled. I felt so good, so right, so *safe*. I—

Mist swirled around my ankles, lapping at my legs.

Strange.

I looked down slowly to find that my fingers had stilled on the strings. Stranger still. I hadn't intended to stop playing. It was just the overwhelming sense that I was already free, that I'd accomplished my objective.

My mind was slow to process. By the time I realized the mist was to blame, it was too late. The luck evaporated from my veins, leaving a horrid hangover in its wake. The air turned warm, humid, cloying. Suddenly, rather than frolicking in a pleasant night wood, I was cowering in a dark forest, feeling eyes on me from all sides.

When nothing emerged from the gloom to confront me outright, I stumbled forward—but now my heart was heavy with fear and my fingers struggled to gain purchase on the lute.

It was almost a relief when the netting snapped around me, jerked me into the air, and hung me from the tree. *Almost.* Because the anticipation was over. But everything else was about to get much, much worse.

The riders didn't take long to reach me. In other circumstances, I might have fought the ropes, cut myself free, and been away again—but these ropes were imbued with magic that prevented that. Another *almost* mercy.

When they came, I knew he was among them. I knew well before they were in my sight. The air sang with his fiery rage, as furious and radiant as a midsummer sun. The young initiates in his party were not immune, though not one of them had the courage to voice discomfort. They'd all sweated through their clothes and looked irritable and exhausted as the party surrounded me.

Bůk cut me down himself, and I shook too violently to stand. He was going to give the order, and I knew it. And this time, he wouldn't spare use of the collar. I would crawl back to the Fated camp and do exactly as he bade as my mind unraveled.

"I'm sorry," I choked out, even though I'd practiced half a dozen lies while I'd hung there. I'd lost my way. I'd been possessed. I'd misread him and thought he might *enjoy* the hunt, so really wasn't it sort of a gift? All of that sounded absurd now.

"You will be," he allowed.

He dismissed his men with a wave of his hand. They fled, greedy for clean air.

He glowered down at me. "You played."

I blinked, mistaking him at first. I thought he meant I'd played a game by running. But no—he stared accusingly at the lute. I had played it, of course. I'd just expected the whole fleeing his captivity part of my transgression to be the bigger deal.

He reached out, touching the collar thoughtfully as I fought to control my panic.

"Please," I choked, even though it was more than obvious that any goodwill or bargaining power I'd accumulated had drained away. "Please don't."

"Then how will I keep you in line?" he mused. He sounded mild, but the air didn't cool a single degree.

I knew better than to trust his bait. His fury was untouched. He towered over me, glaring down with a fierce and terrible beauty that painted my flesh with goosebumps.

What could I say? I certainly wasn't going to shrug and tell him I supposed he was right and it was time to flay my mind after all. I gritted my teeth against the challenge of inventing my own custom punishment that would both satisfy him and not kill me. A tall, impossible order.

In my frantic search of the surrounding area, my eyes snagged on his horse. Hanging from the saddle was a worn leather strap. The image of that strap wrapped around his hand, of it lashing out to kiss my skin, flashed in my mind. I looked away again quickly—afraid he would follow my gaze.

Naturally, it was too late. His dark pleasure rippled through the air.

Our eyes met. We both knew the answer, but he didn't move a single muscle. One corner of his lips curled up in a cruel smirk. He was going to make me *ask* him to punish me. And for all I knew, he would refuse and compel me anyway.

I couldn't form the words. I stumbled toward the horse instead, my destination blurring with angry tears. I jerked the strap from its hook and brought it to him. My breath hitched when he failed to take it.

"Please," I whispered.

The blazing air cooled just slightly, mirroring the satisfaction in his eyes.

Yet still he waited. His brow knitted together as though in deep thought. I saw the moment he decided it wasn't enough. My heart skipped.

"Make me believe this will help you learn your place, kitten," he purred.

I took a shaky breath. Was he *serious?*

He crossed his arms.

Yes. He was serious. And if I found it this hard to humiliate myself *without* compulsion, how hard would I fight if he actually used the collar? I would break myself in minutes. I knew it in my bones. It *couldn't* happen, no matter what it cost my pride now.

Prickles of raw humiliation rippled through me as I sank to my knees. I held the strap up and forced myself to look at him.

"Please," I said. "Teach me what happens when I disobey you."

I'd meant to make it a performance. To tell myself that I was merely on stage playing a role. It didn't work. When I met his eyes, I wondered if the mist was still fucking with my head —because a stab of heated desire roiled in my belly. I hated myself for imagining his strong arm holding me down, his teeth grazing my skin as he took me hard and fast.

Blood rushed to my cheeks. I couldn't stand it. I broke eye contact, even as I feared that doing so would mean failing this undefined test.

But to my surprise, the inferno surrounding us receded in a chilly rush.

He plucked the strap from my hands and pulled me to my feet. His strong fingers cupped the nape of my neck, his thumb digging in with a slight warning pressure. He guided me to the trunk of a fallen tree. Then he released me and waited, staring expectantly. I closed my eyes and bent over the tree, steeling myself for pain.

Nothing happened.

When I looked back, he raised an eyebrow and looped one finger lazily in the waistband of my riding leathers. I fought to swallow as I tugged them down—baring my ass to the gods, devils, and Bŭk—and resumed the position.

The zip of air before the leather struck was my only warning.

A furious sting erupted in the strap's wake, and I cried out pitifully. To my deepest horror, an answering ache resounded between my legs. I told myself when I trembled under his gaze in that cave that this was not at all what my fantasy had been, not *really*—but my body said otherwise now. I was appropriately incredulous. Did the strange, uncivilized thing at my core —the voice that always said to push, always tempted me to reach for trouble—*enjoy* this?

The strap struck again, lower. The first welt was fire now, the second an angry biting sting.

No. Whatever the hunger inside me was about—whatever my broken mind dreamt of on empty nights, this was *agony*.

Fuck. Him.

"Was it *wise* to run?" he gritted out through clenched teeth.

Another strike before I could answer. Two more in quick succession when my breath hitched, and I failed to find words.

"I *said*—"

"No!" I cried. "No. It was— I was—"

The words turned into a shriek as his next strike seared the back of my thighs.

"—scared," I hissed.

"Not scared enough, kitten."

He punctuated the snarl with a *thwack*.

"I'm sorry!" I sobbed.

I was furious with myself for meaning it. I didn't *want* to be sorry. I wanted to be angry. But the taste of his rage in the air made me queasy. I didn't like that he'd honored my requests—first by not using the collar, and then by letting me take the tattoo in place of the brand—and that I'd taken the very first chance I had to show that no part of that respect was mutual. This is what I'd always done. This is who I was. The scoundrel, talking sweet and then fleeing into the night. Only this time, I'd been caught. "I'm sorry, I'm *sorry.*"

"Not sorry enough," he said, though there was less heat behind the words now.

He delivered a fresh blow diagonally across the welts that had already accumulated, and then another crosswise to complete the X.

I sobbed in earnest, praying to gods I knew and others I didn't, that he was finished.

The strap stilled, but his hand on my lower back held me in place. My insides twisted. I could feel his gaze surveying his work. The air grew thick with the sizzle of his pleasure. I whimpered.

Bůk's thumb traced featherlight across the freshest welt on my ass, from top to bottom.

"Did you enjoy that?" he mused.

My breath shuddered. I wanted to shout something fitting, such as, "*No, obviously not, you soulless rancid hellspawn.*" But as his thumb reached my thigh and skated along the contour of my ass toward my pulsing center, a fresh panic washed over me. He was two seconds from finding out the answer for himself—and my body would not lie.

I stood abruptly, spinning to face him. Pretending I wasn't caught between a demon and a tree. Pretending my leathers weren't around my ankles. I lifted my chin with a fury only the threat of utter destruction by way of humiliation could have breathed into my soul.

"Are you satisfied?" I spat.

His smirk returned. Whether at the question, my sudden anger, or the fear that hitched my words, I didn't know. Perhaps all three.

He was too close. The tendrils in my chest tightened and twisted. My body was entirely out of sorts. My pussy thought we were on an adventure, and my heart thought we were in battle.

He lifted the strap between us. I opened my mouth—to protest? To plead? I don't know. No sound came out. He flicked the leather, so the tip caught my lips. Just hard enough to sting. Enough that my eyes burned.

I longed, absurdly, for him to press his lips to mine to swallow that sting. To bend me back over the tree and use a different tool to finish this job.

"Are *you* satisfied?" he mused silkily. "You're the one who got on your knees and begged me to do that."

Heat flooded my cheeks. I closed my eyes. Because he was right. I *had*. If the gods were watching, they would have had mercy and smote me right then. But even they must have turned away from this.

Bůk allowed me a moment to drown in my shame. And then he reached a hand around and slapped my searing ass cheek lightly with his palm before stepping back.

"Get dressed," he commanded. "We'll be in the saddle from dawn to dusk tomorrow. You need sleep."

His sudden lack of proximity left a ripple of cool air and emptiness behind. The world spun as I bent to lift my leathers, trying not to think about how the saddle would feel in my current state. I wondered how covertly I could heal. It was a struggle to get my pants back up my thighs. When I forced them over the fresh welts and fixed them on my hips, my world exploded again in agony.

"Get on the horse," he said. A hot breeze stirred around us to match the fire in his eyes. His almost-playful demeanor vanished. He wasn't teasing anymore. He *was* still furious. "And if you heal yourself, the next round will be *much* worse. Do you understand?"

Did he read my fucking mind? Or was it just that obvious that a healer would make quick work of vanquishing her own pain? I swallowed, the fight gone out of me. "I understand."

The horse was too tall, the saddle too hard, but I gritted my teeth and climbed.

He leapt into the saddle behind me and compressed our bodies together, reaching around on either side to take the reins.

"Wait," I whispered hoarsely, spotting my lute on the forest floor.

He stiffened. I turned to look up at him with pleading eyes, uncertain how even to begin to bargain here. I hadn't forgotten that he'd confronted me about playing my instrument before he'd even mentioned the fact that I'd run.

But to my surprise, Bůk flicked his wrist with a grunt. A tendril of shadow drew the lute to my lap.

My murmured *"thank you"* was lost to the night as his horse leapt into action.

I stroked the polished wood, careful not to disturb a single string. I focused on the pleasant sensation at my fingertips to distract me from the friction of my terrorized ass grinding against Bůk and the saddle. The fifteen-minute ride back to camp was the most excruciating quarter hour of my life to date. Not least so, because I knew that tomorrow would be a hundred times worse.

Chapter 7
Ero: A Ride to Remember

Bardic Advice from Eroithiel von Dua to future generations: The ability to follow orders is often overrated.

I was right. The next day was worse.

I slept on a thin mat next to Bǔk's—having failed to collect my own Fated-issue tent and bedroll in my eagerness to flee. I woke to find my hands in soft leather gloves. I tried to pull one out, only to further discover unforgiving metal bracelets looped around each wrist with tiny locks cinching them in place.

I frowned at my lute. The gloves were meant to prevent me from playing. The tendrils of magic in my chest raged against the insult.

I sat up, trying to calm my fury, only to get a sudden and forceful reminder that my ass was in a dire state. Flames erupted along the welts, and I yelped, tipping forward onto my hands and knees to relieve the pressure.

I'd never dealt with pain of any duration before. Not since I'd learned to control my healing well enough to nip hurts big and small in the bud with song.

I sucked in several breaths, straining to slow my racing mind so I could think.

And then Bůk arrived.

The tent flap blew aside, and before I could adjust my position or turn to face him, his hand clapped my ass, which I'd only just served up in the air.

I cried out. He laughed. It was the first time I'd ever heard the sound, dark as night and rich as molasses. I might have enjoyed it if my fury hadn't consumed me.

"Do you like the gloves?" he asked, stepping deeper into the space and reaching out to cup my cheek mockingly.

The movement was not gentle. I was grateful for that, and the warning in his gaze. Because only fear could have prevented me from snapping. I couldn't afford to antagonize him again so soon.

With monumental effort, I swallowed every retort on my tongue and managed a mild, "They've made your point."

He grunted. A single pull on the tent's drop string collapsed it into his waiting hand. That fast, we had an audience of dozens. The sharp morning sunlight made me flinch. I remained on my hands and knees at his feet, cringing at the curious looks.

Bůk stalked to his horse, which was tacked and waiting a few paces away, and jumped on. I feared he would pull me into the saddle in front of him, as he had the previous night, forcing a day of excruciating friction *and* proximity. But when he'd settled, he draped a spare saddle mat behind his seat and turned to reach for me. I wished for nothing more than the ability to leap up without his waiting hand. I did not possess it.

My legs screamed in protest just from the two steps I had to take to reach the beast. Grumbling, I took his waiting hand and swung up onto the mat.

Although the mat was marginally better than the hard saddle, we weren't fifteen minutes into the punishing ride before I'd fisted his shirt in both hands and soaked the fabric through with my tears. I shifted and squirmed, attempting to sacrifice my right leg and then my left for any chance of relief for the other—even trying to hold myself in the air with my knees—certain I would pass out from the rhythmic thuds against my raw ass before the ride was complete.

Would he catch me if I fell? Punish me again for slowing him down? Let me fall and be trampled by the others? I didn't want to find out.

While I focused on surviving my personal predicament, the party came to an abrupt stop. I hissed when Bůk's sudden jerk on the reins slammed me back into my seat. His hand shot back, fingers digging painfully into my thigh in warning. The message was obvious: *Silence.*

There was one terrifying beat of stillness, during which I assessed our party. It was the same small collective that had overtaken my group in the ruins. Apparently, these were the chosen ones who got to wade into dangerous territory before the rest of the faction followed.

The beat of stillness ended. Hellfire rained down.

It was an ambush, and we'd ridden in blind. This time there was no wardrobe to dive into. But also this time? Bůk was on *my* side. Relatively speaking.

Flər turned out to be a few hells of a caster. His instant incantation blocked the flames that would have cooked us all. Through his shield, I still felt the blazing heat of the inferno, but I didn't get burnt. The man who'd stolen my crossbow leapt up to a crouch in his saddle and loaded *my* weapon. A series of shots fired into the woods.

Bůk lurched out of the saddle—leaving me crashing forward into the void he'd left. When I righted myself, he stood impossibly far up the path. Our assailants' cries of surprise gave away their positions, but by then, it was too late for them anyhow.

I watched in horror and awe as Bůk's shadow grew from that of a man to that of a beast. His actual frame seemed larger too, though not nearly proportional to the shadow. A wave of fire washed from his feet outward in a perfect circle, illuminating our assailants on either side of the path even as it set them aflame and drew their screaming cries.

My stomach fell. I froze. Bůk's expression grew *thirsty*, not even remotely satisfied by the destruction he'd already wrought. He turned like an apex predator to seek new targets beyond the flames.

I felt fingers clawing at my neck for a full beat before I realized they were my own. Then my mind caught up. In my trance, I'd apparently decided I could not wear this *thing's* collar a moment longer. Fear of Bůk pierced straight to my heart. I'd just watched him roast ten spirited fighters as an effortless appetizer, and every insult I'd spoken—every quick retort I'd issued in the last two days—the way I'd dared to *run* from him, played on a horror loop in my mind.

He was right. I *hadn't* been scared enough. I was now.

I half leapt, half fell from the saddle. To do what? Not run again. Gods and devils.

I froze, realizing there *was* no escape. Not now. I still had a semblance of a survival instinct. What would he do to me the next time I crossed a line? There *would* be a next time. If I was born for one purpose, that purpose was crossing lines.

I struggled to catch my breath. This was *not* the time to panic. Yet, here I was, panicking.

A loud thunk next to me yanked my attention back to the battle. The man who'd claimed my crossbow lay dead at my feet, one of his (my) own arrows stuck grotesquely into one unseeing eye.

How was that even possible? Arrows couldn't—

A fresh volley of cries interrupted that thought. Right. Fight now. Think later.

Bůk's ring of fire sizzled another group of hidden soldiers. How many *were* there? I thought he'd cooked most of them already. But no, through the flames came at least two dozen more. Their party was massive. Too large for the handful of us, even with Bůk slaughtering them in scores.

I grabbed my crossbow, turning it unsteadily in my shaking hands. There were only a couple of arrows left. Fuck. I didn't even know how to *draw* the thing. Even if I managed it, I'd be as likely to shoot someone from my party as I would be to hit an enemy.

I flirted briefly with the idea of hiding behind a tree and simply turning myself over to the victor. But no…I'd inked the Fated tattoo on my wrist. There was no wiping that away. My new reality was this, for better or worse.

The burning need for my lute sent my tendrils writhing. If something didn't change, we were all going to die. I lifted my hands to assess the gloves.

"Bůk!" Flǝr wailed, and my head snapped up again.

He was surrounded by the enemy. The others were in no better shape. The only thing saving them was our assailants' apparent desire to take prisoners. Surely, they would have already been felled otherwise.

I swallowed. The time for idleness had long passed. I was no archer, but I had *magic*. And I wanted to live.

My song started soft. A cappella. Not my favorite way to do things, but I had little choice. It was my best battle song. Two overlapping melodies, one to bolster those who would keep me safe, the other to distract those who would do me harm. Would that put Bůk and his people on the right side of the music? I could only hope.

The tendrils in my chest twitched like feral cats being asked to play nice without the enticement of a treat. I needed my damned lute. I *longed* for my lute.

To hells with it all.

I clawed at the gloves, dashing them violently against anything I could reach. The panicked urge to fight imminent death with stronger chords of protection outweighed even the fear of what Bůk might do to me for disobeying him again. (Though only just.)

In the end, the gloves were no match for my tailspin. With the aid of a knife from a fallen man's hip, I tore them to shreds.

At the first strum of my lute, my tendrils *soared*. The soft song rose with a fearsome swell. Words changed on my lips to a language I didn't even know. I sang in tongues. I screamed the lyrics. I let the magic unfurl.

Flər's assailants stood briefly stunned, but the jester showed no such hesitation. He lifted his blade and slew them in short order. The others engaged around us had mixed success. They all gained an edge, but some were quicker to use it than others.

It was Bůk's reaction that paralyzed me. His shadow doubled again in size, spilling over the treetops. It wasn't just factionites who cried out. The panicked hisses and squawks of woodland creatures fleeing chilled my bones. Despite my horror, I did not slow my song. I played louder, sang the words *at* Bůk, and watched the magic work.

Bůk's flames abandoned their tidy wave formation. They sailed through the dark trees in flaming balls of vengeance, flushing out every hidden fighter, torching people I'd not even known were there.

They all died screaming.

Bolstered by the turn of fortune, my song reverberated with refreshed confidence. The battle was over in minutes. The Fated around me roared in the throes of victory and adrenaline. Someone pulled me into the celebratory throng—and I, at the height of my magic-drunk euphoria, allowed it. I hugged, I high-fived, I shouted insults at burnt corpses. (That was a bit much, I admit, but I was thrilled not to be among them.)

I raised my hand as the crowd spun me toward another party-mate, ready to celebrate with him as I had with the others. But his angular face was still, his green eyes troubled, and he didn't seem to see me at all. It was Brü, the one who commanded the little group.

I followed his gaze. Bůk faced away from us, his body tensed. He was framed by two thick trees, one hand on each, both aflame and glowing red. His shoulders heaved. For a split second, I thought he was sobbing. But no. He was sucking in breath after breath, overcome with rage.

Oh. Shit.

Brü's hand closed around my elbow. He frowned down at me. "Mount up, initiate."

I looked from him back to Bůk, letting out an unintentional groan as one of the burning trees collapsed. A flaming branch glanced off Bůk's shoulder. He didn't even notice.

"Ero, right?" Brü asked in a tone that lived somewhere between stern and empathetic. "Listen, he won't be able to ride. We'll meet him at the next village. Our path is clear now. I *will* need you to mount up."

I didn't ask how he knew our path was clear. Or *if* he really knew. It could have been a guess. I suspected from his certainty, though, that it was not. Someone in the party might have read one of our now-dead adversaries—a mind worker or a necromancer or some such.

It didn't matter. I wasn't about to disobey a superior's order. I had enough problems at the moment.

I took a deep breath, nodded, and moved for Bůk's horse.

Brü called after me like an afterthought, "Do try to heal yourself and any factionmate for whom you can spare the energy, Ero. And good work. Your song saved a few asses."

He turned away without waiting for my response. Brü had a natural charisma, in that I immediately wanted to please him. Which annoyed me. And yet, in much the same way I'd glommed onto the Huntress party when I'd sought safety in numbers, I knew I didn't want to face these woods without Brü and his team. Nor did I wish to go anywhere near the raging Bůk.

I touched my lute hesitantly. I chanced one last look Bůk's way, only to find the place he'd stood empty. Through the tattered gloves, I played again, blanketing our party in healing melodies.

Guilt, dread, and relief mingled in my belly as the cuts and scrapes faded from my hands...and the welts faded from my ass. I was only following orders, I told myself. Yet the tattooist's words and Bůk's both swirled heavily in my mind.

Lord Austvix's wrath is fearsome. Bůk's is deadly.

If you heal yourself, the next time will be much worse.

I took a steadying breath as the melody faded and Brü's orders to mount echoed around the clearing. Bůk's saddle was still warm. It was comfortable now, too. The others formed up around me, several issuing passing words of thanks for my songs.

For a moment, I allowed myself to feel the familiar and intoxicating joy of belonging. For a moment, Bůk wasn't there to take it away.

Chapter 8
Bůk: Tormented Indeed

Demon Binding Code 1.1: In accordance with this agreement, the hellspawn shall be granted a human body and confined to earthly form, free from and untrackable by the Hells until all terms of said agreement have been fulfilled. Should the Bound breach the code herein during its period of service, Torment shall have full reign.

By the time I felt the breach, it was too late to rein it in. And thanks to the gods-damned bard, I couldn't have even if I'd wanted to. Her song jabbed at my psyche, shattering my control and amplifying my instincts until everything that followed was as good as inevitable.

I was a weapon and nothing more.

There were civilians woven in among the factionites in the Huntress party. I know, because I felt their deaths like bursts of mage fire in my skull. The last sane thought I had before my contract's cold, inky magic ripped coherent cognition from my grasp was that the Huntress *knew* my limits and had intentionally included these people in the raid party— either to protect her factionites, assuming she expected me to hold back in self-preservation, or to put me out of commission.

Neither option meant good things for the Fated. We were being outplayed.

The Huntress's purpose quickly became irrelevant to me, however. Her party was slain to the last soul—and my ability to perceive anything beyond pain winked out.

Brü once asked what happens when madness takes me. The truth is, I could never recall enough to articulate the experience. This time, however, I was blessed or further cursed to maintain a bare shred of awareness.

The heat came first. Licking from head to toe, sinking its claws deep into my flesh and raking them to the discordant melody pounding around me. It didn't matter that the bard no longer played. I heard her anyway. My flames danced to her cursed beat.

Now, demons rarely complain about fire. We are from it and of it. We wield it and bend it to our will. But just then, I lost whatever immunity I had. Like a bard who woke to find her voice gone. Every blazing flame burned me as readily as it would have a human—and they were inside me, so that was a bit of a problem.

I threw myself into a body of water. I don't know where the water came from or how I got there, only that it was there and I experienced the faintest measure of relief as I sank into its icy depths. My body died in a matter of minutes, the way weak human bodies will when they are deprived of oxygen. One might think this was better, but one would be wrong. Untethered from my flesh, the psychological pain became my entire existence. I would have built my body anew from sheer will had the binding not done it for me.

I reincarnated on the bank, slicked in boiling mud. All I could do was scramble back to the water, grasping again for a tiny shred of relief as the air attacked like so many angry hornets.

This time, I didn't drown. Piranhas found me first. Their razor-sharp teeth tore my brand-new flesh from my brand-new bones and soon, I was once again a heap of freshly made human in boiling mud.

This went on for some time.

With each reincarnation, I tried to hold my place in the mud—knowing that eventually, the boiling torment would subside. That I would regain control. But here's the thing about humans. When they find relief—a way to stop their torment, even briefly—they will flock to it again and again and again. No matter how dire the consequences. No matter how counterproductive. Humans are weak, and because *they* are weak and I existed in human form, I was similarly weak. Or so I told myself.

The point is, I paid for the lives I took outside the bounds of war. I paid, and I paid, and I paid.

Not that it did anyone any good. Did it bring the dead back? No. Did it help my faction or harm its enemies? Not a bit. But vengeance without gain—isn't that about as human as it gets?

After an untold stretch of time, knowing that I needed to claw my way out of the torment cycle and back to sanity, I reached for a place to focus my thoughts.

I started with Lord Austvix—the Fated's warlord, the man who'd bound me. But his face wavered and slipped from my grasp like a freshly caught fish. The bastard's magic protected him even from my thoughts.

I reached for Brü next, knowing full well that was no use. He was the nearest thing I had to a friend. My mind wouldn't allow *comfort* at this stage. Electric shock chased each flash of his endlessly patient face away.

So I moved on to Aelith, Brü's water witch of a lover. She hated me more deeply than he knew. The only thing she desired *more* than Brü's cock was my death—and I wasn't even sure *she* knew that. But I did. I tasted it in her energy, in the way she tensed when I neared, in the way her teeth clenched and her chest tightened when I spoke. Her dedication to her gods infuriated me, because I knew she would sacrifice Brü if the heavens demanded it. And he knew it too, and he didn't *care*.

The mere thought of Aelith flooded my chest with fury. The heat grew worse—not better. In my rage, I boiled the water around me. Several piranhas died, which I suppose was a small bonus. But so did I, this time cooked alive in my own anger.

I woke again in the same mud, in the same agony.

This time, the bard's face lit up my mind. I reached greedily for the sight of her tears, but saw instead the challenging set of her jaw as she snapped at me.

I screamed my frustration, water pouring into my mouth and choking me as I wailed. I'd punished her, gloved her hands, made her ride with a reminder of my lesson written across her ass—and when the party needed more than we had, she'd *still* played despite my orders.

Stupid. Brave. Infuriating bard.

She'd saved Brü and the others even as she'd destroyed me.

I scooped up fistfuls of mud in my brand-new hands, howling with need. But I didn't let myself go back to the water this time. How many times had I died by then? Ten? Twenty? How much time had passed? A day? Two? The silt squished through my fingers in sickening snakes, sizzling as it fell back to the ground.

My stomach growled. Exhaustion tugged at my eyelids.

I needed to return to the camp. If I left them waiting, they would be in further danger—and if they bore losses because of my absence, my contractual torment would continue in a ceaseless cycle. Not to mention, if the bard died, I'd be that much further from solving the Finchton problem.

It was time to get myself together.

With great effort, I stood.

I wasn't ready, and I wasn't better—yet. But I would be. Until then, gods save anyone who had the misfortune of standing in my path.

Chapter 9
Ero: Taking Action
for the Faction

"What is the opposite of cutting off your nose to spite your face? Dealing with your face to indulge your nose? What if your face deserves spiting, but your nose really just needs a win right now too? What I'm saying is, maybe it's fine to compromise now and again. Maybe." - an excerpt from the journal of Eroithiel von Dua, 1313 B.A., before the Great War

I slept alone for two blissful nights. We sang around campfires and retold the story of the battle until it grew into the legend every hard-won victory deserves to be. I put the words to song and enchanted the civilian tavern-goers. On the third night, we used their tips to buy barrels of mead. Everyone relaxed into the revelry.

Well, almost everyone. Brü stood apart from the others, brooding against the inn wall. I frowned. Approaching him would risk puncturing my own rare bubble of joy, but I couldn't unsee him. And I couldn't shake the whisper of dread his countenance conjured.

Sighing, I approached.

Brü watched me, his gaze openly curious. He didn't mask his melancholy—so I wasn't subtle with my prodding.

"What's wrong?" I asked.

"Bůk," he answered simply.

The name sent tingles down my spine. While the others were around, all aglow, I could convince myself that my brief flurry of mortal terror upon seeing Bůk fight was a temporary blip on my path to this new reality of warmth and belonging with the Fated. Acknowledgment of Bůk's continued existence put a wrench in that fantasy.

"He should be here by now," Brü said.

I settled against the wall next to him, watching the others muster around the mead with raucous delight. Clearly, they were unconcerned—and just as clearly, they did not expect to have an early morning tomorrow. I chewed my lip, curiosity getting the better of me. As always.

"What happened to him after the battle? He was...off."

"He killed civilians." Brü winced, scrubbing a hand through his mussed hair. The way he gave me information—directly, without hedging or dancing around it, had the annoying effect of making me like him more. As if to underscore that winning trait, he went on. "He was already in a frenzy, and that can be hard to come down from. But it's a lot harder when he's breached his contract."

I stiffened. His contract? That *was* interesting.

And then something clicked. In the cavern, before I'd taken the Fated marking, I'd *been* a civilian. Coloring a fake tattoo on my arm hadn't changed that. Was that why he hadn't killed me? Had my garbled pleas been unnecessary?

I glanced at the darkened trees. "So he's just out in the woods...burning things?"

"Trying to come to his senses, more like. But if he'd had any success, he would be here by now. We're opening ourselves to attack by waiting. He wouldn't do that if he'd regained control."

"Will we go after him?"

"No," Brü said firmly. "Colonel Astrada knows that would only risk further delay. I think she would just order us forward, but after the ambush...we don't know what we're walking into. Bůk has senses the rest of us lack. We rely on them, unfortunately."

"So...waiting is dangerous and moving forward is dangerous," I summarized.

He nodded grimly and surprised me by confiding further. "The real trouble is, Bůk regaining his senses enough to turn up doesn't mean he'll be ready to perform on the road. And we *need* him ready." He sighed, scrubbing a hand over his face in a way that suggested he'd been locked in an exhausting cycle of comparing several equally poor plans. And he wasn't even the colonel. "Never mind. You should join the others and enjoy the night while—"

A brief round of whooping and cheers interrupted Brü, drawing our attention back to the fire. A shape had emerged from the trees.

My heart stuttered.

Bůk.

But that wasn't what the whooping was for. A sultry line of costumed entertainers had emerged from the tavern at the same moment to join the circle. They'd made their rounds each night, seducing factionites—dancing, flirting, sneaking off into the shadows to do more. The party was about to begin in earnest.

"Ero?"

I startled. Brü stared at me. Whatever he'd just said, I hadn't heard him. He registered my frozen expression with grim understanding.

"He has...other things to worry about," Brü said, barely a murmur, though his tone stopped far short of trying for reassurance. He knew damned well that even if Bůk didn't opt to... well, act like Bůk tonight, I was still back at my captor's mercy now that he'd returned. We all had our problems.

"Come on," Brü said.

Together, we moved away from the inn wall into the throng of cheerful people at the fire. Brü and I took seats on the opposite side of the ring from Bůk. Even from a distance, I saw alarming changes in him. His pupils glowed scarlet. His cheeks were drawn, his gaze hooded.

Somehow—*somehow*—the seductresses making their rounds managed not to skip him. They were brave. They flirted. They *touched* him. He issued terse responses until they moved along, some looking relieved and others disappointed.

"What does he...need?" I breathed to Brü when I caught him watching Bůk intently.

"To fuck one of them through a tree and get it over with," Brü grumbled.

I snorted. I'd thought the answer would have to do with potions or...I don't know, meditation?

"Knitting works too," Brü went on, continuing an impressive run of uttering totally unexpected nonsense. "Though he hates it, so it's a bit of a two steps forward, one step back deal. Carving figurines is better, but if he nicks himself with the blade, it might be two steps forward and *four* steps back."

Brü realized he'd lost me. He finally looked away from Bůk and met my eyes.

"He needs to ground himself," he explained. "But his binding is determined to torture him for his breach. To pull out of it, he needs a task that fully occupies his mind." Brü smiled ruefully. "Sex is by far the best."

I blinked. Wow. I knew the coital arts were useful for getting the mind off general problems. I'd never pegged them as a salve for magically induced psychosis.

"If that's what he needs, why isn't he...?" I trailed off, cocking my head at the latest woman to settle next to Bůk.

"Because he can be a bit intimidating in the...uh, act." Brü pressed his lips together, as though that were a vast under-statement. His amusement faded in favor of a grim frown, though, as Bůk shooed away the latest flirt. "The problem is, if they run, his instinct will push him to give chase. He would catch them, of course, and then...well, depending on how far gone he still is, things could get out of hand. If one died, he'd be back to square one. Even if they didn't, he would still have to deal with the weight of whatever harm he'd caused in his rage."

My vision dimmed at the edges. I knew too well how Bůk's chases could end.

I swallowed the memory and shrugged dismissively. "Like he cares."

Brü had been leaning in conspiratorially. He sat up straighter then. "He does." He shot me an assessing look. "If he didn't, it would make it several hells of a lot easier for us all."

Why did I feel chastened? I had *plenty* of reasons to ques-tion Bůk's character. He'd been a brute to me without showing a scrap of the internal conflict he apparently had for these women. And he was a *demon*. That didn't exactly scream moral code.

"So, all he needs is a willing partner who can't run and for whom he won't be punished if he causes accidental harm?" I asked.

Brü snorted. "If we're wishing on stars, sure."

He kept talking. Something about more realistic options, each with significant downsides. Lost time. Potential for failure. Weak returns. But I didn't listen. I stared at Bůk.

The firelight framed his rigid muscles in a tantalizing glow. His hard glare made love to the embers. I couldn't help but recall the way it'd felt to have those eyes on my exposed ass—the horrible, wonderful anticipation as he'd surveyed his work and traced his thumb across the welts toward my too-telling arousal.

The memory already had me wet. For half a minute, I let myself imagine it. Dubious though my connection to the Fated might be, wouldn't it feel good to play the hero? *And* to get this grotesque fantasy out of my head once and for all? And! To kill *three* birds with one arrow, might it even balance the score with Bůk, since I'd technically played him into madness while disobeying him yet again?

I winced, not totally able to convince myself of the last bit. I'd be safer staying out of sight and out of mind, I reasoned.

And then Bůk's gaze snapped to me.

As though he'd heard my thoughts, his eyes arrested mine. The tendrils in my chest went taut even as the ache between my legs pulsed. I wanted him the same way that tiny part of me always longed to jump off a cliff when I neared one's edge. Deep need reverberated through me, distant thunder before an inevitable storm.

Much like it had when I'd spotted that leather strap, a

certainty bloomed in my chest about what would happen next. I'd always had more daring than sense. And didn't I *owe* myself this one small thing? A fantasy come to life.

I stood, realizing dimly that Brü was still talking. Poor guy. He deserved to unload to someone. Normally, I would have been a decent choice. I answered his confused look with an apologetic smile, then strode away and skirted the fire to stand before Bůk.

Bůk glowered up at me. That *should* have snuffed out my desire. Instead, it stoked it.

"Let me help," I said. My voice did not shake. I was being a *hero*, dammit.

For a moment, the world paused. Towering over Bůk, I felt... powerful. My insides swelled with the sensation. It was foreign and tempting and wholly without precedent. I hungered in a way that had nothing to do with my aching clit. I sucked in a breath. Maybe I needed to examine this sensation...later.

Something of my power trip must have shown on my face, because Bůk caught my wrist and squeezed. Hard.

The smirk died on my lips. Bůk twisted my arm and pulled me roughly into his lap so that I faced back toward the fire. Like any prey, my chest trilled when I could no longer see his eyes. His hand settled at the hollow of my throat. His lips grazed my ear.

"Walk away, kitten," he growled. "Or I'll take you up on that."

I tried to twist in his arms, but there was no give, so instead I craned my neck—exposing more of it in the process—to look up at him. Could I really do this? What *exactly* had Brü meant by "intimidating in the act"? Bůk was intimidating *out* of the act. *Could* I handle him?

"If I take you into the woods," he said, speaking to the night without looking at me—but also without loosening his grip, "it's no game. You will not run."

I reminded myself to breathe. For some reason, my body stopped handling that function on its own.

"I couldn't, could I?" I whispered, raising the hand he'd not arrested to touch the collar gingerly. "Aren't I your safest bet?"

The red swirled in his irises as he searched my eyes with his penetrating glare. What was his issue? When I ran out of other plausible explanations, I was left with two awful possibilities. First, he feared he would *actually* kill me. Second, he didn't *want* to fuck me. The former was terrifying—the latter, somehow, worse.

"No," he said. "I still have a use for you. Go back to Brü—"

The rejection pierced my heart and made all the recklessness in my body surge to the forefront.

"I healed myself," I pushed, too thrilled by the adrenaline coursing through me to listen to something as pesky as my survival instincts. "On Brü's orders."

Bůk's jaw clenched.

"And I've played at the fire every night. I suppose I could stay and do that some more instead if you—"

The surrounding air heated, as I'd known it would. My logic, which had retreated to a locked box somewhere far from my pulsing and possibly scorned womanhood, shouted at me to—at the *very* least—stop taunting the gods-damned demon. But I was incapable. I'd never felt more alive.

I hummed so quietly it was barely a tune. My magic caressed the melody.

Bůk's reaction was immediate. The hand he'd draped across my throat squeezed, instantly taking my air away.

I froze.

"If you're so determined to taste me," he growled, "ask nicely."

His grip eased, though his hand remained in place. Finally, he looked down at me. I stared into the once-onyx depths of his eyes, now bright red like embers. I'd always been drawn to danger. But this? This was...something far beyond.

I inhaled slowly to steady my breathing and said, "Fuck me until you're sane again, Bůk." I licked my lips and added, barely above a whisper, "Please."

The words hung in the night air for a pregnant moment. I couldn't sense his emotions at all. I couldn't read him. Even the shadows swirling in his eyes stilled.

And then he stood like I wasn't in his lap, and I fell unceremoniously toward the ground. I braced myself for impact, only for his rough hands to snatch me from free fall. He slung me over his shoulder like a sack of grain and stalked toward the woods.

The last thing I saw before the dark swallowed us whole was Brü's horrified face across the fire ring.

Chapter 10
Ero: In Over Every Head

Bardic Advice from Eroithiel von Dua to future generations: Be cautious, but don't forget to live a little. Like, if you get a chance to fuck a demon... don't quote me here, but... you know. You *know*.

Bůk walked for several long minutes. Long enough that I needed to shift for comfort on his shoulder. He answered the tiny motion with a stinging slap to my ass—and I couldn't prove it, but the dark laugh that followed felt like a direct commentary on the way I consumed the spark of pain like a pleasure wine.

By the time he stopped, we were far from the camp. He put me on my feet, my back to a tree, and stood too close. He pinned me with a warning. "Stay."

Heat flushed my cheeks. There was nothing I was so prone to do as disobey a direct order. It was in the building blocks of my soul. But I humored him this time.

He extracted a heavy metal chain with two iron cuffs from a

satchel at his hip. A tiny spark of fear wormed its way through my lusty exterior. Brü had said that Bǔk refused to fuck the entertainers because they might run. No one was *running* from those.

"They're for me," he grunted, reading my expression. Or my mind? Could he *do* that?

He looped the chain around a low-hanging tree branch, dangling the cuffs above our heads. He fixed one onto his own wrist, and at his prompting grunt, I helped with the other. Then my gaze dropped to his pants—which was perhaps too direct, but his enthusiasm already strained eagerly against the strange shadowy fabric. There went the fear that he wasn't interested.

"No...foreplay necessary?" I breathed.

"Your tears are my foreplay."

My gaze snapped to his. How was he—chained to a tree—still in control of this? For fuck's sake.

"Are you going to do something stupid, or are you going to get on your knees now, kitten?" he growled.

The words simultaneously enraged my mind and lit a blazing wick between my legs. Nice. Good. At least I was *consistently* contradictory.

"Both?" I said, as the heavy drunkenness of power finally bloomed in my chest.

"These chains won't hold me if I don't want them to," he warned.

I would call that a silly boast, but I'd seen him during battle. He was probably right.

"You *do* want them to, though," I shot back, sinking in slow motion to my knees without breaking eye contact. "If you lose control, you return to your little mental torture chamber."

"Careful, or—" he started.

But I didn't let him finish.

"What do you need from me?" I demanded. "And I don't mean here, in the woods." I ran my fingers gingerly along his length, pausing at the tip. To ensure I made myself crystal clear, I added, "I know what you need right *now*. But why did you collar me? At the fire, you said you still had a *use* for me. I didn't miss that."

His jaw ticked in warning. A thousand dark promises shone in his eyes. He could break the chains and take me—but if he did, he might thwart himself. Still, I acknowledge that I was pushing my luck.

"I said—" I started, pouring cockiness into my tone just to get under his skin.

"Translations," he snapped.

I blinked. Because...what the fuck? Selling me to some rich barbarian with musical sexual tastes, sure. Tormenting me for his own pleasure, I wouldn't even question. But *translations*? How bizarrely mundane.

"Say more," I ordered—but, sensing that he was in danger of combusting, I began the slow process of unlacing his pants to tease the promise of imminent relief. I pressed my lips against his cock through the straining material.

"You're from Finchton," he gritted out. "The accent. I recognized it in the cave. Your people speak in riddles. Invitations to tea go six fucking wordplays deep. We have letters, and we need to know their meaning *now*."

I stared up at him, mouth partly open. And yes, I was surprised, but the gesture was also a bit intentional—because I knew what he wanted, and I deeply enjoyed keeping it just out of his reach.

"I'm going to make you regret every fucking second—" he started.

I loosed the last tie, reached inside, and drew him out and into my mouth in one quick motion. His words dissolved in a groan. I traced my tongue around his head a few times, then drew him deeper.

Now, I was more of a student than a field specialist when it came to sucking cock. I'd spent many a long night listening to women more experienced than I swap stories and recount in shocking detail the things they'd done to tame this variety of snake. But I'd had limited opportunities to practice. The men I'd experimented with were too impatient for that. One batted me away and bent me over when he'd realized I was a novice. Another held my hair and set a choking pace and then refused to meet my eyes as I'd spit the resulting mixture of vomit and cum into a washbasin.

Those men had been mistakes. No better than fodder for a few bawdy lyrics.

This moment, however, was not about giving immediate or perfect pleasure. That was quite freeing. So what if I was bad at it? So what if it took all night? Even better. Let him suffer.

I paused, breathing around his shaft without moving.

The air rippled as his anticipation morphed into irritation.

I chuckled, which probably felt better than he deserved. Only when his warning growl reached me did I resume motion.

I tried not to think about how good he tasted. As if I needed one more piece of evidence that my soul required a thorough cleansing from the gods. But until I could find a temple to fix me, why shouldn't I enjoy this?

"Use your hands, kitten," he ordered.

I trailed my hands up his inner thighs at a glacial pace, holding his gaze as I did so. Saying *fuck you* with my eyes while I literally fucked him with my mouth. With one hand, I cupped his balls. I took deep satisfaction in the sound he made when I wrapped my other hand around the base of his cock.

The tendrils in my chest gave an unexpected jolt. For a fraction of a second, I was afraid we were about to be attacked. My magic burned with readiness. But...no. There was no threat. It was just that rush of power again. I could squeeze. I could destroy. I could bring him to his gods-damned knees. I positively burned with that high.

When I looked up to check his face, I found him frozen, staring so intensely at me that my stomach flipped. I didn't look away, though. I pumped his shaft and trapped his sensitive tip between the roof of my mouth and my tongue, keeping a perfect rhythm like the good little bard I was. His balls tightened in my hand a second before he came.

I didn't release him. I swallowed the salty brine and kept going, teasing his flesh with hums and puffs of breath until the temperature spiked around us.

"Are you satisfied?" I mused. It was hard to speak with his cock in my mouth, but I managed. I'm determined like that.

"Stand up," he ordered.

I chuffed, annoyed that he was coherent enough to issue the command. I *felt* like I'd done better than that.

With a final slow breath, and perhaps the lightest squeeze to remind him I actually held his balls in my hand, I released him and stood.

"The key is around my neck," he said.

I searched his eyes. Still red. My mental victory lap fizzled, replaced by alarming doubt. He wouldn't have cum if it'd been *that* bad, right? He didn't look angry.

"Something wrong?" he purred.

That quick, he had the power again. Even though the

chains still held him. Something in his voice told me I was being naïve.

I reached for the key tentatively, and despite the certainty that he was leading me into a trap, I said, "Your eyes don't look better."

A cold smile curved his lips. "My pleasure doesn't help with that. I just wanted to see your mouth do something useful for once. Now unlock me."

A strained breath slipped through my lips. For a moment, I'd almost lost myself to the fantasy. I'd almost forgotten who Bůk was. I averted my eyes so I wouldn't have to watch him enjoy his victory as I lifted the key and unlocked one wrist and then the other. The air sizzled around us the moment the second cuff came off. I had to shield my face to protect it from the rush of heat.

What was *that?*

When I dropped my hands, he was rubbing his wrists. They were mottled red and raw. The cuffs weren't tight, and he hadn't tried to fight them, so that was odd.

"Undress," he commanded.

I dropped the cuffs, peering up to see if he was serious. But of course he was. This was exactly what I'd offered him.

The red in his eyes briefly glowed brighter.

Fuck.

My body seemed to remember that I was keeping company with a demon who had the option to mind flay me into doing what he liked a beat before my brain did. I dropped my fingers to my shirt and tugged it off. My boots and then pants and underthings followed.

"Put those on," he said, pointing to the cuffs.

A chill rolled down my spine.

"I don't think that's a good..." I whispered, then trailed off. "You know I can't run."

"You put them on like you're told, and I'll do this the nice way," he said. "If I have to put them on you, I won't. Pleasure or pain? It doesn't matter to me. Which do *you* prefer?"

His thumb traced the leather strap hanging from his belt. I hadn't noticed it before. He smirked accusingly. My cheeks blazed.

"Can you read minds?" I didn't care that asking meant tacitly admitting my depravity. This was the third time I'd gotten the impression that he knew too much of my mind— things he couldn't possibly have guessed *so* correctly.

"Desires, kitten." Bůk said. "I can read *desires*."

He moved closer, encircling one of my wrists gently with his thumb and finger. His lips grazed my forehead, and I could tell he wanted me to look up at him, so I did. His red eyes shone with malice. He lowered his voice to a silky rumble. "When you were in that wardrobe, I could smell it on you. You would have been thrilled to suck my cock to save your life."

A traitorous prickle of tears sprang to my eyes. Because he was right. And I couldn't think of anything worse than his knowing it.

"In the woods," he continued, "I might not have been as hard on you, but you enjoyed my strap a little too much. I needed to make sure the ride was the real punishment."

My tears spilled over. Embarrassment and shame twisted my insides.

I needed to get away from him. This was a fucking mistake. I needed to run—and I *couldn't*. It was one thing to indulge myself and let him use me for our mutual benefit. It was something entirely different to hear him recite my innermost secrets

—truths I would have taken to my grave rather than admitting out loud.

"Please stop," I said.

"You said you could handle this," he taunted. "Were you *wrong*?"

Oh, fuck him.

If there was one thing I would never admit.

His hand moved ominously for the cuff, but I raced him there. Call it a twisted type of self-preservation. I snapped one cuff into place and groped for the other.

A wave of nausea stopped me. The cuff was spelled.

The tendrils in my chest receded sharply from the assault of the metal, like a pet with a trampled tail. A hollow chill gripped me. I couldn't bite back the whimper that spilled from my lips.

Bůk watched me closely as he reached to help with the second cuff, his gaze settled even as my breathing became erratic and my tears flowed faster.

"There they are," he purred, pausing long enough to trap my chin in his fingers. His tongue flicked out and ran slowly up my cheek.

The air swelled with his arousal. He wasn't kidding. My tears *were* his foreplay.

I was too busy quietly panicking to be indignant. The cuffs were *dampeners*. Of course they were. They were for him—to keep him steady while he worked out his demon rage. But on me, they *attacked* the musical knot in my chest that gave me life. This was out of bounds. It wasn't exhilarating sex. It was *murder*.

"Please," I cried. *"Please!"*

He was considerably taller than me, and with my hands in the cuffs, I couldn't put my heels firmly on the ground. I swayed on my toes in my panic.

"Bůk, I—I—"

Bůk dropped to his knees. My breath ceased to exist. Seeing that man kneel before me did things to my insides I couldn't explain. A horrid symphony of empty pain clashed with a rush of powerful pleasure.

No! my head shouted again, though the rest of me had already abandoned the fight.

Bůk didn't use my own slow-burn tactics against me. Quite the opposite. He lifted me off the ground and flung my legs over his shoulders, pinning my back against the tree with his face buried in my pussy. His tongue took me before I could cry out again. Even my head shut right the fuck up then.

I was instantly blind to the forest and the rest of the mortal realm. Blind to the pain of being separated from my magic. His tongue swirled against my clit with perfect pressure, like he knew exactly what my body needed. And then it snaked into me...but the lapping pressure on my clit didn't let up. I writhed, trying to look down at him to confirm what I felt.

Holy fuck. Holy fuck. Holy. Fuck.

I'd *seen* his tongue. It wasn't—but yes, right now it was. Forked. One side swirled in perfect rhythm outside and the other plunged in, curling forward to hit a spot no one had ever touched.

I came unraveled, pulsing around him in a pathetically short amount of time. I cried out, throwing my head to the side. Our shadows in the moonlight stretched across the trees in uneven waves. His loomed unnaturally large.

I wasn't fucking Bůk, the man. I was fucking Bůk, the *demon*.

There was little time to grapple with that, because he didn't let up. I keened and cried, desperate for a chance to catch my breath—a mercy he refused. Soon, I didn't want it anyway. He withdrew his outer attention from my sensitive bud and traced every curve and valley instead, tickling and lapping, and playing—all while inside, he drove deeper and harder. A fresh wave of need grew until I bucked my hips, silently begging for him to finish it.

Only he knew.

He knew exactly when I was on the edge of tipping, and he stopped. *Now* he was getting his revenge. He teased me to the precipice of release once, twice, thrice...each time freezing to blow cool air over my pulsing need.

I cried. I begged. His warm tongue trailed slowly over the cold, bringing temporary relief—but not release. Inside me, he curled to graze that secret place. Just barely. Telling me he knew where I wanted him and driving me mad with his refusal. Then he thrust again, mercilessly, until my legs trembled.

"Bůk, I'll—I'll fucking—I'll—"

Kill you? Crawl on my hands and knees and grovel at your feet if you just let me finish? I couldn't decide.

His low chuckle vibrated against me. That nearly did it too.

Any promise I made now, I would inevitably break tomorrow. We both knew that.

I had no power.

I sagged in defeat.

And then he gave me everything at once—the swirling suction, the curling friction, the hot breath.

I came screaming. Stars burst in my peripherals. I blinked at the forest, unable to see straight.

"Stop!" I cried then. "I—I—"

But my pleas no longer resembled words.

"Try meaning that, and maybe I will," he taunted.

I didn't mean it, and he didn't stop. He didn't even slow.

His tongue pushed me through the wave of pleasure,

answering my growing hysterics with amused flicks and merciless strokes. He shoved me through the agony as my body screamed for respite and started the build of tense pleasure all over again.

"Haz!" I cried out, my god's name wrenched from my lips in a fit of pathetic sobs.

Bůk stopped then, just long enough to glower up at me. "He's not welcome here. You call my name, or you take it in silence."

Silence then, I vowed.

I sucked in a breath, but his tongue was already back at work *everywhere*.

At some point, I realized I was crying his name. Another vow broken.

I came apart again, and again, and again.

And. Again.

Chapter 11
Bůk: New Resolve

Bůk's Personal Code, Item 3: Thou shalt not be distracted by a mortal.

I don't know how much time passed in the woods. I lost track of the number of orgasms I wrested from the bard's writhing body before she went limp in my chains.

I crossed back to this side of sanity before she passed out. I remember that much. Perhaps I should have stopped then—but I didn't *want* to. She was so swollen and slick and sensitive, and the rest of the night had been so horrific, I took what I wanted. An unhurried taste of what she'd so unwisely offered.

Or...had it been unwise?

I marveled at the need to wonder. Not once while she was conscious had she *stopped* desiring more. Not when she cried out, not when she begged like she'd been driven to the brink of madness. Not even when her body showed signs of giving up. Through all that, she still *wanted*.

Now I listened to her soft shuddering cries as I removed the dampeners from her wrists. She curled into me. *Terrible* instincts. But I held her in my arms, glad she wasn't awake to open her mouth.

In the silence of the night, everything that'd led to that moment caught up with me. The ambush in the woods. The feeling I'd gotten right as it'd begun that we would not walk away from it. Well—*I* would. I couldn't help but walk away from it. Immortal being, and all. But for a moment, I'd been certain I would be the sole survivor from the Fated camp, waking up alone to report the losses to Colonel Astrada.

A strange feeling nagged at me. By rule, I didn't care about individual mortals. But the thought of Brü—and even Tavish, Hammond, and Nigel—slain to a man filled me with something like...was it frustration? I mean, fuck Flər. They could have done me a favor there. But the others? People took getting used to. Starting over would be so tedious.

The bard moaned in her sleep. I paused, wondering if she would wake. She didn't. Her flushed cheeks, stained with dry tears, glistened in the moonlight. Her pink lips parted to allow a few shaky breaths to escape.

My infuriating kitten wasn't so bad like this. Unconscious. Soft. Serene. I smirked. But my amusement faded quickly. I knew the bard harbored some fascination toward me—a purely sexual desire that made her foolish. What I hadn't realized before tonight was how much she hated that part of herself. Nothing I'd done to her body had hurt her nearly as much as the truths I'd told.

I traced my thumb over her cheek. To my vast irritation, my cock stirred. How did humans ever accomplish anything with bodies this needy? I couldn't fathom.

The burning urge to pin her to a tree one last time, to relieve my ache with something sweeter than my hand, surged like a tide. I gritted my teeth and kept moving. My lines might not be godly enough for Aelith, but I had them. The bard had had enough—and she wasn't in a state to *desire* more.

With a slow inhale, I looked up at the stars. They glittered over the forest, embossing our path in silver. I searched again for the Huntress in the whisper of the evening breeze. I hadn't been able to read her in the air before, and there wasn't the faintest hint of her there now either—even in the silence and calm. Had she learned to shield me out? Or was my mind somehow *still* too scattered?

I bristled. If the Huntress became a bigger problem for the Fated, it wouldn't matter if I solved Finchton or not. Austvix hadn't traded a sliver of his eternal soul without contingencies. Should he die at the Huntress's hands, I would be obligated to offer *her* the opportunity to claim my contract—with the huge disincentive that she would negotiate her own rules. If she accepted, Austvix would regain his soul, and *I* would be at the mercy of a new binding...with one less warlord on the playing field. If the Huntress refused, I would be banished back to the Hells and have to face my problems there almost empty-handed. A mere sliver of a demigod soul wouldn't fix what I'd broken, even if it would allow me to torment Austvix for eternity.

No, I needed this deal to *succeed.* I needed the souls of Austvix's siblings. Whole, complete souls. Demigod souls. A currency that would not only pay my debt but buy me a station so high above those I was indebted to that *they* would have to flee the Hells to save themselves from *me.*

I gritted my teeth. Everything moved slowly on the human plane. That didn't bother me when it felt like we were on the right track. I was hidden here, unreachable. For now. But the Huntress wasn't even Austvix's strongest sibling. *She* shouldn't be able to give us this much trouble. Had I placed my bet on the wrong warlord?

A sharp intake of breath interrupted my self-pity. The bard stared up at me through glassy eyes. Her body tensed in my arms. A bleary fear spiked—nectar to my soul—and I watched her face contort as it raced from thought to thought like a hummingbird with an entire field of flowers. I could only guess what she was thinking, but I supposed she was taking stock. Making sure she was unharmed. Wondering if we were finished.

Despite the dark desire snaking through my lower belly that told me I *could* feed her fear and that I *could* tease joy from this, I didn't want to give her the power to derail my contemplation further.

"You're alright, kitten," I rumbled. "Rest."

Her quiet stare made the hairs on the back of my neck prickle, though I looked straight ahead. The desire emanating from her now had a new flavor. It was almost enough to make me look again to see her expression. She desired *approval*. Mine. Which was laughable, because I was certain that if I gave it, she would immediately make me regret it.

I had little time to consider this, though, because her body's need for rest quickly eclipsed all else and she was once again asleep in my arms.

The blip—the fragment of need—had the unwelcome effect of pulling another bard from the depths of my memory. The fair one. The one whose song still haunted my dreams every single night.

She'd looked disturbingly like Aelith, but even gentler. There'd never been a spare scrap of fight in the woman. Only naivety and an earnest desire to save her family. A desire that a devil had taken advantage of. And then at his request, I'd tormented her.

I wove through the trees, indulgently watching the rise and fall of my new bard's—of *Ero's*—chest. Why couldn't I have met *her* in Hell? I could have made an *art* out of torturing her. With the soft one, it'd been like trying to condense something that was already as small as it could be. To tease emotion from her, I had to offer hope first. And then crush it. Over and over. It felt hollow and forced and wrong.

Ero's braid came partly unraveled. I ran a finger through the tangled tresses. She slept on.

On my final day in Hell—the day I'd ruined everything—I'd been given the soft bard and a set of instructions. The devil was bored. The girl was a shell. No one wanted to give him anything for her, but he couldn't enjoy something so clearly devoid of life. He wanted me to restore her. At least a little. Enough for him to trade for something better.

My fingers closed around the tangled hair. Tightly. Ero whimpered in her sleep, but she didn't open her eyes.

I'd tried my old tactics on the girl. I'd teased her with false promises to inspire hope. But she had none left. I couldn't make something from nothing, couldn't stir up what wasn't there to begin with. So I gave her a lute instead, and we made a deal. If she could remember how to play a joyful song—the only thing I'd ever seen her happy to do—I would give her a chance to run. She didn't believe me, of course. I had to make it real, and I had to prove it to her. I made a deal with the keepers of the gate while she watched. We signed in blood. All the soft one had to do was play her song, and then I had to let her go. Give her a true path out. The gatekeepers wouldn't stop her. She would get a head start. If I caught her, she stayed. If she made it out, no one from the Hells would ever find her again.

I reached the edge of the clearing. The fire had gone to embers. Almost everyone had gone to bed. Only Brü sat up, looking haggard and miserable with Aelith asleep on his lap.

I nodded to him. He nodded back, perhaps relieved, perhaps just tired. I didn't want to interact with Aelith, and Brü seemed just as keen to avoid that. He jutted his chin at a tent at the edge of the encampment, and he waited to rouse his lover until I'd carried Ero inside it. There was only one bedroll. I didn't care to go back out and find Ero's things, so I didn't put her down. I simply crawled inside and held her.

I closed my eyes.

Like that would make the memories stop.

It didn't.

The soft bard *had* remembered her joyful song. And she'd been smarter than I thought. I'd mistaken her timidity for lack of wit. She played the song with magic woven through so that it echoed in my head, unrelenting, making it impossible to think. I never found the first trace of her. The chase was no chase at all. I'd lost her the moment I made that deal—the moment I'd underestimated her—and I knew I would pay dearly for it.

So I'd fled. I scoured the planes for a soul to balance the scales. Instead, I found a warlord with a prophecy about a demon and a deal that outstripped my wildest dreams.

I don't know what magic the soft little bard used. But ever since it got inside me, the faintest hint of bardsong has itched that scar deep in my mind that I've never been able to scratch.

I looked down at Ero. My kitten, with her sharp claws and her colorful tangle of magic and her warring desires to fuck me and drive me mad.

I longed to whisper cruel orders into her ear—the kind the collar wouldn't let her refuse or play coy with. To watch her crawl. To watch her beg. To watch the fantasy snap and genuine fear take hold. To do everything the soft bard never actually deserved until she'd tricked me and left me to pick up the pieces.

I touched the collar.

Its power rose seductively and sang soothing promises, lapping at my finger like an eager pet. I pictured Ero on her knees, taunting me with that little smirk, delaying my gratification just to show me she could. When we made it to camp, perhaps I would order her to her knees. Make her stay there for hours. Keep that mouth open wide and ready. Use it over and over while she pretended not to love it. Leave it until her lips cracked and bled...or until her desire finally faded. Whichever came first.

The air in the tent grew so humid with my musing that Ero coughed violently.

It broke the spell. The cool night air rushed back in.

Fuck.

And *that* was why I couldn't hear the Huntress. The bard was in my head.

I looked down at her, finally seeing the problem for what it was. Even asleep, her colorful tangle of magic roiled with life, needling me. The urge to work out *how* to break her tugged at a part of my mind that had been dormant for too long. A part I *enjoyed.* Yes, it would be satisfying to play with her. But if I wanted to focus, that wouldn't help.

Tomorrow, I decided. Tomorrow, I would give my kitten to Brü to tend until we reached the base camp. Then I would get answers about Finchton and release the bard back to the wild where I'd found her—to remove the distraction from my path once and for all.

If that magnanimity didn't balance the Fates in my favor,
what would?

Chapter 12
Ero: Not Friends, Not Lovers,
But a Third Worse Thing

Bardic Lesson #111: Don't trust demons. (Fucking obviously.)

I woke in his arms.

For a moment, it was nice. Warm. Comfortable. Secure. These were feelings I'd learned not to take for granted in my life on the road. Bůk's powerful arms formed a cage across my chest that I could have imagined being happy to live inside.

And then...the night before came flooding back.

You would have been thrilled to suck my cock to save your life.

My cheeks blazed. And the words didn't stop there. Humiliation built with each stinging memory. Each of his filthy—accurate—accusations.

Fuck.

Bůk's breathing remained heavy and even as I deftly extracted myself from his grip. The frigid air taunted me with its emptiness. Did I *want* to crawl back into him and forget everything? Maybe. But I wouldn't. I didn't want to face his mocking smile. Didn't want to hear what fresh, cutting things he would say when he saw my contentment. Definitely didn't want to be foolish enough to mistake what any of this was and hope for—

What?

A deep, familiar ache blossomed in my chest.

What *did* I hope for? A friend? A lover? Someone who would care if I got hurt? That's what I'd *always* wanted. It's why I'd joined that doomed adventuring party to find a book that would point me to my father and maybe, if the Fates smiled on me, to a sister or a grandmother or...just *or*. Someone whose desire to see my face had nothing to do with the songs I could play or the hurts I could soothe.

I reeled with that longing.

Haz's saggy left. I needed fresh air and one hundred percent less proximity to the demon I'd allowed to—

A different memory flashed at that half-thought. A forked tongue. The certainty that if he didn't stop, I would die, and that if he *did* stop, I would also die but *much* less happily.

Double fuck.

I shoved out of the tent and stumbled into a flurry of light and people and activity, the camp already in full swing. It was exactly the splash of cold water I needed.

As I staggered toward the main firepit in search of breakfast, I gleaned from snippets of conversation that we were to mobilize around midday.

I failed to find food, but I spotted Brü and started for him, figuring *some* task could use doing and that he could point me toward it. A soft hand caught my elbow before I reached him.

I was startled not just by the touch but by the feeling that accompanied it. Like I was being caressed by *water*. I turned to the woman—a willowy blonde with kind eyes and a holy necklace that looked like an ice dagger with wisps of frost billowing from it. Was she an elemental? Could elementals even look so… human? I stared dumbfounded, trying to figure her out instead of doing a normal thing like saying *hello*.

Her smile told me this happened often.

"Hullo, Ero," she said softly. "Do you mind if I heal you?"

I narrowed my eyes. If I were hurt, I could heal myself. I didn't—

The soreness hit all at once. My muscles screamed. My wrists burned. And that was to say nothing of the raw sensitivity between my legs. The shock of it was almost worse than the pain. How had I not felt any of it before? Had Bůk worked some demon sorcery to keep it at bay? Further, how had this woman known when I hadn't?

"It's no trouble," she said. "Brü asked me to find you."

"Um…sure?" I said. Because while I *could* heal myself, her eyes were liquid gold and eager to please, and I didn't need to expend the energy if she was willing. Plus? I was curious. And —I realized with a start—I actually *trusted* Brü.

My curiosity was handsomely rewarded. The heal washed over me, a warm ocean spray lapping against my skin with a cold undertow that drew the pain away. It'd been so, so long since I'd received anyone else's magic this way. Not since I was a child. And never quite like this. It ate away the strain in my whole body, gently strengthening as it went.

I groaned.

The dimple on the woman's pale cheek deepened as another wave came stronger than the last. Her fingers trailed up my arm and over my shoulder. The sensation cascaded down my back like a billowing cloak. But her fingers froze when they reached my clavicle. The comforting wave receded abruptly.

I opened my eyes and saw her troubled gaze trained on my collar.

Somehow, this embarrassed me. Like I'd chosen the wrong accessory for an event.

Her eyes, so open and friendly before, chilled. "He really used it." She sounded appalled but not surprised.

When our eyes locked again, I steeled myself. I knew how fast "friendly" could turn to something else. To mean, superior, judgemental.

Only she didn't look any of those things. Just contemplative.

"If you need—" she started.

"She doesn't," a gravelly, bored, too-familiar voice interrupted.

Bůk's hand fell possessively on my shoulder from behind. And now, whatever the outcome of my new almost-friend's moment of contemplation might have been, it curdled and hardened into something I could read quite clearly. Hatred.

"Bůk," she said through clenched teeth.

"*Aelith*," he bit out in return.

Each had a hand on me. And suddenly it was too much. I took an abrupt step aside. I ought to have thanked Aelith for the heal. I felt better than I had any right to after last night. Only I didn't want to squander the refreshed energy on a standoff in which Aelith might accuse Bůk of cruelty and Bůk might, in turn, reveal my debauched desires...at which point, I could never show my face to anyone in this faction again.

"Brü!" I called. "What needs to be done before we go?"

To Brü's credit, though he was too far away to have witnessed the particulars of our exchange, he didn't miss a beat upon seeing the three of us and hearing my desperation. Good old Brü.

"Gather your tent and tack your horse," he ordered. "Then listen for my call. We ride out two hours before the others to scout, so don't forget to eat."

"Yes, sir," I said.

And then, coward that I was, I ran into my tent and let the flap fall behind me without looking back.

I never sought food. I stayed in my tent for as long as I could stand it, then ducked out as the time to leave approached —refusing to look around in case Bůk or Brü or Aelith happened to be near. I tacked the horse Brü had assigned me and gave her little scratches and loaded her with my things.

When Brü's muster call rang out, I steeled myself and walked to my probable doom.

Bůk wasn't there.

Thank Haz for small favors.

Aelith slipped into the circle to kiss Brü while we assembled. She did so without show and without embarrassment. Then she came to me.

"Here," she said, holding out a bundle. "I didn't see you at the fire."

Her offering included bread and jerky with a steaming skin of what smelled like lamb stew, all wrapped in a woven travel net. Saliva pooled in my mouth—but a sharp doubt nagged at me, too. *Why* was she being nice? Because Brü asked her to? Why would Brü ask her to? Because I'd "fixed" Bůk? Some internal ledger burned to know whom I owed for what.

"Thank you," I said uncertainly.

"Safe ride," she answered with a serene smile as she bounced away.

And...Bůk never showed.

We rode out, pretending we didn't have questions. Except for Flər, who marveled in exaggerated tones how nice it felt to ride in this exact company without, for example, a cloud of nasty dark energy around to block out the sun. I rolled my eyes. Not that I didn't agree with him. I did for once. I just hated him more than I wanted to bond over our mutual love of Bůk-free space.

The ride was uneventful, though long. Aelith's gifts became necessities by our seventh hour in the saddle. I drained the stew and savored the last crusts of bread as we finally halted atop the chain of hills that would serve as our new camp. It was a suitable spot. We were exposed—but anything that approached would be visible for at least half an hour before it reached us.

Brü talked us through the plan. A mid-sized party would join us later that night, with the rest of the train rejoining by tomorrow evening. Once the full company had gotten a night of sleep and a meal, we would repeat our inchworm progress —this time with a different scouting party taking the lead and us traveling with the forty or so factionites in the second wave.

I reached for my tent, but Brü paused as he passed. "If you wouldn't mind, a song of vigilance and rest would go a long way."

It was an odd request. Usually, one would play for either vigilance *or* rest—but this sort of discordant melody was exactly my niche, and I was surprised Brü had both noticed and chosen to encourage that. I nodded, and he was on to Flər with orders to gather firewood.

I wanted to ask about Bůk—just to ensure it was safe to play my lute. But I hadn't seen him all day, and I knew it would be hours before either of the lagging parties neared, so I didn't bother.

The songs poured out of me, easier with each passing moment and every passing smile. I sang while Flər built a fire and while the tents rose—some for sleep, others for gathering because the breeze hinted at rain. I loved rain. The promise and threat of it teased my song into something so rich that before I knew it, Brü stood over me with a drunk, heady smile. "I think that's enough, or we'll have them jousting in their sleep. Thank you, Ero. Play whatever you like now."

And I did. More hours passed in bliss. Someone cooked. Someone opened a leftover keg of mead. When I needed breaks, I started popular tavern ballads and let the others carry them through.

The second party arrived around dusk, and I was so caught up in the company and the fire that I didn't even notice Bůk at first. When I spotted him, he stood alone by a tiny copse of trees at the top of the hill, watching me.

I slid my lute onto my back, eliciting groans from those who hadn't had their fill.

But the coward I'd been that morning was gone. I felt whole and confident now...and determined.

I made my way to Bůk.

His expression darkened as I approached—but that was so Bůk-coded, I didn't take it for the warning it was. I leaned one elbow on the tree next to him and looked up at his scowling face without fear.

I didn't like that I'd spent the day afraid to face him. It ate at me. So I forced myself to maintain eye contact and shove down all the thoughts that threatened to make me look away.

He watched me with cool curiosity.

"When we reach the base camp," I said, "I'll do what I can

to decode your letters. In return, I want access to any historic tomes in the Fated's possession."

That was more than fair, no?

In my mind, we were beyond the collar now. Bůk had already shown his willingness to forego its use. If I didn't provoke him, and he didn't use it, it stood to reason that we could forge new ground and come to an equitable—

The world flashed before my eyes. One moment, I was leaning against the tree, laying out my proposal. The next, my back was smashed against the bark, and Bůk's fingers squeezed my throat. He'd spun me around the tree to a place where the others couldn't see. We had privacy that I very suddenly and very much did not want.

"I'll say this *once* for your benefit," Bůk said. His tone was flat, and his gaze bore into me. "Only once. So I suggest you listen."

I couldn't exactly do otherwise. I fought for breath through his hold. My lute pressed against my back, in danger of being crushed as his weight pinned me.

"Do you know why collars like this—" his pinkie finger slid demonstratively between my throat and the silver and leather, "—still fetch such a good price?"

I managed a jerk of my chin.

"Because they *work*," he said, closing his fist, taking away my air. "Because they only cause madness in *animals* that are too simple-minded to understand that fighting the compulsion will destroy their minds. But people? They can understand. They can *choose* to obey—if they're not too stupid or too stubborn."

He loosened his grip enough for me to gulp in a single deep breath. I looked around wildly. Why hadn't he said this in the cave? Or when he'd caught me in the woods? Why now, when we were—when we were what? On nearly good terms?

His timing didn't make sense.

Until it did.

"*Get on your knees*," he ordered.

The words weren't just words this time. The command snaked through me like a caster's fire, prickling at the base of my skull.

The bastard *compelled* me.

There was a single beat—a suspended moment where the choice was mine. Obey or fight.

But even as my anger rose, his warning sent me reeling. Did he *know* the collar wouldn't cause madness so long as I didn't fight it? Or was this an experiment?

It didn't matter. I couldn't risk it.

My knees hit the ground.

Hatred and fury flared white-hot through my body. Tears blurred my vision. I stared hard at the hilltop beyond his feet. Why *now?* Why at all, really, but especially why *now?*

He cupped my cheek. My heart trilled with a burst of adrenaline.

"*Look at me,*" he ordered.

I listened. I looked up at him in wonder, too hurt to care if he enjoyed my tears. Though the prickle of compulsion was still there, I barely felt it when I gave in quickly.

Bůk studied me right back, still with those empty eyes. It wasn't normal. The air around us was just air—devoid of his usual stir of emotion. How could he do this and feel *nothing*?

I felt everything. It was every acquaintance who'd ever left without saying goodbye. Every casual promise forgotten. Every lover who'd spurned me.

Betrayal.

How many times did I have to learn this lesson? How many times did I have to remind myself not to trust someone just because I wanted to? Because they were pretty or kind or interesting or a good fuck?

"I'm not your friend," Bůk said, as though to underscore my point. "I'm not your lover, Ero. I'm not someone you get to *negotiate* with. You belong to me. Do you understand?"

Ero. Not *kitten*. Why did that chafe?

I gave a jerky nod.

"I said," he bit out, "*Do you understand?*"

The prickle returned—the feeling that if I didn't answer, I would come apart from the inside out.

"Yes," I gasped. "Yes, I understand."

His hand fell away from my face. For once, I didn't trust myself to speak. My tendrils stretched in every direction, keening their agitation. One rogue tendril snaked up, wedging itself between my throat and the collar, tugging in outright defiance before a shocking jolt from the enchantment chased it away.

I needed to right things with Bůk—*somehow*—to return to that shaky ground we'd inhabited before, when he'd agreed not to—

He never agreed, the voice inside my head taunted. *You just assumed he wouldn't because he hadn't before.*

I sucked in rapid lungfuls of air, breathing so hard my throat strained against the collar. The constriction made my panic worse, so I closed my eyes and forced measured breaths instead. Too aware of his eyes and judgment on me. Too afraid that what he saw would delight him and make him want to do it even more.

But when I opened my eyes, Bůk was gone.

I knelt alone in the dirt. The warmth I'd felt all day—the confidence I'd gained—shattered.

I got unsteadily to my feet.

When the tide of disjointed emotions finally subsided, I stumbled back to the fire. The flames danced, distorted through my tears. I ignored calls for more songs.

I hated Bůk and then myself and then Bůk again in a spinning kaleidoscope of broken thoughts I couldn't escape.

When a soft hand took mine, I didn't need to look up to know it was Aelith. Her calm, watery touch had already become familiar.

"Is there anything I can do?" she asked.

"That depends," I said. "Do your gods know how to kill a demon?"

She smiled.

Chapter 13
Ero: How to Kill a Demon and Other Problems

"If you anger a man past logic, you can expect that he will eventually return to his senses. If you embarrass a man, it's best to assume he will not." - a fragment of correspondence from a Temple Mother, preserved in the journal of Eroithiel von Dua

Aelith turned out to know a lot about killing demons.

Or neutralizing them, anyway. She was happy to recite lore and imagine aloud with glee how satisfying it would be to see Bůk's soul trapped inside a relic or sutured to a boar's ass or sold back to Hell. The firelight crackled merrily as she wove a dozen beautiful plots.

And then with a sunny sigh, she said words I desperately didn't want to hear. "But we can't. He's off limits."

"*Why?*" I demanded.

"We're all pledged to Lord Austvix." She shrugged. "No one in the faction can act against Bůk in any serious way. Trust me, I've *tried* to find a loophole. Bůk's contract is self-enforcing, as

I'm sure you've noticed, so in Lord Austvix's eyes, an act against the lord's demon is an act against the lord himself—and there are consequences for that. Anything from caning to hanging. Nothing fun."

"Fuuuuck." I groaned, resting my chin on my knees.

Aelith smiled sympathetically. She nudged my shoulder with hers. "It may be scant consolation, but he'll avoid you if you're with me. I can make him *quite* uncomfortable."

She flicked her fingers demonstratively, sending a volley of ice shards into the air with a seductive smirk.

I managed a weak smile. I already adored Aelith—but I wasn't in the market to annoy or avoid Bůk. He was the kind of problem that required a more permanent solution.

Pondering my collection of poor options, I caught some of Aelith's ice on my fingers and watched the shards melt. "How does the whole water elemental thing work, anyway? I've never seen an elemental in human form."

"Austvix," she said with a one-shoulder shrug, as if his name alone explained everything. While she spoke, she filled a small vial with the moisture welling at her fingertips. "He's sort of a collector...or a curator, I suppose? He can transfigure willing souls."

She handed the vial to me with a wink. "In case you ever need a quick fix."

I examined it. The vial had a slight glow. *Holy water.* Interesting.

But I didn't spend long considering the potential weapon. My attention snagged on what she'd said. Had Lord Austvix transformed Bůk too? If so, what had Bůk looked like before? Based on the battle in the woods, he must have been a huge, shadowy beast. Ten feet tall with leathery skin and a forked—

Aelith leaned over me to snatch two mugs of mulled wine from a passing cart. She handed one to me.

I blinked. Right. Not thinking about Bůk right now.

"So…you were willing?" I prompted, taking a long drink. The potent aroma of cinnamon and clove mingling with the wine took me to whole new planes.

"I was," Aelith confirmed, smiling distantly at some private thought. "I actually met Brü in my original form. He was in a swamp battle. Almost died inside me, in fact."

I choked through a swallow. "How romantic?"

Aelith snorted. The shine in her eyes promised a hundred song-worthy stories. I yearned to shake at least one out of her —but Brü caught her attention then, and the way he looked at her made *my* cheeks heat.

"We should get our rest," I whispered conspiratorially. (You're welcome, Brü.)

Aelith squeezed my hand and arched a knowing brow. "We *should*. We'll work on your demon problem in the morning?"

I forced myself to stand and issue bland words of agreement. I didn't mean them, of course. Now that I knew Bůk was "off limits," I couldn't drag Aelith or anyone else into my trouble. I would have to work on my "demon problem" alone.

Nevertheless, I looked forward to spending more time with Aelith. In the space of a day, she'd become the one bright spot in my dark, thorny mess of a situation.

I floated to my tent on a cloud of warm feelings—perhaps partially due to the wine. My night had ended almost as well as it'd begun, I noted—Bůk's antics aside.

The downpour the clouds had threatened all day hit moments after I crawled into my bedroll. It didn't take long for the whoosh of the storm to lull me.

Regarding Bůk, I thought blearily as I drifted toward sleep, my best bet was probably to incapacitate him long enough to run. Even though the thought of leaving for good was suddenly *much* less appealing than it'd been pre-Aelith, I couldn't justify staying. And even though the thought of what Bůk would do to me if I failed sent an electric spark of conflicting desire and fear straight through my core, there was no winning alternative.

I tucked Aelith's vial of holy water into my meager rucksack and hid it under my blanket for safekeeping. The *last* thing I needed was for Bůk to find it.

By the time sleep came, I still had no real plan—but I *had* spent quite a lot of time imagining in stark detail epic successes that ranged from seeing Bůk on his knees begging for mercy to seeing Flər framed for my crimes and caned before the faction.

I fell asleep smiling.

I did not wake up smiling.

It wasn't morning. The rain had stopped, but it was pitch black in my tent. It was the *poing!* of my lute string that alerted me to imminent danger. I shot up, registering that someone was in my tent. My first thought was Bůk.

"Shit, she's awake," a deep voice warned.

It was not Bůk.

The voice sounded wrong—unnaturally deep and distorted, likely through spellwork.

I reached automatically for the dagger in my boot. I wasn't any sort of expert with it, but I trusted my survival instincts to guide my hand.

The man's gloved fingers closed around my wrist before I could swipe at him. His other hand clapped over my mouth just as I opened it to scream.

"Still and quiet, love, or I'll—"

I didn't wait for the end of that threat. His masked face was only inches from mine. I whipped my head forward so that my forehead connected with his nose. A satisfying crunch sounded before his curses filled the air.

"Shut the fuck up!" a second voice hissed from outside. "Haz's sack, *grab* her."

In the grapplefest that followed, I fought like my life depended on it. I'm glad it didn't...because I lost. My blade might have found skin before I went down, though. I earned a fresh wave of curses and felt something warm and wet drip onto my leg before a vice-tight arm around my neck forced me to release the weapon, and a fist gripped my hair.

That fist led to yet another round of cursing as the enchantments in my braid lashed out protectively. Although the man released my hair, the grip on my throat remained firm.

Through the scuffle, my second assailant's words reached me. "Calm down, initiate, or this will go much worse for you."

Initiate?

Shit.

It wasn't an attack. It was...initiation?

The hands—there were four now—turned me over, bound my wrists tightly behind my back with a spelled rope, and tugged a bag over my head. My magic wasn't cut off the way it'd been with Bŭk's manacles, but it felt drunk and unstable. I didn't dare try to reach for it. I cried out, but the sound echoed as if I were inside a sealed metal box. No outside sounds entered. All I could hear was my own ragged panting.

And then something small and sharp pierced my neck, and the world blurred.

I granted myself one kind lie as I drifted away from consciousness.

This is going to be fine.

Hours later, I woke to Brü's gruff "road in five" on the other side of my tent flap. The mid-morning sunlight drove hot pokers into my eyes.

A whirlwind of the previous night's activities fought to reassemble as my head pulsed.

Coming to with my face in a pool of water.

Being held under for an agonizingly long time, only to come up for too-short reprieves before going back under.

Being shoved to my knees on a bed of sharp pebbles. Attempting to stand. Earning lashes for the effort.

Counting aloud to one hundred before I was allowed to rise.

Running, racing the other initiates who wore barely translucent scarves over their eyes—like the one they'd put on me while I was out—knowing that whoever crossed the finish line last would earn a bonus humiliation. Listening to the initiate who lost choke back sobs as our tormenters passed a wooden paddle and competed to see who could score the loudest yelp.

Dawn had already teased its arrival by the time they split us apart to return to our tents. I was tired and achy, though as far as hazing went, it could have been worse.

But when we entered my tent, the man who guided me knelt beside me and placed something around my toe. My wrists were still tied, and I was far too tired to fight him. He untied me when he finished, but the euphoric rush of my magic returning never came. Instead, my tendrils remained pinned in a tortured, drunken state by the crude magic of the toe ring.

"That's for breaking my nose, cunt," he whispered. "Tell the others, and I'll make sure you regret it."

Then, he was gone.

I sat up, examining the toe. The makeshift dampener was a thin gold chain, too tight to slip off, but not tight enough to cut circulation. I trembled, touching it. It seared my finger. I cried out, then quickly bit my sleeve to stay quiet. The absolute last thing I needed was to draw attention to myself. I still didn't even know who my assailants were.

Unfortunately, I couldn't heal with the ring fighting me. The cuts and bruises from last night would stay. It was no raw, welted ass, but it would make the day's ride rough.

A horn called us to muster. I ground my palms into my eyes, trying to shake the last remnants of sleep. The day's scouting party must have departed hours prior. My group was to ride the second wave this time. I took only a moment to gather myself and my things before I yanked the string that collapsed my tent.

Bůk stood right outside.

I pretended not to see him. Probably my least convincing performance to date. Dread gagged me as I shouldered my things, keeping my eyes firmly on the ground, and skirted around him to reach my horse.

Mercifully, Bůk said nothing.

Our party was large enough for me to lose myself in the line of riders, and I did so. We rode through a miserable drizzle with little conversation. The rider next to me—I think his name was Tavish?—had the good sense to fade into the scenery.

For once, when Brü requested I play a song, I didn't need Bůk to grumble about it before I gently refused. I told Brü my throat was sore, and though he gave me a concerned look, he asked nothing more of me.

We ate in the saddle as usual. I'd not woken up in time to get provisions, so I fell back on a meager stock of jerky that'd come with my faction-issued tent and bedroll.

When we stopped for the night, there was no fire. The storms were already upon us, and the camp looked as miserable as I felt. I considered finding Aelith and asking her to heal me—but I was so tired, and for all I knew she was in the larger party and wouldn't arrive for hours still. So instead, I zipped myself away to await the night's hazing.

The thunder roared. The lightning followed with such searing intensity that a tiny blossom of hope snaked its way through my chest. Perhaps they wouldn't come. Perhaps it would wait for another night.

No such luck.

A blade slashed through the top of my tent and sliced it to ribbons. I should have been afraid of what was to come—but all I could think was, if they left the dampener on, I wouldn't be able to heal myself or mend the tent. When they finished with me, I would sleep in the freezing rain.

My assailants had not grown more creative overnight. The assault followed the same beats. A near drowning, excruciating kneeling, counting aloud to the moment of relief, and then— the race. I poured every remaining drop of my strength into outstripping my fellow initiates. Last night, the only reprieve I'd been granted was during the loser's torment. Even more than I needed to avoid the extra punishment, I needed the rest.

I could tell through the blindfold that I was in or near the lead. Pained grunts behind me coddled my exhausted brain with soft promises. But apparently, I'd broken the wrong man's nose. A truth I realized when my ankles locked mid-stride. I was falling before I knew why. I tried to bend my legs to catch myself on my screaming knees, but that failed too. My cheek hit a rock with an explosive blow. A foot came down on my shoulder. Another on my calf. The initiates I'd been so triumphant to outrun were trampling me. I pushed myself up out of the mud, but my legs still wouldn't work.

And then they did. All at once, the interference evaporated. Naturally, it was too late. I dove forward, threw everything I had into one final burst—but everyone else was already across the line.

Despair and humiliation warred inside me. I didn't make it fun. I lay lifeless as they joked and rained punishing blows with their wooden paddle. Only when thunder shook the air and lightning struck too close for comfort did they call it.

I'd survived. So that was something.

I'd let them pummel me without giving one single worthy cry they could enjoy. That was even better.

Back in my tent, I waited for the man who'd shoved me inside to untie my wrists. I promised myself I *would* find Aelith in the morning. She would fix it. Nothing was permanent, except the anonymous names I would mentally add to my list of people to dismember in the future—whenever I had time.

Only the man wasn't finished.

"Hold her still," he said.

His finger hooked into my waistband. That single touch dispelled the numbness I'd gathered around me like a blanket. Fear trickled down my spine. My hands were tied. My magic was out of reach. I couldn't stop what he was going to do, and I knew it.

Their voices were faint through the roar of the rain. I could make out only snippets.

—*the codex*—

—*give a* fuck—

—*Bůk*—

More unintelligible bickering.

—leaving—

No. It started as a cry in my head. The one who was arguing —who was stopping the other man from doing what he wanted to me—was going to leave.

A deafening crack of thunder made all three of us stiffen. The lightning that followed illuminated them. The second man was angled away, already half a step from disappearing into the night. But I stared at his masked face, a horrified plea frozen in my eyes. I saw the ink on his neck where the fabric around his mask had torn. I stared at it, searing the pattern into my memory just in case.

After a long, hesitant beat, he turned back. He yanked his companion away from me. They exchanged a few more heated words I couldn't hear, and then my reluctant savior shoved the other man out of my tent.

They'd never untied my wrists. I lay there on my belly, sucking in deep breaths, sobbing as the rain washed the mud and blood away.

When a shadow fell over the tent again moments later, I was sure it was the man whose nose I'd broken returning to finish what he'd started. That he'd shaken his friend and circled back. I promised myself I wouldn't make it easy. He might win, but I would hurt him too. A bite, a kick—anything. I would mark him, and then find him later and squeeze the life from his body.

I writhed in my bindings, scrabbling for leverage.

Except when the figure spoke, it wasn't the distorted voice of my assailant.

"Who did this to you?" Bůk growled.

His fury heated the air. I looked up just in time to see the soaked remains of my tent hiss steam and burst into flames.

Chapter 14
Bůk: Mine

Bůk's Personal Code, Item 7: Aelith is the worst.

I *was* in a good mood. As good as moods got in this place, anyway. The storms kept the camp quiet. The quiet made space for the wind to speak. And speak it did.

I finally knew what the Huntress wanted.

Having put the bard firmly in her place the previous night —a victory I'd assumed after leaving her mewling in the woods and confirmed earlier when I saw her so cowed that even her magic shied from me—I'd gone for a long ride alone.

The clouds hung heavy overhead, ripe with anticipation. Haz's interest weighed heady and acidic on my tongue. Plots were thickening. Luckily, I had the whole day to breathe them in. While I did, I tasted the Huntress's desires amplified by every soldier who wished to please her.

The Huntress wanted *me*.

Why? That was more complicated to parse. My contract with Austvix was ironclad. I couldn't help the Huntress nor work against Austvix. My existence had not been a secret before, so her sudden interest was suspect at best. If this were about neutralizing me, she would have wanted to do it before. So, there were still plenty of mysteries afoot. But Colonel Astrada was right to worry. As long as the Huntress's desires remained singular, our party would be in grave danger. The good news was that the Huntress's closest riders—now that we'd killed the first wave—were several days' ride away.

It was late when I returned to the camp. There was no point in rousing Astrada before morning. Tomorrow, I would share what I knew and leave the next move in her capable hands.

I'd just settled in my tent with that plan in mind when a violent wave of anguish choked me. Its cadence flashed scarlet and tasted of burnt amber. I knew immediately that it was the bard.

I was on my feet and back outside before I could fully comprehend the situation. Her distress was not a result of idle anger. That much was clear. The bard wanted to kill. She wanted it so loudly, so painfully, that I knew something had to have happened just now. If the Huntress's desires had been a faint whisper in a gale, Ero's were a tornado.

Concerned that her life was in danger—which would be terribly inconvenient—I stalked to her tent. A gaping hole at the top let the rain flow in. Ero lay on her stomach with her hands bound behind her back. Her sobs grew more furious with each choked breath.

I stiffened. Heat climbed my neck despite the freezing rain. The position I found her in had appeal. The fact that she'd been put there by someone else did *not.*

"Who did this to you?" I demanded.

My first thought was Flər—but I knew better. He wasn't this bold. He was the sort of man who wanted to be thought well of, who acted on his basest desires only when he was certain no one would know or judge him for it.

The air heated with my growing fury. The bard and I were instantly enveloped in steam. I might have reined in my temper had the moonlight not illuminated the cuts and bruises on her writhing arms. But it did, and the tent caught fire.

Who the fuck had touched her? It was no secret she was mine. Not a cherished possession—but a possession all the same. Someone was going to die for this.

It was her scream that finally grounded me.

Right. Humans could burn.

I lifted her bodily from the wreckage, kicking the flaming tent into the mud to extinguish it. A flick of my wrist summoned my shadows, which gathered her meager collection of things from the mess. They trailed behind us as I stalked back to my tent. I deposited her on her feet—forcing a gentleness I didn't feel in the least.

"Who?" I demanded again.

Her gaze snapped to mine. Her desire didn't change. She wanted to kill me just as badly as she wanted to kill whoever had done this to her. Perhaps I'd been *too* convincing in the woods.

Too bad. I wasn't sorry.

"Untie me," she said through clenched teeth.

"Then tell me—"

"I don't *know*." She stumbled back, her jaw set. "It's not your problem. Untie me. I'll handle it."

I frowned, not liking the tone any more than I liked the situation.

"Careful, kitten," I warned.

A hint of fear flashed in her emerald eyes. But her expression remained hostile.

Fine. I could humor her. I cut the rope binding her wrists. It was imbued with amateur spellwork—something designed to confuse and distort magic. Oddly though, when it fell to the ground, her usually colorful and chaotic tangle of magic remained muted and gray. Just like it'd been early that morning when she hadn't been able to meet my eyes. Was that because she finally feared me enough to mind herself—or was it something else?

"What's wrong with you?" I asked.

She laughed, bitter and cold. She had no trouble meeting my eyes now. "Fuck. You."

Something far more dangerous than anger stirred in my chest. Intrigue. She *wanted* a fight. She burned for it. She knew how outmatched she was, and still, she pushed.

Fine.

Wish granted.

"Undress," I ordered, pushing my words to weave into the collar's enchantment.

Her eyes flared. The nectar of pure hatred mingled with a dark desire even I couldn't fully untangle. She wanted to destroy something—apparently even if the only thing available to destroy was herself. For a moment I feared she would fight the collar. I wasn't prepared for that. I wasn't even sure what to do if she tried. I *needed* her mind intact—and I was banking on her to care enough to keep it that way.

Luckily, she did.

When she finished shedding her clothes, she crossed her arms. Not out of modesty. No, she didn't bother to hide her chest, but rather framed it with her defiant stance. Her nipples pebbled in the cold, begging for a warm touch. On cue, my predictable body itched to provide said touch. *Haz's whole bare ass.* It was *not* the time. I needed answers. Besides which, where her hatred had been intermingled with desire in the past, it was *just* hatred right now.

"Tell me what happened," I said evenly. At the immediate pursing of her lips that had *fuck off* written plainly across them, I grew impatient. "Speak, or I'll ask again, and you'll tell me from your knees."

Sensing exactly how much she didn't want to be touched, I refrained from reaching for the collar to underscore my point.

She looked away. But she spoke.

"It was initiation," she said in a disinterested monotone. "Last night and tonight. I wasn't the only one. Like I said, it's *my* problem."

I frowned, examining her as she avoided looking at me. There were bloody cuts on her knees, mud and bruises on her arms, and—I circled behind her—thin angry welts on her back, trailing down to bruises that covered her soft ass and thighs.

I took a few slow breaths. It would be exceedingly inconvenient to burn a second tent tonight and have to shake Brü down for a spare. The temperature rose, but only by a few degrees. I was *trying*.

"What's wrong with your magic?" I pushed.

Almost as soon as I said it, though, I saw the answer for myself. She followed my gaze to her foot and didn't bother to speak. The tiny gold chain cinched around her toe caught the lamplight. Its chaotic aura had been lost in the mess of emotions before. I singled it out easily now.

The spellwork was criminal. It wasn't just weak, which would have been forgivable and expected of a homebrew. It was unstable. It clawed at her, forcing her own magic to hold a constant shield against it.

"Sit down," I ordered.

"I'll go to Aelith."

"You will sit the fuck down," I said, louder than I'd intended —but I didn't use the collar again. Yet. "Aelith won't be able to remove it."

A headache dawned with a fresh realization. Even though Aelith wouldn't be able to remove the spellwork—because she wasn't adept at enchantments—if *I* removed it...I would need a healer on hand. Preferably a strong one with the ability to soothe serious burns quickly. Aelith was the only one who clearly fit that bill.

Well, fuck me sideways.

"I'll get her," I sighed.

Ero looked surprised. I didn't bother explaining myself. I pointed at my bedroll, indicating that she should sit, all of my irritation plain on my face.

Then I fetched the biggest thorn that'd ever graced my side.

The camp's hazy aura glowed umber and sage. Soldiers cowered in their tents, miserable from the twin assaults of unrelenting rain and isolation. These were social creatures. Forced to keep their own company for even short stretches, their misery sang.

I found Aelith with Brü, of course. At my call, he poked his head out of his tent like an initiate who'd been caught with a painted entertainer in his bunk. I didn't bother with niceties.

"Ero's hurt. She needs the elemental."

Brü asked a flurry of questions that I ignored. Further talk was unnecessary. The smug blonde strode out of the tent without a hint of resistance. She put on a wonderful show of concern—as usual, giving me nothing tangible to point my hatred toward, though hate I did.

I explained the situation on the way back to my tent—and Aelith put voice to my observation as we entered. "They know better than to do anything that would interfere with the initiates' ability to perform their duties."

"I broke his nose," my feral kitten explained. "He took it personally."

Of course she wanted to talk now that Aelith's infuriating eyes held hers. She'd also stolen one of my shirts while I was gone. It went almost to her knees.

"Still—" Aelith started.

"He tried to do more," Ero said specifically to Aelith, desiring my absence more loudly than ever. "The other man mentioned the codex, and..."

Aelith's lips parted with a naïve little gasp. As if she were somehow blissfully unaware that half the men in this company were one dark room and one unguarded hole from breaking the codex on any given day, despite the threat of castration or death per Lord Austvix's rigid rules. Humans were human.

"I don't know who they were," Ero added, clearly frustrated. "They had masks and some sort of voice enchantment."

"Lars Wendlin," Aelith said, glancing pointedly at me. Two guesses why. The holy one wouldn't have to go about the messy process of lobbing accusations if I simply killed the man.

"Are you sure?" Ero asked quietly.

"Broken nose, minor leg wound, cuts and scrapes," Aelith said, focused on Ero again. "I healed him last night."

Well, I had a name. I didn't know Lars from the next man, but he ought to have known of me—and failing in that regard was his problem. He would regret it tomorrow.

While Aelith teased out useless details from my suddenly loquacious bard, I examined the tiny gold chain on her toe. I needed to be sure that breaking it wouldn't do something irritating like kill us all. Even amateur spellwork could be explosive when tampered with. But I found no such roadblocks. So, desiring nothing so much as an end to this night, I directed a surge of fire into the metal without bothering to warn the women.

Ero's scream pierced the night air.

It was over in less than two seconds. The molten gold dripped into my waiting hand, inert and devoid of its magic. Aelith's rage overshadowed even Ero's pain, but she made the right choice. Rather than attacking me, she performed the necessary heal. As quickly as the toe beneath my finger blackened and burned, it reformed and returned to its original state.

Aelith kept both hands on Ero's shoulders, drawing every hurt and scrape from her battered body. Absurdly, it occurred to me how perfect a pair Aelith and I might have made had we not been immortal enemies. What I could destroy, she could restore. What she could restore, I could destroy again and again. Beautiful symbiosis.

"She's coming with me," Aelith said coolly, puncturing the image.

"She's not," I said, already bored with the argument she wanted to have.

"Bůk—" Aelith started.

But Ero put a hand on her arm.

I arched a brow, curious what my kitten intended to do.

"I'm fine," she said. "Thank you, Aelith. But I need to talk to him."

Aelith hesitated. What Ero could possibly be to her, I didn't know. I watched them have an entire conversation with a look. Then Aelith stood. We locked eyes. She raised her hands and shook them once, as though to rid them of mud, and tiny droplets of holy water splattered my things.

Cunt.

"Goodnight, Ero," Aelith bit out.

She left without further ado.

Ero looked up at me. I couldn't read her face. That simple fact sparked a familiar thrill. I'd purposely pushed her in the woods—so she would fear and hate me enough to stay out of my way and out of my head. The best thing to do would be to maintain that. What I *wanted* to do was draw her back to me, so I could do it all over again.

I turned away from her, considering how to proceed.

"He's mine," she said to my back, as though she hadn't been able to force the words until she didn't have to say them to my face.

I humored her, keeping my back to her as I directed heat through the tent to dry the cleric's mess. I picked up Ero's things, which had fallen in a heap just inside the tent. Her lute, her bow, a handful of provisions and potions.

"Did you hear me?" she said.

Her voice trembled. I smiled. But I said nothing. The shirt she'd stolen rustled when she stood, and I looked at the things in my hands absently while I waited for her to approach. She touched my shoulder, featherlight. I turned to face her, intentionally drawing it out.

The heal had worked wonders. Her skin glowed. Her eyes gleamed. Her hunger to destroy soared, no longer tamped down by pain. I *liked* this version of my kitten. I liked it so much I didn't bother to tell her that Lars was mine. She could take her crack at him first. Fine. And then I would finish it. Spectacularly.

A sharp inhale drew my attention back to her face. She was looking at the things I held. The tiniest spark of fear and the way she looked away again immediately told me this wasn't the typical concern for her precious lute. I looked more critically at the items in my hands. Among the potions was a vial... of holy water. Something I wouldn't have even noticed had her panic not given her away.

I deposited the rest of her things and turned the offending item between my fingers. It was sealed. I could feel the vile substance within, but it couldn't reach me.

She stepped back, but I matched her.

"Bůk...I..."

"Shh," I soothed. "Lars is yours. Tomorrow."

The fresh fear in her eyes didn't waver at my concession. Good. I'd decided my path. I deserved a little fun.

"Get in the bed," I said. "You're safe tonight. We'll talk about this—" I lifted the vial and lobbed it through the open tent flap into the night. "—later."

She wanted to speak. I saw the words form and die. Her turmoil was too sweet. Cracks formed in her single-minded desire. She wanted to sleep. She wanted to *feel* safe. And finally, for the first time all night, she *wanted* me to touch her—to reassure her.

I trailed my fingers down her cheek indulgently. It was so easy. She melted into the soft touch. I guided her to the bedroll and held the cover up while she climbed in. Then I got in behind her, wrapping my arms around her body, enveloping her in my warmth.

I drifted to sleep with the sweet taste of her nerves on my tongue. Tomorrow, Lars would pay for ruining my night and touching what was mine. Then, my kitten would find out what happened when she played with fire.

Chapter 15
Ero: Hear No Evil

Bardic Advice from Eroithiel von Dua to future generations: Don't assume you know your own strength before you test your limits. Maybe not even then.

I thought the most significant thing that would happen the next day was the confrontation with Lars Wendlin. But life is full of surprises. Good old Lars came in a solid second.

When I woke, I felt eyes on me. The hair on the back of my neck stood on end. My spine prickled. The tendrils in my chest rose, on high alert. I turned to look at the only other sentient being in the tent, confident I would find him staring at me. I did not.

Bůk slept on. Head back, lips slightly parted, inferno of a chest bare to the morning chill. The scar from the holy water in the cave cut a jagged line on his hip. He looked like a gods-damned piece of art.

As that very thought formed, I heard a distinct scoff.

I sat quickly, scanning the tent, but there was no one and nothing else there. I blinked. Unease carried me to my feet.

A long moment passed.

Nothing happened.

I shook dried mud from my clothes and pulled them on, leaving Bůk's borrowed shirt on the floor. I combed my hair out and wove it into a fresh braid, humming quietly to lace it with magic to shield against fire and ill-intentioned hands. Then, I scooped up my things and ducked out into the morning light.

It was earlier than I'd realized. Brü stood by the fire, but most of the camp still slept. I needed to figure out who Lars was and exactly how I intended to handle him. I approached Brü with that in mind—wondering if I ought to ask directly or have him point me to Aelith—but he slapped a small book into my hand without so much as a hello.

"What—"

"The codex," he said. "I suggest you read it during our morning ride. We're back on lead today."

I looked at the little book, perplexed. I was already on edge from the phantom eyes following me. Now I bit my lip, worrying that I'd unintentionally gotten into some sort of trouble with faction leadership.

"If there's going to be a fight," Brü said, more to the satchels he was dumping, rearranging, and repacking than to me, "I wouldn't want to know about it. On the road, I'd be duty-bound to shut it down until we're back at the base camp."

Slowly, I smiled. "I see."

"Huh. Some of this isn't going to fit," he said, nonchalant and still not looking at me.

I peered at the items he held, a random assortment of loot

gathered along our way. Why he didn't shove it onto one of the carts—

"Do me a favor?" he asked. "Just hold on to these for the day."

He held out a wispy silk vest that felt like chainmail when it brushed my fingers. It was clearly of fae origin, though I'd never felt a material like it before. Next came a handful of potions labeled in careful scrawl—strength, constitution, speed. Then a few sharp throwing knives in quick-draw sheaths.

I wanted to hug him. If *I'd* been a swampy water elemental and he'd almost died in *me*, I was pretty sure I would have made a deal with a warlord to become a hot blonde for him too. *Get it, Aelith.*

They treat you like a child.

I stiffened.

The voice was deep, dark, male and...inside my head? I shot looks in several directions, but I didn't expect to find the speaker this time. Dread pooled in my gut. I knew without knowing that the voice was just for me. I didn't know how or why, though.

What are you? I thought.

Nothing.

Brü stared at me with concern in his thoughtful eyes. I realized what I must look like—clamming up at the not-quite-mention of my fight to come—and what that might lead him to assume. So, I forced a smile. I was *not* going to let anyone think I was afraid of Lars Scum-of-the-Faction Wendlin.

"I'll keep it all safe for you," I said, matching Brü's conspiratorial tone.

His concern appeared to ease. He waved me off with a

reminder to review the codex, and I ventured to the mess tent to gorge myself on breakfast foods.

Our ride that day was uneventful. Bůk didn't join us at the outset. He was bent over a map with Colonel Astrada when we rode out. But he caught up with us as we neared the end. I was dutifully flipping through the codex when his horse pulled astride mine.

"Studying?" He smirked.

I shot him a quick, assessing look. He seemed to be in a good mood, which was rare. Particularly considering the minor holy water incident hanging over us.

"Just making sure I don't get myself into trouble."

He snorted. "A book isn't going to help you with that. You have a penchant for trouble."

I bit back a smile.

You allow him ***to control you. So weak. Such a disappointment, Eroithiel.***

I swallowed. The voice hadn't spoken all day. Not since it'd mocked me that morning. I'd never lost the feeling of being watched, but after so many quiet hours in the saddle, I'd let it fade to the back of my mind.

Now, it'd used my *name*. I didn't love that.

"Something wrong, kitten?" Bůk's tone remained light, but I sensed the suspicion in it.

I don't know why I didn't want to tell him about the voice. I mean...I guess in general, one wouldn't want to advertise signs of madness. But something deeper tugged at me. A sense that it would be dangerous for Bůk to find out about this.

Brü called us to a halt.

I let out a slow breath, glancing sideways at Bůk. "Did you mean it last night? Wendlin is mine?"

Understanding dawned on his face. My distraction worked.

"All yours," he confirmed.

I nodded and made a point of focusing my mind on Wendlin. If Bŭk wanted to read my desires, he was welcome to. I just needed to focus them on Lars for now. Mercifully, the creepy voice did not interfere again.

We set up camp. I threw myself into the many tasks that needed done and made an art of avoiding conversation. I prodded a few times at the presence I still felt watching, hoping to goad it into giving me something I could use to identify it. It did not rise to the bait.

Finally, the second party arrived. Bŭk left at Brü's request so I could play protections into place. It took longer than it should have. I struggled to hold the tune. If Brü noticed my distraction, I assume he chalked it up to nerves.

The carts arrived with the rest of our company in tow a few hours later. By then, I was ready. Not necessarily in a "prepared to win a fight" sense, but certainly in a "prepared to start one" sense. Good enough.

I dropped the things I wouldn't need in my tent, swallowed all three of Brü's potions, and returned to the fire feeling my inflated senses ripple with anticipation.

After a miserable night hiding from the rain, factionites crowded the raucous community space. I scanned faces and listened to conversations until I heard what I was after. It didn't take long.

"Lars! Tell the one about the troll!"

I followed the eager man's eyes and found my mark. He was tall, lean but fit, and had floppy dirty blond hair that he had to push out of his eyes several times as he deflected his companions' entreaties to entertain them. In case I needed further confirmation that this was my guy, the man sitting next to him had ink snaking down his neck that I recognized all too well.

Wendlin wielded an understated command of his pack. Even the larger, meatier men deferred to him. They arranged themselves around him in a way that showed the pecking order quite clearly.

There were no women. That was also telling.

Even though Wendlin didn't have the build of a grappler, experience reminded me he was stronger than he looked. Nerves trilled in my belly.

Is one mediocre alchemist all it takes to undo you, Eroithiel? the dark voice taunted inside my head.

My teeth clenched. I thought as hard as I could in its direction, *"Tell me who you are and why you're here, or fuck off."*

The voice did not deign to respond.

Irritated anew, I closed the distance between Lars and me before I could talk myself out of it.

He looked up. I'd already been ninety-nine percent sure Aelith was right when she'd named him my attacker last night —but the look in his eyes at that moment took my certainty to one hundred. A predatory mixture of amusement and disgust colored his face.

"What do we have here?" he drawled. "Where's your lute, Princess? Going to play me a pretty tune?"

At the word *princess*, the tinderbox that was my patience torched.

"No, I was thinking I might castrate you for what you tried to do to me last night."

The surrounding conversations died.

One flash. One flash of utter appalled outrage was all I got. He was so quick to mask it. His expression settled back into languid confidence almost instantly.

"Oh, Princess, don't do that," he said. "I told you I can't let you out of initiation. It wouldn't be fair. Even if you act like a little whore and promise to—"

My fist connected with his mouth before he could finish presenting his twisted version of events. Pain lanced through my hand. Possibly thanks to the strength potion, because I'd hit him harder than I'd ever hit anything in my life.

Which wasn't terribly comforting, considering he lurched to his feet barely fazed.

"You're going to fight me, you stupid piece of shit," I said, "or I'm going to report you to Astrada for attempting to rape a factionmate."

Wendlin's amusement vanished. In my experience, rapists didn't like the word rape. It made them feel dirty and wrong. *Good.*

He stood, a silvery whip appearing in his hand. "Your word against mine, Princess."

"My word is that you're a small, weak coward and an opportunist. And you can deny it, but I think even your friends know who's telling the truth."

We moved, step mirroring step, until we found space. This wasn't what I'd planned. I'd expected to challenge him, goad him into accepting, and then...I don't know. Perhaps go to a nearby clearing somewhere and establish rules and stakes and do this duel style. The punch had brought things to a head a little more quickly. And now everyone was watching.

"I knew you were a soft little thing," he taunted. "In case you wondered, your lies won't make you any friends."

His hand didn't move, but the whip shot out. It came too fast to block, snapping against my shoulder. The tip singed my cheek. I sucked in a gasp, but managed not to cry out.

I palmed two throwing knives. He couldn't kill me. It was in the codex. If he did, Astrada would punish him and then deliver him to Austvix for probable execution. I didn't *care* if I lost, I reminded myself. The point was to expose him. I'd already achieved that objective.

A *meaningless objective.*

I bristled at the voice, flinging both knives at the same time.

Wendlin didn't even flinch as he deflected them and answered with another crack of his whip. This time, I anticipated it and dodged—though there was still no visual warning. He was fighting with magic, not brawn.

I realized belatedly that I should *try* to do the same. I reached for my tendrils, willing them to do what I needed rather than whatever chaotic thing they chose for once.

They stirred...but they did nothing.

"I'm bored and I want a drink," Lars drawled.

It was the only warning I got. His whip swirled into action again—but it was merely a distraction. Six tiny blades flew from his off-hand. Two came for my knees, two for my arms, one for my face, and one for my stomach.

Time froze.

I lifted my arms instinctively, shielding my face. But I still would have been skewered five different ways had the disgusted voice in my head not pushed me one last time.

Fight, Eroithiel. Or just die and get it over with.

The tendrils in my chest unfurled. Fury uncoiled from my core and burst out, knocking the blades from the air and riding my rage to and through Lars Wendlin.

For a moment, I didn't realize what had happened. I felt his flesh part, felt his heart sizzle, felt the sluice of his brain liquefy. But it wasn't until I saw his very dead, very bloody corpse hit the ground that I fully comprehended what I'd done.

There she is.

The voice and the eyes that had followed me all day vanished with that final pronouncement.

The screams reached me then. They echoed around us. Hands gripped my arms. I didn't fight them. A cloud of heat reached me from one side—Bŭk—and Aelith's voice rose above the din, but I couldn't focus on her words.

I'd killed a factionmate.

I was so...so fucked.

Chapter 16
Ero: Speak No Evil

Bardic Advice from Eroithiel von Dua to future generations: Even when the bastard deserves it, spare a moment to plan your revenge. The consequences of your actions can be such a headache otherwise.

"*D*on't speak."

Although Bǔk didn't raise his voice, his order cut through the cacophony of the crowd. It was laced with compulsion—so I had no choice but to obey. Which meant I couldn't defend myself.

The dead man's friends fought to reach me. Bǔk conjured a mote of fire to keep them at bay. The smoky stench of burning grass and leaves raked at my eyes.

I watched in a daze, their shouts and struggles removed as though they were a show and I its audience.

"*Kneel.*"

I was too hollow to question Bǔk's reason for giving that

132

order. For giving orders through the collar at all. As if I would have resisted him right then. I was one stiff breeze from collapse. I knelt.

He caressed my hair, offering silent praise despite my lack of choice. Then his thumb squeezed between my throat and collar—holding it like I couldn't be trusted not to attack.

A prickle of embarrassment broke through the numbness. Half of our company had just watched me obey Bǔk like a mindless pet, and more were arriving every moment to see what the raised voices were about. They would find me kneeling at his feet.

I sucked in a breath—ready to look up at him to show my disapproval in whatever way I could, since I couldn't speak it— but he gave a subtle jerk of the collar, momentarily taking my air away.

It was jarring enough to give me pause. For now. I didn't have the energy to fight Bǔk. So instead, I closed my eyes to block it all out.

I killed someone.

I killed someone.

I killed someone.

The cadence of the jeers and shouts changed when leadership arrived. A woman's sharp voice rose above the rest. "What is this, Bǔk?"

By the pin-drop silence that followed, I knew the voice belonged to Colonel Astrada. The woman who would probably decide my fate any minute now. I'd only seen her from a distance, but her commanding tone was exactly what I'd imagined.

A man on the other side of the flames shouted with raw fury before Bǔk could speak, "She killed Wendlin, Colonel! Everyone here saw it."

I opened my eyes, looking up at Colonel Astrada. Her tight bun and her stiff uniform told me all I needed to know about her relationship with regulations. I was triple-fucked.

She frowned down at me. "Explain yourself, initiate."

It felt like the dream where a monster stands over you and you want to run, but you can't move. Or shout, but you can't open your mouth. Helplessness was my least favorite flavor. I gritted my teeth in frustration, imagining Bůk's face melting as loudly as I could. Let him read *that* desire.

"She won't speak," Bůk said.

Colonel Astrada's gaze snapped up to him, and her tone turned to ice. "Excuse me?"

"Wendlin attacked her last night," Bůk said calmly, ignoring the protests from the men he'd neatly boxed out with his flames. "She confronted him. They fought. He struck to kill." Bůk shrugged one shoulder, as though he was sick of telling the same dull story twice. "I ordered the bard to defend herself. She did. Wendlin didn't survive."

My incredulous gaze shot to Bůk. What was he *doing?* He hadn't ordered me to do anything. I'd started this fight—and my magic had ended it.

A swarm of angry butterflies trilled in my stomach at the thought. *My* magic had done this. The tendrils I coaxed into bolstering my songs every day, that I had to push and cajole to heal—had gutted a man like it was nothing.

Holy shit.

Colonel Astrada's mouth tightened. "And why can she not tell me this herself, Bůk?"

I sucked in a sharp breath. The closest I could come to vocally agreeing with the spirit of Astrada's terse question. The thumb Bůk held between the collar and my throat tilted, intentionally tightening the collar until I could barely breathe.

"Because I ordered her to be silent," he said, as though that were explanation enough. "I brought her into the faction on business for Lord Austvix. She wears my collar. She follows my orders. If there's a problem, Colonel, I will address it."

The look Colonel Astrada gave Bůk put her on a special shelf in my mind, inhabited previously by Aelith alone. A party of two who showed absolutely no sign of bending in the face of Bůk's considerable intimidation. They were stronger women than I. The words the dark voice had spoken in my head that morning taunted me now. *You allow* him *to control you. So weak. Such a disappointment, Eroithiel.* In that moment, I couldn't help but agree with the shadow's assessment.

"Bůk, you are out of bounds," Colonel Astrada said softly. "Remove that collar, or I will have my guard put her down."

Black spots danced in my eyes from the lack of oxygen as Bůk's grip tightened further still—this time, I think, unintentionally. But he remained outwardly calm. After a beat, he released me altogether. I fell forward on my hands and knees, gulping in the smoky air and choking on it.

Bůk met the colonel's gaze—not with the superiority or dismissiveness with which he always seemed to look at me—but with respect. And regret. "I can't do that, Colonel. The situation is what it must be to serve Lord Austvix."

Panic coursed through me. She was going to have her men kill me, and I wouldn't even get to plead my case first.

"Be still," Bůk ordered.

I froze. It didn't stop the feelings, which spilled down my cheeks in the only way they could now. My anger blazed to new heights. The tendrils in my chest—I pictured them differently now, bloody and hungry—stirred with fresh desire.

No, no, no. I pleaded with—them? Myself? Fear of what I might do if Astrada's people came for me overtook everything else. It was all coming to a fever pitch when she finally spoke again.

"I see," she said.

She brushed ash from her pristine cloak, frowning in deep thought. I couldn't begin to guess at the power dynamics at play. I could only hope they worked out in my favor.

"Then you take responsibility for your factionmate's death?" Colonel Astrada asked, her tone returning to business and suggesting a purposeful topic shift.

"Yes," Bůk answered without hesitation.

She took stock of her audience. Everyone was watching. I didn't need Bůk's senses or abilities to read the crowd and understand that no answer was going to please everyone. I didn't envy the colonel. She grimaced.

"Raise the whipping post," Colonel Astrada said.

A fresh cry of outrage from Wendlin's crew sounded. Murmurs blanketed the crowd. Astrada lifted her hand for silence. She frowned at Bůk. "You will report in ten minutes. Bring what you need."

"Yes, Colonel," he said.

And then he yanked me to my feet and pulled me away from the crowd.

The compulsion dissipated when we entered his tent. He didn't have to say anything. My ability to speak simply returned. The only barrier then was deciding which of my many, many thoughts to voice first.

I started with a nice all-encompassing, "What the fuck was that?"

"You're welcome," he answered.

He turned away, wrenching a small satchel from the ground as though it weighed much more than it appeared to. He reached inside. Although it looked like his hand alone would fill the bag, he extracted the manacles and the long chains he'd used in the woods. His dampeners. My tendrils lurched at the sight.

"What are you doing?"

"Making sure I don't kill a man for doing his job."

He meant the whipping post. Gods help the factionite tasked with whipping Bůk. And what else? The codex, which I'd been so pointedly gifted that morning, mentioned that executable offenses—such as killing a factionmate—that happened in the field were to be litigated before Lord Austvix himself. But Bůk couldn't be killed. So what *would* happen?

Which brought me to another salient point. *Why* Bůk? Why not me? I harbored no delusions about Bůk's character nor his feelings. He wasn't the 'sacrifice myself for others' type.

"Why did you lie?" I demanded.

He paused then, letting the chains fall, and turned to give me his full attention for the first time since he'd stepped to my side at the fire. His hard look softened infinitesimally. His onyx eyes bore into mine. My breath caught in my throat.

"Only I get to punish you," he said simply.

"F-for killing Wendlin?"

Saying the words aloud sent a ripple of alarm through me that had nothing to do with Bůk. As though the statement made it real—again. And I hadn't just *killed* Wendlin. I'd cooked his heart and liquefied his brain.

A grim amusement danced in Bůk's eyes. "No. Wendlin was already dead the moment he put his hands on you. Your killing him tonight merely saved me the effort." Some of the amusement faded in favor of his usual put-upon frown. "Granted, I would have been more subtle about it. Killing him in the middle of the camp's evening festivities was…certainly a bold choice."

I winced. I might have pointed out that it actually hadn't been much of a choice—more of a strange anomaly even I couldn't explain. But that was need-to-know information. The last thing Bůk needed was more knowledge to use against me.

The way he looked at me made those thoughts fizzle out. I could feel him digging around in my head. I feared what he would find there.

"I guess I should be grateful," he said in that low, dangerous tone straight out of my nightmares. "At least when you come for me, I know it won't be a surprise."

I swayed, dizzy with the accusation. The obviously true accusation. Also, the one I'd been stupid to let him see, first with the holy water and again not twenty minutes ago when I'd made love to the mental image of his face melting. "I—"

"No, kitten." He put a single finger to my lips. "No lies tonight."

When his hand fell away, I licked my lips and tasted his earthy flavor mixed with ash. He was about to take *my* punishment—and we hadn't even settled our other scores. The ledgers were a mess.

"Time to go," he said. "If you value your life and the lives of your factionmates, I suggest you don't contradict anything I told Colonel Astrada tonight."

I nodded, physically unable to speak. This time, I couldn't blame the collar.

"Good kitten," he said.

He picked up the chains and slung them over his shoulder. Then, he strode from the tent without a backward glance.

I took a moment to gather myself. To remind myself that I

was still alive—for now—and that somehow, I'd escaped whatever fate Colonel Astrada might have rightly given me for killing Wendlin. The fate I had waiting for me with Bůk, however...

Well, that was a problem for later.

Chapter 17
Bůk: A Simple Challenge

Bůk's Personal Code, Item 3, Revised: Thou shalt only be distracted by a mortal when it doesn't interfere with the mission. Then it's fine.

I hadn't exactly expected the whipping to be a grand time—but I underestimated Colonel Astrada's ire. As I approached, a young officer stopped my progress toward the sight of the spectacle-to-be and guided me into a tent at the edge of the field. Although the young man's face was carefully expressionless, his fingers trembled on my arm—and his desire to let go and run was palpable. I offered him no reassurance.

Colonel Astrada waited inside. I stepped in and noted the immediate silence. A sound barrier.

"Explain," she ordered, dropping the careful stoicism she'd held at the fire. "Now."

I met the colonel's eyes, appreciating once again the tight spot she was in. To lead a company of individuals with varying strengths and abilities—many that physically far outstripped her own—knowing that one of them could turn on her at any time. I, chief among them.

"She's from Finchton," I said. "Lord Austvix is no closer to—"

"Explain the *collar*, Bůk."

I assessed her. I hadn't exactly hidden the artifact, but neither had I advertised it before tonight. In truth, I hadn't thought much about what anyone else would have to say about it. I shrugged. "The bard was with the Huntress party. We need information that she can't be trusted to provide without—"

"That's a thin excuse," Colonel Astrada interrupted impatiently. "A truth serum would achieve the same results. As it stands, the bard is a weapon you can point at whomever you like without facing contractual consequences. She's a loophole."

I scratched the back of my neck. I could have explained that I hadn't actually known my kitten was *capable* of much harm until I'd witnessed the scene tonight. I could have denied the desire to find a loophole in the first place and reiterated my dedication to the Fated. Instead, I shrugged again. "Wendlin was owed a trial, but he deserved what he got. I'm sure Ero wasn't the first initiate he attempted to take advantage of." I arched my eyebrow. "I didn't know him from Haz before tonight. I have no intention of using the bard to cause problems."

"But you could," Colonel Astrada said. "And Lord Austvix will be warned. I only wanted to communicate as much to you. You may go."

The stiff nod toward the tent flap, the hard eyes, the tight jaw—none of it could mask the primal fear that hid just beneath the surface of her words. If I decided to push limits, I could destroy her. Sure, I would face consequences. But that wouldn't help her. She knew it. I knew it. What she didn't know, and I did, was that I had no desire to harm her. A good leader with a level head was difficult to find. And as far as leaders went, I found her among the most tolerable of them.

I left the tent without another word.

Only to find Aelith standing next to the hooded man who awaited me by the whipping post...coating his cane in holy water.

Fuck.

Colonel Astrada wasn't *that* scared after all. This was a choice. I begrudgingly toasted her in my mind. Scared perhaps —but brave.

I donned my dampeners and let them get on with it.

I woke before dawn with my face in the mud and a soft melody scratching at my psyche like nails on slate. I groped blearily for the source of the music, but even that slight motion lit my shredded back on fire. I groaned into the mud.

"It's working," my kitten said quietly. "Just a little longer."

I gritted my teeth. The music was marginally less awful than the boiling wounds—which wasn't saying much. I closed my eyes. The dampeners were still on. My shadows pooled angrily beneath my skin. The post and the crowd were gone. They'd gotten their show.

Ero's song was the only sound in the dark. I tried unsuccessfully not to slide back to Hell, tormented by my own foolishness. For minutes or hours—I couldn't begin to guess— flashes of that fateful chase riddled my jittery mind. The hollowness after. Being destroyed by ill-timed empathy. By a bard. By—

"I'm going to take them off," Ero said.

I reached to stop her—knowing that I wasn't ready. But no screaming pain answered the motion. I twisted at the waist, testing the raw skin. It didn't feel *good,* but the wounds were no longer bleeding or burning. I stilled, and she retrieved the key from my neck and unlocked the manacles one at a time.

My connection to my higher senses surged back to life. The skin on my back—aside from the parts where remnants of holy water still lingered—began to knit together and smooth over.

When my body settled, I sat up.

Ero watched me, something unreadable in her expression. Her green eyes pulsed with unmanageable thoughts. Even her desires were a tangled mess I couldn't discern.

"Why are you here, kitten?"

Her nerves flared to life when I held her gaze. Despite her colorful cloak and the way she effortlessly commanded a crowd with her songs, it struck me that a bare moment of focused attention was enough to undo her. Did no one ever look this closely? As if to prove my observation true, she slid her lute onto her back and looked down, ostensibly to adjust the strap. But when her eyes darted up again—a quick check—I was still watching and waiting. She swallowed.

"It was supposed to be me," she said, looking away again, unable to meet my eyes. "I just…"

I waited, but she didn't finish. She felt guilty. The irony of that considering what I'd done to her—and still planned to do —was delicious.

"Look at me, kitten."

Her struggle fascinated me. I could have said it again— ordered it—but watching her warring emotions play out was so much sweeter. Finally, she looked. I caught her chin before she could drop it again.

"Wendlin deserved what he got," I said slowly so each word could sink in. "And you were magnificent."

The flare of alarm in her eyes told me her turmoil wasn't just about me. She'd seen a side of herself tonight that she wasn't sure she liked. Pleasure seeped into me like a tide drawn by her existential strife. When she bit her lip, uncertainty etched in every detail of her expression—I pushed.

I leaned forward, pressing my lips to hers.

Her desire rolled in like a spring storm—sudden and fierce. I chuckled against her lips. She was so eager, so nervous. I sucked her bottom lip into my mouth and bit down until her alarm added to the sweet melody. I didn't draw blood, but I let her wonder if I would.

My body ached for a release. The night had gone sideways, sure, but she was right here, begging for it—and I wasn't going to deny myself now.

I pushed her back on the ground, drinking in her wide eyes and the protest she almost but didn't quite utter. She didn't want to deny herself either. She just thought she should. And she was probably right...but I took away the temptation with another kiss. Her lips parted eagerly, granting my tongue entry.

I pushed my hand down her pants, swallowing her gasp when my fingers slid through her arousal. Then I pulled them out, wrenching my mouth from hers and holding the glistening fingers between us. "Is this for me, kitten?"

She whimpered, looking away. Her lips parted, drawing in a breath. She wanted to run. Shame and embarrassment clawed at her, pulling her desires in several directions. I smiled, trailing the fingers around her kiss-swollen lips so she could taste herself, then wrenched her chin toward me and forced her to look me in the eye.

"Open your mouth," I said, low and guttural.

To my surprise, she obeyed. I pushed the two fingers inside, pressing them to her tongue. Her lips closed. She sucked them clean without having to be told.

But she also closed her eyes.

My dark chuckle was her only warning. I pulled my fingers out of her mouth, lifted my weight off her, and flipped her over in one quick motion. She tried to move, but I held her face to the ground.

"No, no, you don't want to look at me," I taunted.

Her alarm spiked. Her desire did too. Like twins, riding the hills together.

I yanked her pants down and freed my cock, sliding into her before she could catch up. She cried out. She also sank back into me, forcing me deeper. I groaned. This would not be the drawn-out ordeal my cock craved. There would be time for that later. It was nearly dawn, and we were out in the open in the middle of camp, and for once, our desires were aligned. I would take it while I had it.

I slammed into her, once, twice, fine-tuning with each thrust to answer her wordless desires until I found the spot that reduced her to a whimpering mess and hit it mercilessly. She came apart, pulsing around my cock. It was enough to push me over the edge. I didn't bother to withdraw, filling what I'd claimed.

She deflated beneath me, sinking into the soft ground. I could taste her languid assumption—but I wasn't finished. I pulled out, pressing my cock to her thigh, and trailed my finger through the mess we'd made. I kept going, sliding back until I reached her ass. I traced the tight ring and smiled when her whole body stiffened. Then, I shoved one finger in up to the knuckle.

"Bůk!" she cried.

The protest tugged a smile out of me—because the aromatic hints of lemon and clove exposed her. As always. Her desire, now underscored with a heady new undertone of forbidden want.

"Are you ready to talk about the holy water now?" I whispered against her ear.

The spike of her panic soothed the last of the night's frustration away. Pleasure burned low in my gut. I pressed in just a little farther, teasing her fear to a fever pitch.

"Bůk! Please!"

I trailed kisses from her ear to her jaw and back, biting down on her earlobe before I spoke again. "Who do you belong to?"

"You!" she cried—too quickly, too easily.

"I don't think you believe that yet."

I teased a second finger through the mess dripping out of her, and she tried to twist under me. I held her still.

"Please," she whispered.

I don't think even she knew what she was begging for.

I let the moment linger. Let her feel every second—her fear, her longing, her fullness. Then I withdrew the sunken finger and let both rest on her ass in warning.

"Tell you what, kitten. You did so well tonight, I'll give you a chance."

Her frantic breaths—her spark of hope—made me smile against her hair. She was so naïve.

"Obey without questioning me for one day, and I won't punish you for conspiring with Aelith. How does that sound?"

She nodded, accepting the terms without thought. A trait I quite liked, actually.

"Use your words, kitten."

"Yes," she mumbled. "Yes, please."

I flattened my hand on her ass, removing the immediate threat of invasion, and traced gentle circles on her soft skin. She relaxed again—right before I lifted my hand and delivered a vicious smack.

"Clean up and come to bed," I told her. "We're still in the lead tomorrow."

With that, I stood and put myself together, leaving the bard panting in the clearing, confident knowing that she would learn—sooner rather than later—what it really meant to be mine.

Chapter 18
Ero: A Spectacular Failure

"We judge heroes based not on their actions, but on the outcome of those actions. This, of course, ignores the role of the Fates. The same action performed twice might save one village and raze another." - a fragment of correspondence from a Temple Mother, preserved in the journal of Eroithiel von Dua

"I need a tent."

"Good morning to you too," Brü mused.

For the second day in a row, we met at the fire before most of the camp had woken. I knew I would find him there. He was a creature of habit. All thoughtful and contemplative—probably hoping for solitude, but that was his problem.

I'd only waited for Bůk's breathing to even out before I'd extracted myself. His body—his scent—was a constant reminder, both of what my body craved and what I desperately needed to escape.

I let him—

Nope, no. Not going there. I refused to think about any of it. I had a mission. Acquire a tent! I needed to reclaim space where Bůk couldn't literally breathe down my neck. That would be a good first step.

Brü arched a brow. "Didn't I issue you a tent a few days ago?"

So, it was going to be like *that* today. A pang of something like gratitude chased my annoyance away, though. At least Brü wasn't angry about last night.

I shrugged one shoulder. "Bůk burned it."

Brü nodded slowly. "That must be why *he* told me you wouldn't need a new one." He made a face like 'distinctly minding my business over here, not asking a single question,' and turned to add logs to the growing fire. But then he tossed me a bone. "I do have extras, though, if you want one."

I bit my lip. While it was good to know that Brü wouldn't automatically side with Bůk, knowing that Bůk had spoken to him about the tent gave me pause. Would something like *this* violate Bůk's challenge? It would be an awfully ridiculous way to lose if so.

"Tomorrow," I said, nodding decisively. "Same time?"

Brü made his amusement plain with a tight-lipped smile. He shook his head but didn't inquire about my logic.

To reward him for not being the worst, I strummed a few energizing chords on my lute. Mostly because I needed them myself—but also to thank him without being direct about it. For the potions yesterday, for not berating me this morning, and—of course—for his willingness to ignore Bůk's requests where I was concerned.

The others trickled in. The usual crew. Nigel, the hawk-eyed fighter, with his curved blades and dozens of visible scars that suggested either a long adventuring career or an unlucky one. Hammond, the brutish barbarian who outsized even Bůk —well, Bůk at his most human, anyway. Tavish, a quiet man whose role I'd yet to discern. And Flər...who, I was pleased to note, gave me a wide berth.

"Is Bůk traveling with another group today?" I asked Brü hopefully as the time to roll out approached with no sign of him.

"Aw *shucks,* I was hoping—" Flər started, and then cut himself off as Bůk appeared at the edge of the fire ring, expression dark as night.

His gaze lingered on Flər for an uncomfortably long beat as the rest of us pretended not to watch.

A teeny, tiny part of me hoped they would fight.

They did not.

Bůk stalked to me, immediately invading my space. I looked up at him tentatively.

"Did you sleep at all?" he asked. His tone was low—not quite a whisper, but clearly not for the group. Which didn't stop them from straining to hear every word.

White lies formed and died on my tongue. *Yes. A little. Enough.*

"No," I said truthfully, if reluctantly. "But I'll be fine."

"You'll ride with me."

A faint smirk twisted his lips as my obvious desire to argue rose. Showing *great* restraint, I ignored the urge and nodded instead. This was going to be unpleasant. But...not unpleasant enough to give up the game.

Bůk cupped my cheek and brushed my forehead with a soft kiss before turning to remove my things from my horse.

I froze. Every single person in our party had just witnessed that. And I realized with a flush of annoyance that that was the point. *Who do you belong to?* he'd asked last night. But when I'd given him the answer he was looking for, he'd accused me of not believing it. Was this him illustrating the point? Showing that he could do whatever he liked with me—including play pretend in front of others?

I stalked to Bůk's horse and mounted, teeth clenched so tight my jaw hurt. If kneeling for him at the fire hadn't already destroyed any chance I had of saving face in the faction, this would. But I couldn't worry about that yet. One Bůk-sized problem at a time.

When he swung into the saddle behind me, he took the reins and rested his hand on my thigh.

I tried to think of anything else. I made a game of it. Songs, places I'd been, Aelith. But the latter led to thinking of the holy water—which, of course, reminded me why I was in this situation—pressed against Bůk's unforgiving form as the horse rocked beneath us. I tried even harder. Favorite foods, favorite stories, favorite insults.

You can do this for one day, I cheered myself on. *He's a crusty lamb shank. He's less significant than a flake of dead skin. He's like if Flar were worse.*

When we hit rocky terrain, the motion shoved me deeper between Bůk's muscular thighs, and his rapidly hardening cock pressed against my ass. It gave me a terrible, wonderful idea. I angled so he would rock directly into me with each bounce. He grew predictably harder, even as the surrounding air heated in warning. I smiled to myself—ready to relent, lest I actually anger him—when Brü raised a hand, bringing us to a silent halt.

I looked around, but I didn't see whatever had given him

pause. Then Brü made a motion—a signal I didn't know, but everyone else seemed to recognize.

My heart lurched, tendrils rising and ready. I reached slowly for my lute.

Bůk's fingers closed around my wrist.

"No," he breathed against my ear before he released me and leapt to the ground.

But Bůk didn't land in the empty pathway he'd leapt toward. By the time his feet hit the ground, Huntress faction-ites were *everywhere*. It was another fucking ambush. They were up in the trees, lying on the ground, crouched in the foliage. Dozens of them—all with their weapons trained on us. It was as though we'd been in a blinding fog and had stepped out to find ourselves surrounded. It had to have been spell-work. How had *none* of us detected it?

Flər cried out, "Bůk, no!"

And the moment of surprise fizzled. Dozens of weapons that had been more evenly distributed swung toward Bůk.

My lute was suddenly in my hands, drawn there by my tendrils without so much as a conscious thought on my part. That was new. I didn't—*couldn't*—stop to think about Bůk's stupid game, or we were all going to die. He'd forgiven me last time. He would just have to do it again.

I struck a chord.

And...then I flew off the horse, high into the air. The gust of wind that carried me took my breath with it. As I groped for purchase, I saw a flash below. Bůk's hands were raised—at *me*.

Had he thrown me himself, or was he trying to catch me?

It didn't matter. I fell. And when I did, there was no ground waiting below. The woods disappeared in a flash as I dropped past a cliff face I hadn't even known was nearby, and fell toward the sea.

The frigid water sloshed cold and angry in the wind. I hit hard—but not as hard as I might have done without the few bare tendrils that bothered to cushion my fall. Most of them forsook me in favor of forming a protective casing around my lute.

I swam hard for the cliff face, praying to Haz and any other available deity that there would be a place to climb out. After several alarming moments of scrambling against the slippery rock, I found a foothold.

Icy water lashed at my back. The wind skated hellishly across my exposed skin. If I didn't get out of the water fast, I was going to go numb. I hoisted myself out with monumental effort.

The climb was slow work, made worse by the wind slicing through me, whipping my drenched cloak this way and that. Had I not been so attached to the damned thing, I might have let it fall.

When I finally reached a ledge wide enough to sit, I collapsed, choking in ragged breaths as my arms melted. I was still close enough to the water to feel its spray. The woods—the trail—were impossibly high up.

My teeth chattered. Thoughts swirled. A familiar voice whispered in my ear. *Leave now.* It wasn't the dark voice mocking me from on high. It was my own. The one that always urged me to leave one town and find the next when things got complicated. The voice that never found anything worth staying for.

Shaking, I folded in on myself.

Had anyone survived? I closed my eyes and saw Brü's rueful smile. Oh, gods. Aelith would kill the Huntress herself if he didn't make it back. The others flicked through my mind, one at a time.

I didn't want to run. I wanted to meet Lord Austvix. I wanted to solve the Finchton letters and learn more about my magic and prove that I belonged somewhere—maybe even with the Fated—and have something worthwhile to show for myself when I finally found my family.

But how *could* they have survived? There were *so* many of the others waiting. We'd been blindsided.

Dots of black danced in my vision.

Last time, they'd seemed to want to keep us alive. To capture rather than kill. Could that be the case this time too? If I made it back, would I find my factionmates alive—possibly even in need of rescue?

I licked my frozen lips. I wanted to play for clarity or luck or rest, but my fingers trembled. They were bloody and cold. I couldn't waste the time or energy it would take to heal them. I needed to go *now*.

I stood shivering violently and forced myself to move, batting each thought that came at me away. *You don't owe them this. This might be your only chance to escape Bůk. Would they come for you?*

I climbed until rough ledges in the rock smoothed into a winding path. It was narrow and perilous with the wind beating against me, but I moved steadily and willed my magic to make up wherever my physicality failed. I made agonizingly slow progress.

When I finally reached the grassy, wooded cliff, I nearly collapsed. But the sound of Flər's laughter stilled me. I blinked. Had he betrayed the others? It was a shitty first thought. And, a second later, it turned out that no—Brü's triumphant voice answered him. I stumbled forward, pushing brush aside, falling into the little clearing they'd made.

Dozens and dozens of Huntress factionites were bound in lines through the trees. They were gagged, but they also appeared to be spelled silent, because none of them made the faintest sound. My party, in contrast, sat around a small fire, enjoying the spoils of their apparent looting. Meat and vegetables roasted on long sticks. Mead overflowed tankards.

They were all fine.

Better than fine—they were *jubilant*.

I sank to my knees. Relieved—yes. But also spent. Also wrapped in the self-pitying thought: No one had come for me. Not even Brü.

Bůk rose. He took his time coming to me. This time, the others didn't watch. Too pointedly, in fact. He must have dangled some interesting threats.

I looked up at him, trying to get my exhausted mind to parse what I had found. He looked entirely too satisfied.

"You threw me off a cliff," I accused.

"You disobeyed me."

That. Motherfucker.

The truth hit all at once. It *had* been an ambush—but it was Bůk and Brü—and possibly everyone else in our party who knew what was coming, not our attackers. Bůk must have seen it—planned it. Only I wasn't told. That's why everyone else recognized Brü's signal.

"You cheated," I muttered, my vision blurring with the desperate need for rest.

Bůk bent, lifting me in his arms. I couldn't have fought him if I'd wanted to. His heat cut through my frozen clothes and sent shivers through me as it warmed and dried them. I groaned, burying my face in him even as I wished I had an ounce of strength left to pull away.

"It was never a game, kitten," he growled against my ear. An electric current of danger chased his thumb down my cheek. "Sleep now. Tomorrow, I *will* play with you."

Chapter 19
Ero: A Lesson from the Shadows

"You can make me say it, but you can't make me mean it." - an excerpt from the journal of Eroithiel von Dua, 1313 B.A., before the Great War

I woke before sunrise. The deadweight of Bůk's arm held me in place, tucked tight against him. His chest rose and fell in a steady rhythm, bare skin pressing into me with a searing heat that was comforting one moment, suffocating the next.

I steeled myself. In what was becoming a morning ritual, I carefully lifted his arm to slip out. He didn't stir. Thank Haz for small favors.

I needed a moment to think. If I could find Brü, I could collect my new tent. Perhaps a potion of luck, too. I crawled out of Bůk's tent, preoccupied with my developing plan—but came up short at what I found.

Doused ash where there should be fire.

Empty trees where there should be tents.

Silence where there should be bustle.

I stumbled across the tiny clearing. The stench of piss and shit and vomit wafted from the woods where the prisoners had been. Spare bits of rope trimmings were all that remained.

They were all gone.

I braced myself against a tree. My faculties that'd been dulled last night by the exhausting climb were back in full force. Including my anger.

Bůk had set me up.

Bůk was toying with me.

And Bůk could fuck all the way off if he thought—

"Good morning," he said.

I rounded on him. He stood just outside the tent in a languid slouch, tugging a shirt over his head to conceal the delicious ripple of muscle I'd slept against. He smiled, but it didn't reach his eyes.

"Where are they?" I demanded.

He padded toward me, in no hurry to answer. I tried to hide my nerves, but I could tell he sensed them by the shimmery waves his pleasure made in the air.

He lifted the end of my messy braid, considering it thoughtfully.

"Bůk," I said, unnerved by his silence. If he didn't want to speak, I would. "Yesterday on the trail, I thought—"

"Remove the enchantments on this," he instructed, tugging the braid gently.

I took a step back. Instantly, his gaze darkened, and the air heated. His temper was quick this morning.

I swallowed and forced myself to hold his gaze as I combed my fingers through my hair, undoing the braid and the enchantments with it—demonstratively. As if to say, *See how reasonable I am? Would you like to try that too?* When I finished, I dropped my hand to my side, searching his face. Despite trying to keep my tone steady, my question came out close to a whisper. "Why did everyone leave without us?"

Bůk ignored my question. He stepped forward, closing the distance between us once more. I leaned back without stepping —only to meet a wall of unforgiving bark. I reached back and gripped the tree he'd backed me into with both hands to steady myself. His breath tickled my forehead. I tried to look away, but he gripped my chin and held me in place.

Bůk's irises glowed black, the tiny flecks of gold and crimson warring for space.

"I'm going to offer you a deal," he said.

He wants your soul a terrified voice inside me chirped. Wasn't that what demons bargained for? Belonging to him for eternity would make this collar look like child's play. I promised myself I would take option two, whatever it was. He'd already claimed my free will. I didn't have to give him—

"Dawn to dusk," he said. "You run. *Each* time I catch you—" he emphasized the inevitably of my multiple failures with an arched brow, "—I fuck you just the way *you* want."

I narrowed my eyes. That was clearly a trap. That sounded delightful?

He smiled at my uncertainty. "The way your *body* begs to be fucked."

On cue, my stomach hollowed. My *body* betrayed me at every turn—particularly where Bůk was concerned. Its desires were much darker than my mind's. He knew that, of course. He'd watched me battle it since the moment we met. And I couldn't exactly lie to someone who could *read* my desires.

"Bůk..."

He remained silent, waiting for me to finish. But I couldn't. Because there was nothing to say. Once again, I had no leverage. I swallowed. And then I remembered his words from before, and a tiny prick of hope broke through my fear.

"You said a deal," I pointed out, scrabbling for purchase.

He nodded, his smile vicious. Slowly, he brought his fingers up to trace the metal bracing on my collar.

"At dusk, I will ask you if you want me to remove this," he said. "I will give you one chance to answer. If I take the collar off, you can leave and never look back. I will remove the tattoo from your skin, strike your name from the Fated's enrollment logs, and never pursue you again."

I took a shuddering breath.

Yes. This was it. It *had* to be. Whatever he did to me today, by tonight, I could be free. Would there be a catch? Almost certainly. But I would be smarter this time. I would see it coming, I promised myself. I would outsmart *him*.

"If you say *no*," he went on, "then I'll know you've accepted what this is. And we can stop with the pathetic games."

He bent forward, boxing me in with his forearms on either side of my head. He breathed against my mouth—the flavor of midnight woods overwhelming me. Our noses nearly touched as he stared directly into my eyes with his devastating onyx glare.

"Do you understand, kitten?"

"Yes," I hissed.

"Then fucking run."

My feet thundered through the brush, grasping for distance in favor of stealth. I slid down an embankment and splashed into a stream.

Perfect.

I would take wet boots if it meant leaving no tracks.

How long would my head start be? He hadn't told me. But I didn't see or hear any sign of him yet, and that seemed like a good sign—even if it'd only been a few minutes.

When the stream curved, I played a quiet melody on my lute and willed my tendrils to lighten my feet. I flew past obvious hiding spots—boulders with dark crevices, tufts of cattails, a tangle of fallen trees. Only when my breathing grew labored did I leap into the thick foliage, wedging myself deeper until I couldn't see anything at all.

I had to elbow vegetation out of the way to raise my lute again for a cloaking tune. When it ended, I closed my eyes. Rest. I could rest. I could catch my breath and—

The gust of wind came at once.

He didn't even pretend.

The plants around me whipped back and forth, lashing me violently before they flattened to the ground under his assault. Whereas I was dripping with sweat from the exertion of my run, Bůk stood as calm and cool as he had been before, head tilted with a pitying smile. The sun was barely up.

"You're not very good at this," he mused.

My heart trilled. I'd been pretty sure until about three seconds ago that I was doing *great.* So this was...an unfortunate turn of events.

Bůk didn't move, but his shadow rippled. I watched it warily, recalling the way it'd grown in the woods before he had. Now it dissipated instead, forming tendrils that rolled toward me like dark fog.

I scrambled back, jumping for a low tree branch. I caught it and swung my body, planning to leap the stream and run once more—even if it proved futile. But the shadows were faster.

They snaked up my arms, encircled my wrists, and held my fingers to the wood.

I dangled there, kicking the air until the shadows caught my feet too.

"Fancy trick," I said through my teeth. "But that wasn't hard enough—right? Maybe you should let me go and try again."

The only sign that he'd even heard was a slow head tilt.

The shadows spread, spilling into my sleeves and up my arms like silken snakes, ice cold and slippery, raising goosebumps wherever they touched. I couldn't help the image I conjured—of those shadows finding the places Bůk had already discovered—of fucking me *for* him while he watched. When I blinked the image away, his faint smirk broadcasted a smug *"message received."*

I flushed. Would he? *Could* he?

I held his gaze as his shadows crawled up my legs, tickling the insides of my thighs—and paused there.

I whimpered.

"What do you want, kitten?"

What *did* I want?

I wanted him to rip my clothes off and fuck me. I wanted him to leave and never come back. I wanted—just for once—to want something simple that wouldn't destroy me.

How much control did I actually have over *which* desires he could read?

That question fizzled as one of the shadowy wisps darted up my thigh and dipped into the evidence of my arousal. Bůk's smirk deepened. He leaned back against a tree with his arms crossed, a good ten paces away, and watched me writhe as the shadow slid slowly through my slick heat, tickling my pussy, and dragging its wetness down the inside of my thigh.

"When I ask a question, you answer," Bůk ordered.

The compulsion gripped me.

Bůk sounded like he had the first time he'd compelled me in the woods. Blank. Devoid of all emotion. That realization—even more than the caress of his chilly shadows or the fact that I was bound and hanging from a tree—made my heartbeat pick up speed.

"What is your name?" Bůk asked, clinically disinterested.

The shadows danced to the clasp of my cloak, the button on my pants, the hooks in my armored fae shirt. Like an eager suitor after one too many drinks, they made quick work of undressing me for him, dropping my clothes to the forest floor.

"Ero," I gasped, tugging uselessly against the shadows—instinctively trying to shield some part of my body from Bůk's stony gaze. The tendrils in my chest seemed *scared* of the shadows. They tangled up, rearing back as if they'd encountered a wild animal.

"Who do you belong to?" Bůk demanded.

I wasn't *trying* to be obstinate. Had the compulsion not pressed an answer off the tip of my tongue before I had a moment to polish it, there's a fifty percent chance I would have said what he wanted to hear.

Instead, I growled, "No one."

A faint gust of warm air served as the first sign that Bůk wasn't totally closed off emotion-wise. But his low chuckle made the tiny hairs on the back of my neck rise.

"You don't think so?" he taunted.

"No," I bit out—then cried out loud as the shadows wrenched my legs apart, leaving me spread-eagle, angled toward him for his viewing pleasure.

As if that weren't humiliating enough, two more tendrils of

shadow snaked against my pussy and spread it open wide—like curtains revealing the main stage.

"*Bůk!*" I cried.

"What is your name?" he asked again.

"E-Ero," I gritted out.

Another tendril teased my wide-open entrance before slipping inside. The cold lit up every nerve as it filled me, eliciting a high keening moan. I couldn't take even a beat to enjoy it, though, because more silky wisps crawled down my spine toward my ass, and fear overwhelmed the temporary pleasure.

"*Please,*" I begged—not even knowing what I was asking for. Please fill me up and make me come apart? Please stop? Please not back there?

I shook with desperation from warring desires.

I expected Bůk to ask again who I belonged to. This time I would be ready. I would give him what he wanted. The words he needed—for whatever reason—to hear. Because whatever he said, this *was* a game. If I had to bend to him in order to get away, I would. It didn't have to *mean* anything.

Only he didn't ask.

The shadow inside me curved forward, tickling the spot I knew he would hit, undulating against my inner walls. I tasted summer. I smelled rain. I invented a new religion.

A light touch breezed across my clit—so faint it almost felt like an accident until it happened again, in rhythm with the motion inside, demanding my pleasure.

The shadows crawling down my back reached my ass, swirling around the tight ring Bůk's finger had breached as he'd threatened me two nights before. I knew it was useless, but I whined a desperate plea anyway. It was too much—I wasn't ready. I couldn't handle it all at once.

The shadow slid into my ass without hesitation.

It was hard to concentrate on any one sensation as the pressure on my clit increased and the rocking inside my pussy grew harder and the shadow in my ass swelled, straining in a way that hurt as much as it thrilled.

I was so full everywhere. So close to the release I needed in no time at all. I was a meager handful of thrusts from oblivion.

"What's your name?"

"B-Bůk!" I cried. It wasn't the correct answer. It *was* all I could say. And technically, he'd only told me to *answer* when he asked a question. I didn't have to be coherent or right.

Thrust.

"That's *my* name, kitten."

Thrust.

"What's *your* name?"

Thrust.

"Please!" I screamed.

The tendrils froze in place. I choked back a sob, feeling the orgasm that had been exactly one thrust away recede from reach.

No.

Fucking no!

I yanked my wrist, thinking of not one single thing except my need to touch myself before I lost the promise of the best undoing I'd ever had. The shadows, of course, did not allow that. My pussy clenched angrily, and I rocked my hips forward —hoping the friction from that one motion would be enough. Only there was no friction. The shadows could touch *me* with their solid and tangible caress, but it seemed *I* couldn't do the same to them.

"What do you want, Ero?"

"Fuck me," I pleaded in a breathy, pathetic voice I didn't even recognize.

The shadows moved again, but the rhythm was all wrong —too slow, torturously so. The cold tendril snaking up my ass thickened, stretching it in agonizing discord with the soft tickle at my clit—which took on a texture suspiciously similar to Bůk's tongue as it traced lazy circles.

Tears rolled down my cheeks. I needed a release more than I'd needed anything in my entire life. More than I needed the book that would lead me to my family. More than I needed water. More than I needed air. Had Bůk requested my soul in that moment, I fear I would have given it to him and asked if there was anything he would like on the side.

The tongue shadow teased me to the edge again. So close, I felt the outline of the wave and knew it would crash down any second. When the shadows froze again, I sobbed plaintively.

"I belong—" I gasped desperately, "—to you."

I opened my eyes. The morning sunlight shocked me with its brightness. The world slid jaggedly into view. Bůk still leaned against the tree, still looked so unbothered staring directly at my splayed pussy.

My words didn't move him.

The shadows began the cycle again. My clit throbbed, too sensitive to withstand more. My whole pussy screamed for release. The cruel shadow stretching my ass barely thickened, but it threatened to split me in two as it poured deeper into me.

"More, kitten?"

"No!"

The shadows dissipated at once.

I fell.

My tendrils caught me—not Bůk. Nice of them to finally show up. I trembled, lying where they left me on the forest floor. He remained where he was, arms still crossed. No sign of feeling, like he wasn't moved in the least.

Dried pine needles pressed into my cheek. I tried to breathe. I wheezed a plea that I'm not even sure included actual words. My next breath came with a mouthful of forest shrapnel. It stuck to my tongue, which was bone dry from so many panted breaths. I spluttered and spat the detritus back out with difficulty.

I don't know how long it took to get my body back under control, but with each receding wave of pleasure, my fury grew. I pushed off the ground—ready for a fight. Ready to goad Bůk until he fucked me for real. Until the air heated with proof that he needed me too. I needed to hit him. I needed him to bend me over and—

The forest was still in the morning light. I was the only movement in the serene space.

Bůk was *gone*.

And so were my clothes.

Chapter 20
Bůk: Is This Yearning or No?

Bůk's Personal Code, Item 3, Re-Revised: Thou shalt not be distracted by a mortal even if thou art relatively certain it will not affect the mission. With very few and very occasional exceptions. (Fuck.)

I plunged into the water, letting the icy waves assault my heated flesh. My cock throbbed—fucking at the water the same way it'd fucked at my pants before I'd fled the clearing, like a rogue battering ram at a siege. It ached, demanding satisfaction it couldn't have because the *bard* wanted it, and I couldn't reward her for crying empty words at me. What good would that do?

I growled a stream of unintelligible curses into the water.

Haz's sagging sack.

I was supposed to be tormenting Ero into submission, ensuring that she would not become a bigger problem—not turning my cock to stone. Yet her sweet cries echoed in my ears. Her lips, parted and panting, danced across the backs of my eyelids. The flavor of her bittersweet melody lingered acidically on my tongue.

Frigid water succeeded in shattering my cock swell, but it did nothing to relieve my frustration. I stood, now only waist deep, letting the chilly wind bite into me. Facing the hard truth.

I *wanted* her.

It wasn't just about neutralizing the possibility that her schemes would interfere with my goals.

I wanted her on her knees, begging.

I wanted her bent over a tree, clenched with the anticipation of my next blow.

I wanted to pull her up by her hair and shove her to her knees and watch those soft lips close around my cock.

Hells, I even wanted her to make that snarky little face that broadcasted her intention to fight so I could watch it freeze and break when I gave her no choice but to submit.

And...just like that, hard again.

A few hours later, I had a full stomach, a soft cock, and a plan.

I scattered the remains of my fire and tossed the deer entrails off a nearby cliff face. At some point during the hunt, I'd regained control. I wouldn't lose it again.

Something nagged at the corner of my mind as I set off down the trail. The Fates had things to say. They danced just close enough to make their presence known without allowing me to grasp them. A flash of a soldier's face here, a flourish of the Huntress's cloak there. A spear of celestial power glittering ominously in a twilit sky. It was all just enough to irritate me without giving me any useful information.

But that was fine, I told myself. I knew the Huntress's game, didn't I? Today wasn't about that.

I cast my consciousness wide—reaching for the bard's essence instead. The newly reawakened beast inside me rippled with anticipation. No holds barred this time. No teasing. I would find her and drink my fill. Glut myself to flush the need from my body once and for all.

It was never a fair hunt, of course. The bard could cloak her physical form all she liked—but her magic? It lit up like a beacon, guiding me true. If she were smart, she would already be far—

I stopped mid-thought, surprised to pick up her discordant melody right away. It was close. Ten minutes' walk at most, not remotely worthy of the hours I'd given her to run. I frowned.

What was she playing at? Had she purposely made it easy to find her? Was she so desperate to get fucked that she'd made the *grave* error of failing to even *try?*

I was still considering the punishment possibilities when the first bolt of electricity cut into my chest. It lashed like a whip, burning through my shirt and burrowing into the skin. Although the burning that might have been agonizing for anyone else didn't faze me at all, the gaping wound wasn't pleasant. I reeled back.

The magic was visible, but faint—like threads of gold only catching the sunlight from certain angles.

Slowly, I smiled. She *hadn't* run. But not because she wanted me to catch her. Because she'd decided to *fight.*

I licked my lips. This was going to be fun.

My skin knitted back together on its own. It didn't take long. The shirt had a dramatic look, but I didn't mind that. Let her get satisfaction from her small win. It would be her last.

I made quick work of dispelling the magic as I proceeded,

akin to sweeping cobwebs from my path. But I moved slowly from there, more vigilant. I noticed and leapt over a patch of flesh-eating slick spelled into the dirt. I ducked under a shimmering tripwire attached to a conjured game net.

My bard had been busy.

When I finally spotted her, I was glad her eyes were closed.

She wore leaves stitched together with that same golden magic—not the living tendrils pulsing around her, but strands I assumed must have been drawn from the air by her lute. I'd debated taking the instrument. I was glad now that I'd left it for her. The barely covered skin was almost more alluring than seeing her spread open wide for me had been.

She was deep in concentration as she hummed a low melody. Her soft pink lips—slightly open—shaped the chords. She knelt on a small grassy peak, surrounded for ten paces all around by venomous rock toads. A few more hopped into the fray as I watched, freezing when they reached their place in the group.

A butterfly drifted into the clearing. No sooner did it breach the space than the closest three toads jolted from their trances and shot out their tongues to catch it. The commotion drew Ero's gaze—her face mildly startled, softening quickly into relieved confidence as she watched them tear the intruder apart. Her trap worked. Her pleasure sparked a rose-wine scent that made my mouth water.

The trap would work on me, too, I realized—if I were foolish enough to walk into it. I could heal quickly, but rock toad venom had psychedelic effects. With enough of it, even I would be incapacitated for long enough to ruin our little game. Not to mention the danger posed by the gold strands blowing in the breeze above the toads—charged with the same lightning I'd already encountered, no doubt.

"Not bad," I said.

My kitten's body stiffened, confirming that she hadn't heard my approach. She let the lute slide onto her back and stood slowly, turning to face me with a confidence as impressive as it was erroneous. I noted that her braid was back, as were its enchantments. Something else to make her pay for.

I took one step closer to the toads, careful to stop short of the nearest golden spell thread. I could taste her desire for my misstep. Surely she knew I would win in the end, but she longed for a minor victory first. She wanted to see me struggle —to work out how to entice the toads from my path or to thunder through them and endure their venom.

Too bad.

I let the fire pool in my hands and *pushed.*

The cyclone cut through the toads, cooking the ones that weren't fast enough to jump out of the way as it raced toward Ero. I met her scream with a smile. She *should* be afraid.

The fire died at the edge of her patch of grass.

"Come here," I said.

The surprise on her face sparked and almost instantly twisted into anger. Poor bard. She hadn't considered this possibility. The most obvious answer. That I didn't *need* to reach her, because I could make her come to *me.*

Her feet moved. She had only a split second to decide— venomous toads or burning embers.

"Hurry," I growled.

Already, my cock pulsed in time with my heartbeat. If she wanted mercy, she would find none here. She cried out when her bare foot touched the blackened trail.

I smirked. Of course she would avoid the toads. If one wanted to see what mortals feared most, one needed only to examine the traps they set for others. My kitten would rather burn her feet than lose her senses.

She ran down the trail, shrieking when the toads—jarred from their trance by her motion—leapt at her. She jumped the last several feet, landing hard and crashing into me. She clung to my tattered shirt. Like I was her salvation rather than the source of her torment.

Her mistake.

I fisted her hair, not caring that thorns sprang from it and dug into my flesh. Blood trailed down my fingers, but amid her cries and pleas—the desires dancing in the air betrayed her so sweetly. She still *wanted* this. And I marveled at that—at her desire to push me until I ruined her.

I allowed her fantasies to lead the way—thanking gods and devils alike that they so neatly mirrored my own.

I turned her over, shoving her face down on the ground— dangerously close to the toads that were now busy tearing each other to shreds, awakened from the stupor she'd played them into and reminded that they were territorial beasts. She fought hard, even though we both knew there was no point. I pinned her between my thighs, finally letting my cock free to claim its due.

"Bůk—" she cried.

Fear permeated the air. Fear that I would give her what she was afraid to want. Fear that her own trap would be her downfall.

"Don't speak," I ordered.

The compulsion elicited a strangled cry. She wanted to beg, wanted to plead her case—and taking that from her teased the agony to new heights. I pushed my fingers under her braid, through the hair at the base of her neck, and fisted hard, wrenching her head to the side so my breath could skate across her ear.

"You want it, so take it," I growled.

I released her hair and let her turn her face away, hiding those pretty tears in the grass while I reached into my satchel for what I needed. One twist of the slippery tinnio pod released the plant's slick gel, coating my cock from tip to base. I wanted to ruin her—not destroy her. I knew that this wasn't the last time I would want this. And if her desires swirling around me weren't enough to confirm the same for her, her dripping pussy would have.

The gel worked its magic. I was already hard as a fucking rock, but a fresh ache added to my need as the gel made my cock vibrate. The hum pulsed in tune with Ero's gasping breaths.

I positioned my cock against her tightest ring, and she fought me—pulling herself just an inch forward—a futile resistance that made me smile. Because her desire for me to give chase only strengthened. So, I did.

Pushing in felt like heaven. I met her gasp with a groan. Despite all her scrabbling, she took it so well, opening up for me as I pressed relentlessly forward. I murmured in her ear, reminding her to relax, coaxing as I drove deeper. Her rose-wine glow grew, a scent and a flavor and a song.

I knew I was overwhelming her, but my kitten could take it. I picked up my pace, nearing release—

And then everything went black.

I woke in new flesh hours later.

It took a long moment to recall where I'd been and why. Another moment to realize... I'd died.

I'd *died?*

I sat up, looking around. There were still a couple rock toads about, but they were scattered now. A few broken threads of magic blew in the breeze. The sun was still up, but it had a hazy glow that hinted at sunset.

I looked around stupidly, trying to piece together what had happened. And then I noticed...

Ero was gone.

And so were my things.

Chapter 21
Ero: Did We Forget "See No Evil"?

"You know those times when a rock toad licks your eye and you go blind and accidentally murder the demon who's buried balls deep in your ass? No? I wish I didn't either. Wasn't my best day." - an excerpt from the journal of Eroithiel von Dua, 1313 B.A., before the Great War

I didn't see it coming. And then I didn't see anything at all.

I was lost in the moment—hating Bǔk, utterly consumed by Bǔk, and frankly a bit scared of myself and the things I wanted him to do to me. I knew the toads were near. I knew what they could do. I just didn't think it would happen.

The tongue hit like a shard of glass, slamming into my eye with unnatural force. The headache was instantaneous—but it was also irrelevant. Because I was *blind*. My magic panicked. The tendrils shot out in a defensive strike against enemies I couldn't see.

Pain pulsed and grew with each heartbeat. The venom spread like fire through my veins.

I shouted Bůk's name before I realized I shouldn't be *able* to do that. He'd compelled me not to speak. But an unbroken stream of epiphanies barreled into me then, each less pleasant than the last. The compulsion was gone. Bůk wasn't answering. Bůk was heavy and still on my back. Bůk's chest was leaking a burning hot liquid that smelled of brimstone and rot.

I killed him.

Shit, shit, shit.

Had my tendrils been as disoriented as my mind, I might have suffocated under Bůk's deadweight. Luckily, they were not. Probably because they were responsible for *skewering him to death*, and thus were not shocked by the occasion. My magic took mercy and shoved him to the side for me. I made an unholy noise as his cock slid out of my ass—leaving me suddenly empty, but also allowing me to breathe again.

The pain in my assaulted eye grew with every second. I groped for my lute, unsurprised to find that Bůk had detached it from its strap during our encounter. My tendrils took mercy once again, carrying it to my eager fingers.

I strummed, coaxing the healing chords out. The cuts and scrapes from our scuffle faded. The aches gradually dulled. But the piercing pain in my eye didn't waver—nor did my vision return.

Trying not to panic, I took stock. The stench of death grew more rapidly than it should have. Tentatively, I pushed my tendrils to feel around me. They were unusually cooperative.

Bůk's form was already deflated and festering, like a weeks-old corpse. He couldn't be dead in a *mortal* sense—so how long did I have before he became my problem again?

I sat bolt upright.

If he were dead, even temporarily...could I remove the collar?

With the confidence of a person who was absolutely certain their harebrained plan was about to work, I reached for the clasp.

The resulting electric shock fused my fingers to the metal and singed its pattern onto my skin, eliciting a cry the nearest town must have heard.

When the collar finally relented, I sagged to the ground.

So much for that.

I sang my fresh wounds almost better before the venom made things...strange.

I had too many arms for one. That was my first clue that things weren't right. Dozens of arms. I felt around me, unsure which ones were real. I grazed Bǔk's melted corpse and felt my way into his little satchel, so deep I stretched as far as I could into it and still couldn't touch the bottom. The rough skin of the rock toads all around felt like sandpaper. They were no threat now, because they liquefied at my touch. The sun tasted azure and then magenta and then chartreuse as I poked it.

I noticed the woods flying past me. Or I flew past them? I couldn't see, but I suddenly had seven or eight other senses to rely on, so that mattered little. I didn't just pass the leaves brushing my cheeks. I swam inside them, turning sunlight into energy. I shrank to the size of a beetle. I grew taller than the forest and thundered through it, snapping centuries-old trees like twigs. I jumped from a cliff and caught a gust of wind to soar into the sky. I became a storm and raged down, frightening the woodland creatures. I liquefied and trickled through the dirt, joining a stream and then a river, floating lazily toward the sea.

When I finally came to, my face was under water. I was

naked, streaked with dirt, and mumbling words I didn't mean to say into the gurgling brook.

The venom was fading.

I pushed myself up, blinking rapidly as I dug my knuckles into my eyes, hoping to make the forest come into focus. It didn't work. I could see a faint light, but that was all.

For a while, I just sat there.

The forest was oppressively *present.* Like it was staring, waiting for me to figure my life out.

I started by cleaning myself in the water and searching for my clothes. My tendrils probed around in Bůk's bag until they unearthed everything I needed. I slipped into my leathers and fastened my cloak. I also found cooked venison. I hadn't realized how hungry I was until I'd devoured most of that.

I'd like to say I felt refreshed then. I didn't. I felt...vulnerable. And not just because I couldn't see. Because I was alone again, and I missed the camp—missed Brü and Aelith and the chatter around the fire and the way everyone relaxed when I played and the way their running jokes made my skin heat with belonging—unsettled me.

I was supposed to be looking for my family. What if I'd found something better? My father—whoever he was—wasn't *good.* I knew that. I knew he was the reason my mother had hated me since my birth. But I still wondered about him. I'd convinced myself that finding him would help me find my place. Was that desire fading?

No. It wasn't.

I groaned. Making it back to camp might mask the empty feeling, but it wouldn't *solve* it. I didn't need my father to care about me. I just needed to know who he was—*why* he'd left me, and why he'd required that I visit the temple yearly to give a drop of my blood to Haz. It wasn't about him. It was about knowing where I'd come from.

I took a slow, shaky breath, and walked. My tendrils spread out before me, guiding my way. I felt where the trees were, sensed the poisonous leaves I wouldn't want to allow near my skin, and dodged them easily. I didn't have a plan. I just *needed* to move.

By the time my legs ached for a break, I could see shapes again. I sat on a huge rock and made a game out of staring at the trees, willing my vision to come back in earnest. I hummed a melody that didn't help at all because it was as melancholy as I was—but it kept me company.

The light above began to fade. Dusk neared. That meant the end of the game, right? I snorted softly. What was Bǔk going to do when he found me? A few hours ago, that question would have thrilled me on some deep, primal level. Now, it exhausted me. I didn't feel like being hunted right now. I felt like being wrapped in strong arms, caressed, *loved.* None of that was Bǔk's department.

I sighed, shifting on the rock to look at a new collection of shadows. I defined the outline of one tree, and then the next, comforting myself with the reassurance that they were becoming easier to see. I was going to be all right. Soon.

One tree was closer than the others. I followed its outlined edges up—but it halted abruptly. I tried again, concentrating harder. Only the rough edges *moved.*

"There you are," he said.

I froze. Not a tree. A demon.

The surrounding air gave me nothing to read. No heat, no chill. I supposed it was a good sign that his fury wasn't palpable—but fear gripped me all the same. I wished I could see his face.

His shape grew as he closed in. He lifted my hand and examined it, thumb grazing the skin where the collar had singed me and hadn't quite healed before the venom distracted me. I flinched at his touch.

"I didn't mean to," I couldn't help whispering. Even if it didn't make a difference. I needed him to know that. I would take credit for my strike when it was time. This one had been an accident.

Bůk cradled my chin, letting one finger fall on my lips, whispering, *shh*. His hot breath against my ear sent sparks of heady desire to the much-played and yet deeply unsatisfied instrument between my legs.

Despite his shushing, I opened my mouth again. He shifted suddenly, scooping me into his arms. My back was against a tree. His lips were on mine. The kiss was deep and thorough and strangely passionate.

I stopped trying to speak. His fingers explored over my clothes while his tongue slipped into my mouth. He cradled the back of my neck with one hand while the other unbuttoned my pants and pushed them down. His talented fingers went to work teasing my arousal until it was all I could think of.

He took me like that—soft and careful and sweet. *Why?* I kept asking myself. But I didn't ask him. He slid into me and filled me perfectly, rocking to a rhythm my soul keened for. And it was so much worse than anything he'd done before, because I ached for it.

Helpless tears cut paths down my cheeks, and I gave in, tasting the soft skin on his throat, sucking, kissing—*needing*. I came hard and cried out against him while he picked up his pace and answered my whines with a satisfied groan of his own.

I opened my eyes, still breathing hard, and realized I could see his face. Relief mingled with the high of the orgasm. He wiped my tears away with his thumb, smiling. Devastatingly beautiful.

His fingers trailed down to my collar. The moment slowed, hanging so I could feel the full weight of the pleasure he'd just used to chisel away my distress. He traced the metalwork with one finger.

And then...he asked, "Do you want me to remove this?"

It was dusk.

I'd survived.

And the deal was still on.

The realization barreled into me. A fresh panic rose. What had he said? *If I take the collar off, you can leave and never look back. I will remove the tattoo from your skin, strike your name from the Fated's enrollment logs, and never pursue you again.*

Did I want that?

I didn't want that.

I didn't want to leave *now*. Possibly not ever. But could I afford to say no? Would I be able to live with myself if I did?

This was a test. The pleasure drained away, and with agonizing clarity, I realized what was about to happen. Bůk hadn't made sweet love to me because he wanted me. He'd done it because he'd read my desire for it and thought he could use it to manipulate me.

The betrayal aspect helped, really, with what I was going to have to do. It didn't make it *easy*, though. Not at all. He'd fucking won. I *wanted* to stay. I wanted him to use me. I wanted *everything*.

And still, I managed to force out the words. "Yes. Take it off."

The air heated at last. His eyes swirled with unfathomable fury. But he didn't move. We stared at each other, locked in an embrace that had started sweet and become cruel.

One corner of his mouth curled up—but his eyes darkened as he growled a deeply satisfied, "No."

My heart pounded.

No? But the *deal.* He'd said—

It hit me then. He'd said he would ask me. That I would have one chance to answer. He'd said that *if* he removed the collar, I could leave—not that he *would* remove it. That was the trick. He'd planned to make me say no, but saying yes didn't mean he would listen—it only meant I hadn't given in.

"Bůk—" I gasped.

He smiled now. "No, don't do that. Don't try to change your answer, kitten. I think I prefer you like this."

I reeled, more off balance now than I'd been at the height of the rock toad's venomous trip. What did he *mean?*

"I can't break you, can I?" he whispered, stroking my face. "You're perfect."

The soft words and touches were at odds with the fingers digging into my back. My breath hitched.

"My own little puzzle," he mused, tone darkening further with each word. "To play with for as long as it takes. Keep holding out, kitten. I *need* that like you need me."

I shook my head frantically. I didn't need him. I didn't *want* him, even if my body did. The humiliation of failing to see his game before I lost clawed at me. I was naïve. I was stupid. This was my own personal Hell.

Bůk's cock grew hard against me. Again. I knew this round wouldn't be soft and kind. And I hated that I thrilled at that promise.

When his lips crashed into mine, I bit back. I drew his blood, and would have kept going—but a metal cuff clamped around my wrist. My magic *reeled,* screaming in protest as the dampener forced it to recoil. The other snapped on.

"Bůk, *no*—" I pleaded.

I hated it. It wasn't part of the pleasure. It was agony—the real kind—losing a vital part of myself.

"Shh," he purred. "This isn't a punishment, kitten. It's for *my* safety."

He ate my reply with another furious kiss. I writhed against him.

But he was right, wasn't he? My magic couldn't be trusted. If he chased me and took me—I might kill him again. I was just as much of a monster as he was. That fact didn't make any of it feel better, but it stopped me from arguing.

His fingers twisted in my hair. "I'm going to make you want things that will make it hard to look yourself in the eye, kitten," he growled. "And then I'm going to give them to you."

I let out a defeated groan, sinking into him. I could have pointed out that he'd already done that. He did it every time he looked at me, even when I knew damned well I should stop wanting him.

He stepped back abruptly. Losing his warmth was a stab to the gut. The fact that I wanted him back? Infuriating. I knew he was going to tell me to run now—and I would do it. And this time, nothing would go wrong. He would catch me, and fuck me, and we would both come apart, and the pleasure would make it all worse and better at the same time. I would lose myself to him.

Or so I thought.

Right before the celestial spear exploded from his chest.

I watched the light leave his eyes this time. His death was instantaneous.

Five of the Huntress's soldiers looked on with satisfaction as his body crumpled where it stood.

I might have tried to fight the women who surrounded me...but Bůk's dampeners remained on my wrists, keeping my magic out of reach.

"Hello, Eroithiel," one of the women said. She glanced at Bůk and back again with a sneer that told me exactly what she thought of the scene she'd just interrupted. An answering snake of shame ricocheted through me.

Then my new captor looked to the others and said, "Take her."

Chapter 22
Ero: Not a Princess

"There's nothing so easy—nor so necessary to defeat—as a hot-headed man." - a fragment of correspondence from a Temple Mother, preserved in the journal of Eroithiel von Dua

After they secured my chains to a tree and stripped me of my things, they butchered Bůk like wild game while I watched. His body cleaved in five, limbs that had chased and ravaged me all day turned to strips of meat. The thirsty ground drank his blood.

None of the factionites appeared to be disturbed by what they were doing. They clearly didn't register any part of Bůk as human. Just a beast wearing human skin. Maybe that was fair?

Even the youngest of the five absentmindedly kicked Bůk's hand out of the way when it broke her pacing route. Her nervous energy permeated the air.

"When can we go?" she asked after rocking back on her heels, twisting her cloak in her hands, and chewing her lip until it swelled all failed to soothe her. If I had to estimate, I'd say she was still an adolescent. On the brink of adulthood, but not there yet. What was she even *doing* here?

"It's late," the leader said. "We'll set up camp. The others should be back soon."

The young one's eyes bulged. "Miri, what if he—" She cut herself off, looking down at Bůk's head in horror. Her pupils pulsed. A few errant golden sparks dripped from her fingertips. "What if he comes *back?* I…I can't do it again. I can't even conjure a *shield* right now."

Miri shrugged one shoulder. "He won't, Sade. And even if he does, he won't touch you. I'll kill him myself first."

Although my Fated tattoo made these women my enemies, Miri's naïve words sparked a prickle of dread in my gut for Sade. If Bůk came back, they were all dead. I suspected that went double for the one whose conjured holy weapon had slain him, even if she was practically a child.

Sade sucked in a breath like she meant to argue, but then she let it slip out and returned to her pacing instead. When she caught me watching, her expression hardened. "What are *you* looking at, demon-fucker?"

Ouch.

Unlike Sade, whose body betrayed every emotion, I forced a smirk to cover the fact that her insult hit home. I shrugged one shoulder, mimicking Miri, and feigned nonchalance. "Just watching some dead women play with their kill."

The girl's hazel eyes shot straight to Miri, tears welling. Shit. I hadn't meant to make her cry.

Miri wiped Bůk's blood from her hands and took her time coming over. She gave me a withering glare, then said to Sade, "Build a fire, yeah?"

The girl stalked off without answering.

Miri looked down at me, her disgust plain. She crouched, coming eye level. I watched warily, waiting for the telling off—or the blow.

Instead, she said, "Not very becoming behavior for a *princess.*"

A chill ran down my spine. I'd known from the moment she'd called me *Eroithiel* that she had an unexpected wealth of knowledge about me. This confirmed it, though. And despite my best efforts, irritation wormed its way into my tone.

"Not a princess," I snapped.

"No?" She arched a brow. "Not Eroithiel Finch, the youngest daughter of Queen Rashada Finch?"

"Not my name."

Technically, that was true. I'd written it once—and only once. When I was five and had just learned my letters. I wrote it inside my schoolbook and watched my tutor's face flicker with a self-preserving concern before she crossed out the "Finch" and wrote "von Dua" instead. The queen (my mother) heard about it anyway. And that day I got my first lesson regarding *who I was* and—more to the point—*who I wasn't.*

I bore the surname of a beloved human merchant from town, known for his collection of bastards. He wasn't my father. But it was believable enough. Even *I* believed it until I was ten, when I found him drunk at a festival and slipped into his booth to say hello, and he told me that there was no need to uphold the charade in private, then ushered me out.

"Okay, Princess," Miri said, smirking with self-satisfaction as she left me to wonder how she knew what she did—even the flawed version—and why it mattered. I did not give her the satisfaction of asking.

They built camp then. I watched. Miri was the de facto

leader. If Sade wasn't her sister by blood, she'd certainly assumed the role. They were aware of one another in a deeply caring way. Even when Miri seemed to ignore the younger girl, she shot regular looks her way. Likewise, Sade gravitated to Miri's side any time her nerves grew especially strained.

The other three were as different as one could imagine—but they fit together beautifully. The hulking, barbaric woman had a laugh that boomed through the trees. The slight one, smaller even than Sade—though definitely older—danced around energetically, amusing everyone. Her eyes darted frequently to the fifth woman—a solemn gray-haired caster—to check for a hard-won grin after each joke. She got one about half the time.

They all *loved* each other. That much was plain. It stirred a sickening jealousy in my gut. This was everything I'd imagined finding for myself. Aside from the minor detail that they loathed me, and I kind of hated them for killing Bǔk and spatchcocking him like a giant chicken. Feelings I chose not to examine further for a multitude of reasons.

Things changed when the others arrived. At the sound of a signaling whistle, the women exchanged looks. By unspoken directive, their personalities receded.

Seven more Huntress factionites entered the clearing, led by a man who dripped lethality. Tattoos covered his bare, sculpted chest. He wore dozens of heavy silver rings encrusted with blood. But it was the way my original band of captors leaned subconsciously away from him that put me on alert.

He assessed the situation, face impassive as he noted my presence and Bǔk's rotting corpse. He betrayed nothing of his opinion until his eyes landed on Sade, and a few nervous sparks sizzled at her fingertips. Then he frowned at Miri.

"I told you not to let her conjure while we were gone," he said.

Miri held a soldier's pose—not obviously afraid, but certainly uncomfortable. I didn't miss the way she positioned herself subtly between him and Sade. And then Miri lied through her teeth. "The demon sensed us. It was then or never, Captain."

He dismissed her with a grunt and issued orders to the others, effectively reorganizing everything Miri's little team had already done. He ignored me almost too pointedly until everyone had settled and food was cooking over the fire. The mouthwatering aroma of simmering stew was tarnished by the stench of Bůk's decay. The captain tipped that balance for the good by collecting a bowl and bringing it to stand over me. I was instantly famished.

"Where is the Fated's next muster point?" he asked, not bothering with niceties. He dipped a spoon into the stew and slurped a huge bite, chuffing around it to cool his mouth. When I said nothing, he arched his brow expectantly. "I'd rather not unpack my tools, but I can make this less pleasant if you'd like."

I considered that. I didn't know where the next muster point was, of course. I wasn't faction leadership. Hell, I didn't even know where the rest of my scouting party went after they left Bůk and me. But why would he believe that?

Miri pretended not to listen as she moved packs from the perfectly reasonable location she'd selected to the arbitrary place he'd ordered them moved.

What would a clever person do here? Clearly, there was a way to play them against one another. No love lost and all that. If I—

Slurp.

My teeth gritted together. *Haz's steaming piss.* Listening to him eat had to be worse than whatever torture he could conjure with those tools he'd mentioned.

"No?" he asked, mouth still half full. "Fine. Get up."

I did not get up. I didn't do anything brash, like taunt him or make a face, either. I just didn't move.

As I'd suspected it would, blood rose up the back of his neck, flushing his skin red. Easy to anger, easy to fuck with. So long as I didn't value my comfort—which I kind of did, but I'd make an exception in this case—this could be a certain kind of fun.

The captain held his stew out to the side and dropped it, like an actual psychopath. The bowl broke, and the hot sludge splashed me.

I took a moment to appreciate his beauty then. I know! Timing. But his abdomen was all bronzed and tight and inked with alluring swirls that accentuated the ripple of muscles. I hoped, for their sake, that at least one of my original captors had gotten a chance to lick him or something before today—because I was pretty confident it wouldn't be long before Bůk returned and made him utterly unappetizing.

Miri surprised me by stepping forward. "Captain, the truth serum is—"

"Put the demon's head in a tank of saltwater," he ordered her, eyes never leaving mine. "Unless you'd *like* him to rejoin us."

Miri motioned to the barbarian and her funny companion, who jumped to follow the orders. A mild alarm bell set my nerves on edge. Would that really stop Bůk? Aelith hadn't mentioned it. The man seemed confident, but men like him often did. I couldn't be sure.

To my continued surprise, Miri remained where she stood

—and spoke again. "Sir, the Huntress wants the princess unharmed."

His eyes flashed. He finally looked up, glowering at his subordinate. His voice carried an edge of warning. "Little Sadie spent herself under your command. Did you squander Greta's energy as well—or might she be available to heal a few minor wounds?"

"I've not tapped Greta today, Captain," she said calmly.

"Good to hear you can *half*-follow orders, soldier." He waved her away. "Elhamine, bring my kit."

A sour-faced woman whipped her hood back and yanked a leather bag from a pile of things. A hatchet hung on one side, a mallet on the other. All manner of bloody blades, fishhooks, and coiled wires dangled from the straps. Gods only knew what he kept *inside* the bag.

He bent and gathered the chain to hold my wrists together, yanking me to my feet. I briefly considered going limp and falling right back to the ground—but Elhamine moved in behind me, ready to hold me up. Her clammy fingers brushed my skin once and gave me a full-body chill. I kept my feet.

The captain gave me a once-over and scoffed under his breath when his gaze snagged on my collar. He cast another withering look at Miri. "Did you even *search* her?"

Miri looked at me—probably to see what her people had missed. My eyes locked with hers. They *had* taken my lute, emptied my pockets, ferreted out every last one of my knives, and collected Bůk's things to boot—but one of them must have recognized the collar's magic and wisely opted to leave it alone. The captain apparently did *not* recognize it.

Miri and I weren't friends, obviously. But I hoped she would read my silent request. After all, he couldn't kill me if the

Huntress wanted me. He couldn't even really hurt me that badly if what Miri said was true.

So let me have this, I silently urged the woman.

"Please," I said, looking up at him again with what I hoped was convincing anguish—rushing to answer before Miri could. "Please don't touch it."

His lips quirked in a cruel, anticipatory smile at my pleading. He reached greedily for the clasp.

The shock ripped through him, drawing convulsions in the most delicious show. He fought to let go, but the angry enchantments didn't allow it for several long seconds. When they did, he tried to keep his feet. He ended up on his knees anyway. For a moment, *I* towered over *him*. The rush was immediate and strong. An inflated sense of invulnerability.

I laughed.

"It's spelled," Miri said, pouring the perfect amount of *obviously* and *wait don't* in—but doing so purposely late.

I hated her, but for a minute I loved her too.

"Van!" Elhamine cried, leaping forward to help him.

He shoved her back, pushing himself to his feet. I knew the next however long would be unpleasant...but at least I would have the image of that rancid face twisted in pain to hold on to.

Hours later, I lay atop Bůk's liquefied corpse in a pool of my own blood and vomit, contemplating whether "worth it" was the right sentiment.

What remained of Bůk's head bobbed in a saltwater tub that pressed against my cheek. In my bound position, the only way to avoid seeing it was to close my eyes. They'd put me on my stomach with my chained arms stretched out and bowed up to attach to one tree, legs spread and tied to two separate trees behind me. There wasn't enough slack to relax into the ground, nor was the setup taut enough to suspend me.

It was expertly horrible.

If I'd had any hope that Captain Van was the lone problem in the party before, that'd been put soundly to rest. I didn't understand Elhamine's magic, but I hated it. It felt like mud polluting a crystal stream. It *pulled* from me wherever she touched, leaving only exhaustion and ache behind. The others, whose names I never learned, came at me in rotation. Asking about the muster point, imparting new wounds when I couldn't answer. Pressing me for details of the Fated's larger plans in a way that implied I was far, far more important and high ranking than I actually was—and punishing me no matter how I answered.

Miri and the rest of her group never reappeared after the torture began. I tried to focus on that, primarily to keep my mind trained on anything whatsoever besides what was happening to my body.

What was the deal with the five women—or the four women and one girl? How had this odd dozen come to be? Why were they all stationed together when the division was so obvious even to an outsider?

That mystery kept me going.

When Van came again in the early morning, I sensed a shift. He was calm again, for starters. He also didn't lead with cackle-faced threats this time. Instead, he settled by my head and leaned against Bůk's tank, bringing a waterskin to my lips.

I drank. Could he have laced the water with poison or some awful drug? Yes. But I needed water, and I still clung to that kernel of certainty that he couldn't kill me if his warlord—for *whatever* bizarre reason—wanted me alive.

"We can go in the morning," he said. His deep voice had a soothing quality that might have worked on another day, in another situation. "Or we can stay here, heal you, and do this all again."

I said nothing, as it was painfully obvious which path he would point us down. I didn't appreciate the false choice.

"Tell me about the Fated's water elemental," he said.

My pulse thundered in my aching skull. *Aelith?* What. The fuck.

I blinked stupidly. It wasn't hard to look mystified, because he'd really caught me off guard. But I had to use every ounce of my scant energy to muster the bite I put into my response.

"My ink is still fresh, you fucking half-wit," I gritted out. "If you think I know anything worth—"

"Then the demon," he said.

I looked up at him. My first impression came barreling back. *Lethal.* And not as stupid as I wanted to believe, either. Yes, he'd missed the collar's enchantments and gotten his due for that mistake. He'd asked a lot of useless questions with a fervor that suggested he expected answers when I couldn't possibly give them. But now...now he was circling like a panther, and all that bluster seemed to have been for show. To wear me down? To exhaust me before the real questions began?

"What about him?" I mumbled.

"The Huntress heard that he's in possession of a weapon," Van said, propping himself up on one arm so his cheek rested against the tank mirroring mine. "We've been through his things and found nothing out of the ordinary."

I searched his eyes. Hoping to read what he wasn't saying so I could work out what he really wanted before I decided what to say. Maybe I would have had a chance, too—if I hadn't been exhausted and starving and in several worlds of pain. But that was probably intentional.

"The collar is his," I said. I blinked back a wince as a stomach cramp begged me to curl into a ball. I couldn't, of course. The ropes wouldn't allow it.

Van's face remained impassive, not even reveling in my pain. It was like he'd become a different man—focused and hard. "It's not the collar."

I squeezed my eyes shut. I was going to vomit again. I racked my brain. I hadn't seen Bůk use any weapon but his own magic, had I?

Desperation clawed at me. Why had he asked about Aelith? And if I couldn't give him what he wanted here, would he return to her? Did I know anything that could harm her?

Elhamine hovered in my periphery. Van motioned her over. She bent, pressing her finger to his chest. Although my magic remained pinned and muted by the dampeners, it prickled at their connection. I could *feel* the sickening, muddy energy flowing from her into him. When she pulled back, the place she'd touched—a little tattoo of a mountain—glowed. Next to it was a swirl of ink, like wind, which was also lit and glowing. Beside those were a flame and then a water drop—each barely visible.

He was a siphon.

My tired mind groped clumsily at the clues. Is that what he wanted with Aelith? Did he have a collection going? Was someone here a fire elemental?

Elhamine tripped backward, her fierce eyes unfocused and dull now. She caught herself on a tree, and I felt the energy shift again, reviving her. But not much. Just enough to keep her upright. She stumbled away without looking back.

Van radiated power now. A sharp bronze energy lit the surrounding air.

The tank glowed translucent gray where he touched it. I stared. The grotesque hunk of head had melted entirely. Not a bit left. Just black, blood-tainted water.

Van flexed his hands. He reached for his hook. "What is the weapon, Princess?"

My breath quickened. I couldn't help it. I could handle pain, but my body was at its limit.

Behind Van, the shadows stirred.

Chapter 23
Bůk: Not Dead

Bůk's Personal Code, Item 2: The only good enemy is a dead enemy.

I woke up cold, naked, and furious.

Again.

I should have seen the celestial spear coming. In fact, I *had*. It'd been one of the many visions nagging at the periphery of my mind as I'd toyed with my kitten.

Which raised the question, what *else* had I missed?

I rose, absently gathering moss and leaves and weaving them with shadow to cover myself. I didn't need my cock out while I sorted the Huntress's vermin.

I wasted no time after that finding the bard's trail. It wasn't easy despite our proximity. The dampeners essentially hid her magic signature. But I caught the trail—and shortly after dawn, I came upon a scene that made my blood boil.

A siphon stood over her, hook raised. Blood and bruises

painted her pale skin. Agony twisted her desires toward survival.

My instinct told me to cook the creature. One quick flame to the back, and all that power would leech back into the earth. But as I lifted my hand, she sensed me. I tasted her relief and then...her *frustration*.

I smiled despite the situation. She wanted her own shot at this man who'd tormented her, the same way she had with Wendlin. Fine. There were more than enough bodies to go around.

I cloaked the key to the manacles in shadow. It crawled unseen across the forest floor while the siphon leaned down and gripped Ero's hair, wrenching her head up.

He didn't notice the temperature rise. I almost abandoned my plan and killed him outright.

"I *said*, what is the weapon?" he hissed.

I paused. I'd been so attuned to Ero's desires, I'd not paid attention to his. After all—he was powerful, but insignificant. He was about to die. Now that he'd piqued my interest, though, I breathed him in.

He wanted a weapon—*my* weapon—whatever that was supposed to be. He wanted power. No surprise there. He wanted to wed the Huntress—wanted to be *worthy* of wedding her. Tiny bubbles of mirth rose up my throat. Good luck with that. The man was delusional, but determined.

I returned my attention to the shadows—*quite* finished watching another creature lay his hands on what was mine. I turned the key in one manacle. Ero didn't miss a beat, catching it before it could fall and alert the siphon. When the key turned in the other, though, she crashed face-first to the ground. I winced. Her magic probably would have caught her had it not been strained and weak from its time in the chains. It wasn't so weak that it didn't lance immediately through the siphon, though.

His cry of pain echoed beautifully through the trees.

I would have stayed to watch her finish him. I wanted to. Watching my kitten rip the man to shreds was second only on my list of desires to doing it myself. But at the man's cry, other factionites outed their locations with flares of panic. And one of those flares had a celestial quality that I owed a very specific end.

I left Ero to her revenge—more than ready to take my own.

I found the earth elemental first. She crumbled at my touch. She was so hollow, bones empty, organs diminished, that I knew the siphon was not a good sort. You might think that came with the territory for a siphon—but not so much. Like vampires and humans, there were plenty of energy siphons who rode a line and took only what they needed to survive. This siphon took *everything.* Greedy little bastard.

Three more Huntress soldiers fell to my quick killing blows. I didn't bother with flourish. I saved that for my assassin, assuming it would be a simple but entertaining battle.

And then I found her.

A fucking *child.*

She stood in a warded cave, aching with the desire to catch sight of a companion whose name she breathed over and over like a personal mantra.

When she saw me, she fell silent. Her desire to be brave painted the air. She wanted so badly to face me without trembling. She didn't manage it. She stumbled back, ready to flee to the deepest part of the shallow cave—but I didn't allow it. I poured flame into the darkness behind her—a fire so intense she had no choice but to dive past the protection of the wards and fall at my feet.

"No!" she cried. "MIRI!"

To my surprise, her anger was still greater than her fear. The depth of her wants echoed inside me. *Kill Van. Kill Van. Kill Van.* In her mind's eye, his face was so pummeled and swollen that I almost didn't recognize him as the siphon.

Appalling.

Terrifying creature of darkness that I was, hovering over this insignificant child—and that child had the audacity to focus on someone else? I already wouldn't get a fight out of this. The least she could have done was be terrified of me.

"You'll see them both in Hell," I promised impatiently.

"No," she spat. And then she *pointed* at me, jabbing her finger to punctuate her words. "Don't kill her. Don't. Fucking. Kill. Her."

Again, the strength of her desire overwhelmed me. I couldn't tell if she was pushing it on purpose—an almost absurd thought, because how could she even know that I could taste it? Perhaps young humans simply felt things more strongly by default? One thing was for sure, though. She *wanted* me to see her mind.

And unfortunately, I did.

I was a fourteen-year-old girl. (Haz's tits. I tried to clear the vision, but it had an iron grip.) *My sister—more of a mother to me than my own mother had ever been, and by far the most badass woman in town—sauntered in, freshly back from deployment. She was Faction. They gave her free ale at the tavern, called her in to set scoundrels right and clear any beasties—even the big ones—that harassed the area. I couldn't wait to join the faction. I bounced up to her, hugged her, whispered, "Pleeeease tell them I'm sixteen so I can join. I have tits now! They might believe you."*

She'd always laughed when I asked before. This time, she didn't. Her smile fell away like autumn leaves (Really? I was even narrating in her infantile metaphors?), and it almost looked like she would cry. I'd never seen Miri cry. Not when our parents died. Not when she'd shattered her shoulder. Not even when the boy she'd been with for two years up and left with some floozy from the next town. And then she crushed me. "You can't join, Sadie. Ever."

My heart fell through the floor. She had to be kidding. What changed? She refused to explain. She just kept telling me to dream other dreams.

A flash, and it was my sixteenth birthday. I wasn't supposed to enter the barracks, but Miri never showed up for breakfast—and it was practically deserted, anyway. I heard Miri's voice.

"Fuck off, Van. Find someone else."

At the sound of a hard slap and Miri's gasp, I ran into the room with a throwing knife already in hand. I'd practiced for two years. I was sure I could hit true. But he moved so fast. Spotting me, pinning me to the wall, squeezing my wrist until it popped, and the knife fell to the floor.

"Oh look, someone else," he said.

A series of horrible flashes. The holy symbol burned into my flesh as he held the searing metal to my back. The temple's holy water poured into my lungs as he shoved my head into the fountain, and Miri—spelled to immobility—watched helplessly.

I could have died, but the goddess accepted me. Gave me the power Miri had refused to harbor. Made me his weapon. And I had to be his weapon, or he would have hurt her. He'd been hurting her all along. I was stupid to seal the promise to him with an oath. I didn't see any other way.

I finally shook the girl's vision from my head. The sunlight needled my eyes, the forest especially heady and present after the prolonged hallucination. My body felt huge and strange.

Right. Good.

Time to kill the kid.

I reached for her. Her hands covered her face. Tears leaked through her fingers. Because nothing could ever work the way it should, those tears buzzed like bees in my throat. Why did this feel wrong when it was *objectively* justified? She made choices. She accepted the holy symbol to save her sister. She joined the wrong faction. She fucking *killed* me. And even if none of that had been true, my entire department was torment. This should feel fine.

Her companions skidded into the clearing then. An irritating interruption, even though tracking them down was solidly on my list of things to do. And now here they were, saving me the effort. Four women, united in their desire to destroy me.

Well, too bad.

I turned on them, raising shadow and flame resplendent with the power of every drop of irritation I'd felt since regenerating an hour before. The air sizzled with my fury. Three of them reeled back. The only one who didn't was Miri. I recognized her from my brief time as a teenage girl.

No matter. She was *about* to be a burnt husk formerly known as Miri.

"Bůk, no!"

My attention snapped to the treeline. There stood my kitten with a fresh, nasty cut across her cheek. She swayed, physically incapable of standing upright without help from her flickering magic. Despite her state, she lurched forward, pushing her energy into the fray—forming a pathetic wall between my flame and the women.

Miri lunged at me. I could have flame-broiled her, but Ero's desire was so strong and clear that I hesitated. Did Miri know something? Did we need her? I couldn't unkill her once the thing was done—so instead, I pivoted.

In a flash, the five Huntress soldiers were bound and gagged with shadow. They fought—some harder than others—but it barely took a shred of concentration to hold them.

Ero was at my side in an instant, gripping my arm.

"He's gone," she said urgently. "He knows where they are."

I tilted my head. Did she mean the siphon? I'd *watched* her skewer him. Surely he hadn't skipped away from that.

"He wants Aelith," she rushed on, holding up her torn elven undershirt, as if that would tell me something. "He can track. He—I don't know—but he's going to find her."

I considered this only briefly. The siphon was going to find Aelith?

"I don't see the problem."

"Bůk," she hissed. "He has a fire elemental. He's headed for the camp. Aelith, Brü—all of them—are in danger."

I sighed. That still didn't explain why she'd interrupted my cleanup job. If we needed to rush off to play save-the-party, we really ought to wrap this up first. And there was only one reasonable way to do so, even if my sniveling little assassin had temporarily given me pause.

"Then let's go," I said, lifting one hand to raise a fresh column of flame.

Which Ero promptly doused with a flurry of rainbow tendrils.

I glowered. "What are you doing?"

"You aren't going to kill them."

My jaw worked overtime to prevent a more biting response. I landed on, "Why not?"

When that simple question brought her up short, I blinked, appalled. Did they not have something we needed after all? Was my bard just having *feelings?* Too bad. We weren't leaving loose ends. That wasn't how war worked.

"Because I— Because they—" she started, but struggled to complete the statement.

I quirked a brow. Her desires were a tangled mess. In them, I tasted the usual syrupy longing for human connection. But that didn't seem relevant here. They were a clear and distinct enemy—not even remotely interested in making a new friend. Wrong strays to adopt, and all that. Feral. Messy. Mean.

"Because you're not," she finished with remarkable confidence for someone I'd spent the previous day chasing and fucking into oblivion.

She looked around us and zeroed in on a fallen tree. She pointed. "Put their arms there, faction tattoos up."

Color me intrigued. Sure, some part of me wanted to put *her* there instead and let them watch as I reminded her who she was talking to. But those bees buzzed in my chest again. I was the reason the siphon had tortured her. I'd dampened her magic so I could play with her without winding up dead again. Instead, he'd gotten his hands on her. I'm not saying I *owed* her —but perhaps I had the smallest urge to go easy for a moment.

My shadows dragged the women to the log and displayed their tattooed forearms in a neat line, per request. Ero stood over them. I saw the slight tremble, the hesitation. But she set her jaw and concentrated until five tendrils peeled away from the rest and shot out, wrapping around each captive's arm like colorful snakes.

When the tendrils receded, the tattoos were ruined. Angry burns in swirling patterns remained on the skin. All five women screamed their pain into the gags, the sound swallowed by my shadows.

Interesting. Someone had read the faction handbook. Had one of our enemies defaced our soldiers this way rather than opting to kill them, Colonel Astrada would be forced to consider them compromised. A life spared was a life owed. It didn't mean the Huntress would disown them—but she might.

I still didn't understand Ero's logic. Dead enemies were far less complicated than live ones.

"Let them go," she said. "We need to hurry. Their horses are close."

Again, I bristled at receiving *orders*. But once more, urgent visions danced just outside of my reach—a flurry of them, changing faster than I could latch on. The Fates were up in the air right now. I didn't know what was coming, but I knew Ero was right. Something hung in the balance. What we did now mattered.

"Then go," I said.

I released my shadows. Screams immediately polluted the air. The women fell against one another, holding their burned arms, holding each other. Ero's gaze lingered for a beat longer before she turned and fled.

I cast one last look at the child who'd slain me and found her staring right back—the only one among them who seemed to have attention to spare for us through their pain. She didn't look angry anymore. Just curious.

"*Bŭk.*" In Ero's exhausted tone, my name was a plea. And once again, some distant relative of guilt bid me to answer her call.

Anyhow, although my reaction to hearing that the siphon might finally free me of Aelith was truly indifference bordering on relief—the same couldn't be said for the rest of our party. So, I followed Ero to the horses, and we rode toward yet another fight.

Chapter 24
Ero: Asking the Impossible

Bardic Advice from Eroithiel von Dua to future generations: Don't try to kill a siphon with your own magic. Siphoning magic is literally what they do.

Everything was slow. So slow. Like moving within the confines of a massive gelatinous cube.

I watched myself order Bůk away from my band of captors. I don't know why I did it. I can't explain what compelled me to mark them instead of letting them die. I understood how things like this were supposed to work. I didn't even *like* them. I just couldn't watch him end their little family.

I don't remember selecting or mounting a horse, but soon we raced through the forest, wet leaves slapping my cheeks, silence echoing with the siphon's laughter.

My body was at its absolute limit. I couldn't convince the tendrils that were already working overtime to keep me in my saddle to so much as clot the blood dripping down my face.

I closed my eyes for just a moment.

My tendrils pierced the siphon. They should have cooked him like they had Wendlin, but his expression flickered from surprise to fury to dark delight in the space of a few seconds.

I couldn't pull back. He drank, freezing my magic in place and drawing it in deeper, slurping it like his stew. His eyes flickered, losing their forest green in favor of an iridescent swirl.

I don't know how I knew it, but I did. I'd just told him everything. He grabbed me, tearing my elven mail shirt like worn fabric. His teeth gleamed when he grinned. "Her mate gave this to you."

It wasn't a question, so I didn't bother to answer. He released my tendrils, and I reeled inside, off balance in too many ways. He was going to kill them all. And more immediately, he was going to kill me.

Only he didn't.

A figure stood behind him, bouncing a ball of fire like a fidgety child. They exchanged words, but I was too busy trying to shake the pins and needles from my drained tendrils to pay attention. I caught only snippets. Locations I forgot as soon as I heard them. Names he shouldn't know rolling off his tongue.

His knife shot out, slicing my cheek. I tried to swipe at him, but I fell over my own feet. He let the blood from his blade drip into a tiny glass vial.

What did he want with my blood? I opened my mouth to ask—

I didn't see the branch coming. Bůk must have ducked it. It swept me off my mount and out of the memory with a bone-rattling blow. I landed hard—my tendrils making a clumsy attempt at catching me, but the numbed ones were still disoriented, so I careened straight into a bush.

When I peeled the leaves from my face, Bůk stood over me.

I tried to tell him we had to go—that there was no time to slow down. No words came out.

"You need to heal," he said evenly.

After a heroic effort to generate the words to explain that my tendrils were half drunk and my energy was depleted and we just needed to get on with it, I managed to gasp a single word. "Can't."

He frowned, kneeling to inspect me closer.

"Go," I said, reasoning that if he went alone, he would be faster. He might even overtake Van on the trail—and if not, he could at least get there in time to stop whatever attack the energy-sucker had planned.

Bůk's onyx eyes danced briefly skyward. He didn't bother to argue. He simply scooped me up and remounted his horse, carrying me along for the ride like a broken doll. We sat chest to chest. My horse was long gone, probably quite relieved to be down one wet noodle of a rider. By the time I rallied enough to protest the situation, we were already at full canter.

I sighed. At least we were moving.

I drifted in and out of sleep as we rode. Van's gleaming teeth haunted the brief wisps of unconsciousness I managed. Bůk's arm held me in place, but his shadows were more attentive. I wondered if they were like my magic—operating with little input from their host. They must have been, because the gentle circles they traced on my aching back and shoulders were very un-Bůk-like.

I'd just descended into a deeper sleep—or maybe I'd been there for hours—when the acrid smell of burning woke me. A blast of heat spiked my adrenaline. I reached automatically for my lute, stunned to realize that not only had I never collected it from the enemy camp—I hadn't even noticed its absence until right then.

Bůk slid it into my hands.

I blinked up at him.

And then I looked around. The woods were on fire, but not

in the wild, chaotic way a natural fire would burn. A rigid line of flames tinged green with magical influence cut the forest in two. I didn't have time to worry about that, though. All around us were the remains of the Fated's carts—ransacked, broken, and abandoned.

No bodies. That was a good sign, right?

"We'll have to go around," Bůk said.

The tension in his tone worried me. I followed his gaze and saw what he'd already registered. The prints in the mud did *not* go around the flaming section of woods. They went straight into it.

I hugged the lute to my chest. Bůk urged the horse—who clearly disliked us now—forward.

What would I do if we found them dead?

I pressed my face into Bůk's chest, breathing through his cloak of shadow and moss to keep the smoke at bay. My eyes burned anyway. The horse rocked beneath us.

My thumb drifted to the tattoo on my forearm. Not the Fated's eye, but the gloved fist. Yes. I was desperate enough to pray. Temple, save me.

"Haz, for the love of war and peace..." I thought in the general upward direction.

What? For the love of war and peace...*what?* Let them be alive? And why would the God of War and Peace care? Wasn't he also the Huntress's god? Wouldn't her devout factionites pray too? Did he keep a tally? Would one prayer weigh the vote in our favor? Or were we just so many baby chicks, pecking at a mother hen who barely knew we existed? And why did one god cover war *and* peace, anyway? They were two distinctly different things. When has this land ever even *known* peace? Clearly, Haz had a favorite child.

We cut a hard turn at what I assumed was the end of the flames.

"They're alive," Bůk said for my benefit, because we were still too enveloped in smoke for me to see anything.

Great, I thought sardonically. *Praying works.*

It took another ten minutes to reach them. At which point I discovered that Bůk had left out a few details. Like the fact that there were only a few dozen of "them" left.

I scrambled down from the saddle despite Bůk's attempt to hold me in place. My lute was already raised. The need to help —to focus on the one thing that I was good at and provide some measure of relief in the face of the destruction I'd caused —overwhelmed me.

But there was no one to heal. Aside from a scant few who looked like they'd been at the back of the fleeing group and had their clothes singed, no one was harmed. Even those few were sipping potions and looking better off than I was. I suspected that meant anyone who *wasn't* here had already turned to ash in the inferno that still raged mere paces away.

I swayed. It was Brü who caught my arm.

His concern was plain as we locked eyes—but mine was more important.

"Aelith?" I demanded.

"She's been in and out searching for survivors," he said.

Something in his tone flagged my alarm.

"The siphon?" Bůk asked, edging in. Although I had more questions for Brü, I was grateful for Bůk's proximity—solely because his giant form shielded me from the waves of heat rolling off the trees.

Brü shook his head. "We haven't seen him or any of the others since the initial attack."

Bůk opened his mouth again, but I was faster. "How long has Aelith been in there?"

The flash of fear in Brü's eyes was unmistakable. The answer was *too long*. Whether that meant Van had gotten to her or the flames had.

"I'm going after him," Bůk said, unlatching his satchel from his hip and letting it fall at Brü's feet.

"I'm going too," I said.

Both men leveled me with remarkably similar glares.

"If she's hurt—"

"Stay with Brü," Bůk growled.

The compulsion barely registered in my war-torn body—but I knew I wouldn't be going anywhere. And if I were honest, I'd already known that. I couldn't even heal myself. The idea that I would be of any use to Aelith after I marched into hellfire was absurd. But I couldn't do *nothing*.

"Bůk," I said. "If you find her...help her. Please."

He frowned. I didn't know the extent of his and Aelith's past, but I knew enough to know that this wasn't a minor request. He looked from me to Brü and back again. The tables had turned. Now it was Brü and I who shared a single expression.

"I'll do what I can," Bůk groused, turning from us without further ado.

And then he was gone—into the flames.

I sagged against Brü, the last of my energy spent. He helped me to a log. The gelatinous cube feeling returned, worse than ever. I answered his questions, drank his potions, and lay against his shoulder vaguely murmuring reassurances I couldn't support about Aelith's safety.

Then, I let the darkness claim me.

Chapter 25
Ero: A Waiting Game

"Power always has a source. Don't forget that." - a fragment of correspondence from a Temple Mother, preserved in the journal of Eroithiel von Dua

I sat in Colonel Astrada's tent, uncomfortably aware of the accusing eyes all around flitting briefly to me and then quickly away again.

I wasn't supposed to be there. Brü was. Unfortunately, the order Bůk laced with compulsion had *not* been merely to stay out of the fire. It'd been to stay *with* Brü.

I'd only dozed on his shoulder for about fifteen minutes. It was long enough for the potions to work. My body was—technically—healed and rested by the time leadership summoned Brü. But there was something hollow about rest potions. I felt like used underthings fancied up in a secondhand shop pretending they're new. That feeling, combined with my numb tendrils that didn't respond to the potions in the least *and* the simmering concern for Aelith—left me a vulnerable, brittle shell.

Colonel Astrada did not help. Her sharp gaze pierced me. She asked me to give a report in Bůk's absence since I had to be in her presence anyway. I recounted our days away to the best of my ability, holding nothing back outside of the events of a more sexual nature. Astrada asked me to repeat everything. Twice.

Brü and Astrada shared a long meaningful look when I finished. Understanding that they would be having an actual conversation in my absence, I stared at my hands.

"Our supplies are gone," Astrada said at last, focused on the whole assembly. "When Bůk returns, we'll move as one for the rest of the trip. If we're fast enough, we can make it in one long day's ride. Every soldier should be ready to leave at a moment's notice. We've taken enough losses. Brü, you can go."

The colonel hadn't said a single unkind word, but the undercurrent of irritation still sent prickles of humiliation through my chest. Brü shouldn't be leaving. He should be staying for the strategy meeting. Instead, he had to babysit me.

Brü guided me out of the tent and back to the log near the wall of flames.

"Sorry," I said, not looking at him as I sank back into my seat, hunching my shoulders against the heat.

I stared hard at the green-tipped flames. The unpredictable pattern of swirls and flickers had a strange, dangerous beauty to it.

Brü stepped into my line of sight—catching my shoulder when I tried to look away. Reluctantly, I looked at him.

"I can assure you," he said, "I would rather be here."

I studied him for a moment. He wasn't the smoke-blowing sort, so the sincerity on his face was a small breath of fresh air.

Of course, his preference probably had less to do with my company than the promise of knowing the moment Aelith returned. But at least he wasn't angry.

"I think we could both use a distraction while we wait," Brü said, dropping on the log next to me. "Ask me a question. Make it good."

He leaned back, resting his palms on the bark, looking pretty pleased with himself. I smiled despite the variety of negative feelings warring for my attention.

"What made you join the Fated?" I asked.

Perhaps it wasn't the most creative question—but it avoided such topical landmines as Aelith and Bůk.

"That's quite a story, actually," he said. "I was set to join the Huntress originally."

He laughed at my expression.

"It's not a secret," he assured me. "I was born and raised in her territory. Right near a border, though, so people in my town tended to split—even families, right down the middle. Some to her, some to Lord Austvix."

I bit my thumbnail. I'd been born in Huntress territory as well, but I'd spent time in land controlled by both the Fated and the Obsidian Alliance at various times since leaving home. In the towns, there was no marked difference. Factionites were treated like a higher caste anywhere you went. But I'd not detected any material difference between one faction's people and another's. They were all a little superior and a little blustery about it.

"I was orphaned when I was quite young," Brü said. "So I didn't have a family to push one faction over another. But I had a friend with a lovely family. Sage. The Huntress sent her brothers into Fated territory to poison the water and salt the fields when we were teenagers. They were both killed on the mission—and Sage's sister and father were killed shortly after when the Fated retaliated and sacked our town."

"Holy shit," I said.

"Yeah. It gets worse. Sage was able to hide, but her mother was assaulted by two Fated soldiers. She heard the whole thing —heard their names, the things they said, the things they did."

This was decidedly *not* a fun story. I braced myself as Brü kept going.

"Sage reported the men to the Huntress, hoping she would raise a complaint with Lord Austvix and demand their heads. The Huntress acknowledged Sage, but told her there was nothing to be done. The rules of war were bent all the time, she insisted. It would be a waste of time to challenge Lord Austvix over a minor infraction. I can see why, of course. The Huntress had just baited the attack and had a lot of grander pieces moving on her game board. But for my friend, it was a devastating dismissal.

"At that point, I lived at a local inn and did work for them. I was fifteen, so not quite old enough for the faction—but I planned to join up after my birthday. Sage stopped by in the middle of the night. She wanted to say goodbye. She was going to cross the border and go to Lord Austvix herself to demand justice. She didn't expect it to go well."

I hugged my middle, already sick for where this was going.

"I decided to go with her." He shrugged. "We weren't faction, so technically we had no reason to expect a violent response—but we were both realistic. We knew it was a possibility."

"What did Lord Austvix do?"

Brü smiled faintly. "He actually saw us—and listened. He had the men brought to his tent to hear the charges. That was already more than we had expected. Both denied involvement at first, but a truth serum fixed that. Everything my friend said was true, and they confirmed it. So Austvix gave them three choices. Execution, castration, or a 'fitting punishment.' Obviously, they chose the punishment.

"He stripped them, tied them to chairs, and put tiny bells on their cocks."

I blinked. *"What?"*

Brü smiled. "Austvix has a cat. It's a fierce little motherfucker."

"No."

"Yes. One guy was hard before the dancers even came out. He must have had a thing for humiliation."

I covered my face, groaning.

"I heard they didn't manage to save his bits and pieces, so he probably would have been better off with a clean castration —but I'm not losing sleep."

"And the other?"

"He went to town to recover and decided to retire from faction life to become a monk. Not sure how his cock fared. The screams were thrilling, though."

I shook my head, trying to piece together my new mental image of the much-discussed Lord Austvix. I didn't hate it.

"Sage and I joined that night," Brü said. "Her mother joined too a few weeks later. They're stationed together pretty far away, but we still write."

"Wow," I said. "Do you—"

"Nope." Brü arched a brow mischievously. "My turn."

I frowned, not at all interested in telling stories about my past. I checked the wall of flame hopefully—just in case Bůk and Aelith stumbled out at the perfect moment. No such luck.

Brü reached into Bůk's satchel, which he wore at his hip. He pulled out a bow—*my* bow—and put it across my lap.

It was strange. Before I'd stumbled into that cave and begun this entire adventure, I'd worn the bow on my back like an oversized fashion accessory for nearly two years. But since I'd been here, it'd become an afterthought. I'd shoved it wherever made the most sense just to keep it close. Now when I touched it, I felt an odd hum. Like it was irritated with me for the neglect.

"Can you shoot it?" Brü asked.

"No," I said quickly. "I mean, I've never tried. I didn't know anyone who knew how. It was a gift from the temple."

Brü's gaze carried some unspoken weight that reminded me of the loaded look he'd shared with Colonel Astrada. Not my favorite look.

"I'm no sharpshooter," he said, "but I can give you pointers. Give it a try. Let me see what I'm working with."

My heart pounded the way a child's might when they first tried a new skill in front of their peers. I didn't want Brü to see me embarrass myself.

"Fine, but no judgement," I insisted. Like that was both an option and a fair thing to say to my superior officer, who had good reason to encourage and expect me to have some small measure of competence with my weapon.

He held his hands up in an *I would never* gesture.

I rolled my eyes. "Where am I shooting?"

Brü picked a tree not terribly far away. It had a nice blackened singe mark that would make a suitable target.

Figuring I wouldn't get any better if I delayed—and that I might, in fact, attract attention I didn't want—I pulled the weapon up, shoved an arrow against the string, fumbled with the drawing mechanism as I'd seen real archers do, and shot in the general direction of the tree.

It hit dead center.

Now, I know what I should have been thinking. One of two things really. Either *"Wow, what luck!"* or *"What a great bow."*

Instead, I may have swelled with undue pride and unexpected glee at discovering I was secretly good at something. It was a little hit of confidence I needed, so why not bask?

"Again," he said.

I froze. Not *quite* ready to let the high fade if it turned out to be a fluke. I raised my brows teasingly. "Isn't it my turn? Don't I get another question?"

"Again," he said, this time using Superior Officer Voice. And while he did not have the literal power to compel me, I recognized the fine line I'd walk if I argued.

Anyway, if it wasn't a fluke, how amazing would it be to discover that I was deeply talented with my own weapon? Never mind that it meant I'd wasted two years I could have spent showing off and doing generally badass things.

The next two shots hit dead center as well, so close to the first that the arrowheads all jammed together.

That was that.

I was amazing. I was brilliant! I was perfection personified.

"Try mine," Brü said.

I frowned at his smug expression, understanding that I was walking into a trap—even if I didn't know how. His bow was a similar model. A crossbow with a mechanical device that made drawing relatively easy. It felt different in my hands, but not different enough—I reasoned—to undercut supreme talent like mine.

The arrow didn't loose so much as snap and tumble. One part fell to the ground. The other disappeared in a sideways arc into the wall of flame.

"Your arrow was flawed," I said.

He handed me another, so smug I didn't even argue. I

needed to wipe that look off his face like I needed my next breath. The next arrow—I'm pleased to say—didn't snap in half. It also didn't go anywhere near the tree.

"Why do you look so cocky?" I demanded.

"Don't be angry," he soothed—which is exactly what every angry person loves to hear. "I had a hunch about the bow's enchantments. I think they're attuned to you."

I considered this. I knew weapons *could* be attuned, but I assumed there was a whole process for that. Not to mention requirements, such as the most basic level of skill with the piece.

But then I remembered the man who'd taken the bow from me in the cave. He carried it into that first ambush—and then turned up dead, with one of his own (*my* own) arrows to the eye. I'd not had time to think about it in the heat of the moment, but I suppose I assumed someone had collected the arrow in the mayhem and shot it back—however unlikely a scenario that was. Had his death actually been the bow's doing?

I stared down at it, more than a little nervous.

"Ero," Brü said. "You talked about the siphon questioning you about Bůk's weapon."

The tiniest flare of annoyance sparked. Bůk's "you belong to me" schtick felt like a power struggle between me and him. If I followed Brü's line of reasoning correctly, he meant to imply that this weapon—by belonging to me, and me belonging to Bůk—could make it *Bůk's* weapon in the Huntress's eyes. There were so many missing links in that chain. So many assumptions. So many questions. Not to mention, the bow had been in Bůk's satchel—which Van's people searched.

"You think my bow is what they wanted?" I said, all of those brilliant arguments ready to lob upon confirmation.

"I think *you* are what they wanted."

I stared. Leaving aside the several immediate reasons I would have protested that idea to begin with, one thing was quite clear. If I *were* the weapon—which sounded pretty ridiculous, even to someone who'd just over-celebrated her own surprising new skill like it was heaven-sent—Van definitely hadn't known that. Nor had the others. They'd openly said the Huntress wanted me alive. They'd separately demanded I tell them about the weapon. There was no doubt they expected it to be something other than *me*.

My head ached. War was stupid. Mysteries were stupid.

"Why do you think so?" I finally asked.

Brü's face softened. "You don't strike me as someone with any formal training. Is that correct?"

I frowned, but nodded.

"You heal as well as Aelith. You liquefied Wendlin without appearing to try very hard. And this powerful instrument— which I suspect has some discernment capabilities of its own— is quite comfortable with you, despite your lack of proficiency with bows."

I picked at my cloak, still not understanding how this all connected. Don't get me wrong. I could see his point. I practiced my music, but I'd never put much effort into anything else. Not even the healing. Really, I'd only latched onto that because I had a tendency to get myself into situations where I needed it—and it was the one thing I could coax my tendrils to do half the time. The music helped, and I liked the music, so it'd become something of a self-perpetuating cycle. Get better at playing, get better at healing.

"Who—" Brü started.

But a shout behind us cut him off. Someone pointed toward

the fire. Even distorted through the dancing flames, I recognized Bůk's shape lumbering toward us.

I leapt to my feet, the bow and its mysteries and *my* mysteries temporarily forgotten.

Brü was on his feet too—and he looked as anguished as I felt when we both saw that Bůk's figure moved alone.

Chapter 26
Bůk: The Demon's Dilemma

Bůk's Personal Code, Item 5: Never run from a fight.

The flames felt like home.

It wasn't just the heat, either. The souls around me hungered—some for vengeance, some for peace, and some for a last chance to resolve unfinished business. As soon as they sensed me, they latched on, trailing along in a ghoulish parade. Their desires pressed in as thick as smoke.

Most people heard enough cautionary tales in their youths to understand that making a deal with a devil or a demon was bad business. But just let them see their own charred bones and feel genuine desperation for a last wish—and oh, how quickly they threw their immortal souls to the wind.

The shit of it was, it was a veritable buffet for me, and I wasn't even hungry. The easy ones I handled for free. With a mere flick of my will, I released tortured souls from broken bodies. My mercy allowed them to pass over without delay. No one was coming to mourn them, anyway. Not here. And while none of them were what I would call friends, they were faction-mates. It cost me little to end their suffering.

I ignored the others. The ones who sought vengeance might enjoy the show if I found the siphon, so they could just keep following. The others would have to choose the spirit path if they wanted to resolve their business.

When I reached the center of the inferno, I paused, feeling around me for living energy. It was scarce. Death crackled along waves of heat intense enough to melt flesh. It only tickled mine. I stood still, demanding quiet that the chattering souls refused to give. After some time, two threads of life force emerged from the babble. One was strong but cloaked—the siphon. The other was so weak I nearly missed it. Water that'd almost gone to steam, a life force I knew too well because it had nagged and chafed at mine since the moment we'd had the misfortune of meeting. *Aelith.*

I turned toward the siphon.

And then I paused. Ero's piercing green eyes, heavy with fear and desperation, pleading for something she knew better than to expect but had the temerity to ask for anyway—tugged at me strangely. As if sensing my doubt, Brü's face slipped in next to hers, pinched with the pained certainty that it was already a lost cause.

I didn't enjoy the queasy sensation those accusing looks stirred. Could they *really* blame me if Aelith got herself killed?

I took one more step in the siphon's direction. He'd killed half of our party. He was a clear and present threat to the others. Prioritizing that made good sense.

On the other hand, he wasn't moving in their direction.

On a third hand, problems like that liked to fester if left unresolved.

One more step.

Aelith's pathetic light flickered. The answering stab of joy in my mind was sullied by those damned bees buzzing inside me. A new and unfortunate sickness. Wasn't it supposed to be butterflies? That's the sort of nonsense soft little bards were always on about. But no, not for me. For me, the angry buzzing became pricks of stinging torment all over my body.

Ah, fuck it.

I pivoted, cutting toward Aelith with smooth efficiency. She was probably too far gone anyway, I reasoned. What a stupid thing to do, entering an inferno like this as a water elemental. I could do the bare minimum. Show up. Maybe even gloat a little. At least then I could say I tried.

I found her at the base of a massive oak, chewing desperately on an exposed root to steal its water. Her blond tresses fell limp around her shoulders. That the hair hadn't burned away told me she was employing the last dregs of her energy to maintain a shield against the fire. It wouldn't last. The oak above her flamed, and her lips blistered from the boiling water.

Aelith sensed me, but she didn't look up. I only knew because her desire to tell me to fuck off flared to life. I took some satisfaction in the fact that she didn't have energy to spare for it.

"I couldn't pass up seeing this before I handled the siphon," I said, leaning casually against her tree.

Aelith's response took so long I thought she'd actually decided to ignore me. But then she sagged against the root and turned her soot-stained face up to meet my eyes. She glared.

"You. Won't." The words were barely a whisper. Each took a hard-fought breath, huffed out on its own. "Handle. Him."

Aelith closed her eyes then, anguished. The words sounded taunting—telling *me* that I couldn't best an enemy?—but there wasn't any pleasure behind the accusation, and despite myself, a stab of doubt coursed through me.

She struggled to form more words. And, fuck me, I couldn't help but lean closer. If she had information about the siphon that I didn't, I wanted it. Needed it, even.

"God's energy," she croaked. Her tongue darted out to wet her lips, though no wet remained.

I frowned. Was Aelith saying the siphon had sourced from a god? If he had, it couldn't have been much. I'd been close enough to feel his power before, and nothing about it had set off alarm bells. Hell, perhaps he'd siphoned from the Huntress. All the warlords had some god's blood. That was what set them apart from lesser mortals to begin with.

Either way, siphoning from a god or one of their descendants didn't *make* one a god. The creature was still mortal. Still beatable. Still going to be beaten.

"I'll handle it," I dismissed.

Aelith winced, nodding her head. "Coming. Back."

For a moment, I thought she meant *she* was coming back. With me. To the party. My first instinct was to taunt her. *Coming back how?* I might have asked. *Is this the part where you beg for mercy from the very demon you've taken so much pleasure in irritating? Are you ready to see how effective that will be?*

But that wasn't what she meant. She meant the siphon was coming back. And she was right again. His energy signature was moving our way.

Perfect.

Plausible deniability.

I'd found Aelith, but the siphon found us. There was nothing to be done. The story told itself. I could dry Ero's tears and pat Brü's shoulder, and we could all move on one annoying elemental lighter.

"Get them out," she hissed. Strong words, a last rallying cry. A demand, not an ask.

I looked down at her. Her golden eyes swam with fierce determination.

Shit.

She wasn't begging. She wasn't even asking for her own life. No, she was invoking the one mutual desire we had. *Them.* Irritating to the last, wasn't she? Refusing to give me the pleasure of clean and simple hatred, even at the end.

As the siphon drew closer, a prickle of danger in my peripheral senses told me that Aelith might understand more than I gave her credit for. Cockiness aside, the power I sensed emanating from the creature now was not of the *"I'll handle it myself and be on my merry way"* variety. Perhaps he'd cloaked some of his power before to keep me from interfering? That would explain why Ero's magic had failed to destroy him. Either way, I could tell now that our clash would be an actual fight. I could even die again. That would be the ultimate irritation—particularly because it would give him time to reach the others.

I frowned more deeply, fully grasping Aelith's ask as her unspoken desires crackled in the air. She didn't mean for me to win the fight so I could get them out. She meant for me to run—to leave *her* here to distract the siphon, whose desires were currently focused on collecting the elemental who'd refused him now that she was near enough to death to reconsider. She wouldn't. But he didn't know that.

I *itched* for the fight. It would be so cathartic to melt the man's smug face. To teach him myriad lessons as I tore his body apart and ejected him from this mortal plane.

But between the bees and Ero's watery eyes and Aelith's

bone-dry ones and Brü's resigned ones—something inside me folded.

"Drop your shields," I growled.

Aelith's eyes popped open. Suspicion and fear warred inside them. Did she think I would waste time or energy killing her myself when the fire was about to do it for me *and* my doing it would trigger a contract response that would serve me up to the siphon in a maddened state? No. She was too smart to think that I was *that* petty. But she also didn't trust me. Which was absolutely fair. I wouldn't trust me either.

Still, I didn't have time for this. "If you want me to save them, I need to go now. Drop your shields."

Keeping up with my impression that Aelith was smarter than she looked, I felt her flicker of hope. Sure, it was tinged with terror. With the fear of her last act in this life being a bad gamble. But to my surprise, she listened anyway.

The flames dove for her like sentient jackals lunging for their long awaited kill the moment her shields fell—but mine were there to replace them, repelling the hellfire effortlessly. Inside *my* shields, Aelith was perfectly safe.

I broke eye contact, certain that if we maintained it, my plan would fall apart, and I would revert to my baser instincts. I bent and scooped Aelith off the ground. Her trembling limbs wound around me—so weak, I knew she wouldn't be able to hold on if I ran. And I needed to run, because bringing her along meant there would be no one left behind to keep the siphon busy. *You're fucking welcome, Ero and Brü. Let's hope your absurd request doesn't get you both killed.*

My shadows cinched her in place. I let the cloak fall around her, one more layer of cool energy between her and the flames that nearly claimed her life.

And I ran.

It tasted like licking grounds from over-brewed tea. Running from a fight? Haz's tits. I would never live this down. And to save *her*. No! To save them. Fuck her. She was a gift to them—and not a single thing more.

We easily outstripped the siphon, who—despite whatever powers he was high on—still needed to shield hard to move through the flames. He'd drained Aelith. I felt that now. Her power coiled around his own far off in the forest while she sagged empty against me. I also sensed the flickering golden light that must have been the god's energy. He had little of it. He would need more if he really meant to fight *me*. Good. That might buy us the time we needed.

The distance between us and the siphon grew as we ran, though his pursuit didn't actually stop until we neared the edge of the flames. I was more relieved than I cared to admit when I sensed him turn.

I crashed out of the fire into the relatively cold air just outside. Ero and Brü were right where I left them, on their feet. Their faces curdled in a way that told me exactly how much they cared about the fate of the water elemental clinging to my chest. I pulled the cloak away and dumped her in an unceremonious heap at their feet.

The emotions changed in a sudden, nauseous wave. Brü fell to his knees to gather Aelith in his arms. Ero simply froze, staring down at them as if this was almost worse than what she'd feared seconds before. Such a strange kitten.

As if hearing that thought and needing to underscore it, she threw her arms around me and buried her face in my chest.

I stood perfectly still.

My kitten's sob—like a shaky dam breaking—had a strange calming effect on my inner bees. I lifted my thumb to feel the trail of hot tears on her cheek.

Gods-damned *nectar*. My cock twitched. I fought the urge to have a taste.

Of course, an answering wave of irritation beat the cock-swell back. Ero's flurry of feelings was about Aelith, not *me*. And anyhow, I would have gotten the tears either way. I didn't have to make a *habit* of protecting the damned elemental. It was a one-time thing.

I nearly said something to this effect, but Colonel Astrada did me the favor of sounding a rally horn. Word of our return must have already reached her, and she wasn't planning to waste time. Good.

I stepped back from Ero before she could say words she would regret—like *thank you*. And when I sensed the same urge rising in Brü, I frowned pointedly at them both, silently communicating something to the tune of *"get your shit together, soldiers."*

"Better mount up," I growled, hoping my tone would shut down any lingering *feelings*. "And use whatever potions you've got left. If the siphon catches up, it's going to be a bloodbath."

Chapter 27
Ero: A Touch of Existential Doubt

"No matter how many places I go or people I meet, it will eventually just be me and the road again. So I find it imperative to stay ready for that eventuality."
- an excerpt from the journal of Eroithiel von Dua, 1313 B.A., before the Great War

The drop came as quickly as the high.

Aelith was alive.

Bůk saved her.

For me? For Brü? Did it matter?

I stared down at Brü, cradling her in his arms, knowing I should feel relieved. But a strange hollow uncertainty tugged at me instead.

Questions skewered me rapid-fire like so many arrows. If I'd never come to the Fated, would these attacks have happened? Would any of the Fated's dead—from those who fell during the first ambush to everyone we'd just lost in the fire—still live? Would Aelith have been in danger at all? And if not, would a civilian town have burned instead? Or would it have just been me, collected alone on the road, quietly taken to the Huntress?

The joke of it was, I wasn't a weapon at all. Whatever the Huntress knew or thought she knew, I was a poor bet. Untrained, undisciplined, unremarkable except by occasional accident. Everyone would have been better off if she'd found that out quickly.

Bůk's attention stilled the edge of darkness threatening to send me into a familiar spiral. He was watching me.

And he'd saved her.

I'd asked him to do it, knowing perfectly well that the two of them would love nothing more than to see each other crumble to dust—and he could have ignored me and gotten that wish. But he hadn't.

I moved to him without thinking about it. Without giving myself a moment to worry about how he might react. The only uncomplicated emotion I felt in that moment was gratitude.

For one golden beat, it became a warm reunion. I cried on his chest. He brushed my tears away. Brü whispered reassurances to Aelith. Aelith lived. We were all fine.

And then Bůk stepped back.

Things moved too fast from there.

Bůk said some terse words, and he was gone. Brü lifted Aelith, and they were gone. Everyone scrambled for horses, grabbing at the meager supplies that remained, calling out to whichever living members of the group they naturally gravitated to, forming plans.

I alone stood still.

A dark gray cloud tugged at me. Emptiness where moments before there'd been so much light. *Why* wasn't I happy?

My lute called to me as it often did when melancholy

threatened—but I was afraid to play for two reasons. First, half of my tendrils remained blunted and numb. I didn't know how the music would react to that. Second, Bůk hated it when I played. It seemed a poor way to repay him for such a huge favor.

But what good was I without music?

My sweeping gaze caught on my bow, forgotten on the log where Brü and I had talked moments before. I moved to the weapon. Its energy purred for me now—more like my lute and less like the thorny hum it'd greeted me with before. I slipped the strap over my head and fixed the arrows at my hip. There were seven. I glanced at the tree, considering whether there was time to collect the ones I'd shot—but they weren't there. In fact, the quiver felt fully packed already. Interesting. Had Brü brought them back? Or was this yet another aspect of the bow I'd never discovered?

The question came with a shame chaser. Brü had been so kind about it, but now his gentle questions chafed. How had I never tried my bow? How did I *not* know it was attuned to me?

"What are you doing, bard?" Flər sneered with his usual inflated bravado as he thundered by on his horse. "The mounts are over there. Are you deaf or slow? We're moving out."

I looked where he pointed. There were only a couple of horses left. There were already several soldiers doubled up. I'd ridden with Bůk so often that I half expected to hear *his* irritated voice next, but he was nowhere to be found.

"Unless you'd like to share?" Flər smirked. It wasn't even flirtatious. It was just mean. My dislike for him was certainly mutual by now, if it hadn't always been.

So I finally forced myself to move—darting for the remaining mares like someone with something to lose. Such as the ability to ride without questionable parts of my body rubbing against fucking *Flər*.

I made it. Flər said something that was probably cutting as I mounted up, but I tuned him out. One side of my saddle was a melted, bloody mess, and the horse had shiny new skin over recently healed wounds. I didn't know if the blood belonged to her or whoever her previous rider had been, and I tried not to think about it. No wonder she'd gone unclaimed. I patted her reassuringly, wishing I had time to bolster the rushed heal. But I'd barely situated my lute on the hip opposite the arrows when we started to move.

Unfortunately, we fell into pairs—and Flər was next to me. Given the option between chattering with him and letting my mind run wild, I chose the latter.

The last few days played on repeat. Bůk's game in the woods. Miri and Sade and the others. Van. Brü's theory about the Huntress.

Why would she want me? I still couldn't make that make sense.

Brü implied it had to do with my magic. Something I'd always wondered about, but had no one to ask. My mother was a legendary Night Walker. On a clear night, looking at the stars, she could travel half a world in a few steps. My half-siblings each had their own unique brands of her gift. The only time she'd ever addressed my lack of their abilities, she'd sneered and told me that half-elves didn't get elven magic.

Only, I had magic. She didn't know that. Even as a child, I'd known better than to share the news after her declaration. Partly because I knew it would anger her if I contradicted what she said—and partly because I didn't know how to *use* my magic, and that embarrassed me.

But why *hadn't* I tried harder? I'd gotten the lute, and my tendrils had liked it—had willingly, on *their* timeline, allowed me to improve its sound and transform it into an extension of us. And I'd just gone along telling myself that music was the beauty I could bring to the world—insisting that was enough.

But what if I had an ocean of power at my disposal, and I'd only chosen to use a few drops? Wasn't that exactly what the Temple Mothers abhorred? Squandering ability was as morally corrupt as hoarding resources. And if I *had* developed my talents, would I have already found the book I was looking for? Found my actual family? For all I knew, my tendrils were just as frustrated with me as I was with them.

"Not going to play, Princess?"

The words—particularly the *princess*—startled me. Flər seemed surprised to suddenly have my full attention. Perhaps it wasn't the first time he'd spoken at me.

"Something wrong?" he pushed. "You look like you've seen a ghost, sweetheart."

At the new pet name, I breathed again. But the seed of doubt he'd planted with that careless word didn't dissipate. I hadn't kept my mother's identity from the Fated to fool any of them. It was the opposite, really. I didn't want *her* to know where *I* was—if she even cared, which was a big *if*. I'd never volunteered the connection to anyone since the day I'd left.

"I don't feel like it," I said, probably three minutes later than was socially acceptable. But who cared? It was just Flər.

"Oh, then by all means," he said with exaggerated deference. "Be useless."

The biting responses I prided myself on keeping at the ready were nowhere to be found. His dig settled right in with my own doubts. Why did it have to be *him* next to me?

Brü's story about Lord Austvix and the rapists he'd punished came to mind, juxtaposed with Flər's bloodlust-fueled eyes in the cavern the day we'd met. *"Mammoth in the room, Bůk,"* he'd said. *"You going to share? I'd settle for the mouth. Promise to give it back in top condition."*

I glanced again at his smug face bouncing along next to me. Alive, when so many had died.

"Does Lord Austvix know you threaten to rape captives?" I asked Flər.

Now *I* had *his* full attention. He shot quick, covert glances at the pairs of riders ahead of and behind us. Then he fixed me with a dark glare, his anger barely concealing the hint of fear that shone bright in those beady eyes.

"That's not what happened," he said.

"It's not?" I looked away, watching the trees pass, tone carefully disinterested. "What exactly did you want to borrow my mouth for?"

"It was a fucking joke, Ero."

"You're a fucking joke, Flər."

His horse kicked up leaves and twigs from the path as he shot forward, startling the riders in front of us as he forced his way through them to move up the line. He left a string of curses and grumbles in his wake. Everyone scrambled to adjust.

I expected confronting him to feel good. It didn't. But when the dust settled, at least it was Hammond at my side instead of Flər. The tank of a man always had a smile on his orcish face. Not a kind one, exactly, but one that suggested he'd just amused himself by beheading an enemy. I'd kind of grown fond of it.

"What'dja do to get under his skin?" he asked, already grinning.

"Just held up a mirror," I said, still too hollow to enjoy the victory.

Hammond's face scrunched up in a way that told me he might have taken the statement too literally.

We rode for a few more minutes, but it quickly became apparent that Hammond was not a "deep inner thoughts" sort so much as a "shoot the shit" sort.

"You lookin' forward to the festivities?" he asked. "None of us wanted to get there this way, but it's nice we won't miss it."

"Festivities?"

"Twilight," he said. "Starts tonight. Bit hard to keep track on the road, but Astrada told everyone. Think she's tryin' to keep the mood up."

I frowned. Twilight was the week leading up to the new year. Had it really been that long? I tried to do quick math, but everything was too fuzzy. If he was right, though, I'd missed my birthday somewhere in the mess of the previous fortnight. Which meant I'd missed a temple visit. I looked down at my forearm. The temple tattoo with Haz's gloved fist looked bland next to the much fresher Fated tattoo.

What I felt wasn't exactly guilt, nor concern. It was just one more snapped tether. The only thing I knew about my father—aside from the fact that he'd thrust me upon an unwilling mother—was that he required that I visit Haz's temple every year on my birthday to tithe a drop of my blood. A requirement even *she* insisted upon, though she patently refused to speak of or acknowledge him in any other way.

Each year, I made the visit alone. I pricked my finger and smeared it on the altar. A Temple Mother refreshed my tattoo, listened to me recount my year, counseled me, and gave me a gift. Some years the gift was only a handful of nuts I might have foraged for myself, or a dull knife I had little use for. Other years, the gift was as grand as the bow on my back or a potion of incredible luck. (An item I'd promptly wasted on a lark to meet a prince, but I was only thirteen at the time.)

Anyway, I kept my expectations as low as possible. Now, I feared I would have to pay a penance instead of receiving anything at all.

"Is there a proper temple in the camp?" I asked Hammond.

He'd still been talking about the Fated's festivities, but he didn't seem to mind the interruption. Many outposts had small shrines or motherless temples. Those wouldn't do. I looked again at my tattoo, the edges faded like rain soaked into drought-starved clay.

"Sure do," Hammond said, grinning mischievously. "Best baker in the realm right next door to that, too. Getcha some gods, and then fuck, I *promise* you've never had glazed buns with candied jam til you've had old Sal's. Sticky buns, she calls 'em. Even Lord Austvix carts 'em in special. You know it's good when leadership can't go one council meeting without a taste."

Hammond waxed on at great length and in great detail, lionizing his favorite treat. I gleaned from his descriptions—peppered though they were with further talk of baked goods and ales—that the camp was less of a tent city and more of a semi-permanent town.

It brought me back to wondering about Lord Austvix. The warlords were all after the castle in Queensdale—which only someone with gods' blood could claim. But it'd been empty my whole life. There'd never been an overlord—only tales of what it was like hundreds of years ago when the realm bowed to one woman. Now the warlords all seemed bent on conquering one another before they took the seat, and that fight was slow and brutal. There were myriad rumors as to why. Curses, superstition, alleged prophecies. But for most of us, it was just background noise. Entire lifetimes still passed in the little towns the warlords ignored.

Was Austvix really as good as Brü made him sound? Or had Brü chosen the one story he knew might make me less likely to fear I'd pledged myself to an evil warlord sight unseen?

My curiosity exhausted me. I caught myself humming a tune, even though I'd not meant to. I glanced at Hammond and saw his grin as he swayed to my beat, no longer speaking. So I kept going.

The deadened tendrils stretched, pins and needles prickling at their tips, like a limb coming slowly back to life. The melody quieted my mind, even if it didn't make things better.

We didn't stop for food. Hammond passed me a hard roll at one point, which I took only because he had several. I hummed even as I ate—my way of thanking him.

It had to be almost dawn when we finally approached the base camp. I marveled at its size. It sat atop a mountain with a soft, curved peak. The tip was fortified with a massive stone wall, but the full encampment spread at least halfway down the mountain, and a second wall stretched out and around, out of sight in both directions, suggesting even more protected area. Strong-looking workers with the Fated symbol burned into their forearms hauled yet more rocks to the wall, fortifying and thickening it as we passed through a narrow gate.

Most of the soldiers couldn't get away fast enough when we made it inside. I watched in disbelief as a sizable group welcomed Flər with laughter and delight. He didn't so much as glance at the rest of the party as his friends tugged him away into their throng.

Was my lowest low tonight going to be being jealous of *Flər?*

Young factionites threaded among us, handing out waterskins and collecting the mounts. Most of the stablehands were covered in glitter, dressed for the festivities. We'd clearly interrupted their fun. That explained the terse attitudes. I dismounted quickly, making it as easy as I could.

And then I stood uncertainly, surrounded but alone. Everyone seemed to know where to go but me. Every direction I tried, something beat me back. Soldiers from our party delivered bad news to groups of hopefuls who'd come to greet people who hadn't made it. My heart lurched. A throng of paid entertainers offered to help riders out of their clothes and into baths. I stumbled back. Yet more soldiers embraced loved ones who were relieved to find them safe. I turned again.

A shadow fell over me from behind. I spun. Bǔk was still mounted. I hadn't seen him during the ride. He looked exhausted and smelled like a singed version of his usual midnight musk.

No one had come to greet him either, I realized. Nor did he seem fazed at all by that. Unlike me, spinning uncertainly in the breeze, he was as self-contained as ever.

"Come on," he said.

He reached a hand down, and I—who owed him a debt that I feared would deeply complicate my ability to deny him anything right now—took it.

I expected to see more of the camp when he nudged his mare forward, but he veered toward the woods that butted up against the stone wall instead. Up close, his shadowy cloak smelled even more strongly of the fire. I choked on the flavor.

It didn't take long to get lost in the trees. The moonless night offered no mercy. Nor did Bǔk, who pushed the tired mount to a canter. We raced through the dark woods—inside the stone wall, but as far from the people who'd built it as we could possibly be. By the time we slowed, I wouldn't have been surprised if we'd reached the far side of the mountain.

Bůk slid from the saddle. I heard a splash and looked down to find stars reflected in a freshly disturbed spring pool next to the horse. Bůk surfaced, wiping his dark hair back from his eyes. He'd either removed the shadow cloak, or it'd simply dissolved.

Bůk's beauty really came through in the dark. Away from the need to pretend at bland humanity. The water going to steam on his skin rose in soft silvery puffs.

A sudden urge raged inside me—for the weight of his body to hold me down, when all I felt like doing was dissolving and floating away. Why? I wish I knew. I ought to have craved what the others had at the gate. Loved ones who went to pieces at the sight of my safe return. Yet now, all I wanted was for someone to hold me accountable. To tell me everything that'd just happened was my fault, that I didn't have people waiting because I didn't deserve people. To make the way things were and had always been finally make sense.

I looked away.

"Get in the water, Ero," Bůk said. No inflection. No warmth. "Clean yourself."

Even the urge to argue was deadened. Had he been the dark, growling, smirking version of Bůk, I might have felt something. But he wasn't. He was just as indifferent to me as everyone at that camp had been. And frankly, it chafed.

I dismounted, carefully setting my bow and lute on my once-colorful cloak—now so heavy with mud and soot it'd gone gray—and then slipped out of my clothes and into the water.

It was hot. Was that because it was a spring? Or had Bůk had some effect on it? Either way, it felt better than anything had in days. It penetrated my chilled skin, lapped at the knots in my muscles. I could have gone under and never come up and been happy to do it.

Bůk moved closer. That prickle of not-quite-worry that he might grab and use me sparked deep in my belly. *And you would like it,* a voice suspiciously like Sade's taunted in my mind. What had she called me? *Demon-fucker.* Not terribly imaginatively, but accurate.

When Bůk did touch me, it was only to soap my shoulders. The enchantments I'd woven into my hair didn't lash out at him as he unplaited the braid. Traitors.

I closed my eyes, letting him wash me. Even when his fingers trailed down my spine and over the curve of my ass, he didn't move closer. His cock remained out of reach. The distance ached. The ache teased my already bruised pride. And although I knew logically that my need for his touch was about *me*—about *my* selfish loneliness, my seeing the little band of survivors from our party disperse into a wider group full of people who cared about them while I had only a demon who mostly despised me and occasionally found me alluring—I didn't care. I still wanted it. I still craved it.

Such a disappointment, Eroithiel.

That dark voice I hadn't thought about in days played back. It wasn't really there. Just a memory. But it cut all the same.

Bůk's hands fell away.

I stared straight ahead, picking the brightest star and focusing on it to keep myself from thinking or doing or even wanting too loudly something that would make me utterly pathetic in his eyes.

The water lapped as he climbed out. I waited for him to tell me what came next. Get out? Get dressed? Spread my legs? I didn't care. I was ready.

But the water lapped again as he returned and waded toward my back. I stiffened with anticipation, my pussy tingling in a way that annoyed me.

Something cold and smooth glided up my arm.

He made his way slowly around me. The cold thing trailed along, over my chest, up my cheek, and rested against my lips. I didn't look at it. I locked eyes with him instead. He snapped the leather strap, stinging my lips.

"Are you ready?" he asked—nonchalant, neither sinister nor teasing. Just matter-of-fact.

"For what?" I breathed.

"Did you think favors were free, kitten?" His words had a cruel edge. It didn't feel right. Didn't feel like him. But what did I know? What did I *really* know about Bůk? I knew the one instance of soft, sensual lovemaking in the woods was just part of his game. Pushing me to say *no* when he offered to remove the collar. Pushing me to willingly give up the last shred of self I couldn't spare.

I searched his blank eyes, my gray cloud of pain returning twofold. I meant nothing to him. I was a possession, and Aelith was a transaction, and he was going to make me feel every bit of that at my lowest low.

But at least I would feel something.

I nodded, holding his gaze.

His voice dropped lower still. "Use your words. I *said* are you ready to pay for her life?"

I ignored the tears welling in my eyes. I didn't even care that they would bring him pleasure. I didn't care about anything.

"Do your worst," I whispered.

And, fuck me—I hoped he would.

Chapter 28
Ero: His Worst

Bardic Advice from Eroithiel von Dua to future generations: Asking a demon to "do his worst" is not the best way to showcase the heights of your wisdom.

Bůk's low chuckle painted a trail of goosebumps down my arms. But I just watched him, tingling with anticipation.

This must be what it was like to be a true penitent—one of Haz's devotees who did more than visit the temple once a year to pretend at holiness. The ones who welcomed the Temple Mothers' wrath when they had misdeeds to atone for.

I had plenty of misdeeds. I'd never atoned for a single one. I made a masterclass of dodging consequences. Letting Bůk—who I knew would derive his own pleasure from the act—deliver the justice I craved was just poetry.

"You will follow my orders without hesitation," Bůk purred, lacing the words with compulsion that made the collar around my throat thrum.

He pulled the strap back, ready to strike. I closed my eyes. Waited. My core pulsed. A resounding *crack* echoed through the night—but the strap struck the surface of the water, not me. I shuddered.

"You will answer when I ask you a question," he went on, tracing incongruously gentle circles on my chest with the wet leather. "Do you understand?"

I didn't open my eyes. I took a shaky breath, and whispered, "Yes."

This time the strap landed. It lanced across my bare chest, lightning to my peaked nipples. I cried out. My hands shot up to soothe the pain, but he blocked them with his forearm.

"Hands behind your back," he ordered.

The chilly breeze sank its sharp teeth into my aching nipples when I dropped my hands. I would never admit it, but there was a delicious release in his compulsion this time. No choice to make. No self to fight. The knowledge, in fact, that fighting his orders would do irreparable harm. It made everything so simple.

A silky shadow snaked around my wrists, binding them together behind me. I looked up at Bǔk, greedy for the way his eyes held mine—no longer indifferent, but hungry. Ravenous. There was power in having him this way, even if he had me right back.

He waded closer, leaning down to invade my space. His hot breath tickled my ear. He didn't so much as blink as he thrust two fingers inside me and teased my clit with his thumb. I groaned at the delicious, unexpected invasion. Wondering for just a beat if this was going to go a different way than I'd thought—if his threats were just foreplay, not a demand for real recompense.

And then his free hand snapped something onto my collar. I

didn't want to look away from him, but I couldn't help it. Curiosity has its own power. I barely had time to register that the thing was a leash, coiled around his fist, before he yanked on it. I stumbled forward, losing my footing. His fingers and the pleasure they teased vanished. I was only under water for a second, but the spring's heat on my freshly terrorized nipples caused me to suck in a lungful of water.

I came up sputtering. Bůk didn't wait for me to recover. He stalked away, leash held firm. I had to move fast to keep up. The silt gave way to hard pebbles and coarse sand. When we made it ashore, the breeze was even colder. I whimpered.

"On your knees, Ero."

I dropped carefully, unsteady without my hands to guide my landing. The sharp pebbles dug into my skin. I winced.

His eyes met mine. "Were you afraid I was going to let you down, kitten?"

I didn't know if he meant with Aelith in the fire or just a moment ago in the water by turning the punishment to plea-sure, but my answer was the same either way—a hurried, "No."

"Liar."

The strap lashed out, catching my arm and licking around across my shoulder. The pain was perfect. It beat back the fog that'd chased me all day in favor of a single, tangible strip of searing red. I melted into it.

"All you wanted today was someone to blame you," he murmured, sounding deep in thought as he circled around behind me. "To tell you how badly you'd fucked everything up. How your weakness got people killed."

Knowing that Bůk could read my desires and having him prove that he'd tuned in when I was busy having my darkest private feelings were two totally different things. My cheeks burned. The urge to argue—to lie, even though he knew damned well that he was right—rose like bile.

"But you've made them love you, haven't you?"

I stiffened at the accusation. That hollow ache that'd eaten at me all day lit up like a poked cavity. None of them *loved* me. At best, they enjoyed me. But when we reached camp and their real loved ones rolled out of the woodwork—who even remembered that I existed? And who *should* have? I was nothing to them. No more than their demon's musical pet.

I might have gotten lost in my spiral again had his compulsion not torn an answer from my mouth. I shook my head, choking on the word. "No."

Three rapid strikes to my ass scattered my thoughts and took my breath away. I tipped forward, instinctively trying to evade the pain, but he laced his fingers through my hair and closed his fist, holding me there. Although he'd unplaited the braid, the dregs of my enchantments lashed out. He didn't flinch as they tore at his fingers. Drops of his blood hit my back.

I panted, chasing a breath I couldn't catch.

"They love you, Ero," he said evenly. "So much that they won't even blame you for letting the siphon go—"

"I didn't—"

"But *I* will."

He released my hair and shoved—pitching me forward with no way to break the fall. I turned my face so one cheek took the brunt of the impact.

I tried to push up and sit back, but his hand rested heavily between my shoulder blades, and he growled, "Keep that ass in the air, kitten. I have plans for it."

"I didn't—" I gasped, "—*let* him go."

Three more quick strikes rained down on my ass, too hard

and fast to be pleasurable—delivering pain that elicited a strangled cry.

"You killed *me* with one blow," Bůk mused in a dark, warning tone, raking his fingernails lightly over the fresh lash marks, eliciting more goosebumps and whimpers. "Are you suggesting that the siphon is *stronger* than me? Harder to kill?"

"No." It came out a strangled, pitiful cry. "But I— I couldn't—"

"Like you *couldn't* let me finish the Huntress's soldiers?" he pressed. "Couldn't or wouldn't?"

"I *couldn't!*"

The fingers tormenting my welts pulled away suddenly, and my whole body clenched. It didn't help. The next blow landed lower than anticipated. My thighs lit up with white-hot pain. A sob tore from my chest. I was ready to plead—to lie, to let his version of the truth reign if it meant he would stop even for a second so I could catch my breath.

But of course he knew that. He walked away, leaving me there with my whole body trembling.

I didn't move. I listened, trying to gauge where he was and what he was doing. He stopped about ten paces away and fumbled with something on his horse's saddle. I took several slow breaths, trying to calm myself.

Did he really think I'd let the siphon go on purpose? He couldn't possibly. He was playing with my mind. But the accusation still tugged at a loose thread in my psyche. I *should* have been able to handle Van. I'd cooked Wendlin's insides, for fuck's sake. I'd killed *Bůk.* Why did my tendrils go weak when it mattered?

It was only then—questioning them—that I realized how quiet they'd been since Bůk had pulled me into his saddle back at camp. I groped for them, suddenly frantic. But they were right where they were supposed to be. Relaxed, inert. Like I was lounging in a pub instead of ass up and hands tied at a demon's mercy.

A jagged suspicion gnawed at me. After the rock toads, Bůk had put his dampeners on me before he would touch me again —concerned that my magic would lash out and ruin his fun. That's why I'd not been able to fight when the Huntress's soldiers came for me. So how did he know it wouldn't be a problem this time? And why were my tendrils proving him right?

A bloom of anger ignited. Which was unfortunate, because I wasn't exactly in a position to use it. It was infuriating to think Bůk knew more about my magic than I did—that he was learning faster.

Bůk's footsteps announced his return. I tensed, but he didn't stop behind me. He settled within my narrow field of vision to the side—leaning his back against a boulder with his Fated-issue cloak in his hands. He fished a knife from the cloak's pocket and used it to dig at the threads holding his sewn name patch in place.

A gust of wind whipped the cloak against his body, raising steam from the contours of his muscles. Despite my anger, a wave of desire tugged at me when my gaze landed on his cock. It was already hard, and I was more than ready. My pussy ached—clenching at empty air.

And then I saw his smirk. Haz's fucking tits. I *hated* that he could read my desires.

He didn't even mock me for it this time—too busy with whatever arts and crafts bullshit he was doing. From behind the sewn name patch, he extracted a sliver of stone. He turned it over in his fingers. I couldn't make out what it was until he flicked a ball of fire onto a pile of logs at his feet. The flames were too close to my face for comfort—hot enough to make my jaw tick—but they lit him up beautifully. If he looked alluring in the dark, he was art in the firelight. I didn't even bother trying to rein in my ripple of want.

Bůk crouched down, touching the burning log until the fire turned a more intense blue. The stone plate in his hand was a black rock with metal inlay spelling out his name. An enchantment emanated from it—something soft and protective.

"It helps identify bodies if our clothes burn," he said, taunting me by answering the unasked question, proving once again how little effort it took to read me. "They're standard issue. You'll get one at the camp. The metallurgist weaves decent protective spells into the stone, too. She'll be interested in whatever it is you do to your hair."

He punctuated the statement by dropping the plate into the fire. It thunked against the log, immediately consumed by the blue flames. I didn't understand the point of his little show— and I didn't like that, because I was sure there *was* a point. But I quickly forgot that I cared when he stood again to his full height and frowned down at me.

"You've been distracting me lately," he accused. The conversational tone was gone as quickly as it'd come. Intermission over, apparently. "So you're going to be silent and still while I listen to the Fates now. Do you understand, kitten?"

"Yes," I breathed.

"Good girl," he purred, which might have been a compliment if I'd had any other choice, but in this case was pure mockery. My pussy didn't seem to know the difference. It pulsed needily once more.

Bůk gave a low, dark chuckle.

He moved out of sight, padding to stand right behind me. Too close. My breath hitched. He sank to his knees, nudging my feet apart until he pressed against me. His thumbs kneaded my ass—which was still up in the air as ordered—and then slid down to spread my pussy wide open. Without further warning, his cock thrust deep inside in one fast motion. I would have groaned, but the compulsion trapped the sound in my throat. I gagged on it—panicking as I fought to breathe around my own cries.

And we stayed that way.

My needy ache returned tenfold when Bůk failed to move again. I was brimful of his cock, but denied the friction I craved. Unable even to beg for it. I tried to think, desperate for a distraction. The Huntress? Lord Austvix? My limp fucking tendrils that seemed not at all concerned by my distress? Nothing worked. Every sensation centered on his cock and how badly I needed it to *move*.

The breeze came and went. Crickets chirped. The first rays of dawn broke. And still, Bůk convened with his Fates—inside me, but utterly removed. The fire crackled on, its heat drying the mud under my cheek.

By the time Bůk stirred again, my mind was as numb as my body. He adjusted, just barely, but it was enough to wake up the ravenous beast between my legs. This time my whine was allowed to escape.

"Who do you belong to, kitten?"

I'd like to say I noticed something off in his tone. The deadened, hollow turn. But I didn't. I was distracted. I *needed* him. I'm neither proud nor ashamed to admit that I would have said anything in that moment to earn a meager handful of thrusts.

"You," I gasped.

He pulled back, and I held my breath—praying to Haz that it was only a windup. It was not. He pulled all the way out and stood up, ignoring my plaintive groan. He walked around to stand in front of me.

"Sit up," he ordered.

I did. It wasn't easy with my hands behind my back and my muscles absolutely atrophied in place from holding the prostrated position for so long. But my tendrils were quick to help for once. Not even attempting to evade the traitor allegations.

Bůk cupped my chin, and his cock pressed against my lips. I opened them eagerly, but he jerked back. I shifted, impatient, grinding my dripping pussy against my heel for any relief whatsoever. But he just glared down at me.

What exactly had the Fates told him?

That question froze me in place. He moved again, smearing my own arousal across my lips. This time, I held still.

Was the siphon going to become a bigger problem? Was I? A dozen tiny fears bloomed, but the anxiety only strengthened my desire for him. I didn't want to think. I just wanted to feel.

He stroked his cock with hard jerks, denying me any part of him. I breathed harder.

"Bůk," I whined.

"Don't be selfish, kitten," he murmured, tipping his head back as his pace picked up. "Haven't I given you enough?"

Aelith.

Fuck.

I closed my eyes—but quickly opened them again. Selfish indeed. I couldn't deny myself the sight of him reaching his peak, even if it absolutely split my pussy in two with need.

"Yes," I cried, almost forgetting to answer until the compulsion wrenched the word from my tongue.

He came apart. I waited for a taste, but I didn't even get that. He aimed his cock down, painting my stomach and thighs with his pleasure. Then he fell to his knees, nudging my legs wider to kneel between them, bringing us eye to eye. I knew without asking that he would not grant me the same relief he'd just had.

He leaned forward, pressing a hard kiss to my lips.

"Are you going to forget who you belong to?" he demanded, and bit my lip before I could reply—hard, feral. Then he kissed me again.

"No," I breathed into his mouth.

Something rustled next to us. I didn't have attention to spare for it, barely even registering the sound. His fingers trailed through the mess he'd made on my thigh, rubbing it into a wider circle.

"I know you won't," he said, almost soothingly. "But if you do, I hope this will remind you. Hold. Still."

His bare hand pressed the white-hot nameplate into the sticky mess on my thigh.

My scream echoed through the woods.

And once again, my tendrils refused to rise. Allowing the motherfucker to brand me.

Chapter 29
Bůk: Toward the Inevitable

Demon Binding Code 2.1A: The bound shall not knowingly pursue any course of action that seeks to harm, impede, undermine, or otherwise trouble his Lord or party.

To be fair, she'd *asked* for my worst.

I carried the sobbing bard through the trees, a little too pleased with myself for rising to the challenge. I felt I deserved this moment too, considering what I'd perceived in the wind.

I was going to lose her.

I didn't know how—but it was coming, and soon. Of all the flavors of fate I'd tasted with my cock's irritating distraction conveniently sated for once, the worst was the bitter flash of her collar lying empty on the ground. No explanation. No fork in the path that might allow me to avoid it. It *would* happen.

And I fucking cared.

That was the worst part.

I held her to my chest, listening to the soft *"I hate you"* murmured in her babble of incoherent rage. She meant it. But I knew better than anyone the other side of that coin. She hated me, but she needed me. She hated me, but she *wanted* me. And that was good enough.

I pressed soft kisses to her temple, fighting the urge to put her down and give her the release I'd withheld before.

There were things to do.

I let the horse go free. We'd already overburdened her enough for one night. We had a long walk ahead. A gentle rain pattered through the trees, gradually soaking us both. That was for the best. I wiped at the mess I'd left on Ero—stopping only when she gave a little cry of pain as I neared her burn.

"Heal, kitten," I ordered softly.

She buried her face in my cloak, hiding from me as well as she could. But I watched her magic work. The colors pulsed, reaching for the ruined skin. Given the prevalence of scars among our party, I reasoned it was unlikely she would manage to fully erase my mark—but a strange tension coiled inside me, nonetheless. The charred skin glowed under the attention of her magic. Its blackened edges softened, the raw seeping red fading as new skin knitted together. But no matter how the tendrils lapped at my letters, the scarred *Bŭk* remained. I relaxed infinitesimally. Ero sagged, a sound of defeat huffing from her soft lips.

A stab of her desire singed the air gold. She wanted to know *why*. Why I'd marked her—but more importantly, why I was so determined to claim her. She ached to know.

But she didn't ask.

I looked at the rising sun. I needed to get back. I needed to get to Astrada and pass along everything I'd learned but couldn't yet make sense of. I also had a surprise for Ero. By lunchtime, Tavish would be by with the books I'd requested—anything the Fated had that she might use to dig at her own mysteries. Anything that mentioned Finchton or the lineages of its citizens. It was that mission that'd brought her to me to begin with. And it was the only thing she'd demanded of me—even if I had punished her for doing so.

I could have told her about the books. But telling her the things I wanted to give her wouldn't answer her question. Why *did* I want her? I didn't know the answer myself.

I paused at a patch of soft grass, laying her down on her back. She needed to dress now that the leg wouldn't be a problem. She wouldn't love it if I carried her back into camp this way. It wouldn't bother *me,* aside from the slight irritation of having to liquefy any eyes that lingered on her nakedness for too long. But it would bother her.

Despite my original intention for stopping, I didn't reach for Ero's clothes. I stood over her, waiting for her to look at me. She wouldn't—or couldn't. So I crouched down, parting her legs to kneel between them once more. She let me, but she also closed her eyes and angled her face away.

"Kitten..."

"I need to go to the temple," she said.

Her matter-of-fact tone begged questions. She'd never struck me as particularly religious, but it hadn't escaped my notice that her bow was temple-marked. She also had Haz's tattoo, though many of the soldiers had his or one of the lesser gods'.

"I'll take you," I said.

She didn't respond. Just waited. Her turmoil swirled. The need to be held, to feel loved. The need to run from me, someone who couldn't possibly give her that—and the equally powerful need to stay, both warred inside her. A perfect kaleidoscope of torment.

I had a sudden, bizarre urge to give her everything. I tried to remember the last time I'd *wanted* to fulfill another's needs. Even with Brü, who I regarded as the closest thing I'd ever had to a friend in my several centuries, my desire to do as he wished came and went. And it mostly came when his desires already aligned with my own.

My very first memory surfaced unbidden. Not childhood—no, that didn't exist for demons. It was my first moment of awareness. I'd come into being to fulfill a devil's need. It took quite a bit of power and a soul stone to conjure a new demon. I don't know which devil did it or why, only that I suddenly existed, and that I was *famished.* My specialty crystalized as I feasted on an entire fresh hellchamber of damned souls.

How many had I tormented that long day that'd stretched on for years? The number was so great it was basically irrelevant. They'd all handled it in their own ways—begging, breaking, going stoic, fighting back. And it didn't matter, because each of them only made me hungrier.

I have no regrets about my origin, what I did for those centuries, or what I continue to do now. My only regret remained the one time I'd shown empathy to the bard who'd fled.

I traced the letters on Ero's leg with the pad of my finger.

Why *her?* Her unasked question turned over in my mind. I used it to torment myself. Why did the image of her collar on the ground turn my stomach? Why did the thought of searching for a new plaything bore me to my very core? Why did the thought of going without now that I'd tasted her sound worse than any other fate I could imagine?

Had I been wearing human flesh too long? Was I becoming

like them? Growing sentimental? This was deeply Brü-like behavior.

Or did I have it all wrong? Was Ero made to torment me in the same way I'd been made to torment the fallen? Perhaps she *had* no father. Perhaps she would discover only a devil and a soul stone and a clever trick when she reached the end of her queries.

Ero took in a slow breath, ready to speak, and I knew she was going to say we should go. She needed her god—but I wasn't ready to hand her over to him yet.

With a snarl, I was on her. Biting the freshly healed skin that bore my name. Reaching for her face with one hand and her pussy with the other. It was already wet and ready, as always. Even through her doubt and uncertainty, this part hadn't been in question from the first moment she'd trembled on the other side of that wardrobe door.

I stopped thinking. I pulled my fingers away from her wet heat and took her with my mouth, lapping up the nectar, exploring every crevice of her sweet cavern with my tongue. She writhed under me, but when her hands found my head, she didn't push me away. She gripped my hair and held me there.

It was my first day all over again, but I was hungry for something different. I slowed further, relishing the taste even as her breathy moans turned to impatient whines. I grinned against her. Her fears weren't unjustified. But they weren't necessary this time. My tongue fell into her favorite rhythm. I dug my fingers into the marks on her ass that she hadn't bothered—or perhaps hadn't wanted—to heal, lifting that ass into the air so I could plunge my tongue deeper.

She came hard and fast, and even though I could have kept going—could have made this another day of consuming her—I let her come down instead.

And then I pulled her into my lap and held her.

We sat in the grass, limbs entwined, still in the silence. The only sound was the rain falling around us. Her wants dissolved. Mine grew. They weren't the kind that could be sated, though. My cock had nothing to do with them. I longed for something quiet and still—something like we had right in that moment but for much, much longer. And that was a fucking joke considering the mess we were careening toward.

When the rain stopped, we both knew it was time to go. Ero dressed. She donned her bow and arrows, then her lute, leaving nothing behind in my satchel.

I ignored the strange ache echoing in my chest that told me we were approaching our end.

The camp hummed with a vibrant silver energy. Between the rain, the full moon, and the holiday, the collective mood rode at a fever pitch.

Lucky for me, the temple stood apart from the busiest section of the camp. It was the first building to be constructed each time the camp moved. This one was only a few years old, but it had the presence of an ancient building. Lord Austvix carted the statue of Haz along from camp to camp, and the stones too—consecrated long ago in his birthplace by his first Temple Mother.

I'd always avoided the holy row, as others called it. I could have left Ero at the turn and walked away. But I didn't. The hollow sense of loss only grew as we neared the place, yet I couldn't turn back until there was no choice.

The nearest trade tent belonged to a baker. It overflowed

with factionites shouldering in for bread to soak up the ale sloshing in their bellies from the night before.

To my astonishment, Ero took my hand as we passed by. As though she worried I would leave now that the temple was straight ahead. We hadn't spoken in hours—hadn't looked at one another. I hovered just on the edge of breaking that silence, but we were almost there, and I didn't want to let her hand go anymore than I wanted to let *her* go.

We reached the bottom of the stone steps at the temple. An overwhelming sense of finality settled. Why did this feel like an end? Why did I care?

Ero looked at me tentatively. "I'll probably take a while."

Her eyes were so soft, her desires so quiet. Why? I wasn't used to having to wonder.

Several thoughts hovered at the tip of my tongue. *Don't go in. Run. Whatever you think you're doing in there, you're not, and it's going to ruin everything. If you promise to leave, I'll remove the collar.* The last one surprised even *me*. I sure as fuck would not be doing that. Not until I had to.

Instead of saying any of the nonsensical things going through my mind, I nodded. "Give Haz my worst."

That earned a flicker of a smile. Which was all it took to have me imagining shoving her back against the stone statue of her god and bruising her lips with mine until she forgot his name.

But she turned, melting away from me, and disappeared into the temple before I could say another word. I had to settle for knowing that even if she convened with the heavens, she would do so bearing *my* mark.

I turned to retreat to my tent to reflect—but Brü and Nigel stood in my path. Hammond spilled out of the baker's tent behind them, holding overflowing baskets of food under each arm.

"Happy Twilight," Brü said. He looked amused, like he already knew my sentiments on the holiday. On any holiday. Humans' silly excuses for letting loose and doing the things they always craved but denied themselves most of the time.

"Happy Twilight," I replied drily.

All three of them laughed. I shook my head. It was a marked difference from the way they'd behaved toward me even just a month or so ago, before we'd set off to claim the abandoned caverns.

Given their *familiarity,* it was probably good that, like as not, Austvix would assign me elsewhere for the next mission. Whatever Ero found in those letters, I would be the one to chase down the new lead—assuming we got one. And the others would probably stay here, enjoying the respite they'd earned.

"Eat with us," Hammond boomed.

My scowl made them laugh again. Haz's tits.

"I need to see Astrada," I said. A true and factual statement they couldn't argue with.

Except they did.

"She's ridden out to meet Austvix," Brü said—sobering a bit. "Leadership wanted him to hear our report directly, so she thought it best to meet him on the road rather than waiting. They're not due back until tomorrow."

Well, fuck. I could have gone to the other colonels with what I knew of Obsidian's strange mobilization and the clash brewing between the Watchers and the Sword Alliance—but I didn't like the other colonels, nor they me, and telling them wouldn't get the news to Austvix any faster. It would merely give them the pleasure of being the ones to report it.

Hammond waved a sticky bun in what I suppose he thought was a tempting way. Brü batted him aside.

"Come on, Bůk," he said. "It won't kill you."

I sighed. That made one thing.

The temple door at my back danced with an energy I deeply disliked. Something was brewing. For all the relief I'd felt in the moment the Fates opened up, the ominousness of not under-standing how or why the things I'd witnessed connected raised my hackles now. Eating sweets and enduring ribbing from— would I call them friends?—seemed a deeply irresponsible way to spend my time.

And yet, what else could I do?

Ero was busy with her god. And soon, she would be busy with her books. I was hungry and needed something to take my mind off the inevitable.

Holiday indeed.

I gestured down the path, silently bidding Brü to lead us. I could eat, perhaps sleep, and then face whatever fresh irrita-tion was headed my way.

Chapter 30
Ero: Oh, My God

"There is no transgression greater than betraying one's own blood." - a fragment of correspondence from the Temple Mother, preserved in the journal of Eroithiel von Dua

The moment I entered the temple, a sense of familiar peace settled over me. The space was dark, cool, and calm. It gave the impression of existing on a different plane from what waited just outside. No sounds from the camp penetrated the stone door once it closed behind me.

The only sound inside the temple was the burble of a fountain in the center of the floor. I drifted to its edge. A spiral of levitating stone steps circled the rim, the stones spaced precariously far apart. Water dribbled down them from an unseen source above, trickling into the carved basin. Seven golden swords protruded from a gauntlet at the bottom of the pool. They pointed up at the ceiling, gleaming in the low light—a perilous trap for anyone who braved the steps. Though why anyone would do that was beyond me. They didn't seem to lead to anything.

An altar stood behind the fountain. Its subtle power called to me. Nerves teased goosebumps onto my flesh. What exactly would my delayed visit mean? The altar felt neutral as I moved to stand before it. Brown smears of dried blood painted its porous gray surface. A gilded straight pin on a velvet cushion lay in wait.

I hesitated. Even knowing there was no choice, and that I was late, and that I would inevitably lift the pin and do my duty—something gave me pause. A feeling like I had pieces of a puzzle and hadn't put them together yet and shouldn't proceed until I did. This spark of doubt was fully at odds with the way the silence teased the tension from my shoulders. The way my tendrils felt normal for the first time in days. They swirled around my middle, perfectly balanced. And yet somehow, this lack of turmoil made me even more suspicious.

I sighed.

Before I could talk myself out of it, I lifted the pin, pricked my finger, and dragged the dot of blood across the altar.

A creak and grind sounded behind me. A slab of stone slid out of place in the wall, and a woman emerged. The Fated's Temple Mother had wild, untamed locks of silver hair spilling down her crimson holy cloak. She put most of her weight on a gnarled wooden cane as she thumped forward.

"Eroithiel," she said—a question, but not stated as such. More like a demand to confirm what she already knew.

"Yes," I said. "Thank you for having me."

"There's no pleasure in it," she snapped.

The comfort I'd felt upon entering the temple melted. I'd met all manner of Temple Mothers over the years. Some warm, some motherly, some quite matter-of-fact and businesslike. But none had ever treated me with hostility.

"I'm sorry I'm late," I said—nervous, even though I'd not exactly had a lot of control over my whereabouts these last few weeks.

"I'm sorry you came at all," she retorted.

I blinked, thinking briefly that I'd misheard. But her lips pressed together in a tight line of barely repressed rage, and she slapped a cloth bundle onto the altar. She wasn't just annoyed with me. She visibly shook with hatred.

I took a steadying breath. "If I've offended—"

"Silence, child. Nothing of Haz's creation could ever offend me," she said, sounding more offended than ever. "Do you come for my counsel?"

I peered at her. I knew the steps. I should say yes and answer her questions and listen to her advice. But I had a strong suspicion I wouldn't like what she was about to say.

She watched me. Her tight jaw, her blazing gray eyes, her white-knuckled grip on the cane. Somehow, the challenge emanating from her finally spurred my determination to life.

"Yes," I said evenly. "I seek your counsel, Temple Mother."

She nodded. "Where have your journeys taken you since your last visit?"

I recounted the names of the towns I'd visited, the taverns I'd played, and the places I'd lived. I always kept careful track, knowing I would face this question. Though this time, it felt like recalling a previous life rather than the last twelve-month. Only when I reached the part where I entered the cavern with the Huntress party did my confidence falter.

"I wore a false tattoo," I confessed. "The mark of the Huntress. I joined with a small party of her followers to seek the book my last Temple Mother spoke of. I'd heard the caverns had old libraries in their depths—picked over for magical books, of course, but the rumors said no one ever bothered to cart out the rest. I'd hoped..."

"Hope is a fool's crutch," the Temple Mother groused. "Haz's true devotees make their own fate."

I swallowed, chastened. I'd heard that refrain more than enough to have seen it coming. I could have pointed out that making my own fate was exactly what I'd been doing the day I'd donned the Huntress's mark. But the Temple Mother was already on to the next question.

Her lips pinched together again, and her hawkish eyes narrowed on me. "How did our lord feel about your failure to tithe on your last birthday?"

"I—" I sputtered. "How would I know that?"

As a Temple Mother, she ought to have known that I wasn't one of Haz's chosen conduits. I wasn't a temple darling, hearing his whispers and enjoying his guiding hand or his commentary. The entirety of our interactions had played out in temples like these, through Temple Mothers like her.

She chuffed softly, as if I were playing at ignorance on purpose. "He spoke to you that day, child. What did he say?"

Darkness obscured the edges of my vision. My head pounded. The voice. The unseen eyes I'd felt watching me the day I'd killed Wendlin. It clicked into place. I opened my mouth, but no sound came out. My cheeks heated. She was waiting for an answer.

What *had* he said?

He'd said that Brü and the others treated me like a child. He'd insulted me for letting Bůk control me. *So weak. Such a disappointment, Eroithiel.* He'd chided me for struggling against a mediocre alchemist—had told me to fight right before I'd killed Wendlin. Only then had I felt his singular spark of pride. And then he was gone, and he hadn't come back since.

I don't know why this realization made me panic.

Gods had always been intangible beings in my mind. I knew logically that there were those to whom they spoke directly. The Temple Mothers, yes—but also people like Aelith, whose magic was holy and came directly from the heavens. But to me, the idea of Haz was just that. An idea. A philosophy. An obligation. Not an irritated, judgmental, tangible observer. And —holy shit. Had he *heard* all of those "Haz's tits" comments? How many times had I gleefully taken his name in vain? Enough that a fresh sheen of cold sweat coated my forehead.

"He..." I met her furious gaze, groping for words. "He didn't like me much, I don't think. But I made him a little proud?"

She assessed me mercilessly. I was no stranger to disappointing mother figures—and yet, the sickening sensation of her gaze cutting through my exterior and plundering around inside me, seeing things I feared even I hadn't fully examined, made me want to run.

"The temple advises thusly," she said. "Recall, Eroithiel, that Haz is your only god and master. Haz is your source of life and your purpose. Serve Haz above false idols and—" she stared pointedly at my collar "—certainly above the fallen."

I nodded silently. What else could I do? Argue that I'd had no choice where the collar was concerned? That my attempt to make my own fate had in fact landed me here? I didn't need scrying abilities to guess how she would react to that. There was always a choice, she would say. Death would have been a choice. Perhaps Haz would have preferred that.

"In the year to come, you will be tested—and you will fail," the Temple Mother went on, each word a sliver of ice slicing into my heart. "You will let your friends down, and worse—you will betray your own blood."

I stumbled back, gripping the altar for support. The pinprick on my fingertip smeared fresh blood.

How could I betray what I didn't have?

"You will disappoint our lord with your weak heart." Her lips curled. "You are as unworthy of Haz's mark as you are of his gift. There is no transgression greater than betraying one's own blood."

"I wouldn't," I argued—unable to take those accusations without defending myself. "I don't *know* my blood, but if I did—"

"Silence!"

The cry echoed off the stone walls. My heart thundered in my chest.

In the quiet that followed, her labored breaths were the only sound. She glared at me—a silent dare to speak again. I did not.

The Temple Mother turned to her cloth bundle, unrolling it partway to reveal ink and needles. I desperately did not want this woman to touch me—much less to be the one to refresh my temple tattoo, but I splayed my arm across the altar anyway, terrified to do otherwise.

"Lord Austvix is good," she said—but this time, I felt like an intruder on her thoughts. She didn't look at me, barely spoke loudly enough for me to hear, as she prepared her tools and jabbed the ink into the faded space on my skin where the tattoo belonged. "Lord Austvix doesn't deserve this burden. Contessa —Contessa is the one who ought to have borne it."

I shook under her grip. Contessa was the Huntress. Contessa Urgway. I'd read the name, but had never heard it spoken aloud—not by tutors, not in the temple. The Huntress didn't *want* it spoken, and so it wasn't.

"But I am not one to question my god. Haz's plans are divine."

I could have pointed out that it sounded like she *was* questioning her god pretty pointedly—but it didn't seem the time. Her needle jabbed into my skin over and over.

"Our choices are our own. Our fates are what we make them," the Temple Mother muttered.

I gritted my teeth. That sure seemed to suggest that I would have a pretty hefty say in whether I betrayed my blood—assuming I ever found them. But once again, I kept my thoughts to myself.

I closed my eyes and bid my tendrils to heal the skin as the Temple Mother worked. She muttered more, but the words were no longer audible. When she finally finished, I looked down, finding two perfect tattoos on my inner forearm. Haz's gauntlet, just marginally darker and more vibrant, sat nearest my wrist. Above it, the Fated eye with seven tiny stars in its pupil stared sightlessly up at me—already having lost its new-ink luster.

The Temple Mother returned to her cloth roll, fastened her ink and needles back into their places, and then unrolled the thing the rest of the way. She lifted a piece of pale polished wood with jagged edges that looked like part of a broken staff.

My tendrils reached for it without my permission, and a chill gripped me when they closed around it. It flew into my hands. The Temple Mother made no remark—only watched with those intense eyes.

I examined the object. It was warm and serene under my fingers, like it'd recently been in a hot bath. A thousand tiny runes swirled around the edge in a mesmerizing pattern.

Although distant echoes of its power sparked, the object itself seemed inert. Dead. Broken.

What was it? And what was I meant to do with it?

I looked up—already dreading having to ask the Temple Mother a question, considering how she'd behaved toward me so far. But she wasn't there. A movement in my periphery made me jump. She was above me, standing at the top of the spiral steps. Her cane lay forgotten. I held my breath. One slip, and those swords in the water would—

Only she didn't slip.

"To Haz, I commit my eternal soul," she said gravely. "I have served, and I will be served."

Then she put out her arms and pitched forward into the air.

The seven swords sliced through her body. She was dead before she hit the water. Her final breath blew out in a garbled gasp. The fountain water ran red.

My cry echoed through the chamber. I lurched forward, one hand raised—but what the fuck was I supposed to do? I couldn't heal that. There was nothing *to* heal.

I gasped for breath, clutching my newest mystery against my chest in a death grip. Its runes tickled the tips of my fingers.

The grinding creak of the stone door sounded again. I looked up, fearing that I would have to explain—that I would have to defend my indefensible position, standing over the temple's dead mother.

A young man peered at me. He wore a student's white robes. I thought he might cry out—to call for help, or at least to call a guard to arrest me. But he didn't look at me at all. His eyes fell first on the fountain and then danced to the altar.

He lunged for the Temple Mother's cloth roll and fished out a small chalice.

"Holy Mother, newest saint, bless me in your death," he said hurriedly.

He ran to the edge of the fountain, dipped the chalice into the bloody water, and drank. The excess ran from the corners of his mouth, splattering his white robes with red.

I stumbled backward, one step and then two more. He didn't seem to notice or care.

But I couldn't run. I couldn't tear my eyes away from him.

Something skittered nearby—a sound like a rat or some other small creature. I didn't even look to see what. Before my eyes, the boy transformed. His bones cracked, his face turned soft and doughy, and hisses of pain filled the air. The red droplets on his white robes spread until the expanse of the fabric took on a solid crimson hue. When he stood again, there was no *he*—only a young Temple Mother. Her eyes were large and brown, her lips soft and pursed, her form deeply feminine.

She looked at me, tilting her head. "Don't you have things to do, Eroithiel?"

I opened my mouth and found it dry. Unlike the dead woman, this Temple Mother's tone was kind. Curious, as if she'd found me in bed late with chores undone—but didn't mind too much.

"I—"

She smiled softly. But in that smile I saw hints of shadow. Her eyes flashed green and then blue and then back to brown. Her lips changed shape faster than I could register. And then it was just her again.

"Go, child," she said. "I will see you next year."

I didn't need to be told a third time.

I ran.

Chapter 31
Ero: Bags, Books, and Bad Ideas

Bardic Advice from Eroithiel von Dua to future generations: A good friend will help you. A great friend will mock you until you help yourself.

The light of high noon blinded me when I burst from the temple door. I dodged the statue of Haz and stumbled onto the pathway leading back to the camp.

I needed sleep—but I knew I wouldn't get it. The world had a sharp, buzzing edge. My collar dug into my heaving throat.

Fuck.

I wanted answers. I wanted to scream. I wanted to stop seeing the angry Temple Mother's face and her limp form skewered on the swords—an image I already knew had burned irreparably into my mind's eye.

I turned toward the woods, planning to put distance between myself and the camp so I could think—but I ran into someone. Hard. It snapped me out of my spiral long enough to breathe as I fumbled through an apology.

Tavish gave me a half-hearted smile. "Happens all the time. I was actually waiting for you."

I frowned. Tavish was perhaps the only person in Brü's little party that I still felt I barely knew. He was everything medium—height, build, features, temperament. I still, even after making a few separate mental notes to ask, didn't know what role he served in the group. And beyond that, I was sure we'd never exchanged direct words outside of basics like "passing on your left" on the trail. Why would *he* be waiting for me?

"Do I need to report to Brü?" I asked.

Tavish smiled. "No."

I looked heavenward, at my wit's end with mysteries big, small, and medium, but he took pity fairly quickly.

"Bůk asked me to gather the tomes you're after." He nodded toward the temple. "He said I'd find you here when I finished. Are you ready to have a look?"

Well, *that* was unexpected.

Something warm and slippery turned in my chest. I'd asked Bůk about the Fated's library—but his wild reaction at the time had pretty clearly indicated I would never see it. Now he'd asked Tavish to curate a collection? Had he gone soft, or was there a catch?

Definitely not the former. Which probably meant the latter. The question was, did I care?

I licked my lips. A sense of doom pressed down on me, urgently suggesting that I was almost out of time. For what? The gods only knew. But the urge to act vibrated just beneath my skin.

"Let's go," I said, swallowing down every question that threatened to betray my inner turmoil.

Tavish nodded toward the path that led beyond the temple,

farther away from the bustling camp center toward a sparse bit of woods with a few scattered tents. We walked in silence.

Although the sun blazed overhead, the clouds to the west promised storms. I picked at the Temple Mother's words as we walked. *In the year to come, you will be tested—and you will fail.* I scratched the skin where the collar chafed. *You will let your friends down, and worse—you will betray your own blood.*

I twisted my fingers together. Initially, I'd assumed the words were an accusation about how I would harm the family I still had yet to find...but could it have been a reference to my mother instead? The family who'd already betrayed *me?* It would make sense. Bŭk wanted me to find hidden meaning in letters from Finchton, presumably meaning they held significance for the war.

But that didn't explain the bit about my friends. I had no friends in Finchton. I had no friends *anywhere* except here. How would betraying my mother let the Fated down?

"This is us," Tavish said, startling me once again merely by existing in close proximity. He pointed to a small tent standing apart from the rest. "Oh—and here. I made this for you."

He pulled a small black leather satchel from his cloak and handed it to me. Tiny silver stitches decorated the seams, and the Fated eye was embroidered on the front. Although well-crafted, the bag didn't look like it would hold more than a potion or two.

"Thank you," I said automatically, admiring the artistry if not expecting to find the piece useful.

Tavish's smile returned, this time with a teasing edge. "Do you know what it is?"

"A...bag?"

He laughed. "It's a little more than that."

He took it back and unclasped the silver latch. A silky black fabric spilled out. It looked like a fancy feed sack—but when Tavish slid his arm inside, it kept sliding. Far past the visible depth. It was like Bůk's satchel.

"I made them for the others too," he confirmed. "It's not the biggest, but it should keep your bow and lute safe. Those are both marvelous pieces."

I cast him a curious sideways glance as I slid my bow, lute, and the broken piece of staff into the bag experimentally. The fabric hugged them in place, keeping them from bouncing into each other.

"Thank you," I said again, but with a bit more *oomph* this time. "Is it plane magic? Is that what you do for the Fated?"

"It is plane magic, but it's just a hobby." He shrugged one shoulder. "Stealth is my actual expertise."

The truth of that was immediately obvious. I'd noticed Tavish—just enough to learn his name—but never enough to really *see* him. Not in the field, not in camp. Hell, I'd barreled into him outside the temple when he was standing in plain sight and then all but forgot he was beside me moments ago as we walked together. He was *good*.

I made a brand-new mental note to pay more attention to Tavish the next time I grew bored during a ride. *Assuming there is a next time,* my nerves interjected.

With a self-satisfied smirk, Tavish pulled the tent flap back and motioned me inside. Stacks of books waited on a table. Not a library's worth, mind you. But at least twenty.

"Do me a favor?" he said, nudging me as I passed. "Don't remove any of these from the tent. Lord Austvix would have my head. He didn't technically sanction this."

I gave him a quick salute, already scanning for the oldest-looking tome. I wasn't exactly sure what a "centuries-old book" would look like, but it seemed fairly safe to dismiss anything with paper too bright or a binding too tight. I opened the cover of the most likely candidate—a worn leather history—and frowned. It was dated 1265. Only 48 years old.

Nevertheless, I searched it.

I'd been born in 1291 amid a tumultuous few years for Finchton. The year before my birth, the bordering human kingdoms to our east and west were at odds. My mother invited the royals of each kingdom for peace talks—only to betray them both. Accounts of the betrayal varied deeply. No human ruler, it seemed, wanted to admit to falling victim to fae tricks. Nor did they wish to lob accusations of wrongdoing at the queen after the dust settled and she managed to maintain power. Yet the fallout had involved an open multi-sided battle with significant casualties for all, including Finchton. In fact, even Finchton's own histories noted that for nearly a fortnight, the kingdom's future hung in the balance.

Simple math told me I'd been conceived at the peak of the tri-kingdom conflict. The accepted story was that my mother had used a charismatic merchant for a bit of good old-fashioned stress relief, then opted to see the resulting pregnancy through. Thus my surname. But the two rulers my mother had fooled were both human men—and so were a fair number of their generals. I'd read enough about war to wonder whether something else had happened in the heat of that battle.

The book I opened confirmed for the fourth or fifth time that the eastern kingdom eschewed the known gods of the land in favor of a mythological unified human god. That made it unlikely that my father hailed from the east, where there were no temples at all and even fewer devotees.

I snatched a different book. A record of lineages. But in this one, the page on Finchton left my name out entirely. It wasn't even included with the merchant's surname. I slammed the book shut and opened three more simultaneously, flipping the pages with my tendrils as I scanned and waited for anything worthwhile to catch my eye. Nothing. Three more books. And then three more after that.

I must have been at it for hours when the first clap of thunder sounded in the distance, pulling me from my cloud of concentration. I shot a quick glance at the tent flap. It was already dark. I blinked, bleary-eyed from the hours of pointless focus. An entire afternoon and evening whiled away, just for another series of dead ends.

"Not what you're after?" Tavish asked.

I gave a small start, having once again forgotten that I had company.

"Stop *doing* that," I groused.

He laughed. "Sorry, but you're good practice. The fae are better at detecting me than most."

"I'm *not* fae," I said, perhaps more grumpily than was warranted.

But then I caught sight of his face. *Really* caught sight. He was no longer medium anything. His hazel eyes were a deep and striking swirl of ochre and sage. His hair, which I was certain had been unremarkable before, had a shiny brown gleam, and his jawline was the stuff of songs. He truly *had* been using his cloaking magic this entire time.

Based on the smug look on his face, he enjoyed my reaction.

Even his voice was two notches deeper when he spoke again. "What exactly are you after in the histories that's so elusive, if you don't mind my asking?"

I stared with open fascination. Tavish was basically a stranger—and apparently by *his* choice—so, my instinct told me to hold my cards even closer to my chest. But in sheer frustration, I laid them on the table instead.

"My father," I said. "Last year, a Temple Mother told me I would find him in a 'centuries-old book.' I've been searching ever since."

Tavish arched an eyebrow. "How old are you?"

"Twenty-two."

"In fae years?"

I started to retort with appropriate fury and remind him once again that I was *not* fae, and that even if I were, fae were not dogs who aged by different year counts. His laughter stopped me.

"I'm kidding, I'm kidding. But seriously...why would information about your lineage be in a 'centuries-old' book if you were born two decades ago?"

I rocked back on the stool. It wasn't like I hadn't asked myself the same thing. And although I'd decided to share what I was searching for, I still wasn't keen on the idea of telling anyone in the Fated who my mother was or why she might be significant enough to warrant inclusion in the more aged rolling histories.

"The Temple Mother didn't say," I said, choosing my words carefully. "But a lot of the histories have entries spanning decades."

"Decades," Tavish agreed. "Not centuries."

I turned my palms up, annoyed by his focus on semantics. "Maybe the 'centuries' part was an exaggeration."

"Yes, prophecies are known for their imprecise language," he mused drily.

Was he mocking me? I narrowed my eyes.

"Humor me," Tavish said. "What were the Temple Mother's exact words?"

I didn't need to pull out my journal. I'd read the transcribed words every night for months after that temple visit—had long ago committed them to memory. Without hesitation, I recited, "The key to your legacy lies in a centuries-old book."

Tavish didn't react at first. And then slowly, he tilted his head. "And the rest?"

"That's all of it."

"But the part about your father?" he prompted.

I shook my head. "I asked the Temple Mother how I could find him," I explained. "I'd been away from my mother for seven years to the day at that point, and I'd had no luck finding him on my own. That was the guidance she gave."

Tavish pressed his lips together. He met my eyes, and I could see a variety of calculations unfolding in his before he said, "I don't mean to suggest you've been on a wild kobold chase, but is it possible that you've misinterpreted… everything?"

I suddenly found Tavish's pretty eyes a bit grating.

"No," I said slowly, as if talking to Hammond after he'd caught the scent of sticky buns. "My entire relationship with the temple is *about* my father. He's the one who told my mother I have to visit every year. If it's not— He's— I mean, he has to be—"

My argument fizzled out. *Did* he have to be anything? He'd never been yet. Maybe his sole contribution to my life was ensuring that I dedicated some part of it to Haz. There were myriad religious zealots out there. And sure, this one had to have *some* measure of power to have made demands of a fae queen—hell, to have impregnated her to begin with. But did that mean the temple was duty-bound to help me find him?

Tavish's tone softened. "I know a centuries-old book, is all I'm saying. So do you. Spelled a little differently, but sounds the same…"

I swallowed hard, refusing to meet his eyes.

What was it about hearing someone else say out loud something sensible that you'd already dismissed? I *had* thought about Bůk in regard to the Temple Mother's words—sardonically—in the cavern the moment I'd learned his name. It'd seemed ironic. But it was also too...too *something*. Too neat? Too ridiculous? Too whimsical for the temple to have made that prediction in *that* way? And even if the Temple Mother had actually *meant* Bůk, how did that connect to my legacy? Was it simply that I was destined to join the Fated? That didn't explain why the Huntress wanted me. Why the old crone of a Temple Mother today had ended her life in response to my visit. Why *anything*.

I shook my head, searching for words.

Tavish took a few tentative steps forward, laying his hand on my forearm. "Do you want to find him?"

I looked hopelessly at the mess of books. I needed Tavish to be wrong. My legacy couldn't be this collar. My legacy couldn't be a demon whose sole purpose where I was concerned was to *possess* me. The very thought made me want to scratch my skin off. And then images from the past twenty-four hours assaulted me. Bůk scrying with his cock buried inside me. Bůk washing me in the rain after utterly destroying me. Me grabbing *Bůk's* hand as I approached the temple like a gods-damned nervous child.

Shit, shit, shit.

How had I relaxed into this? Was I *letting* him become my legacy?

In a flash, I had a bad idea.

"No," I said, sitting up straighter and looking Tavish dead in the eye. "I don't want to find him. I want to fuck you on this pile of books."

Screw the brand on my thigh. Screw the Temple Mother.

Screw Bůk. If Haz's devotees were called to make their own fate, then I would. And I would make sure it wasn't *him*.

For a beat, Tavish stared at me, and I stared right back. Then his lips twitched—and for one fraction of a second, I thought he was going to agree.

He was not.

"As fun as that sounds," he said, clearing his throat as a shit-eating grin took over, "I'm not especially interested in the eternal torment side of the equation. Sorry, pal."

Heat bloomed in my cheeks. Of course. Anyone I touched would face Bůk's wrath. How incredibly selfish to even suggest putting a factionmate in that position.

Oh, except maybe Flər?

No.

I really did need sleep. And maybe to shoot something.

"Fine." I slapped the table with an open palm, giving up. "Let's find Bůk."

Chapter 32
Bůk: One Night of Humanity

Bůk's Personal Code, Item 113: Mead is a double-edged sword. Proceed with caution.

The bonfire flames were soft and distorted.

It occurred to me as I squinted at them—trying to fix my vision—that I had never *actually* been drunk before.

Sure, I'd had my share of mead. It was a staple among the Fated. At most, it smoothed the more irritating edges of the world down. But whatever quality the drink had that caused humans to act like fools? It'd never penetrated my defenses.

Until that night.

In my ill-advised bid to accept the companionship of my factionmates, I allowed the barbarian to lead. For every drink he consumed, he dictated that Nigel and Brü would also consume one—and I would consume three. I should note that from the outset, I read Hammond's desire to cheat at this already-skewed game. But I didn't care. If this was how the humans wanted to celebrate their holiday, why not?

And then the stars climbed into my skin. The Fates no longer whispered from the outside. I breathed with Astrada's breath. I dripped down Lord Austvix's neck in so many beads of sweat. We rode hard and with intention. We would arrive by early morning—and I knew that because I was everywhere.

"Another!" Hammond cried.

Nigel filled Hammond's tankard and my three. Brü's already lie forgotten on the ground. Nigel's was suspiciously absent.

Nevertheless, I drank, curious if I'd just found a new way to access the Fates fully that did not involve burying my cock in a bard. Indeed, the sparkling night brightened and expanded as the additional spirits went down. I was the Huntress, with two men servicing me simultaneously while I screamed my pleasure. I was Hadrian Sai, rallying the Obsidian Alliance troops with promises that the Fates had smiled upon us. I was—

"There you are," Tavish said.

I blinked at all three of him. Behind them, three sets of irate emerald eyes glittered down at me like poisoned suns. The flavor of Ero's stormy rage interrupted the jolly air. It rippled with discontent.

Haz's sweaty tits. Hadn't I fucked the existential crisis out of her already? I *knew* the temple would ruin things.

"Fucking Haz," I grumbled.

Tavish and Ero exchanged a look. I noted her hand on his arm. I sat up straighter, flames already dancing on my fingertips. Tavish quickly put a solid two paces of space between them. I blinked—not *about* to let him off that easily. The flames bounced on my fingers. I wasn't going to—to do what? I looked again at Ero, frowning. What had I just been thinking about?

"Are you...drunk?" she asked.

I tapped my fingers together, extinguishing the flames. "No?"

Hammond, Brü, and Nigel burst into laughter.

Those alluring green eyes rolled, and I heard sarcastic words muttered in a vanishingly low tone. Something about *my fucking legacy.*

Whatever. I caught her arms and pulled her to me. No thought, only desire. I wanted to feel her. I wanted to taste her. Why, in the end, should humans even try to face the irritations of the world without fucking about it? My cock was definitely up for the job.

"I want you," I breathed against her ear.

A shiver ran through her. Over her shoulder, I caught Brü's expression—a rabbit frozen in a hunter's sights, watching me. Ero's dueling desires clouded the air. Oddly, the primary desire still seemed to be my demise. Sure, she'd grown wet at my touch, and wetter at my words—but something kept her from relaxing into it.

Frowning, I released her.

I tried to use the Fates to prod around, curious what my latest transgression had been, or—more likely—what ideas Haz had stirred in his devotee. But the Fates quickly clarified that *they* were in control.

For a good thirty seconds, I was paralyzed by a vision of Marcellus Vesper and Naeve Andarnus—the warlords who led the Order of the Sword and the Scholars' Collective—shaking hands. Neither looked happy. Naeve looked positively disgusted. I was quite certain that I *should* pay more attention to the circumstances, the details, the general warnings inherent in that vision. But I was also, again, quite drunk.

"Is your bard going to play for us?" a silky voice asked, interrupting my wobbly attempt to hold the vision.

I blinked. We had an audience. Quite an audience, in fact. The fire ring had filled out at some point—never mind the thunder growing louder by the minute. The intrusive voice came from a woman whose name I didn't know, but I could see from her necklace that she belonged to the little troupe of players Hammond had been boasting to all night of our bard's talent.

And this was why people shouldn't talk.

I reluctantly stumbled back, leaving Ero's immediate bubble.

For once, she seemed to have no desire to wield her lute. Her gray cloud of internal conflict stood firm. But Hammond and Nigel and even Brü tugged her forward, cajoling and fawning like mischievous children. Their encouragement eventually won her. She cast a look at me that was not exactly permission-seeking, but certainly held some basic awareness of the potential disaster inherent in accepting the bid to play. I sighed. I'd fully given in to the festivities for everyone else, so fuck me, I supposed. I made a private show of plugging my ears with two ribbons of shadow.

A flash of amusement appeared in Ero's eyes. It was gone as quickly as it'd come. I didn't love how the shared moment warmed me. It warmed me in a way that said, *"danger."* I was feeling too many things, especially where the bard was concerned. But she danced away, and the problem was mine alone.

I sank to the soft ground, leaning back against a stump. Watching her.

Eyes tugged at her—all around, wanting. Whether it was sex or song or a drop of attention, they collectively yearned for her. Something slithery urged me to rip the leather from her thigh and let them all see who she belonged to.

And that was before her fingers strummed the chords.

It was foolish to imagine her music's effect could be stopped by blocking sound. The vibrations drew goosebumps to my skin. The hot, raw desire her voice fostered in her audience teased the alcohol from my skin into the air and dragged everyone around us into my haze. I didn't even realize it was happening. Several soldiers near me passed out cold.

Even as Ero's glistening lips curved around the lyrics of her song—something that typically made her near giddy with joy—her newfound darkness continued to swirl. I won't lie. I was positively transfixed. In fact, my attention was so thoroughly captured that I didn't hear Brü the first several times he said my name. Only when Ero paused to adjust a lute string and Brü stepped in to block my view of her did I finally take notice.

"Are you capable of handling this?" he asked.

I tilted my head. Lost. But the shape of Brü's desire filled in the blank. He feared what my drunken state would mean for Ero. I was equally grateful and irritated. It was none of his business—and it was good to know how much he cared. The bard had a propensity for getting into dangerous situations. She needed as many friends who cared as she could get.

And yet.

"Fuck off," I said.

"Then swear an oath not to compel her until you're sober."

I narrowed my eyes—partly because Brü's face kept doubling, and partly to do some light intimidation work—but he didn't look away. And then I sensed Aelith's approach. I blame that for my quick fold.

"Fine. Hurry," I groused.

His knife came out in a flash. A dot of blood from each of our fingers and a few words later, I'd annoyingly agreed to check my power over the collar until I was fully sober once more. On pain of madness, etc., etc.

Everyone around the fire clapped and stomped to a beat. I knew this was Ero's exit song. She did this when she wanted to slip away. Started a popular, high-energy tune that everyone knew so they would naturally take over and she could escape.

The first droplets of rain plocked around us. It wouldn't be long before everyone else had to leave too. I stumbled out of the fire ring, positioning myself in the path to block Ero's way back to the camp.

I needn't have bothered. When she ducked out of the spotlight, she came straight to me.

"Start walking," she ordered.

I barely repressed a smirk. I didn't need the collar to make her regret that tone. I could already taste her neck. One bite, and I'd have her. Turn that turmoil into—

She gripped my elbow, steadying me. I looked down. My feet were off the path, tangled in foliage. I blinked up at her.

"Haz's fucking tits," she growled.

"I'll fuck your—" I started, seeing the perfect opportunity for the most hilarious joke I'd ever conceived of.

Cold water hit me full in the face.

And then it hit again, extinguishing the resulting flames.

I opened my mouth with compulsion coiled on my tongue, but the pinprick on my finger pulsed just in time to remind me about the minor blood vow I'd made to Brü.

Still. My fury was apparent.

"Can we just *go?*" my kitten hissed.

The contents of her waterskin dripped down my blazing cheeks. The Fates pulsed inside me. A fresh warning. I was going to lose her anyway, but if I didn't tread carefully, it would happen sooner—and much less cleanly.

I sagged, the momentary fury dying as quickly as it'd come. As she looped an arm around my waist and guided my swerving footsteps back to the path, I looked down at her and asked what I probably should have asked a while ago. "What happened?"

Ero didn't respond right away. I could see her conflict in neon swirls. She wanted to confront me. She didn't want to waste her time if I was too far gone.

At a fork in the path, I guided her toward my tent. Was that incredible presence of mind enough to prove my sobriety? I chanced a sideways look at her. It did not seem so. But her desire to have it out rose to a fever pitch all the same. Thank Haz for her impatience.

"Why did you make me wear the collar?" she demanded. "You could have tied my hands and brought me along like any other prisoner."

I looked skyward. *This* again?

It was my turn to take my time. Now definitely wasn't the moment to explain my deeper issues with bards. Nor the time to reveal that I could see magic and knew that hers was wild and colorful and stronger than it had any right to be. Probably not the time to tell her how annoyingly alluring her face and body were either.

"I wanted to," I said at last, shrugging away the rest.

She stopped in the path, causing me to sway. Her jaw locked. Her eyes blazed. Angry tears lit those green jewels. My insides twisted.

"I'm serious, Bůk. The Temple Mother told me—" She took a strangled breath, fighting for calm. "She told me I would find the key to my legacy in a centuries-old book. I need to know what she meant. Do you know something about me? Do you— Is— If—"

She let out an animalistic groan and shook her head. Giving up. It washed out from her like a tide. Whatever confession she'd hoped to drag out of me, she'd decided she wouldn't get it. Which was probably fair. I didn't know what she was after. I wasn't a secret vault of Ero knowledge. If we were part of some great destiny, someone had forgotten to inform *me*.

Yet I caught her wrist as she made to stalk off and spun her back to me. Because I couldn't let her go. It wasn't a want anymore. It was a necessity. I needed Ero like Hammond needed sticky buns. Like Brü needed Aelith. Like Tavish needed to watch his fucking back, because I'd just remembered the way he casually disappeared earlier when I'd intended to smite him for touching what was mine.

Ero's hope returned briefly—and then died all over again as I stared down at her without giving the answer she craved. But when she tugged to get her arm free, words spilled out of me unbidden.

"Do I know something about you? I know your nostrils flare right before you say something mean," I said. "I know the air tastes like citrus and spice at your first drop of arousal."

Her mouth opened, but I put my fingers over her lips.

"I know I could chase you for an eternity and never tire of the way you give in but never quite give up." I don't know how her braid ended up in my hand, but it didn't attack me—and that seemed like a good sign. I closed my fist gently around it. "I know you torment my dreams with songs I can't stop hearing. I know you made my old dreams stop."

Actually, I hadn't known that until right then. I hadn't thought about it in some time. But it was true. When I dreamt, I dreamt of Ero. I no longer dreamt of chasing the Hell-fled bard.

"I know you're going to leave," I went on, barely audible

now. The mead chose a terrible time to make everything fuzzy again. It pulsed behind my eyes, but I forced out the rest. "And I don't want you to."

"What?" Ero demanded.

I kissed her. Not in the possessive, consuming way I'd kissed her several times before—the way that promised I planned to take more. No, I kissed her with stars and moonlight inside my skin reaching out for her. Begging.

Her desire morphed into a delightful delicacy she produced better than anyone I'd ever met. A war within a bard. She wanted me, and she hated me, and it was my favorite flavor.

"Tomorrow," I whispered against her lips.

She nodded. I knew she'd misunderstood. She thought I meant we would talk more tomorrow—not that she would *leave me* tomorrow. I couldn't clarify because her lips moved against mine, and I didn't want them to stop. Not when we were finally almost aligned.

I lifted her. Her legs wound around my middle. We swayed, her tendrils and my shadows both working overtime to hold us upright. The rain soaked us. People streamed past, but no one paid us any attention.

There was still time. Maybe the empty collar didn't mean what I thought it meant. Maybe she would demand its removal. Maybe she would convince me. Maybe she'd devised a new scheme with Aelith. Maybe after it was off, she would still be mine.

I clung to that lie as I carried her into my room and laid her on my bed. As I stared into those glassy eyes that finally burned for me, even if the tiny crease on her brow remained, I felt light —almost *happy?*

I lay flush against her, assuming this was the part where we would do all the things I didn't want to be finished with.

But the stars were leaving, fleeing my body one by one and taking their power with them. The darkness at the edge of my consciousness surged in. The world swayed. Ero made a soft chuffing sound, her lips on my neck.

"Just sleep," she said. "It's almost tomorrow now, anyway."

A tiny, doomed part of me jolted at that—but I was already too far gone to protest. Soon, I was asleep.

Chapter 33
Ero: Letters from Finchton

Bardic Advice from Eroithiel von Dua to future generations: Some clichés exist for a reason. *Do* actually be careful what you wish for.

The morning dawned freezing cold and gray. Bůk's room smelled strongly of mead and brimstone. He slept like the dead. One particularly harsh snore woke me.

The previous night, I'd managed—with significant help from my tendrils—to roll him off me after he passed out. I'd considered looking for another place to sleep, just so I could have space to think. In the end, I'd been too exhausted, and he'd been too warm.

Now, his strange words plagued me. *I know you're going to leave, and I don't want you to.*

I wanted those words to be comforting. They implied I wouldn't be stuck forever, collar or no. That maybe I would actually find what I was after. And maybe it would take me away.

I sat up, once again considering slipping out of the room before Bůk woke. The choice fizzled when someone rapped on the door. Bůk didn't stir, and I didn't answer—hoping it would go away. But after one more cursory attempt, Tavish wrenched the door open.

Bůk sat abruptly, grumbling and glowering.

"Lord Austvix—" Tavish said quickly, with emphasis, as though the name might protect him from Bůk's wrath "—won't call council for a few hours, but he sent me to deliver these."

He held up a bundle of letters. My heart fluttered.

This was it. The reason Bůk brought me here. The thing he *actually* wanted from me, whatever he'd said or implied last night in his sappy drunken haze.

A rare spark of hope ignited in my chest. Maybe *my* answers weren't what would lead to my leaving. Maybe his were. If I could help him solve whatever mystery had tangled up the Fated's plans, maybe he would *choose* to let me go.

A subtle heat spread from Bůk, leaching the morning's chill from the air. I glanced sideways. I hadn't exactly expected him to be turning cartwheels after last night's festivities—but I was surprised at how irritated he looked. Wasn't this what he'd been waiting for?

"Thank you," I told Tavish when Bůk failed to speak.

I stood and reached for the letters.

"Don't touch those," Bůk growled.

I looked at him again, frowning now. His eyes were still glassy. He wasn't just hungover—he was still half drunk. I held my hands up in the universal sign of surrender. But of course when I chanced a glance at Tavish for solidarity regarding Bůk's strange behavior, *he* was already gone. The bundle of letters lay on the ground just inside the door.

"Any...particular reason I shouldn't touch the letters you dragged me halfway across the continent to decode, or...?" I said, arching an unamused brow at Bůk.

His cloudy expression grew darker. His voice was low and gravelly with the remnants of sleep. "It can wait."

My brief glance to the heavens for help produced none. "For fuck's sake, Bůk. Wait for *what?*"

He stared at me. The air churned. Hot and cold, humid and dry. Every breath was something new. I didn't know what to think. He looked tormented. He looked awful. He looked like he had no plans whatsoever to explain himself. Had I been any less frustrated, I might have felt bad for him. But I couldn't muster that today.

"If you don't trust me, use the collar," I said. "I don't care. If you want answers, give me the letters."

Another wave of heat.

What was his fucking problem? He'd not hesitated to compel me before, and now was the most obvious time to do so.

"Never mind," I said. "I need air. Have someone get me when you're ready—"

"I'm sorry," he said.

I froze. Bůk—*Bůk* had just apologized? To me? I blinked, not even exaggerating my surprise.

"I saw things last night," he said slowly, as if selecting each word with great care. "The war is coming. We need these answers badly."

Sarcasm coiled like a snake. "So you want to wait...because this is urgent?"

Irritation rippled in the fine lines around his eyes. Yet he still didn't bite back. What in every single corner of Hell?

A prickle of dread broke through my confusion. Bůk said he

saw things. Were his visions aligned with the Temple Mother's warning? Did he fear I would betray the Fated? What power did I even have to do that? And if Bůk was so worried about it, why couldn't he simply make sure I didn't?

Bůk closed his eyes and groaned. "Just get them."

Resignation? A second shockingly out of character move from Bůk.

I still didn't understand his hesitation, but I didn't give him a chance to change his mind. Hungry for information, I pounced. I scooped up the bundle of letters and carefully untied the twine, pulling it open as quickly as I could without risking rebuke for endangering the paper.

The air stagnated, an apparent manifestation of Bůk's discomfort. But I no longer cared what he wasn't sharing. I just wanted to see the letters that had commandeered my fate.

Some part of me hoped it really was seven-layered Finchton wit that had undone these warlords. For all the hatred I felt toward the royals and most of the highborn, the place had made an art of language. That much, I could appreciate. I probably even owed some of my lyrical talent to them.

No. Scratch that. I owed Finchton nothing.

The first letter was addressed to a highborn, based on the diamonds etched on either side of the letters. The name itself was a pet name—likely one of dozens the recipient had, each specific to a different friend. That was typical. I skipped down to the signature.

And my blood went cold.

Queen Rashada Finch

These weren't military missives or official documents or even highborn gossip. This was a letter from my mother to one of her friends.

I tried to breathe. Bůk had, by some miracle, *not* compelled me to share every single thought or discovery I had about the letters. Which was good, because I didn't want to side quest through a discussion about my unfortunate bloodline right now. I hoped he would attribute my shock to the fact that I was holding a letter from the queen herself.

The letter was dated 1291. My birth year. I swallowed a heavy lump and read my mother's opening lines. *I have the most awful news and the most wonderful need. A parasite has entered my court. In lieu of your typical blessings, I wish for a clever cure—as I know you are so adept at removing the miss from misfortune.*

In the margin, a faded pen had scribbled, *traitor? creature? scorned lover?*

But as I read on, through tears I hated almost as much as the woman who'd penned this letter, I knew those guesses were wrong. This was not a matter of Finchton's penchant for wordplay, which barely showed in my mother's hurried prose.

These letters were about a *baby*. They were about *me*.

And the reason that was shrouded in confusion was that no one—not even the most pragmatic soldier in this company—expected a mother to describe her child the way my mother had described me.

Letter after letter. Plea after plea.

my cruel fate

the heavens' scorn

a cursed weapon

I choked, forcing myself to focus on that last letter.

Into my hands a cursed weapon has fallen, which I fear I've no interest in having or using or even knowing. Should Trident provide an adequate solution, you, sir, might name your price up to and exceeding my own hand.

I read it twice. There was no love lost between my mother and the king. A strictly political marriage—he, a powerless figurehead in the arrangement. But Finchton did not allow polygamy among royals. So, would she have banished the king? Shattered the alliance that marriage had brokered? Or worse— *killed* him? Just to be rid of me?

My hands shook. I'd always known she hated me. That came as no surprise at all. But I'd also thought it was my fault —something that grew and solidified after I was born because of who I turned out to be. That I was not grateful enough, or too whimsical, or too strange for her taste. That maybe I could have won her if I'd just been different.

I couldn't decide if it was a relief to learn otherwise.

I turned from Bůk, mind riddled with questions. Could he read anything in my desires that would give away the truth? Just in case, I gave a half-hearted attempt to center my desire for the queen's death. Let him do with that what he would.

I flipped through more letters. They were all similar. There would be plenty to pick apart later, if I got the chance. It sounded like my mother had searched far and wide for someone to help her get rid of me. But why hadn't she simply ended the pregnancy? That was the part that made no sense. A pregnancy wasn't hard to end. The right herbs would have done it early on, and the royals had no shortage of healers who could have helped at any point after. And barring that, she might have just thrown me out of a window after my birth.

Unless.

My tendrils curled around me, comforting, like for once they were fully on my side. I thought of the way they'd lashed out at Wendlin when he'd come for the killing blow. The way they'd ended Bůk instantly when he was inside me and the rock toad had taken me by surprise with an attack.

Brü guessed the Huntress thought I was a weapon. She'd had these letters. *She* had figured it out.

I took several shallow breaths.

I still didn't have the answer. The final piece. What *made* me a weapon? Why couldn't my mother kill me? Why did she want to? Why did the Huntress have her letters? Why did Lord Austvix steal them? Why were they both chasing my mother's mysterious problem like it mattered?

Was my mystery also Bůk's mystery? If I told him everything, would he be just as determined as I to solve this last bit? Or would he turn me over to Lord Austvix and wash his hands of the rest?

"Anything you'd like to share?" Bůk asked.

I looked up. I felt oddly liminal—one foot in his world, one foot in hers. And, fuck. Bůk saw my tears. His eyes blazed with a curiosity that I knew would quickly become demand. If I didn't give him something, he would take everything.

I wanted to trust him.

But I didn't.

"It wasn't a traitor," I said, nudging the first letter—a plan forming as quickly as the words to enact it. "It was a baby. She was pregnant when she wrote this."

Bůk's brow furrowed.

Even a demon couldn't imagine a mother hating her child that much. Why did *that* tear a new rift in my long-dormant wound?

The heat in the room suddenly turned oppressive. A hollow ache pulsed in my chest. I let the pages fall to the bed.

"What's wrong?" Bůk asked.

I shook my head. "Where did the Huntress get these?"

I looked down at the pile, trying to make that part make sense. These had gone all over the continent—to powerful friends far and wide. Who had cared enough to gather them?

"Tavish believes they were found together in Finchton,"

Bůk said. "Never sent. A spy in the Huntress's inner circle brought news of their existence, and they all turned up at once. Why?"

He knew something was wrong. Any fool could have seen that. I was nearly hyperventilating. But he didn't know *what* was wrong. And that was good.

"The queen wanted to get rid of her child," I said, trying to sound steady. "It's— I just don't—"

I swallowed. I needed him to believe I was overcome with emotion for that. For some faceless princess I'd known from a distance. But even as I fought to keep the last shred of this new angle to myself, another realization slammed into me. Bůk *would* find out. One conversation with either Brü—who'd deduced from a few disconnected details that I was the weapon the Huntress wanted, or Tavish—who knew what I wanted to find in those books, who had watched me focus on entries about the queen when I'd *told* him I was looking for my father. They were all going to put it together. It was only a question of when.

"I need air," I said—knowing I was fucked. Bůk wouldn't let me leave. He couldn't. He couldn't possibly avoid using the collar now.

I lurched for the door. As expected, he came after me. But his hand closed around empty air. He was slow, still fighting off the mead. I listened for his inevitable command behind me— but I didn't stop moving in the meantime, and the command never came.

I ran. His footsteps thundered behind me.

"Ero, stop!" he called.

Still no compulsion.

I moved faster, turning into a busy part of the camp. It looked like a town center. Semi-permanent structures made of wood and stone lined the streets. There were few people out this early, but the ones who were there paid us no mind.

Bůk paused to retch. The moment I saw him distracted, I dove between two buildings. I crouched in the shadows—wondering if it was a fool's errand. He'd found me so easily in the woods. I should have kept moving. I should still—

A sound startled me from my tortured debate.

A meow?

I looked back toward the street. A snow-white cat sat just outside the alleyway shadow staring right at me. Its glassy blue eyes glittered in the morning light. Its long fur swayed gently in the breeze. Stunningly pretty, but also eerily ghostlike.

Slowly, the cat's ears went flat. A low guttural yowl stilled my tendrils.

This was no alley cat. Was it a shifter? A familiar? An intelligent beast in its own right? I moved one hand slowly toward my belt, searching for my knife.

The cat's growl deepened, threatening, and it crouched.

"Pax!" called an unfamiliar masculine voice with a lilt of polished command.

The cat sat up immediately, giving me one last withering glare before it darted away.

Bůk skidded into the spot the cat had just vacated, looking more furious than I'd ever seen him. Sparks dripped from his fingertips. Dark promises danced in his eyes.

And somehow, he *still* didn't compel me.

The voice boomed again. "Bůk?"

Several sets of hooves clopped on the cobblestone. Bůk looked over his shoulder. I stood slowly, flattening myself against the building. There was no way out of the alley in the back. It was a stone wall with a steep cliff face behind it. I would have to dart past Bůk to flee again.

The party of riders stopped behind Bůk, making my single path out more complicated.

And there, I finally caught sight of the esteemed Lord Austvix.

He was as tall a man as I'd ever seen. Even though he wasn't standing, I could tell by the way he dwarfed his horse and the others around him. I was accustomed to seeing warriors—even great ones—so I didn't understand the immediate flare of fear that lit in my middle. The way my whole body went rigid like spotted prey at the sight of him.

My tendrils went mad. Scrabbling at the stone behind me, stretching for the back of the alley. Urging me to run.

When Bůk turned to Lord Austvix, I tried to follow my gut. I darted out of the alley, planning to pivot back toward the camp with Bůk distracted.

But while *he* was looking at Lord Austvix, his shadows were not. One caught my ankle, sending me reeling. I fell hard, and the shadow yanked me back, depositing me on my hands and knees at Bůk's feet.

I chanced a look up, expecting Lord Austvix to be somewhat bemused by our squabble, perhaps—but the fury on his face stopped my heart. His cat sat behind him on the saddle, still as a statue, matching his glare.

Lord Austvix spoke to Bůk, but his eyes never left mine. "Is this some sort of coup attempt, demon?"

I breathed. Once, twice. Waiting for Bůk to answer the nonsensical question.

Finally, he did. He sounded every bit as perplexed as I felt. He drew out the words, like someone audibly holding up their hands in surrender. "No, my lord?"

"Then take that fucking collar off my sister."

Chapter 34
Ero: O Brother, Who Art Thou?

"I guess you could say my brother and I got off to a rocky start." - an excerpt from the journal of Eroithiel von Dua, 1313 B.A., the night before the Great War

The wind rushed in my ears.

That word pulsed like a drumbeat.

Sister.

Bůk pulled me to my feet. His erratic emotions stained the air. I took several labored breaths, trying to find the words to ask every question Austvix's statement begged.

Sister.

Who was our father? How could he be sure who I was? Why did he look so hostile?

In retrospect, I should have given more weight to the last question—but it was only an afterthought. I was too curious to be properly afraid. Nevermind the gargantuan warlord glowering down at me.

Sister.

Bůk's fingers brushed the back of my neck, gently curling into the collar. His warm breath tickled my ear. The moment hung heavy, frozen frame by frame. His shadows enveloped my tendrils. His thumbs grazed my skin. The spicy cinnamon flavor of his angst tickled my lips.

"Run," he breathed.

The latch clicked.

The collar fell.

And I...froze.

My body wanted to listen to Bůk. My tendrils strained against me, trying to force me to follow his advice and flee. But I couldn't.

I looked up at Lord Austvix in silent awe.

Sister.

"How—" I started.

And then Lord Austvix's magic washed over me. The assault stole my breath. My tendrils rose to shield me, but for once, they were outmatched. They grappled anyway, writhing against his. But he had more, and they were stronger, and naïve or otherwise, I simply didn't believe my brother would kill me —and I didn't know how to force my magic to fight without that minor motivator.

Bůk's flames flared between us, momentarily forcing our tendrils to rear back. Lord Austvix turned his furious gaze on Bůk.

"No!" I cried. "Please!"

I don't know why I intervened. I'd already seen Bůk die several times. He would have been fine eventually. But at my shout, Lord Austvix's eyes swiveled back to mine. This time, I saw my death there. This time, my tendrils did too.

When his magic came for me, mine erupted. It spilled out

in a flash of scalding energy. It poured into my brother, stronger by every measure than the burst that'd eviscerated Wendlin. Even as it happened, I fought myself. Cried out inside, terrified that I would destroy the brand new family I had only just discovered.

But Lord Austvix didn't falter. The power lashing out of me glanced off him, finding no purchase until it lanced into the half a dozen guards and handful of onlookers around him, who promptly crumpled to the ground.

I stared in stunned silence.

Somehow, he'd deflected my magic, or I had diverted it. Had my panic done this, or had his defenses?

It didn't matter, because I spotted something that made my heart collapse.

Brü.

His blood painted the cobblestones. A steady bloom of crimson saturated his shirt and dribbled down his neck.

So many wounds.

In a flash, the world resumed its speed. Shouts and cries echoed around us, calls for help. But there wasn't time. Fading heartbeats all around me played their music out of sync, threatening to disappear.

"No," I panted, falling next to Brü, already reaching for my lute.

You will let your friends down, and worse—you will betray your own blood.

I fumbled with the strings, forcing a chord, all the while expecting a final blow to level me from behind. I'd been no match for Austvix during our brief struggle, and my burst of magic had hurt everyone *but* him. If he wanted to kill me, now was the time.

I stared at Brü's pale face. *I'd* done this. My magic. My power. My failure to harness what the Fates had given me.

I played, forcing everything else—the fear, the guilt, the anger—from my mind to focus on the singular task of knitting Brü's wounds back together, of shepherding the blood that remained in his veins along their vital path to keep him alive.

When no killing blow took me, I let the heal wash out to the others. No, I didn't know them. But their pulses cried out for help just as loudly as Brü's—and I didn't want to be the one responsible for their deaths. It gave me the same sickening feeling I'd had with Wendlin. I didn't want to kill *anyone.*

Hot tears stained my cheeks. Only when the first verse finished did I chance a break long enough to cry out, "Get Aelith!"

I hoped one of the faceless onlookers would have the wherewithal to listen. And one must have—or perhaps she'd already been on her way. Midway through my third verse, a wave of cool aquatic serenity washed over me. It beat back some of my panic even as it finished the job I couldn't quite do alone.

Brü's eyes blinked open. He took a shaky breath, but Aelith was already there, scooping his head into her lap, burying her face in his bloody shirt—the scene from mere days ago in reverse. The pitch of her panic told me how close a thing it'd been. And I wanted to dissolve into the cobblestones right there.

Hands pulled me back. Bůk's hands. I turned—ready to collapse mindlessly into him, frightened and overwhelmed with the need for one safe place. Desperate for it to be him.

"I'm sorry, kitten," he whispered.

His dampeners clapped onto my wrists.

My magic receded in a cold rush. It was just as bad as the

first time, in the woods. But worse now, because it was a betrayal.

The pain in Bůk's eyes was nothing to my fractured heart. I'd *almost* believed he felt something human for me. Almost. And maybe he had. Enough to warn me. Enough to tell me to save myself. But not enough to stand with me now.

I looked around at the crowd—hoping, I suppose, for one friendly face. Several of the guards were getting to their feet, some combination of my heal and Aelith's having stabilized them. Two still weren't moving. Several weapons were drawn, but all eyes were on Lord Austvix—waiting for orders.

Lord Austvix strode forward, the heat gone from his eyes. He was all business and no fury now. He took the chain connecting my cuffs from Bůk.

"Wait for my summons, demon. I have questions about how all of this came to be." His brow furrowed, as if he might ask some of those questions now after all, but then with a small shake of his head, he said, "Nevertheless, I suppose you've done well. You'll have your reward soon enough."

The way he jangled the chain when he said that last bit made a wave of disgust rise in my chest. Did he mean to *gift* me to Bůk? His own sister? Nevermind that Bůk had already claimed me in every way that mattered. Austvix didn't know that. And how fucking *dare* he? So much for Brü's stories of his chaotic goodness.

Austvix turned. The crowd immediately parted to allow us to pass. I looked back at Brü. His eyes were closed again, his cheek resting against Aelith's stomach. She met my gaze instead. There was something unreadable in her expression. Her golden eyes were tired and sad and full. Of questions? Accusations? My heart ached.

I couldn't exactly stay and talk it out. My alleged brother tugged once on the chain, and I stumbled after him.

No one followed.

I had to move fast to keep up with his grand strides. My emotions ricocheted all over the place. Guilt, fury, curiosity. It was a whole mess. But we hadn't gone too far before I found my tongue again.

"Lord Austvix?" I said tentatively. I had several pressing questions for this man.

"I can silence you," he said coldly. "Or you can silence yourself. Your choice."

He didn't look down at me. His focus remained straight ahead, moving us down the street toward gods only knew what. I had no doubt that he both could and would take my voice away if he wanted to. That didn't shut me up, of course, but I recognized the need to choose my next words carefully.

We rounded a corner and came to a halt at a gate. It led into a tunnel that'd been carved into the stone face of the mountain. A guard opened the gate, and Austvix pulled me through. It clanged shut behind us.

The dark swallowed us. All the fear that Aelith's heal had tamped down swelled again—and then redoubled when I realized we were in a dungeon. Cells on either side stood empty and waiting. A dank, mildewy smell wafted from them.

Time was up. I had to ask. It was now or never.

"Who is our father?"

Austvix stopped then. He finally looked down at me. His expression was a hybrid of disgust and disbelief. I tried to see in his face what Brü saw, what Aelith and the others believed that made them speak so highly of him. His face had a grand, leaderlike quality. A powerful jaw, electric eyes. The air of someone who had his life decidedly in order. Enviable. In that half second, I thought I could imagine *their* Austvix. Even if it was just a fantasy—a story painted over reality.

Then, one corner of his lips quirked down in a clear dismissal. He wasn't going to answer me.

"Please," I whispered. I sucked in a breath before he could stop me. "I've been looking for him—for you—my whole life."

Austvix's eyes went heavy with put-upon irritation. As if I were a chore he'd been tasked with, and someone else—anyone else—ought to have handled it before it fell at his feet.

He sighed.

"Our father is Haz, the God of War and Peace himself," Austvix said with an unmistakable note of acerbic distaste. The very same way I might have sounded revealing my mother's identity, if pressed.

I didn't have long to question that, though, because as he turned away, he added, "And you'll get to meet the rest of our siblings in a few days. They'll be invited to your execution."

Chapter 35
Bŭk: An Unlikely Alliance

**Bŭk's Personal Code, Item 7.1: Aelith is still
the worst.**

You'll have your reward soon enough.

I stood rooted in place, Austvix's words raising gooseflesh like shadows whispering over raw skin.

My reward.

Ero's soul.

My contract guaranteed that when Austvix killed each of his siblings—the task I was contracted to help bring to fruition—that he would capture and trade their souls to me in exchange for the piece I held of his.

I should be salivating. Beyond the promise of a demigod soul, Ero was the best puzzle I'd ever encountered. Why *wouldn't* I want her in my possession for eternity? A prize that could scratch the itch that lived at the core of my being—that wanted only a worthy challenge to keep it satisfied.

Only I didn't want it.

I wanted *her*. Alive. Here, on this plane, driving me to the edge of madness and then pulling me back again—over and over. Begging me to chase her and fulfill her darkest desires. Lying against me after, content and exhausted.

I watched him drag her away.

I couldn't follow—and I mean that literally. Austvix told me to wait for his summons. Thanks to my contract, an order from him was as good as compulsion. The irony wasn't lost on me. That was why I'd put the dampeners on her to begin with. With one silent gesture from Austvix, I'd betrayed her like it was nothing.

Why couldn't she have just fucking run? There'd been a moment. One breath. She could have gone, and I could have stood between them long enough to give her a chance. But she hadn't.

I picked up the collar. It was still warm, but there was no life in it now. No hum promised to bend another to my will. Until someone donned it again—if that ever happened—it was just an inert accessory.

I looked around me. Brü and Aelith were already gone. The remaining crowd dwindled. No doubt, the story of what happened would saturate the camp in the space of an hour. Fucking humans. The cacophony of their desire to tell, tell, tell echoed in their wake. Not the first hint of concern for the bard, nevermind how they'd all fawned over her at the fire ring, begging for their favorite songs.

I cut a quick path to the woods before I could do something stupid like smite them all.

I should have tied her to my bed the moment I saw the vision. The collar on the street. I could have stopped it if I'd stopped her. It'd just happened too fast. I couldn't compel her because I'd made the vow to Brü. I couldn't have guessed that I would do something like that, because it was a boneheaded move, and I wasn't usually boneheaded. Chalk that one up to Hammond's influence. Again, fucking *humans*.

I scrubbed a hand over my face. Smoke tickled my neck. Behind me, a trail of embers threatened to become a full-blown fire.

Maybe the forest wasn't the best place to feel things.

Maybe running away from the problem wouldn't solve it.

Gritting my teeth, I turned back.

An hour later, I'd come to three separate yet equally irritating conclusions.

First, I couldn't let Austvix kill Ero.

Second, he would suspect subterfuge if I tried to stop him.

Third, and worst of all...I probably needed to talk to Aelith.

I stood outside her hut on the healer's road, appreciating one last moment of peace, knowing that I would inevitably yearn to burn half the camp down in a matter of moments—an unavoidable side effect of dealing with the elemental.

I tried one last time to think of an alternative plan. Brü would have been preferable. But Brü genuinely seemed to like everyone. He wasn't the strongest candidate for convincing Austvix that my intentions were true. If *Aelith* supported me? Austvix couldn't possibly fail to take note. I needed the surest thing I could get.

The door swung open, nearly knocking me off the stoop. I caught a brief glimpse of Aelith's face before she spotted me. Her jaw was already set, her eyes doing that shiny thing more characteristic of cats than humans. A warning to living things to avoid if they wished to remain living. And again—that was *before* she spotted me.

I took a step back. Dying right then would have been exceedingly inconvenient.

Brü appeared at Aelith's elbow, looking haggard and in dire need of sleep after the friendly fire in the street. His turmoil—always alive and well when Aelith and I met—hit a fever pitch when he noted our squared-off stances. His desire to flee elicited a smirk from me that Aelith *may* have misinterpreted. Her irritation flared into a delicious vintage of rage.

Aelith opened her mouth, but I held up a hand.

"A sound barrier would be ideal," I said, nodding toward the people milling about the street.

Even that mild suggestion stoked Aelith's desire to argue. To her credit, though, she didn't. After all, if she meant to confront Austvix—which I could smell all over her now, thank the Fates—she didn't want half the camp pressing their metaphorical ears to the door. Without a word, she retreated into the hut. Brü gave me a tentative searching look before he followed. I supposed that was my invitation.

Aelith's room was large but modest. As was habit for most of us, her personal items and gear remained packed for quick mobilization. The only items on display were pieces of art that gave the room a bit of flavor most of our quarters lacked and a few tinctures in neatly labeled bottles.

The moment the door closed and the runes glowed golden, promising the privacy I'd asked for, Aelith rounded on me.

"What did Austvix mean when he said you would have your reward?" she demanded without preamble.

"Ero's soul," I answered just as bluntly. And no, I wasn't *enjoying* myself exactly—because I obviously wasn't thrilled with the situation either—but I *did* take some small pleasure in her rippling outrage.

Aelith shot Brü an *"I told you so"* look, and drew her holy symbol from her pocket. As if I were the one to fight. As if she could.

This was why the righteous elemental drove me mad. Why would I have come here to rub my win in her face? My joy in tormenting her abruptly fizzled. If Aelith truly believed that I intended to collect, what must Ero think?

At any rate, the reaction confirmed my suspicion that I would make no progress with Austvix on my own. *He* certainly wouldn't believe that I'd had an attack of conscience. He'd never known me to have one.

"We need to talk to Austvix," I said. "Together."

Aelith's sharp eyes narrowed further still.

"If I do it alone," I went on, the initial irritation I'd felt at the realization creeping back into my tone, "he'll think I'm trying to outmaneuver him."

"And what *are* you doing?" she growled.

I leaned forward, edging into her space as heat crawled predictably up my neck. "As much as it will pain you to hear, elemental, I'm doing the same thing *you're* doing. Trying to keep her alive."

Aelith may have scoffed, but Brü believed me immediately. I didn't have to look at him to know. His desire to run relaxed into a mess of relief, an eagerness to play peacemaker. This was what made him a good leader.

Aelith tightened her grip on the holy symbol. "We don't need your help."

This was what made *her* an abysmal party member.

"You do," I said. "Because Austvix traded me something he

can't afford to lose. He won't change his mind just because you tell him you *like* her."

"He'll change his mind because she's not one of *them*," Aelith spat. For a moment, her hatred of the other warlords blazed even brighter than her hatred of me. Impressive. And then she pressed on with her nonsense. "Austvix isn't one of them either. He's reasonable—and *good*. He'll listen."

I crossed my arms. "Then why didn't you go to him already?"

Color rose in her pale cheeks.

"Enough," Brü said. His tone was pained but still carried authority. We both looked at him. "Bůk, please explain your plan. Aelith...please let him."

I gave her a cantankerous smile.

And then I explained.

We approached Lord Austvix's chambers together with unearned confidence. I suppose we all had the sense that a cause big enough to join Aelith and me was a cause that couldn't fail.

The first part of the plan was simple. I would stand outside. Austvix still hadn't summoned me. Brü and Aelith would convince him to do so.

The door had barely closed behind them when Austvix called out, "For the love of Haz's cursed children, get in here, demon!"

Perplexed both by his exasperation and quick acquiescence, I entered. And the plan immediately went to shit.

For starters, the room was already populated. Hammond, Nigel, and Tavish sat on a bench looking rather sheepish.

It took a moment for me to grasp their shared desire.

They'd come for her too.

Something turned in my gut. I wouldn't call it butterflies. Bats, maybe. They cared about her. Enough to confront a warlord. Maybe we could actually handle this.

"She *will* die," Austvix said—pointedly, as though repeating something he'd already had to explain more times than he cared to. "And you all need to hear that now."

Maybe not.

Several voices spoke at once. Aelith, Nigel, and Brü all fought for the next word. I hung back, taking a moment to assess. Austvix's foul mood tasted of singed roses. He was not a man who was accustomed to being backed into a corner—and he showed the strain of that now. His magic, unlike Ero's chaotic mess of rainbow tendrils, liked to arrange itself behind him in the shape of sharp iridescent wings (like a fucking angel). But now, it writhed around him in a protective shield instead.

"Whatever you think she is—" Aelith said, failing in her battle for calm, but winning the floor against Brü and Nigel, "—she's not. She's not the Huntress. She's not Lady Gwendolyn or Naeve Andarnus."

Another day, seeing Aelith's quiet fury leveled at Austvix so directly might have been pleasurable. But just now, it concerned me.

The golden hue of Austvix's already thin patience darkened by several degrees at the sound of his sisters' names. Pax, who'd been sleeping in the corner, stood, stretched, and padded over to sit at his feet. I watched the feline with trepidation. It was a relatively small creature, but I'd witnessed the damage it could do on more than one occasion.

"I'm sure Eroithiel will be flattered to hear how deeply

she's drawn you all in," Austvix said. "But that *is* what she's done. That's what *we* do. We are godsent. Our wiles—our charm—it's all part of that. We are alluring—"

"Humble, too," I said.

Austvix rounded on me, eyes blazing. "It's not a joke, demon."

"It's a little bit of a joke," I muttered.

He turned to his human audience in frustration. "The Temple Mother prophesied that the seventh sibling would be *my* end—unless I got to her first. Has knowing her for the space of *one* expedition won you all so thoroughly that you've changed sides? Do you forget our purpose here? Am I looking at the seed of the seventh faction in *my* war room?"

That hit the mark.

Immediately, conflicting emotions plagued the room. Not a single person present would willingly betray Austvix. Not even for Ero. Well—*I* would, if I had any control over the matter. But I didn't need to share that. I wasn't here because I believed in Austvix's righteous mandate. I was here because he was my path back to power.

"You *did* get to her first," Tavish said, taking advantage of the beat of silence. "She's here, and no harm came to you. The Temple Mother spoke to her, too—and she's been chasing a mirage ever since. My lord, if you would just talk to her..."

Austvix sighed heavily.

"She would fight for you, if you gave her a chance," Brü added.

"She already has," Nigel pointed out.

"She's nice," Hammond said, pounding his meaty fist against the bench for emphasis.

Austvix's desire to tell us all to get the hell out peaked. And then his eyes landed on me again—this time, with a dawning realization. I didn't actually fit in this group. A group that was determined to keep alive someone who he knew I had specific and strong reasons to want dead.

I saw his intentions shift a moment before he spoke. I was about to become his scapegoat. And to my surprise, he was going to out himself in the process. Not what I'd planned—but I would have to adjust.

Austvix tilted his head, ignoring everyone else in the room, holding my gaze. Just as I'd suspected, his defenses were up. Like Aelith, Austvix longed for the morally righteous path. Unlike her, he was willing to use morally questionable means —such as making deals with demons—if he thought doing so would increase his odds of achieving his ends.

"I haven't heard from you, Bůk," he said coolly. "Are you here to argue for my sister as well?"

"Yes," I confirmed.

I might as well have drawn a weapon. His suspicion sharpened acutely.

"You think I should reconsider her execution?" he asked with an uptick in his tone. It was obviously a leading question. We both knew where it was going.

"I do," I said, perfectly willing to play my part.

"And where would that leave me?" he demanded with an acidic *gotcha* in his tone. "Waiting to spend eternity with my soul splintered in your hellchamber?"

No part of my senses managed to evade Aelith's fresh spike of rage. I'd purposely left out this detail when I explained the situation. Only Austvix and I and the Temple Mother who'd overseen our contract knew about it. We were the only ones who *needed* to.

Everyone stared at us.

"Rewrite the contract," I said evenly. "Take her out of it."

Austvix glowered. More certain than ever that this was a coup, though he couldn't quite figure out how. But I'd already fractured his soul for collateral. Of course he didn't expect me to give up something for nothing now.

"Why?" he demanded.

"Because I'm not going to be the reason you hurt her," I said. My voice rose in volume without my explicit consent. "Because you've granted everyone from a Hell-fled demon to a *hideous* water elemental safe haven. Because Ero has spent her whole life looking for her family, and this is a pretty perverse twist—even from the perspective of someone whose existence was designed for torment."

Silence hung in the air for one long beat.

"He's in love with her," Aelith said. She sounded perplexed, as if just putting that together for herself.

Austvix and I both shot her disgusted looks. Although technically, I suppose she was being helpful.

Brü, Hammond, and Nigel looked away. Tavish might have too. He was suddenly imperceptible.

The thing about Lord Austvix was, he wasn't a typical human. He was reasonable. But some dilemmas, even reason couldn't fix. Although my inner beast purred at the flavor of his turmoil, the uncomfortable strings in my chest tightened— because I wasn't sure we were winning this battle.

"Thank you all," Lord Austvix said, his tone painstakingly formal and freshly removed. "You may go now."

No one moved. Except for Hammond, who stood. But he sat back down when he noticed everyone else's stony expressions.

Austvix nodded the nod of a man on the unpopular side of an argument. The nod of a man who had resigned himself to selecting the best of two terrible options in the face of a mob who would tear him apart either way. The trouble was, I didn't know *which* option he'd chosen.

"I'm going to have a word with my demon," he said pointedly to the others. "And then I will speak with my sister. You can all consider your concerns heard. Do *not* question me again."

This time, everyone stood. Except for Hammond, who stood only after looking around to assure himself that everyone else had.

They all filed out. Their sideways glances at the uncertain outcome mirrored my discomfort.

Lord Austvix sagged when the door shut. Absent the others, I more clearly tasted the heavy burden he grappled with. It wasn't just about Ero. The losses to our party, the threat of battles to come, the murky sense that the Fates were toying with us—all tugged at him. Death by a thousand cuts.

"Tell me how you found her," he said. "Just the important parts."

So, I told him. I told him about the moment I first saw her. The pathetic band of fringe Huntress factionites, and the way she'd hidden herself among them with that iridescent magic and a weapon I knew didn't belong. I told him of the slaughter, of hearing her accent, of my fear that letting her slip away would be detrimental. That explained the collar. I told him about the ambush, the Huntress's clever play, Ero's song, my resulting madness, and eventually the siphon.

I skipped a few things. The fucking, mostly. It seemed prudent to skip that. Luckily, he hadn't bid me tell him *everything*.

By the time I finished, Lord Austvix existed somewhere far away mentally. He did that sometimes. His flavor hollowed, like icemelt in an empty drink.

"I see," was all he said. And then, coming somewhat back to himself, he met my eyes. "You will not speak to Eroithiel again, Bůk. However this goes—*that* will not happen."

Just like that, my little group's half victory turned to ash in my mouth.

The order was not brotherly concern for the bard. That much was clear. Austvix's fear that I would still find a way to use her to outplay him—the way he'd been so certain I had when he saw that collar on her throat—remained palpable. She was his foretold end. I was the choice he tortured himself for making every night. Of course he expected his own downfall to involve me.

"You're dismissed," Austvix said.

The fragments of protest died on my tongue.

I left.

Chapter 36
Ero: Kitten

"Family is complicated." - an excerpt from the journal of Eroithiel von Dua, 1313 B.A., the beginning of the Great War

I sat in the dungeon questioning my life choices.

I started with my birth—which wasn't *technically* my choice—and cataloged every questionable decision up to and since the foolish idea to seek my father. Why couldn't I have just been content playing at pubs? Why did I need to meet a man who'd never wanted me to begin with?

The god. The god who'd never wanted me to begin with.

Haz's left—

Nope. Even curses were tainted now.

A huge iron key glittered mockingly on the wall across from my cell. I suspected it didn't actually go to anything, that it was a mere ornament to spark false hope. Just like the Temple Mother's advice. Not that it mattered either way. My tendrils were numb but for the occasional painful spark of protest when they grazed the dampeners. I couldn't have reached the key even if I'd tried.

I curled on my side, cheek pressed to the dirty stone floor. It wasn't night yet, but I was sick of being awake. There was no safe place to go in my mind. Not music—which felt hollow without magic. Not Bůk—whose murmured apology still felt like glass shards in my chest. Not even my friends—who I suspected couldn't be called that anymore since my magic had nearly ended Brü. I hugged my lute to my chest and closed my eyes.

A rustle sounded in the shadows. I winced. I'd heard it off and on since Austvix left—a rat digging for a scrap of food, perhaps. Not that I'd had any evidence that prisoners here *got* food. Breakfast and lunchtime had both passed in silence, and my stomach remained empty.

The scrabbling sound came again, only this time it was followed by a faint *mew.*

I bolted upright just as the tiny creature triumphed. It burst into the cell next to mine from a crack between the wall and the floor. The kitten was Lord Austvix's Pax in miniature—no bigger than a rat, but just as vibrantly white save for a single black ear.

"Pspsps," I whispered.

In general, I wasn't fond of cute creatures. Particularly since the infestation of shifter moles in Bęrk. (Trust me, once you've reached out to pet a puppy and barely escaped with your fingers, you start to see *cute* quite differently.) But this tiny beast had the same magnetic draw as the one from the alley— minus the threatening yowl.

The kitten trounced through the bars without hesitation and pressed its cold wet nose to my finger.

A tear cut a hot trail down my cheek as I scooped the little guy up. Like he was mine. Like he'd always been mine. Why was I *crying?* For fuck's sake.

I cradled him to my chest and choked back a sob as his warm body vibrated with pleasure.

I supposed there were worse things to encounter on the path to imminent death than a kitten. One last moment of comfort was nothing to sniff at.

As if to provide a direct and immediate answer to that thought, a door hinge shrieked. The kitten pierced my chest with its razor-sharp claws. I'd like to say I was brave and valiant and jumped to meet my captor with vigor—but in actuality my terror tasted like acid, I trembled, and I clung to the kitten as if it were my final lifeline.

Lord Austvix strode into the tunnel, framed by the dying sunlight. Not a guard in sight.

He was an objectively beautiful man. All hard lines and pleasing colors. I had an absurd desire to bargain for my life by promising to write him a song. *I can make them love you. It wouldn't even be hard.*

But they already loved him, didn't they? A pang of jealousy tickled my gut.

"Is he yours?" Austvix asked, jutting his chin at the kitten as he approached my cell.

I looked down at the little beast to escape his piercing gaze.

"Yes," I said. Even though I'd only just met the kitten, it felt true.

Austvix sniffed. On cue, Pax appeared from nowhere and curled around his feet. I stole a glance at the intimidating feline. He, in turn, stared assessingly at the kitten and ignored me entirely.

Austvix leaned his forearm on the bars, looking down at

me. Millennia passed before he spoke, and when he did, he sounded uncertain. "You've made friends here."

I swallowed. *Not many,* I thought petulantly. Bůk was no friend. And the others—well, they would probably be relieved if Austvix killed me before I could accidentally cook any of them.

The intensity of Austvix's stare won. I looked up, meeting his eyes. Instead of answering his non-question, I asked, "Are you going to tell me why you want to kill me?"

He tilted his head. I had the distinct sense he was staring *into* me, just like the Temple Mother. My tendrils rippled with electric awareness—but their power remained out of reach.

"Because I have to," he said.

I stared. What the fuck did *that* mean?

"One of Haz's children *will* eventually take the Queensdale throne." He looped one finger around the bar and ran his silver rings down the metal in a musical stroke. "But not before the others die. It's our birthright and our curse."

For one blissful second, I was too angry to be afraid. From my mother's palace—where I'd been born a pariah—to *this?* Six siblings. Every dream I'd ever had come true. And they all wanted to kill each other, starting with me.

"Did Haz tell you that?" I asked. "That you have to kill the others? Or is that something you all came to on your own?"

Austvix smiled patiently. "The Fates aren't always clear, but they were in this case."

"Fuck the Fates," I muttered.

To my surprise, Austvix dipped his chin in agreement. "We share that sentiment. I hope it brings you comfort to know that you won't have to spend your next hundred years at war for a throne you almost certainly couldn't win. And that when I kill you, there won't be any games—no spectacle. I'll make it quick."

My fury blossomed into something prickly and hard. "It would bring me comfort if you—you know, *didn't* kill me."

He met my anger with a ceaseless calm. I detected sadness in his stupid gray eyes. And somehow, that made him much worse than a villain I could simply hate.

"I don't want to rule anything," I said. "I don't want a throne. Ever. I want a family. If you kill me, I hope that haunts you."

And that was true. No part of me wanted to be in charge— to make choices that would affect millions of people. To sit on a throne and demand loyalty and know that whole lives and livelihoods would change in a series of unfortunate ripples at my every edict. I wanted to wander. I wanted to meet people and bring them a tiny bit of joy and hope they remembered my name. Even if that sounded too small to say aloud.

I hunched over, pressing a shaky kiss to the kitten's head. What if I died before I got to name him?

"You don't want to rule *yet,*" Austvix challenged.

There was no heat in the words, but his wary judgement made me bristle. With barely any provocation, I gritted my teeth and pulled myself to my feet. "Okay, *Lord* Austvix. What exactly makes you the most worthy leader among us?"

The bite in my own words bolstered me. I'd forgotten how *tall* Austvix was, and I still had to look up to glare at him, but doing so felt a bit righteous.

His sad smile grew cold. "Not a thing beyond the process of elimination, *Princess.*"

I blanched. That fucking empty title.

"If you get to meet the others," he said, shrugging, "you

might understand. But it's nothing to me either way. I don't need you to like me."

"I want to," I said, sounding very much like I wanted the opposite—but I pressed on before I lost the chance. "Brü told me why he joined the Fated. You sounded almost worth knowing."

He snorted. "Brü flatters me, I'm sure."

The familiar sound of steel on leather raised my hackles again. Austvix pulled a long blade from its scabbard. The metal gleamed black with an oily finish. But it was the overwhelming terror I felt immediately upon seeing the blade that shook me. It had to be an enchantment. I was afraid to die, but I didn't think Austvix meant to strike *now*. No, the sword itself was the problem. It whispered rhythms that made my hands shake. It gleamed in the shadows as if it belonged to them and yearned to get out.

The kitten writhed against me. I realized too late that he was affected too. He jumped to the ground, and a fresh fear choked me. That he would run and I would never see him again. Instead, he cowered behind me.

Austvix nodded to himself. "Show me yours."

I barely heard him. My mind was still screaming at me to run, apparently forgetting that I was locked in a cage and could not. Thoughtlessly, I fumbled for my knife and tossed it at his feet.

Austvix pursed his lips like I was being intentionally—rather than accidentally—stupid. "Your blessed weapon, Eroithiel."

His expression was neither cruel nor friendly. He seemed... curious. And the tiny shred of self-preservation inside me begged me to latch onto that.

I pulled the bow from my satchel and extended it toward the bars.

Austvix reeled back, putting two full strides between us. I thought briefly that he was joking. He was not. His face twisted in a way that told me my weapon affected him as much as his affected me.

Pax hissed.

"Sorry," I said—mostly to the cat. I pulled the bow back.

Austvix looked at it warily from where he stood. He seemed to be trying to work something out in his mind. "Who did you kill with it?"

"Nobody. I didn't even think I could shoot it until a couple of days ago. I shot a tree."

Absently, I pulled the sheath of arrows out. Austvix's expression darkened further.

"Then whose soul is in there?"

I stared. "What?"

He grimaced and took two painful-looking steps forward to return to his place by the bars. He reached through, plucking one arrow from my sheath. He held it with two fingers as if it were a flesh-eating slug. "You killed *someone.*"

I blinked. Could Wendlin's soul be in there?

And then it hit me.

"When we were ambushed," I said, "one of your men had my bow. I found him with the arrow in his eye."

Would Austvix believe that? Or would he think I'd killed one of my fellow soldiers on the sly and blamed it on the bow?

Luckily, he only nodded to himself like what I said made sense.

"Did you say his soul is *in there?*" I pressed, more than a little horrified.

He replaced the arrow and looked at me again. The tiny divot between his eyes deepened.

"If you're going to kill me anyway, you might as well satisfy my curiosity first," I pointed out.

He made a face as if I'd finally made a point he would accept. "What do you want to know?"

"Start talking, and I'll tell you when to stop?"

His lips quirked. "Well, our father has a sense of humor. We all have these." He ran his finger along his blade, and I swear I could feel it in my spine. "They're designed to steal souls."

I blanched.

"Specifically each other's souls, but the weapons aren't picky. They'll take what they can get."

I carefully set the sheath and the bow on the ground. The kitten took the opportunity to dart back into my hands, and I lifted him to my chest again.

"What about the broken staff?" I asked, holding the furball firmly with one palm as I fished the rune-covered wood out of my satchel. "Your Temple Mother gave it to me."

Austvix looked at me like I'd just exposed my privates.

"If one manages to convince our illustrious siblings to *choose* a ruler," he said, his tone making it clear he thought there was a better chance of convincing the world to duplicate itself so we each had our own copy to rule, "then the staff will *allegedly* help the chosen one keep the peace. A powerful but ultimately useless object. I wouldn't keep it where the others could reach it unless you're offering it to them, though."

I considered that. Haz was the god of war *and* peace. Ostensibly, then, he'd given his children a choice. *They'd* chosen war. With all the righteous certainty of one who'd never met most of them, I blamed them pretty harshly for that.

"If you all want to kill each other, why would they agree to come here for my execution?"

"We signed a treaty," he said. "It's to everyone's advantage to know who's left on the field. So, if one of us dies in battle, the victor is supposed to host a peaceful visitation. Likewise, if one of us captures another, the victor is required to allow the others to witness the execution—so long as they agree to a peaceful visit."

"How civilized."

If my sarcasm bothered him, he didn't show it.

"I'm sorry it has to be this way," he said. "Truly. You're the least awful sister I've met. But I have thousands of people relying on me. I won't gamble with their safety."

Hopelessness settled deep in my gut. We were cordial—but we were still at an impasse. How was I supposed to argue with him? I didn't want to die. But that wasn't good enough, was it? If what he said was true—if what the *Temple Mother* said was true—he was making the right call. And the right call was *my* death.

Once again, my eyes burned.

What was the point of this? My existence? My life? My death? Why had Haz bothered with me if none of it meant anything?

"Well, thank you for explaining, I suppose," I said listlessly, ready to turn away again.

The screech of the door stopped me. Footsteps pounded on the stone floor.

"Sir—"

"I told you I wasn't to be disturbed," Austvix said in a tone that brooked no argument.

"The Huntress," the soldier panted. "The Huntress approaches."

I turned in time to see Austvix go pale.

"How long?" Austvix asked.

"Sir, they're already at the pass. We have an hour at most before they reach the gate."

"An *hour?* Where are our scouts?"

Even in the heat of the moment, I noticed the way the soldier pressed forward. In my mother's court, the messenger would have cowered—stumbled back—prepared to flee. Because she would have punished him. Why did it make my insides ache to know my brother was *better* than her? And yet, he was just as determined to be rid of me.

"Dead, sir," the man hissed. "Huntress traitors came to warn us. Our riders rode out to confirm. We wouldn't have known at all otherwise."

"How many did she bring?" Austvix demanded.

The soldier didn't need to say the answer aloud. Even I saw it in his terrified eyes. "My lord, it appears to be the whole faction."

Austvix's mouth settled into a grim line. "Then the Great War is here."

Chapter 37
Ero: A Leap of Faith

"Fuck the Fates." - an excerpt from the journal of Eroithiel von Dua, 1313 B.A., the beginning of the Great War

I shivered at Austvix's words.

The "Great War" was supposed to be a nebulous threat that existed in some distant future we never quite reached. It wasn't supposed to happen *now*. It certainly wasn't supposed to happen to *me*.

Austvix slid his sword back into its sheath.

I sagged. The immediate relief from its absence washed over me, leeching tension from every muscle—even with the threat of imminent battle hanging overhead.

And then Austvix turned away. He was about to be out of my reach, possibly for good.

I sucked in a breath. I couldn't leave it like that. I shoved my bow and arrows back into my satchel, knowing Austvix would feel the same surge of relief I had. And I took advantage. Before he could step away, I reached through the bars and grabbed him.

He froze.

If his magic was anything like mine—and I hoped it was—the fact that it hadn't lashed out was a good sign.

"Let me fight," I demanded.

His eyes were already distant. One foot here, one on the battlefield. He had a hell of a lot more to worry about than a sister he already planned to kill. Yet still, he hesitated.

"Two against one," I whispered, tightening my grip. "I won't take my bow. Just let me play for you—and the others. *Please.* I need them to survive this too."

The waiting officer bounced on his heels. We didn't have time to waste. Not even these few seconds. I knew that. If Austvix said no, I couldn't press him without risking my friends' safety further.

"Fuck the Fates," I growled. "We decide, and I want *you* to win. Let me help."

I thrust my piece of the holy staff through the bars. The only offering I had. Perhaps it was a meaningless gesture, considering we were on the precipice of a bloody death. Considering we were already entering the war, and peace seemed far out of reach. But the leap of faith felt right.

Austvix stared at it for a long moment. He didn't take it. "Bring your bow," he groused. "But if you get a clear shot at Contessa—swear to me you'll *take it.*"

My breath stuck in my throat. He wanted me to swear—not that I *wouldn't* turn on him—but that I would shoot a sister I'd never met.

I tried to make quick work of justifying it. Clinging to crumbs. Brü's story about the Huntress. The fact that the rancid siphon served her, and she let him. But even if it didn't paint a *glowing* picture, it didn't mean I wanted her dead.

With a sigh, Austvix pulled his arm from my grasp.

A desperate hiss escaped me. *No.* It wasn't a choice between my sister's life and her death. It was a choice between Austvix and standing on my own—being the youngest and only factionless sibling in a war I never asked for. Now wasn't the time for neutrality.

"I swear," I said.

He'd already taken two steps away, but a flick of his wrist opened the lock on my cell.

He was letting me go. He was letting me *fight.*

"Keep up," he said. "The demon has the key to the cuffs."

He didn't need to tell me twice. I slung my satchel over my shoulder, struggling a bit with the kitten as I did so. I whispered a frantic "Stay here, baby."

"He won't," Austvix said impatiently over his shoulder. "And he can look out for himself. He's not entirely a cat."

I blinked.

Austvix was already halfway to the mouth of the cave, Pax at his heels. My new furry friend wriggled out of my grasp and bounded after his elder. Something akin to horror bloomed, even as my heart melted at the sight. If not "entirely" a cat, what *was* he?

The gate screeched as Austvix wrenched it open. Right. Questions about my beast could wait. I lurched after my brother before the gate could close and lock me in again.

The kitten—or *whatever the fuck it was*—fell in at Pax's side.

"Troop status," Austvix demanded of the officer.

"Mustering," he replied, his relief at having Austvix snap into leader mode palpable.

"Specialty forces?"

"By the gates."

"Ten minutes," Austvix said. "Leadership to the square, battle formations."

The officer saluted and took off at a sprint. Austvix caught my shoulder, steering me sharply toward the gates.

"If we survive this," Austvix said, "we talk terms. I want to trust you—"

"Likewise," I said quickly.

"—but I don't."

"Same."

Without slowing at all, we exchanged uncertain looks. When I faced forward again, I saw them all. Brü—with Aelith's arms around his neck, her lips pressed to his ear. Hammond, Nigel, Tavish, and Flər with their heads bent together, talking intently. And Bůk. Grim and standing apart from the others, as usual.

Other small clusters of soldiers waited nearby, but Austvix marched directly to my people.

Two white blurs shot ahead of us, Pax in the lead with Lyric —a name I suddenly knew, rather than chose—hot on his paws.

Austvix stopped next to Brü. "Take the bard. Return her to the cells when you're finished. Fire wall in the moat, two layers deep—three if there's time. Angle them to the gate."

"Yes, sir," Brü said.

And then Austvix was gone, giving more orders and winding his way back toward the square.

There was one pregnant beat of silence. Then everyone moved at once. Well...almost everyone. Aelith's arms encircled my neck. Brü gripped my shoulder. Hammond clapped his axe blade with a thundering twang, muttering, "told ya I helped" to Nigel, who shook his head and gave me a little salute. I caught

Tavish's face from the corner of my eye—and almost let my attention slide right past him—but caught it and forced myself to stare instead. He laughed.

Only Flər and Bŭk hung back. Flər pointedly sharpened his blade, his expression pinched with disgust. That didn't surprise me. Bŭk's stony silence did. He held the key to my cuffs out to Brü, refusing to meet my eyes.

"Tell the bard to play," Bŭk said. "We can hit four or five layers if the music is right."

Despite the warm reception from the rest of the party, my stomach hollowed at his chilly words. As if to punctuate them, a frigid breeze emanated from Bŭk. Was he *mad* at me? Now? I should be mad at *him*. He'd handed me over to my brother for slaughter. How dare he act like *I'd* done something wrong.

Brü unlocked the cuffs and tossed them to Bŭk. Aelith planted a kiss on my cheek, temporarily drawing my attention away from my demon problem. I looked into her watery eyes and let the calm confidence she pushed into me take root. That, coupled with the immense relief as my tendrils finally roared back to life, made my power hum with anticipation.

Forget Bŭk's sour mood.

We had a battle to win.

I squeezed Aelith tight before she released me to plant a huge kiss on Brü's lips—which Hammond gave a raucous cheer. Then she loped off to find her place in the formation.

I grabbed my lute.

I didn't need to be told to play. I would have with or without Bŭk's permission, because I had something new to prove. Namely, that I was a sister worth keeping alive.

We rode through the gates toward the danger, the Fated's first line of defense. My nerves grew with each step, but so did the feeling of invulnerability. I was...half a god, right? That had to mean something. That had to—

I promptly tripped over a tree root and crashed into Hammond's back.

Brü saved me from the ribbing that might've fetched by choosing that moment to explain the plan. Our team would lay a wall of fire in the moat surrounding the camp. Tavish and Nigel would watch the pass for the first sign of the Huntress faction to give us time to get back to the gate. Flər would conjure whatever enchanted traps he had time to set. Hammond would clear fallen trees and other forest debris that might help the enemy cross the wall of flame. And Bůk and I—well, everyone knew our jobs.

I'd barely struck my first note when Bůk abandoned any illusions of humanity. His shadow doubled and then tripled, spreading in all directions to blanket the forest floor in unnatural darkness. And then his body burst into flames.

I didn't know what they meant by "layers," but I played like I'd never played before. I didn't *ask* my magic to join me. I pulled it into the strings. Bůk shot into the night, filling the barren moat with flame. He moved so fast I made a ridiculous noise—remembering the first time I *thought* I could run from him. He hadn't even tapped into this power to find me.

Absurdly, a pang of sorrow hit. Would he ever chase me again? The breeze tickled the bare skin of my throat.

I swallowed and poured the emotion right back into the music.

It was only minutes before he approached again—from the other direction. He'd run all the way around the perimeter of the mountain base. Sure. Why not? Inhuman speed, bolstered by madness, apparently made that possible. He leapt the gate pass, leaving the road to the camp entry clear, then dashed by us again in a blur of flame and shadow. In his wake, the wall of flame grew higher—a searing red stone base beneath it. On his second and third passes, he ran on the stone, building the wall higher still.

The heat quickly overwhelmed the rest of us. We wended our way toward the main road, where there was still a narrow pocket of cool air.

"Why doesn't he do the road too?" I called to Brü. I couldn't sing anymore anyway, not with the ash in the air. My chords would have to do the job alone.

"He can't hold it long enough," Brü shouted back. "They would just wait him out. We're forcing them to bottleneck."

In the end, Bůk was right about the layers. He was on the fifth lap when Nigel's whistle warned us of the Huntress's approach.

Hammond shoved one final fallen tree into the flames. Flər, Nigel, and Tavish rejoined Brü and me.

And then I saw them.

Thousands of fighters in formation, marching toward us.

"Retreat to the gates!" Brü shouted.

Everyone but Bůk listened. I hesitated—but Brü tugged my elbow, calling over the roar of the hellfire, "He's not coming, Ero. He has to hold the wall."

It made sense. I couldn't even see Bůk's outline inside the ball of flame anymore. Unless he could put himself out on a whim, which I doubted, he couldn't possibly follow us back into the camp. The others ran for the gate.

Words hovered on the tip of my tongue. I needed to say *something* to him. But what?

"Ero, we *need you*," Brü shouted.

I was out of time. I ran after my friends and left Bůk alone with his wall of flame.

Chapter 38
Bůk: The Siphon

Bůk's Personal Code, Item 3, Re-Re-Revised (Final): Thou shalt only be distracted by her.

In the years to come, the songs would call Lord Austvix clever. Say he'd played it all perfectly. That he knew exactly what to do.

The songs would lie.

In that moment, Lord Austvix's death and the deaths of everyone I knew on this mortal plane hung in the balance. Half one way, half the other. Not a soul could have told the outcome.

Brü was right to take Ero away. It made holding the wall of flame harder—but once a fire caught, it liked to burn. Nature was on my side, even if the heavens weren't.

The Huntress's forces rushed the line screaming battle cries. They tried to break through the flames with shields and magic. A few fire adepts even made it—albeit alone. But my flames worked as intended, funneling most of the bodies toward the gate. And the rest? I eviscerated.

I listened to the Fates. Waiting. It was all I *could* do. I couldn't be in two places at once. I couldn't go to Austvix and help him defend the camp, or the Huntress's forces would come from all sides and overwhelm us.

The fighting raged in earnest nearby. Metal clanged on metal. The cadence of archer volleys and the beat of marching drums gratified the void I had where a soul belonged.

My flames burned brighter as I drank it all in. Mortal folly. That's all it was. Ending each other's fragile lives in the name and service of immortal demigods. Those sickly sweet notes of hubris all around strengthened my power almost as effectively as the maddening bardsong had.

It was all going so well.

And then the siphon arrived.

His energy signature cut through the fighters, moving alone with concentrated focus. Toward...Ero.

I faltered. His desires, his intentions? Crystal clear. He wanted to find her and drain her. He'd already had a taste— and now he had her scent like a hound in the hunt. This was his test. His proof to the Huntress that he was worthy of her.

She's not my problem, I reminded myself.

The words rang comically hollow. She was, in fact, my *main* problem. A spray of blinding color in an otherwise dull existence, taunting me with want for something I didn't deserve and couldn't keep. She was the biggest thorn in my side, and the only thing in this world worth having.

Letting her retreat to the gate without so much as a shared look had, perhaps, been my cruelest move yet. Because I knew she still wanted me. It followed her as readily as that unknowable tangle of rainbow light.

But unlike the siphon, I held no delusions about how my obsession with a demigod would end. Her interest? Her desires?

Those would fade as her power grew. When she opened her eyes and saw me for what I was, I would be in a whole new world of trouble. I'd already made nemeses of the devils. The last thing I needed was the ire of a fledgling goddess.

The siphon stopped abruptly.

He'd spotted her.

His elation rose like a beacon, undulating with satisfaction as he turned, cutting a path directly toward her.

Foggy images hung in the air—the Fates' nonsensical whispers taking form. Ero could fight or flee—but she wouldn't. Not with something to prove. Not with her foolish desire to please her brother blinding her to her own doom. He would drain her, take her to the Huntress, and—

Fuck.

I released my hold on the flames.

The moat still burned, but the structure creaked with the promise of inevitable collapse. I wouldn't have long. If the wall fell—if I *let it*—the first Fated casualty would be on my head. And then I would be no good to anyone.

I cut through the night, hunting the hunter. Half a dozen plans formed and died. Madness clawed at me. I'd abandoned my post. The contract was swift. I had to get to him before it got to me.

I poured myself into human form directly in his path. He reared to a stop—confused.

"Do you think the Huntress is really going to be yours?" I taunted. "You know she doesn't put her real lovers on the front line."

The siphon's confusion morphed into a smug grin as recognition dawned. He knew what I was doing. Playing on his emotions. Trying to distract him.

Fine by me. It would still work.

"She wants to keep *them* safe," I pressed. "The one with the pretty red hair? The one who can melt stone?"

His expression didn't falter, but I didn't need visual confirmation to taste his doubt. I wasn't bluffing, and he knew it—because I'd seen the Huntress's other lovers. The night I'd drunk the stars, I'd lived in her head. She didn't give two fucks about him. Or, if she did, she had a lot of additional fucks to give for others. And he wanted them all.

"She sent you after her weakest sibling." I grinned. "Because you're not strong enough to take Austvix—and she doesn't want to get her hands dirty."

The siphon shook his head, laughing as he tried to move around me—determined to tune me out. I stepped into his path again. I met his steely frown with a lazy smile, nonchalant as I landed my killing blow.

"Drain me, and you'll be able to take Austvix instead," I said.

The siphon froze. "And what's in it for you?"

"Freedom." I shrugged.

Now, I *was* bluffing. But slowly, his desires morphed. I had him. Ero's scent faded from his mind's eye, and a thicket of thorny greed took its place.

"I can't act against him," I said. Truth. "But you can use my hellfire to bring him down." Partial truth. It might work—if the elemental didn't seize the opportunity I was about to present to her on a silver platter.

A beat. The siphon's conflict raged. He wanted Austvix—wanted to surprise his lover with a bigger get than she thought possible. Logic told him to move on, but the poor fucking sap couldn't listen.

He lumbered toward me.

I pulled at the Fates. *Show me.* Would Aelith understand

what I was doing—flooding his system with flame to make him her perfect prey? Was she even powerful enough to do what I needed her to do?

Because if not, they were all going to die tonight. And by morning, I would belong to Contessa Urgway.

And my kitten would be lost forever.

Chapter 39
Ero: The Huntress

Bardic Advice from Eroithiel von Dua to future generations: You miss every shot you don't take. And several of the ones you do.

I played until my fingers bled.

All around me, the battle raged. It wasn't like the skirmishes on the road. It wasn't quick, or exhilarating, or romantic. Each heartbeat that winked out—whether Huntress or Fated—snapped fresh threads of my psyche.

"What are you *doing*, Ero?" Brü's strained voice penetrated my fog.

He swung his sword in a masterful arc at a warrior twice his size and as broad as a boulder—but it glanced wide, somehow missing its mark. His adversary had no better luck with the counter. They looked like green initiates in their first sparring match.

My music raged on. I was playing for...peace?

Shit.

That wasn't right. It was supposed to be a battle song. I fumbled with my lute, willing the music to turn. It *fought* me. Not my oft-finicky tendrils, but my own instrument. *That* was a first.

A low, tiny growl rumbled near my foot. Lyric stared at something in the distance. I followed his gaze and caught my first glimpse of the Huntress.

She stood on a plateau halfway down the mountainside, directing her forces with calm assurance. I jammed a looking glass against my eye.

Magnificent silver and black curls spilled over her emerald robes. Her heart-shaped mouth quirked with a confident smile as she issued orders. My *sister*. Stunning. Perfect. *Mine.*

Why couldn't I have them all? Not just Austvix. The others too. Why did it have to be this way?

A massive rock from a trebuchet smashed into the cobblestone path only a few paces away. A volley of arrows followed. One took out the warrior fighting Brü. His own faction's arrow. But it could have just as easily hit Brü.

Right. She was my sister. But she was trying to kill *my* friends.

I couldn't let the Temple Mother's words ring true. I couldn't let them down. Not even for my family.

I dropped the lute to my hip and lifted my bow.

I had the shot.

The Huntress was no more than a dot in the distance, but my bow *purred* with confidence. I drew and released.

My arrow shot into the fray. It sailed past the thousands of fighters engaged in battle, ignoring everything else in favor of its target—the Huntress's heart.

I whipped the looking glass back to my eye.

The Huntress held my arrow in her bare fist, staring

straight at me across the impossible distance. She winked and snapped it in two. Like we were alone in a room together, not standing on opposite sides of a battlefield.

I dropped the looking glass.

Something told me I'd just messed up in a brand new way. Made a choice I couldn't take back. I slid the bow onto my back and lifted my lute again.

But then, the smoking column of flames collapsed. The sight punched me in the gut. *He'll be fine*, I promised myself frantically. *He dies* all *the time.*

Fear snaked through me nonetheless. Without Bůk holding the Huntress's forces back, we were about to be overwhelmed.

I spun to Brü—seeking his guidance. War was *not* my specialty. I didn't like it, I decided right then. I didn't even *want* to be good at it. But I could follow his orders, right? I could *help.*

Brü stood immobile. Pale. Open-mouthed.

Aelith had been coming toward us, but she must have stopped when the wall fell. She stared toward it past Brü, watching something neither of us could see while he reached for her. Horror grew in her eyes.

"No," she breathed.

Her skin took on a blinding sheen, like the sea on a sunny day. It was too bright. I had to look away. When I forced myself to look again, she was no longer Aelith.

She trickled through the grass, under Brü and past him— water come to life. The trickle grew into a wave. Aelith surged high, crashing over the battle and washing half its participants down the mountainside and away from us.

Holy hell.

She was magnificent.

I could have composed a lifetime of ballads about the way it felt for all of those struggles to cease at once. The beauty of the quiet in their wake. But she wasn't finished—and neither was the battle.

Van stalked forward, the only being able to best the current. Flames engulfed him, but they didn't *hurt* him. He smoked, hot with brimstone and fury.

With Bůk.

No.

His eyes glowed with Bůk's madness, Bůk's flames raged around him, and when he lifted his arm to wield at the camp— I abandoned every hope I had.

We were *going* to die.

I'd never seen water angry before that moment. But Aelith rose, a monsoon of rage, to meet the siphon.

The battle Bůk and Aelith had both been aching for since I'd met them played out before my horrified eyes. Steam hissed where they met. Van's face strained with concentration, faltering here and there with madness that only seemed to bolster his strength, even as it fractured his focus. But the water answered every blow, dousing what he lit, throwing him off balance when he moved.

Brü fell against me. I held on to him with numb fingers.

"Ero..." he whispered. Tears welled in his eyes.

"How do we help?" I demanded.

We watched Van break the wave and lurch forward— watched Aelith dissolve and reform before him, sweeping him down once more. The steam and wind and fire swirled until we could no longer see them at all.

Brü's grip dug into me. He rested his forehead against mine.

"We trust them," he said.

So I tried.

It ended eventually. The storm died in an anticlimactic fade, the way storms do, leaving no obviously living beings behind.

We found the siphon's naked body, burnt to a blackened husk.

We didn't find Bůk. We didn't find Aelith.

The Huntress's forces must have retreated. The mountainside was bone-dry and empty, a silent tomb. As our people surged over the fields to seek survivors, catalog the dead, and recover resources, all Brü and I could do was wait. We came to an unspoken agreement not to discuss possibilities. Unfortunately, we *had* to discuss one thing.

"Lord Austvix told me to bring you back to the dungeon after the battle," he said, the apology in his eyes excruciating. "I'm sure—"

"No, you're not," I said, aiming for a light tone and missing it by a healthy margin.

I wanted to believe my brother would come around on the idea of keeping me alive. But neither of us knew for sure. And although I wouldn't share my doubts with Brü, I wasn't feeling great about my role in the battle, either.

What was *wrong* with me? I'd sabotaged our own fighters. I hadn't *meant* to, but that didn't mean it didn't happen. And I'd be lying if I said it was an enormous shock. That it went against my own feelings. It had, in fact, followed my feelings perfectly. I'd wanted the death around me to stop, and I'd stopped it.

Would Austvix know that?

Would he blame me?

I walked arm in arm with Brü until we reached the cage door on the side of the mountain. We shared a wordless exchange. I squeezed his arm, and he squeezed mine back.

The door swung open. Austvix stood waiting. Nerves

tingled in my belly. I hadn't expected him to come right after the battle. Didn't he have two thousand more important things to do? I'd never been a warlord, but it seemed like they would have a lot to do.

"Come in, Ero," he said. Like I'd knocked on his castle door rather than stumbled into his dungeon. He dismissed Brü with a wave.

I stepped inside warily. The cage clanged shut behind me.

"I'm sorry," I said—rushing to speak before Austvix could set the tone and tell me I'd failed to impress him. "I know I'm no good to you. I tried to kill her—and I'll be honest, I don't want to try again. Ever. I don't want to fight my siblings. I don't want any part in this war. I might be useless to you, but I'm *not* dangerous."

"Are you finished?" he asked.

I looked skyward, even angrier with myself for expecting anything different from him. Why shouldn't he treat me with contempt? I'd begged for a place on the field—and I'd let him down, possibly getting Aelith killed in the process.

Only his words weren't contemptuous. He smiled gently and gestured to the cell I'd been in that morning. I turned to walk in—and then stopped.

Miri, Sade, and the three other Huntress women I'd marked in the woods stood watching us.

"They said you saved them?" Austvix said.

"I…" I grappled with that wording. *Saved* was a pretty strong term for what I'd done. "I didn't let Bůk cook them?"

Austvix nodded. "Well, they came to warn us about the Huntress's approach."

I stared.

Austvix gave me a moment to do the math. No, I hadn't killed the siphon. No, I hadn't shot the Huntress. Hell, I hadn't even played my battle song correctly. But in a small way, I *had* saved his ass. If you carried the five and squinted a bit.

"Contessa retreated to lick her wounds," Austvix said. "We'll do the same. And Ero?"

I braced myself.

"I want you on my side."

My brother clearly did not expect me to throw myself into his arms at that simple statement. Or ever.

But that was his problem.

I smashed my face into his chest and held on tight.

Chapter 40
Ero: When Turnabout Is Fair Play

"They say all is fair in love and war, and what I have with Bůk is usually one or the other." - an excerpt from the journal of Eroithiel von Dua, 1314 B.A., during the Great War

It took Aelith weeks to reform, but it only took Brü two days to find signs of life. A jar of water that was—I guess *her*—glowed for him. He promised she would be alright upon seeing that, and I accepted it.

I had no such premonition about Bůk.

In fact, Bůk returned to the camp in total silence much sooner than Aelith. I was among the last to find out. He'd already been back for two days when Hammond mentioned him. At my emotional response, Hammond showed his unique brand of confusion at the fact that I hadn't known.

Bůk never came to me.

So I never went to him.

We were petulant children in a standoff. Forces in a power struggle that'd been derailed.

I spent my days talking with my brother—when he had time —and reading his war journals when he didn't. There was so much to learn. Our "cats," for example, were—as he'd mentioned —not *entirely* cats. Much like our magic, the beasts were soul-paired. Lyric really *was* mine. And not just because I'd claimed him. I nuzzled him now, at least somewhat confident doing so was safe. Apparently, he'd been there since the moment I'd received the broken peace staff at the temple, completing my passage into demigoddery—demigoddessness? Whatever. The little guy just hadn't gotten his feet under him in time to catch me.

After a lifetime of searching for answers, those weeks felt like my due.

And then one morning, I stepped out of my little hut and watched Brü pick up a very fragile, very pale Aelith to crush against his chest. He spun her, and even though her laugh was a mere echo of what it had been, she was *there*. Alive.

Whether it was that sight that made me shiver or the icy breeze that followed, I looked away from them briefly—just long enough to see Bůk's back disappear into a shadow.

I'd be lying if I said he hadn't been on my mind. That I didn't fall asleep every night replaying his dark words, his forbidden touches, in a torturous loop. Pretending I still wore his collar, and imagining what he would tell me to do. Not that any of that was very effective bedtime story material. I rarely managed to fall asleep before dawn.

I traced the brand on my thigh. A lump formed in my throat. For someone who'd insisted so vehemently that I *belonged* to him, he'd sure given me up quickly. Witnessing Brü and Aelith's bliss—which, I reminded myself, wasn't even what I wanted—made his chilly abandonment chafe all the more.

Fearing that I could only bring the reunion down, I silently retreated to give the lovers their moment.

Don't worry. I didn't sulk for long.

Three nights later, I left Aelith's room and walked through the moonlit camp with a bounce in my step.

Because Bůk wasn't going to get the last word.

The demon who'd found me, collared me, claimed me, betrayed me, saved me, and then had the audacity to pretend I'd never existed—had another thing coming if he thought this was over.

He wouldn't get a chance to explain himself, either. I was done begging for answers. He'd had time.

I heard his heavy breathing through the door. Not quite a snore. Just a deep, unshakable sleep. If ever there was one thing I could count on—it was Bůk's heavy sleep.

I reached into my satchel and took out the things I would need.

Even though his door whined on its hinges, Bůk didn't stir. I poured the powder I'd acquired from Tavish onto the floor just inside the room. My tendrils stirred it into the air. For a moment, it glittered unassumingly.

Abandoned knitting projects and carved figurines strewn about the room spoke of Bůk's most recent journey back to sanity. I tried not to think about who or what else he might have turned to for help.

I approached the bed and frowned down at him, experiencing one singular moment of hesitation. What if everything that'd happened between us really *had* just been Bůk's deep investment in fulfilling his contract with my brother? What if he never actually *wanted* me and he'd removed me from the contract only to maintain peace with Brü and the others? What if what I was about to do was the crazy thing?

Then, I spotted the collar. It stuck out from beneath his pillow, hanging loosely in one huge hand.

I traced the brand on my thigh again.

No, I wouldn't let doubt stand in the way. He *wanted* me—and I would make sure he choked on that desire.

I pulled my Fated-issue nameplate from my pocket. It glistened with imbued magic. Not much. Just enough to freeze the holy water coating my name.

In one quick motion, I mounted Bůk, sitting on his bare burning abs with my knees on either side of him. His eyes popped open. But he couldn't move, because my tendrils lit the powder in the air—and the air solidified.

In the last second before we were frozen in place, I shoved my nameplate against his chest. Right over his heart.

He tried to shout, but the powdery vacuum swallowed the sound. I couldn't move. He couldn't move. We couldn't even breathe. The plate hissed against his skin.

Angry black singe marks appeared on the walls and sheets all around us, but the fire couldn't catch without oxygen to consume. My tendrils vibrated with triumph.

Lyric bounded into the room. I don't know *how*, because doing so defied every conceivable law of motion. But the solid air didn't faze him. He trounced right over to Bůk's satchel and disappeared inside, probably after a bite of jerky.

Bůk tried to turn his head to see what I was looking at. He couldn't. Satisfaction rippled through me.

And then...the powder burned out.

My tendrils encircled Bůk's wrists and ankles to keep him from lashing out. I put my hand to his throat, letting the name-plate fall aside.

"Don't fight," I warned.

Would my tendrils kill him if he did? I wasn't sure. I also wasn't sure if the brand would survive his whole death, dissolving, and rebirth process. Aelith suspected it would. He had other scars that persisted—and their common tie was holy water. But I didn't want to test the theory yet. I doubted I would get a second chance at this.

Although Bůk's eyes blazed, he held perfectly still.

I leaned closer to whisper against his ear.

"I don't know what you want anymore—and I don't care," I said. "You belong to *me*."

I gave him one beat to digest that truth before I crashed my lips against his.

The rest could wait.

The peace staff. Austvix's troubling prophecies. The Huntress. My other siblings. The Temple Mother's words that lingered in the back of my mind. Haz.

Tonight, I was going to claim my demon.

Bůk's tongue pushed into my mouth hungrily, proving that I wasn't alone in missing this. He rolled us over. His weight pressed me into the bed, and my inner beast purred. He fisted my hair and pinned my hips with his. I closed my eyes, drinking it in.

When he pulled back, his shadows clasped over my mouth in a tight gag. Delicious fear sliced through me. He nipped at my throat, almost certainly leaving marks, and his cock—eager and hard—pressed against my thigh.

I didn't want to wait, so I didn't. I pushed with my hands

and magic, shoving him to exactly where I wanted him. His delight soaked the room in midnight chill.

I pulled him into me. I set the pace. I squeezed my pussy around his cock, broadcasting *mine* with each rock of my hips. There was plenty to say—but we didn't need to yet.

We finished together. We collapsed together. And we lay there, panting in the afterglow together.

Somehow, none of the words I'd been burning to say for weeks felt important right then. His shadows settled around me, holding my body firmly against his, saying everything that needed to be said. My tendrils explored him lazily in return.

As dawn approached, Bůk's breathing evened out again.

Mine did not. I'd hoped tying up this one loose end would make some of my internal cacophony quiet down, but there was still so much to think about. The war, my family, my friends—all flitted through my mind in an anxious kaleidoscope, keeping sleep just out of reach.

At some point, I settled on the Huntress's taunting smile from the battlefield. Sleepily, without even meaning to, I thought at my father. *Do you even care about any of this?*

His answer came immediately.

Of course I care.

I froze.

He'd *heard* me. He'd *answered*.

The promise of sleep evaporated. I gripped Bůk, holding onto his steady heat. Haz's presence hung in the room. I hadn't felt him before, but I did now. What should I say to him? Would he answer my questions if I asked them? Was this the time to petition him for a small assist with the whole peace part of his domain?

It couldn't hurt to try.

Will you help me end this war? I thought.

Yes, Eroithiel. But everything has a cost.

Pink dawn light illuminated the room. The shadows began to recede. Bůk rolled in his sleep, casting his arm over me.

I'd like to say I had no desire to know or prove my worth to Haz. To a god and father who'd been intentionally distant, who'd left me to flail about the world on my own when the tiniest bit of guidance could have changed everything. But I would be lying. Need pooled deep in my belly.

What do you want from me? I thought.

Anticipation whirred in my chest. What if he told me to hunt the Huntress? What if he told me to sever ties with Bůk or with my friends? What if he told me to sacrifice myself?

Haz allowed my nerves to spiral for several long moments. When his voice came again, the words pierced my heart like twin arrows.

Kill Austvix.

Acknowledgments

Thank you first to my Radish readers, whose enthusiasm for the serialized chapters of *The Demon's Collar* made telling Ero's story incredibly fun and fulfilling. You were my first readers on this pivot to dark romance, and I'm not sure this book ever would have existed without you.

A big thank you as well to my ARC readers. You valiantly answered my dark, smutty call *and* made it this far—all before the final proofread! What you do for authors is fantastic; I appreciate you so much for being here. And of course, thank you to every single reader who heard "demon MMC" and came running. You *are* my people.

On a personal note, a resounding thanks to the other two-thirds of my favorite group chat. You know who you are. You put up with each and every one of my rabbit holes—from football (sup Joe Burrow) to that month I liked chess to that time I became briefly obsessed with Imagine Dragons to my never-ending obsession with Taylor Swift, and...now to my Lyra Sterling persona. Y'all rock, and y'all know it.

A big and special thank you to my mom (who better not be reading this) for the many times she swooped in to help with the children and to provide general mental rescues. To my dad, who taught me to measure twice and cut once—which, weirdly, *does* apply to writing as well as the carpentry I will never, ever attempt on my own. (Sorry, Dad.) And to my writing friends, *all* of whom inspire me daily.

Last but *certainly* not least, thank you to Mr. Sterling, whose D&D world is where Ero was first conceived, and whose growly prowly love frequently inspires whole new worlds. Dark Bandit for the win. You, sir, are my favorite Dungeon Master.

Until next time, thank you all for going on this adventure with me. <3

Yours,

Lyra Sterling

About the Author

Lyra Sterling lives in Ohio with her soul cat, her husband, their children, another cat, and a dog. She writes spicy dark romance to escape the horrors of the world...in favor of better horrors. For an early look at works in progress (get your serialized chapters of book 2 in The Bard's Demon series and exclusive flash fiction!), check out Lyra's Patreon or sign up to receive Lyra's newsletter at www.lyrasterling.com with future publication news and ARC opportunities.

patreon.com/LyraSterlingAuthor

threads.com/@lyra.sterling.author

tiktok.com/@lyrasterlingauthor

instagram.com/lyra.sterling.author